Dedication

To my wife and soulmate Martha:
You make me a better man every day. I can't wait to see what we do together for the next 100 years.

Cover Design
Aleaca / 99Design
Vesna Tisma

"Outside of a dog, a book is man's best friend. Inside of a dog, it's too dark to read."

— GROUCHO MARX

(Quote discovered by Shane Etter)

Amy,
Hope you enjoy The Time Twisters! Cheers,
Ken

Kim Megahee/The Kimmer Group
Gainesville, GA
www.AuthorKimMegahee.com

Publisher's Note: This is a work of fiction. Names, characters, places, and incidents are a product of the author's imagination. Locales and public names are sometimes used for atmospheric purposes. Any resemblance to actual people, living or dead, or to businesses, companies, events, institutions, or locales is completely coincidental.

The Time Twisters/ Kim Megahee. -- 1st ed.
ISBN 978-1-7340190-3-2

Acknowledgements

I'd like to thank Army Rangers Major Randall E. Batson (retired) and Colonel John Cornelson (retired) for reasonable battle tactics and military behavior, of which I was blissfully ignorant. If there are any areas where the book misrepresents the way things would actually have happened, the error is in my interpretation of their observations.

I could not have done this without the support of many people, I'd like to thank Hazel Megahee (MegaMom), Phoebe Boychuk (editing), Michelle Williams (editing), Mark Malatesta (sage advice), the folks at 99Designs (gorgeous book covers), Shane Etter (best writing advice I ever got), Laura Megahee, Megan Megahee, and the rest of my family. There are way too many close friends who encouraged me over the years to mention, so let me just say that I am blessed with far more loving friends and colleagues that I shall ever deserve.

Most of all, I'd like to thank my amazing and beautiful soulmate wife Martha and our little buddy, Leo the stubborn, redheaded toy poodle.

THE TIME TWISTERS

Kim Megahee

The Kimmer Group

Gainesville, GA

CHAPTER 1

10:45 p.m. – July 21, 2011 – River North district, Chicago, IL

Congressman Blake Phillips was in the prime of his career and he knew it. At the age of fifty-six, he was in decent shape for his age. He had salt-and-pepper hair with grey eyes and laugh lines on his face.

Standing five foot nine, he was usually well-dressed, well-groomed and looked like a corporate executive. His gray sweat suit and athletic shoes made him look like any other businessman on the way back to his hotel from the gym.

He stood motionless on LaSalle Street, between West Illinois Street and West Hubbard Street. He stared through opera glasses at the upper floors of the apartment tower a hundred feet away.

His logical mind understood why Smith insisted he be here to witness the event. Otherwise, if all went as planned, Phillips wouldn't remember the deal they made and his promise to pay the silver-haired mercenary ten million dollars for his services.

His emotional mind was another story. His stomach was still queasy from the time jump. Everything around him was antiquated. Even the air felt different. It was unsettling, like suddenly appearing as a character in an old movie. And Smith's warnings not to interact with anyone didn't make him more comfortable.

Waiting was always hard on Phillips' nerves. He saw Smith on a balcony a few moments ago.

What's keeping him?

His stomach rolled over again and he wished he were somewhere else.

Smith appeared again and threw something off the balcony. *The girl!* Through the glasses, Phillips watched her body fall from the apartment balcony, drifting slightly as it rolled. It smashed into the sidewalk.

Careful not to be the first person there, he slipped the opera glasses into his pocket and ran to the body. A small crowd gathered and he craned his neck to see around and over shoulders.

Her arms and legs lay at grotesque angles. Blood and tissue were splattered on everything within ten feet.

Oh, God!

His stomach roiled again as he turned his head and swallowed the bit of vomit that came to his mouth.

A pale woman clutched a handkerchief to her lips. “Did anyone see what happened?”

“Not me,” said the man who reached the scene first. “I saw her out of the corner of my eye… right before she hit the pavement. Did anyone call 9-1-1?”

“I did,” another woman said. “Not that it’ll help. Look around you. There's no way.”

She looked up and scanned the towering apartment building. “I wonder if she jumped or maybe got drunk and fell off the balcony? Regardless, we shouldn't touch the body. It's a fatal accident scene now. The police will be here any second.”

Phillips left the growing crowd and walked to the warehouse. There was nothing more to learn. He heard the sirens of approaching emergency vehicles as they reverberated off the buildings of midtown Chicago.

After walking a block, he became dizzy and disoriented. His stomach heaved and he vomited into a potted plant in front of a bar. A waitress ran over and yelled at him. He waved her away and staggered to a utility pole. He clung to it until the dizziness stopped, then continued down the street.

When he reached the abandoned warehouse, Phillips slipped through the door he and Smith forced open earlier.

He made his way to the rendezvous point. He reminded himself not to venture too close. Smith would jump in soon, and it wouldn't do to be in the exact spot where he arrived. If Smith materialized into the same space his body occupied, Phillips would be dead.

He fought off another wave of nausea and shook his head in irritation.

Now isn't the time to be squeamish – not with Smith returning at any moment.

He needed to be calm and collected. If he wasn't, a man like Smith would eat him for lunch. Or worse, share his weakness with Rho.

The building's dust irritated his nostrils and sinuses. He checked the time. It was 11:01 pm.

He should be here by now.

He willed his body to relax.

As his eyes adjusted to the darkness, he perceived a shadowy figure leaning against a steel column ten yards away.

Alarmed, he fumbled for his phone again to cast light on the figure. Before he could draw it from his pocket, a penlight beam focused on his face and destroyed his night vision.

Phillips shielded his eyes with his hand and squinted.

Smith's voice came from behind the light. "You saw?"

He's already here.

"I did," Phillips said. "Would you mind turning that off, please?"

"Sure," Smith said.

The light winked off and the two men approached each other. Smith towered over Phillips by five inches and stopped just inside Phillips' personal space. Phillips took a small step back.

"Yes," he said, his voice little more than a croak. "I saw."

"You need a breath mint," Smith said. "Are you going to faint on me?"

"No," he said. "I'm fine. Let's go."

"In a minute. Do you agree I've carried out my end of the bargain? Is there anything else to do?"

"No. I agree you've fulfilled your contract." Phillips waved his arm at the room. "Now, can we get out of this filthy place?"

Smith ignored the question.

"And the rest of my payment will be delivered when we return, right? Half up front and half upon completion is what we agreed."

"Of course," Phillips said. "But, I do have a concern about reversal. Are you sure no one can come back and reverse our changes? It's no good for me if it isn't permanent."

"Yes. After about a week, it's impossible to return to this time – not for another twenty-five years."

"So after a week the changes are permanent? Are you sure?"

Smith shrugged. "One hundred percent. For the next twenty-five years, anyway. By then, it won't matter, will it? I think we're good."

Phillips nodded. "Then make it eight days. I need to know it's permanent. You have my word you'll be paid then."

Smith laughed.

"Your word?" He shook his head, shrugged and then chuckled. "Okay. That'll do for now. I believe you'll honor our agreement. You've everything to gain by paying me. And everything to lose if you don't."

"As do you," Phillips said.

Smith shrugged and nodded. "As for your opponent, I don't think you'll see him on the TEV when we get back to our time."

Phillips smiled at the thought. The technology that made TelExtraVision possible was not new. A small company combined television, the video telephone, and online computer access into one high definition device and branded it. He owned a set, but only used the television functions. He kept the other activities separate.

"That would be a pleasant result," Phillips said. "I presume you will be around for other specialized work as needed later?"

"I'm open to proposals. It depends on my availability, the price and the risk."

"I understand. I don't forget my friends, and you've proved your reliability more than once."

"Yes, I have," Smith said. "What's next?"

"We wait. In a few weeks we'll have the elections, and a new administration will sweep into power. Led by me." He paused and smiled. "Me. And I'm taking this government in a new direction if I have to drag it, kicking and screaming."

"I'll be happy to help in any way I can, Mr. President-Elect."

CHAPTER 2

6:25 p.m. – June 11, 2036 – Defense Logistics Agency Satellite Office Building, Telegraph Road, Alexandria, VA

It was the end of a long day for Major Marc McKnight. His normal day included a workout at the gym, hand-to-hand combat sparring with his team, reviewing potential missions, coaching his team members and getting up to speed on the science of time travel. He liked the structure and the discipline of his schedule.

None of that happened today. Today, he skipped all those activities to play his part in their move from Langley to new offices on Telegraph Road. The complex there was an aged elementary school the Army bought and converted to offices for a team that needed isolation. Now it was being used as a staging area for the move to the new DLA facility on Fort Belvoir campus.

McKnight started the day at Langley, ensuring that everyone on the team was accounted for and visited by the movers. Then he drove his pickup truck to Telegraph Road. As the team arrived there, he directed traffic.

Satisfied that all his people and their stuff made it to their respective offices, he closed his office door and surveyed his own unpacked boxes scattered around the room. *Nope, not yet.* He stretched his six-foot-one frame, reaching first for the ceiling and then touching his toes. Left and right twists of the torso and side bends helped make him more comfortable. He dropped into his desk chair, turned toward the transparent office wall and put his feet up on the credenza. He was tired and it was the first time today he had a chance to sit and think. He was glad the move part was over. After he unpacked, he could get some real work done.

A few short years before, the science of historical research changed forever. Doctor Robert Astalos, an MIT physicist, stumbled onto a time travel mechanism that allowed him to visit time periods in the past. The technology was limited – he could only reach time periods that were a multiple of twenty-five years from the present. Nonetheless, it opened the door to study select past events, especially those shrouded in mystery.

The US government classified the technology and Congress established the HERO team to research and validate history. Retired General Mike Drake was asked to provide strategic direction, overseen by Senator Lodge's committee on New Technology. Astalos continued to work with the team, creating support tools and diagnostic applications.

HERO was an acronym. It stood for Historical Event Research Organization. As a project name, McKnight considered it inane and stupid. But he was in the Army and he followed orders. His orders were to help General Drake select Army and civilian talent for the mission team and to command it. Team selection was complete and their first mission, though unorthodox and rushed, was successful. Now they were planning and scheduling subsequent missions.

It was a dream job and a career maker if he did his job well. But he didn't really think about that aspect much, because the work and technology were interesting and so were the members of his team.

Until today, the HERO Team operated out of a crowded facility near Langley Virginia. In six weeks, they would move to a permanent home in the DLA Headquarters building a few miles away. Today, he'd been on his feet for twelve hours as they moved from Langley to this office on Telegraph Road.

He sighed. *Only in the Army would we move to temporary offices six weeks before moving to permanent offices.*

It wasn't bad, though. This building had room for Doctor Astalos' lab, office space for all, a kitchen and conference rooms. It had everything they needed for the short term. Back in Langley, the team was scattered throughout the complex. Here on Telegraph Road, they had everyone in one block of offices. It would make working together much easier.

Best of all, their offices now had a receptionist/office manager. Her name was Cindy Ginn and she came well recommended.

His phone rang. The ring tone was a familiar one. He answered and said, "Hi, Megan."

"Hey, yourself," she said. "Did I call at a bad time?"

"Not at all," he said. "It's actually a good time. We moved into our new office today. I finally got to sit down for a minute. How are things down in Georgia?"

"They're good," she said. "But I'm feeling a little bit ignored. Are you angry with me?"

"No, of course not. I'm sorry – It's been crazy busy. Is everything okay?"

"Yes," she said. "But I haven't heard from you in a few days. I thought you would have called sooner. I have a remedy for that if you'd like to hear it."

"Sure."

"Like I told you the other day, I'm between jobs now and I'm looking for something else. Don't you think that now would be as good a time as any for me to come to Washington?"

"I'd love you to, but there are a lot of things going on right now. We have ongoing projects, plus another office move in a few weeks. After we get that completed would be a better time for a visit."

There was a brief moment of silence from Megan's end of the line. "Marc, I'm not talking about a visit. I'm talking about moving in with you."

"Oh," he said. He pulled his feet off the credenza and sat up straight. Images of home life raced through his mind – moving out of the Bachelor Office Quarters, skipping gym visits to work around the house, coordinating schedules with Megan, cooking at home, and several others. *Am I ready for that?*

He searched for the right words. None came immediately.

"I'm getting the feeling you think it's a bad idea," she said, unable to hide the disappointment in her voice.

"Nothing about you is a bad idea, Megan. It's just that I've never lived with anyone before. And it's a big step for you to uproot yourself from your family and friends and move to a place where you don't know anybody."

"Yes, it is, but it's what people in love do when they're apart."

"But are you sure we're ready for that? I mean, I do love you. Don't misunderstand that. But we've been in different towns through our entire relationship. What if you moved up here and it didn't work out between us?"

"That's the big risk, isn't it? But you can never know how much time is required to make sure you're compatible. At some point, you just have to take the leap and see what happens. I know that's contrary to your personality, but it's how love works."

"I know, but—"

"How do I like my coffee?" she said.

"Huh?" He paused and smiled. "A splash of French vanilla and one Splenda."

"Correct, and you like yours black, or barefooted as you like to say. I could go on and you know it. We know each other very well."

McKnight shifted his weight in his chair. "I don't know. It seems like such a big step."

"So you need time to think about it? Maybe consider your options? You know, my parents knew each other for less than a year and it's lasted for forty years. We've known each other twice that long."

"Don't get me wrong, Megan. It's just that—"

"You're sending me conflicting signals, Marc. I thought being in love was a good enough reason."

Someone knocked on the door. "Hold on a second," he said, and put his thumb over the phone's microphone.

He kicked off the credenza to spin his chair around and sat upright at the desk.

"Come," he said.

Captain Winston Tyler stepped into the room.

He removed his thumb from the microphone. "Megan, I have to go. Tyler's here and we have some work things to do. I'll call you back."

"Okay. You need to know that this disappoints me and we need to finish this discussion. I love you. Tell Winnie I said hello."

"Me, too. Bye." He disconnected the call.

Tyler saluted. "I'm not interrupting anything, am I?"

"No, not at all." McKnight returned his salute. "Your cousin says hello."

"That was Megan? How is she? Everything okay?"

"Yes, she's fine. It's all good."

Tyler grinned. "Great. You wanted to see me, sir?"

"Yes. As you were. Have a seat, Winnie."

Tyler dropped into one of the two side chairs.

Tyler and McKnight were roommates at West Point. The two men were friends from day one at the Academy. But no two officer candidates were as different as Tyler and McKnight. Tyler was fair-skinned, blond and blue-eyed, McKnight was one-eighth American Indian with dark brown hair and brown eyes. Tyler was barely five-foot-nine to McKnight's solid six-foot-one. Where Tyler possessed an outgoing personality, McKnight was introverted. Tyler grew up in Atlanta in a prosperous neighborhood, while McKnight spent his formative years on a farm in rural Oregon. Tyler gravitated toward mission planning and McKnight showed expertise in leadership and decision-making.

During their time at the Academy, they found they worked well together. After graduation, they teamed up for a couple of successful projects. Tyler was McKnight's first choice to join the HERO Team when it was formed.

"Winnie, I just wanted to comment on the great job you did coordinating the move. Everyone made it into their new offices and, as far as I can tell, nothing got lost. Not bad."

"Thanks, Marc."

"You can start the planning for the next move with Lieutenant Wheeler at your earliest."

"Yes, sir. We've already set up a meeting for tomorrow to get started on it."

"Good. At ten thousand foot level, what are you thinking?"

"A heavily armed convoy, sir," Tyler said. "The technology is important and needs to be protected, even for a short trip."

"Sounds good. Here's another option. Go with a small team for protection, but keep the move totally secret – the secrecy mitigates some of the risk incurred by using a smaller team."

Tyler frowned. "I'm not crazy about that option, sir. Is there a reason why we should take that risk?"

"Unfortunately, yes. I'm getting my ass kicked by General Drake for the budget. Doctor Astalos has some new ideas that need researching and some of our operating budget has been reallocated for that purpose. It's not optimal, but the General and Senator Lodge agreed to the shift in resources."

"I see."

"Captain, I'm not telling you what to do. Just look at the costs of the options and the associated risks and make your recommendation. If we have to overrun the budget, I'll find some way to deal with it. Understood?"

"Yes, sir."

"Okay. We'll need a briefing about a week before the move to go over the details for the team. That's all I have." McKnight mentally checked an item off his to-do list.

Tyler stood. "One more thing, Marc. I was talking to Sarah earlier today..."

From McKnight's perspective, Tyler's attractive fiancée made it her mission in life to find a match for Tyler's best friend.

"Uh-oh. Another blind date? I've been seeing Megan for quite a while now. I, uh…"

Tyler grinned. "Not this time. We figure Megan is more woman than you can handle. No, she wanted me to ask if you've heard from Barbara Howard lately?"

The mention of Barbara's name brought her to McKnight's mind and a smile to his face. He could see her blonde hair, her quick smile and her dancing blue eyes.

"No, I haven't," McKnight said. "Why?"

"Sarah hasn't heard from her in a while and hasn't been able to find her. She's getting concerned and we thought maybe you might have heard from her."

Tyler looked more worried than he sounded.

"No, I'm sorry, I haven't." McKnight said. "Did she get a new job or something? Maybe a new boyfriend?"

Tyler shrugged. "We heard she's dating around, but no serious boyfriend that we know of. But she usually checks in with Sarah every other week or so. It's been two months. Sarah called her parents out in California but wasn't able to get in touch with them as of yet."

"Really? That doesn't sound so good."

"Yeah, that's what we thought. We're pretty much out of ideas about finding her, short of calling the police. That's next, I suppose. We'll wait another day or so before doing that. Let me know if you find out anything."

"We didn't have many friends in common. Just each other. But I'll try all the options I have for contacting her."

"Good deal. Thanks. Well, I've got to go. Sarah's waiting downtown for me. Have a good night." He opened the door to leave.

McKnight held up his hand. "Let me know if you guys hear anything, okay? I'd like to know."

"Will do. I'll share anything we find out. See you later, Marc."

Tyler left the room.

McKnight sat still and stared at the closed door. He thought about Barbara. Inexplicably, he could smell her perfume – a trick of his memory. She was an amazing girl and he wondered how he let her get away.

But he knew how.

Barbara was ready for a deeper relationship and he wasn't. She got tired of waiting and broke up with him. They remained friendly and he wanted to stay close, but she didn't. Staying away from each other for a while was necessary, she said, for her to get over him and get herself back on track. He hadn't seen her for nearly a year.

He drew out his phone, looked up her number in the address book, and called it. He got a recorded message – the number was no longer in service. He frowned. *Well, that's weird. These days, people don't ever change their numbers.*

Well, he hadn't tried to call her lately. There was no reason to expect her to keep him abreast of what was happening in her life.

He sent an email to her and got a quick response. The message said the email address didn't exist on the domain. *That's even weirder. Either she really wants to leave this part of her life behind or something is wrong.*

He wondered if she had met someone, had a whirlwind romance and left for some exotic location. It was certainly possible, but out of character for Barbara.

McKnight pulled himself to his feet and stared out through the transparent wall. *I need to call Megan back soon. She was pretty ticked off.*

He looked at his watch. *I need to go work out. Clear my mind.*

He looked again at the unpacked boxes. *The least I can do is to unpack one box.* He pulled the tape off the closest box and opened it.

CHAPTER 3

12:40 p.m. – June 12, 2036 – Defense Logistics Agency Satellite Office Building, Telegraph Road, Alexandria, VA

Trevor George took another bite of his ham and cheese sandwich and washed it down with Diet Coke. He glanced at his watch. He had about twenty minutes before his meeting with Doctor Astalos. The inventor of time travel had an open slot in his schedule and accepted a meeting request to talk about future enhancements to the time travel technology. As an investigator, Trevor wanted to know and understand the tools at the Team's disposal.

He glanced around the office. *And I still need to get unpacked and clean this place up.*

Trevor was in his mid-forties, with a boyish face, twinkling brown eyes, dimples, and brown curls that spilled over his ears. His own apartment looked a lot like the office. In fact, his whole life was in a state of flux. It all happened so fast.

Just a few months before, he was a cold case investigator for the Atlanta Police Department. After being pulled into a fifty-year-old murder case and working with Major McKnight, he jumped at the chance to join the HERO organization when invited. Now, he was living in Virginia and trying to get up to speed on a new job as a civilian employee of the US Army.

Like McKnight, he thought the acronym for the organization was pretty lame, but that didn't dampen his enthusiasm for the possibility of traveling to the past and witnessing history firsthand.

The job change caused plenty of upheaval in his personal life.

His mother and his fiancé weren't happy with his career choice.

In college, Mom pushed him toward a pre-law degree. She was appalled and mortified when, upon graduation, he defiantly entered the Atlanta Police Academy.

His fiancée, seeing herself as the wife of a successful attorney, had the same reaction.

In truth, it wasn't that he disliked the idea of being a lawyer so much. It was breaking away from his mother and fiancée trying to control his life. It had the desired effect. His mother now barely spoke to him and his fiancée found another potential lawyer.

Trevor would also miss his friends at Open Mic Atlanta, where he played saxophone on Wednesday nights. After a couple of failed attempts in local clubs, he found a band looking for a sax player and started gigging with them around Alexandria.

On balance, the new job and the move to DC were worth it.

The work wasn't the only incentive for taking this new position. There was also Kathy Wu, whom he met along with McKnight on the cold case. She was the civilian mission planner General Drake selected to work alongside Captain Tyler on the HERO Team. Trevor had never met anyone like her before. She was fascinating, beautiful, funny, and possibly the smartest person he had ever met. He liked her fondness for quoting lines from old movies at the most inappropriate or awkward times.

They were about the same age and hit it off right away. They grew up with the same music, the same current events. It felt very natural to spend time together and just talk. And they worked together very well. He wondered where the relationship might go from here.

Trevor thought she was warming up to him, but he wasn't sure he was ready for that. Kathy was strong-willed and he wasn't sure about starting a relationship with a woman who might try to control him. He had been there before and didn't like the ride or the result.

But he had to admit there was something there. He felt it and he was pretty sure she did, too.

His reverie was interrupted by an alarm on his phone. He looked at it and turned off the alarm. *Fifteen minutes before the meeting with Doctor Astalos. I need a notepad.*

Despite all the new personal productivity apps in phones and laptops, Trevor never adopted any for his business life except for communications. He found the act of writing things down with a pen engaged his thinking brain and taking notes pushed facts directly into his memory. Once he wrote something down, he remembered it without referring back to the notes.

He tossed his napkin and empty Coke can into the trash and headed for the reception area. In addition to greeting guests and answering the phones, the receptionist also managed and stocked the team's office supplies.

The receptionist Cindy was introduced to most of the team the day they moved in, but Trevor hadn't yet met her personally. He walked down the hall and entered the reception area.

Cindy sat at the desk. It didn't take an advanced degree to notice she was attractive. She had blonde hair that curved to accentuate her face and was about thirty years old. She wore a conservative navy-blue skirt and her white blouse tastefully accentuated her breasts. The matching jacket and a small white purse hung on the coat rack in the corner and an aged cell phone lay on her desk. She smiled at him as he entered.

"Hi, Ms. Ginn. I don't think we've been properly introduced. I'm Trevor George."

"Oh, I know who you are, Mr. George. You have closed the circle."

"I beg your pardon."

She smiled. "I've met the rest of the HERO Team already. You were the only one I haven't met. Until now."

"Well, now the circle is indeed closed. It's nice to meet you." He waved toward the offices. "I understand you have some admirers here already. I heard you blew the whistle on Mike Smith."

"I didn't do anything, really. My girlfriend and I were out for the evening and ran into him in the Hard Rock Café."

"How did it come about?" he asked. "Before this, time travel technology was a well-kept secret."

"Yes, I know. He was a little drunk and hitting on us. When he gave up and started talking to another girl about the time travel technology, we left. I had never heard about it and neither had my girlfriend, but it sounded like something that should be classified. I called my former boss – Senator Owen – and told him about it. I wasn't prepared for his response."

"Oh, he was on the Senate Intelligence Committee, right?"

"Yes. He told me not to mention it to anyone else and thanked me for telling him. The next day, two agents from INSCOM were at my door for an interview."

"INSCOM? What's that?" Trevor asked and smiled. "I'm relatively new to Washington and haven't heard all the acronyms yet."

"Basically, military intelligence. I don't remember what the acronym stands for. Anyway, I hope I don't run into Mr. Smith again. I heard he lost his consulting position with Senator Lodge and there was talk of jail time. I don't think he's happy with me."

"I'll bet. But the word got out anyway?"

"Yes. We weren't the only people who overheard Mr. Smith. It turns out that an anchor for one of the major news channels also heard him and bought him a drink. The next day, the existence of time travel technology was revealed on their morning show."

"Ouch."

"Yes, well…anyway, Can I help you with something?"

"Yes, a couple of things. I have a meeting in a few minutes with Doctor Astalos, but I haven't seen him today. Do you know if he's here today?"

"Yes, he went to lunch with Kathy, but he did comment that he had a meeting with you when he got back. I'm sure he'll be here then."

"Cool. Also, I'll need to take some notes. Do we have any notepads?"

"Oh, yes, of course." She jumped out of her chair. "They're here in the supply room. I just unpacked all the supplies and organized them. Right this way."

She brushed past him a little closer than expected and stepped into the hallway. He followed her as she turned into the first door on the left.

"I didn't even know we had a supply room," he said.

She laughed. "Of course, we do. All the supplies are here and you can find them by the tag on each of the drawers. See?" She pointed to the labels on two of the drawers. "The notepads are here, for future reference." She opened a drawer and handed him a notepad.

"That's great, thanks." He leaned against the door jamb. "Wow. You sure are efficient. Are you from here in Alexandria?"

She smiled and mirrored his posture against the tall filing cabinet.

"No, I worked for the Governor of Oklahoma for six years and a year with Senator Owen here in Washington. Senator Owen was my boss I mentioned earlier. That's where I go my top-secret clearance."

"Working for a Senator is a nice position. How come you left that job, if you don't mind my asking?"

"Oh, I don't mind. Senator Owen lost his election in 2034 and took a job as a lobbyist. When the music stopped, there wasn't a chair left for me. I was able to find part-time work for a while, but then my savings were almost gone. Finding this job at DLA was a life-saver for me."

"I'll bet the Smith incident didn't hurt your chances for the job. I'm glad to hear it. And we're glad to have you, Ms. Ginn."

"Oh, call me Cindy, please."

"Sure, Cindy. Please call me Trevor. I'm much more comfortable with that anyway."

"So, Trevor, what do you do for fun?" Her body language suggested more than friendly interest behind her words and his imagination flared. Those eyes and lips would be hard to resist if they were accompanied by an invitation.

Trevor told Cindy about his new band and how much fun it was.

"Oh, I love to hear a good saxophone player. Do you play jazz or what?"

"Well, it's mostly a combination of several styles. We–"

Doctor Astalos and Kathy Wu walked by the supply room at that moment.

"Hi," Trevor and Cindy said, almost in unison.

Doctor Astalos responded with a hello. For some reason, Kathy looked irritated.

"Trevor," Astalos said, "I'm available to meet whenever you're ready. Just come on down to my office."

"Yes, sir, I will."

Astalos continued on down the hall toward his office.

"Do you have everything you need, Trevor?" Kathy asked and stepped past the open door as if she didn't expect a response.

"Yes, I do," Trevor said, though he wasn't sure he understood the question.

He turned toward Cindy. "Thank you, ma'am, for the notepad."

"No problem, Trevor. I'd love to hear your band play sometime. Let me know when and where."

"Sure thing," he said.

"I'm really looking forward to working with you, Trevor," she said and walked back to the reception area.

"Me, too," he said and strode down the hall after Kathy with his notepad in hand. It took a bit of effort to catch up to her.

"How was lunch?" he said, matching her stride.

"I'd love to hear your band?" she said and walked faster.

"What?"

They reached her office. She stopped and said, "Really? She's really looking forward to working with you?"

He stopped and looked at her. She stood there in the hallway before him, her long blue-black hair pulled back in a ponytail and her hands planted on her hips. She looked professional, stunning, and irritated – all at the same time.

Trevor couldn't identify the emotion lying beneath the expression on her face. He opened his mouth to speak, but nothing came out.

She looked at him for a long moment, as if waiting for a response. Then she rolled her eyes, dismissed him with a wave and stepped into her office.

"Is there something wrong?" he asked.

"Not at all. Don't forget your meeting with Doctor Astalos. He's waiting for you."

Shaking his head in confusion, Trevor continued down the hall and around the corner to Astalos' office in the Lab.

"Sorry, sir," Trevor said. "It took a little longer than I thought."

"Yes, I'm sure it did," Astalos said, his eyes dancing with mirth. "She's a rather striking young lady."

"Cindy? Yes, she is."

Astalos grinned. "I was talking about Kathy."

"Oh, of course. Yes, she is, too."

"It's my opinion that Cindy noticed that you noticed her."

Trevor looked toward the door. "She did? I mean –"

"As did Kathy."

"What?"

"I think she is interested in you."

"Who?"

Astalos laughed out loud. "Yes. Can you not tell?"

Trevor looked flustered. "What? I'm sure you're mistaken, Doctor."

"Maybe. I'm pretty perceptive when it comes to that stuff. Comes with age, I guess. You know what else?"

"What's that, sir?"

Astalos leaned forward and smiled, his eyes twinkling with amusement. “Two very attractive women in one office. You, sir, I think, are in deep trouble.”

CHAPTER 4

8:30 p.m. – June 13, 2036 – Science Forum Studios – Smithsonian Institute, Washington, DC

The studio director pointed to the stage and said, "Science Forum with Julie Cameron. Live in 3…2…1…"

The attractive blonde commentator sat erect behind her broadcast desk. She shuffled her papers and smiled for the TelExtraVision audience.

"Good evening, ladies and gentlemen. I'm Julie Cameron and this is Science Forum. For the last year, the scientific community has been absolutely abuzz with the revelation that time travel is not only possible, but some daring individuals have actually traveled through time. And no one is more knowledgeable about this subject than Doctor Robert Astalos, the inventor of time travel. Tonight on Science Forum, we'll be sharing with you portions of my exclusive question and answer session with Doctor Astalos. Here's that program now…"

The scene changed to a pair of chairs separated by a coffee table, with a curtain as a backdrop. Julie Cameron and Doctor Astalos sat casually in the chairs.

She turned to the man and said, "Doctor Astalos, you've become a celebrity over the last few months because of…well, your discovery of course, but also for your down-to-earth style and your marvelous ability to communicate such a complex subject to the rest of us. Thank you, sir, for taking time out of your busy schedule to come and talk with us tonight."

The old man smiled at the commentator. "Thanks for having me, Julie. It's my pleasure."

She nodded. To the camera, she said, “Tonight, we’ll be asking Doctor Astalos a series of questions that we received from you, our viewers. And there were a *lot* of questions. Are you ready, Doctor?”

“Yes, I am.”

She produced a small pile of index cards and selected the first one. “Okay. Here’s our first question. A student from Virginia writes the following: ‘I’m a little confused because I read you started as a grad student at MIT in the year 2000 at twenty, but also that you are one-hundred-six years old. By my calculations, you should only be fifty-six. Could you please explain that?’ And you say, Doctor Astalos?”

“It confuses me too sometimes.” He laughed and took a sip from a glass of water. “I am one-hundred-six years of age because I lived through the period of 2000 to 2025 three times. In the year 2025, I had just turned forty-five when I accidentally sent myself back to the year 2000. By the time it was 2025 again, I was seventy and traveled again to the year 2000 on purpose. When 2025 rolled around again, I was ninety-five years old, and that was eleven years ago. Does that help?”

The commentator raised her eyebrows at the camera and turned back to Doctor Astalos. “Wow. I’ll bet there are a lot of stories around those two trips.”

“Not that I’m willing to tell,” he said and winked at the camera.

The commentator laughed and said, “Well, we’ll have to come back to that one.”

“No, we don’t,” he said and grinned at her.

She giggled and waved to dismiss further pursuit of the subject.

“Well, moving on along, here’s our next question.” She laughed again – the interview was going well.

“A science teacher from New York asks this question, Doctor. ‘I read something about time being folded and that it is easier to travel back a multiple of twenty-five years than it is to travel back one year. Could you elaborate on this topic?’ What about it, Doctor? What can you tell this viewer?”

Astalos nodded and took another sip of water. "Yes, I can elaborate. The viewer is correct, but we don't know why. A certain amount of power – a relatively small amount, actually – can travel you back exactly twenty-five years. If you want to travel back twenty-five years and a day, the power required is a little higher. Twenty-five years and a week requires still more power, and power requirements go up exponentially after that. There is a limit, however…I don't think I'm allowed to talk about that. Theoretically, it would take about the same amount of energy to travel back fifty, seventy-five, one hundred or more years as it would to travel twenty-five years. That's why many believe time is folded and the 'crease' is at twenty-five years."

"Very interesting, Doctor Astalos," the commentator said. "I'm curious. Regarding that last question – each of those year intervals are multiples of twenty-five years. What about the zero multiple? Do the physics still work?"

Astalos smiled. "Very astute, Julie. Yes, the math holds true. The zero multiple works as well. Next question?"

The commentator smiled broadly. "Forgive me, sir, but one more clarifying question. If you set your Time Engine for another location, but not another time, it seems to me the Engine will effectively function as a transporter."

Astalos frowned. "That's an interesting observation, Julie. Your suggestion seems to make sense, but I wouldn't try it without a lot of testing first."

"Then, are you saying it works?"

"No. I'm saying I wouldn't try it without a lot of testing first."

"Has your organization tested that particular scenario?"

Astalos drummed his fingers on the arm of the chair and shifted his position. "Let's save that question for another time. It's a complex subject and I want to address as many questions from your audience as I can. What's the next question?"

The commentator looked disappointed. "I'm sure that question will be asked again. Are you sure you don't want to cover it now?"

"I'm sure it will," Astalos said. "But I'd like to make the best use of our time here. Next question."

She selected the next index card. "This question comes from a hairdresser in Georgia. Here's what she says. 'What do you and your other…selves call each other? I mean, you're all named Robert, right? Like, how do you keep up with who's who?' My, that's a very good question."

Astalos laughed. "It was disconcerting at first, but I think it worked out pretty well. My father's name was Robert, so everyone called me Robby when I was young. I went by Robby until I was about thirty. But by then, I was published and thought I should be a little more reserved, so I started calling myself Rob. When I got to be about fifty-five, I switched to Robert. As it turns out, it was a good idea. When the three of us worked together, we took up the names we were used to. Thanks for asking. Next question."

"Thank you, Doctor. Now, this next question is very interesting. I can't wait to hear your answer for this one. A bank finance officer from Gainesville Georgia asks, 'Why didn't you buy a bunch of stock in 2000 that was big in 2025 and get rich?' I love this question and I'll bet most of our audience wish they had asked it. I *know* they'd like to hear the answer."

"That's a fair question. It's a dangerous business, time travel. If you're not careful, you can make a subtle change that, on the surface, is innocuous, but has a catastrophic effect on the future." He paused and took a sip of water. "For example, the act of buying a lot of stock might keep an incompetent executive from being fired when they should have been and they end up running the company out of business. Or my stock purchase might influence the direction of the company away from what will make them successful. Do you see what I mean? It's extremely risky to make changes because there are just too many variables to control.

"Before the first travel accident, I didn't believe we could affect the future by changing the past. But, as a by-product of my work over the last eighty-five years, we proved that you can.

"Based on that fact, we restricted our contact with each other to the time travel and interstellar drive research and stayed away from conversations about the future. We took great pains to work together as employees, not family members. By that, I mean we rarely socialized with one another outside our research. The idea was to reduce the idle discussions that might lead to revealing future events.

"To be honest, I have to say we weren't a hundred percent successful." His gaze fell to the floor before him and he paused for a few moments. He seemed defocused, as if he was lost in a memory.

The commentator reached over and touched his arm. "Doctor Astalos, are you okay?"

"What? Oh, sorry. I was just reflecting on how lucky I am that I haven't caused a significant shift in history. Or at least none that I'm aware of. Of course, things are different now in at least one area. There are three of me here now instead of just one."

"I see what you mean. Thank you, Doctor."

"Yes, Julie. Let's move on."

The commentator shuffled her cards and selected one. "Here's a really good question from a physics major in Pasadena. Are you ready, sir?"

"As ready as I'll ever be," he said.

"Okay, here it is. 'How did you do it? How did you invent time travel? Can you share any details about it?' Now, *that's* a good question!"

"It is," Astalos said. "And, due to the nature of this program, I'm going to stay away from the technical aspects of the work. I hope that's okay. And I didn't invent it…I just found it."

The commentator's mouth dropped open. "Are you kidding?"

"Not at all. Let me explain." His eyes sparkled as he spoke. "When I started my graduate work at MIT, I had a dream to invent an interstellar drive that could propel man to the stars at speeds faster than the speed of light. I believe man is destined to explore. In the 1500s, brave men and women sailed from Europe to the Americas in search of foreign lands, rich with opportunity and adventure. Today's foreign lands rotate around other stars.

"This idea fired my imagination. I vowed I would do whatever I could to help mankind make those journeys. It's been my dream since I was a boy. I'm still working on it, and I *will* make it happen.

"Anyway, back to the story. I worked on my Engine in the same lab at MIT for twenty-five years. On March twenty-first in the year 2025, I flipped a power switch to run a test on the drive and was catapulted – for lack of a better word – back to my lab on the same date in the year 2000.

"I don't know who was more surprised, me or my twenty-year-old self." Astalos laughed out loud. "You see, what I experienced was a flash of light, a mild electric shock and a brief sensation of falling backward through a field of stars. What my twenty-year-old self experienced was the sudden appearance of a stranger out of nowhere. Can you picture that? You're in your lab working and this guy appears out of thin air and falls over backward, knocking over a chair and scattering research papers all over the place." His thin shoulders were shaking with laughter. "I believe I startled him, but I guess I looked so familiar to him that he wasn't too frightened. Well, at least not much." He paused a moment to compose himself.

"Anyway, I had to prove who I was before he…" Astalos hesitated. "Er… I mean I, uh…" He laughed again. "You see, it does get confusing, doesn't it? I had to prove who I was before he would believe we were both the same person, coexisting in the same time space.

"Put yourself in my shoes. I was in quite a predicament because I didn't understand how it happened and had no idea how to get back to 2025. It took a while, but after we both recovered from the shock of it, we worked together on my drive. After all, I was stuck in the past, so I figured I might as well make the best of things, and maybe together we could develop the drive faster.

"That was my hope, but it didn't turn out that way. In the subsequent twenty-five years, we reproduced my experiment and determined the cause of the accidental time travel. We corrected the problem that caused the travel, but the interstellar drive still didn't work. Since Rob and I accomplished a lot together, we supposed it might go even faster if there were three of us. After a lot of soul-searching, we decided to go back to the year 2000 with a purpose. So, when the time of the original accident rolled around again, we both went back to 2000. He jumped first and then me. This time, we really unnerved my younger self. He was shaky there for a while."

Astalos paused and wiped his brow with a handkerchief. When he began again, his tone was serious. "Something else happened, too. This time, there were witnesses to our appearance. Two professors and some students heard the ruckus in Robby's lab and rushed in right after we showed up. Word got out because it was obvious we weren't all just family. That and the fact Robby was unconscious – he fainted dead away at the shock of me and Rob arriving out of nowhere.

"We never considered there could be any negative potential to our work. The government was concerned about the technology falling into hands of terrorists or other enemies so they swooped in and took all our research – and us – under federal control. They classified everything. The secrecy was the downside. The upside was that our budget and other resources grew quite a bit."

He smiled. "When Robby regained consciousness, we all worked together. Before we finished, we perfected the Time Engine and invented the return beacon and some measurement devices. This allowed us to travel back in time with a softer landing and to return to the present. Well, that's the gist of it. It started out with an accident and has evolved into what we are doing today."

"Doctor, that's quite a story. Are you ready for the last question?"

"Yes, of course."

“Very well. We’ll be approaching our last question a little differently. Time travel is a controversial subject and our last question is more political in nature. In the interest of fairness, we provided Doctor Astalos with the question in advance. Are you ready, Doctor Astalos?”

“Yes, I am.”

“Very well. The last question comes to us from Roger Durbin. Mr. Durbin is the founder and managing director of CASTT – Citizens against Space and Time Travel. Mr. Durbin asks the following question. ‘What is your relationship with the HERO project, and what is it that gives you the moral right to travel through time?’ And he added a follow-up question. ‘If the HERO project is supposed to be peaceful, why would the military appoint a general with an aggressive reputation like General Drake to lead it?’ That’s it, Doctor. What is your response to Mr. Durbin’s questions?”

“Thank you, Julie. Let me say that I do agree with Mr. Durbin on one important point – I don’t believe anyone has the moral authority to manipulate time. But there needs to be a little more truth and understanding around what the HERO project is. After the military took over our research, we stopped work until the legal issues were sorted out. Senator Lodge lobbied his peers for and got the Historic Event Research Organization Act through Congress. Its mandate is for researching historical events, not changing the past. Senator Lodge and his committee provide Congressional oversight and retired General Michael Drake was asked to run the HERO mission.”

“Doctor Astalos, thank you for clarifying the mission of the HERO project. But what about his follow-up question about General Drake?”

“For that question, I recommend Mr. Durbin check his facts. First of all, the President appointed him, not me or the military. Secondly, I have known Michael Drake for quite a while now. He is anything but aggressive. Assertive, yes, but also thoughtful and deliberate.”

"Doctor, I've wondered about this myself," the commentator said. "I heard that the troops call him The Dragon. With all due respect, that nickname doesn't sound very thoughtful and deliberate."

"Julie, you're confusing his leadership approach with his fierceness in battle. I won't permit Mr. Durbin or anyone else to question Mike Drake's motives. Mike received the Silver Star for his actions as a young lieutenant in Afghanistan when more than 200 Taliban overran his team's position. When the smoke cleared, he lost five of his men, but his heroism saved the rest. He killed nine of the enemy before running out of ammunition, then seven more in hand to hand combat. That action earned him the Dragon nickname. It's a title of valor and heroism, not of aggression."

"I see, Doctor. Thank you for your frank response," the commentator said. "But, since there is obviously some connotation or misunderstanding of General Drake's reputation, why appoint him to run this project?"

"Well, Julie, to get the answer to that specific question, you'll have to ask President Taylor. It was her call. Believe me, I am sympathetic with the underlying concern Mr. Durbin and others have about altering history. Mike Drake agrees with that mission and is the right man for the job."

"Thank you, Doctor Astalos. It's been a wonderful and information session and you have been the perfect guest."

"You're welcome, Julie."

She turned to the camera. "That's about all the time we have, ladies and gentlemen. Again, I'd like to thank our guest, Doctor Robert Astalos, for finding time to chat with us here on the Science Forum. And especially I want to thank our viewers for the questions from their emails, tweets, and other social media posts."

The taped interview ended and the program switched back to the commentator at her broadcast desk with a large smile on her face.

"And there you have it – our exclusive interview with Doctor Robert Astalos. You can see the entire interview on the Science

Forum website. That's our program for tonight, but I have one final note to add. At the end of the interview, I expressed my concern over keeping the technology safe and ensuring that no one will be able to change history. Doctor Astalos said, and I quote, 'Don't worry, Julie. You can be sure no one will abuse the technology while General Drake and I still draw breath.' I don't know about you, but I will sleep easier tonight. I'm Julie Cameron. Remember to send us your comments by email, tweets, and other social media posts and we'll see you next week on the Science Forum. Thank you, and good night."

"And…that's a wrap!" the studio director said. "Good job, everyone."

CHAPTER 5

7:15 p.m. – June 17, 2036 – Army Mule Pub, Old Town, Alexandria, VA

Captain Winston Tyler looked at his watch for the fourth time in ten minutes. McKnight and General Drake were late. He sat with the team in a booth in the back of the Army Mule Pub. This was their first social event together.

Even in the pub, they were still at work. Kathy and Trevor talked about historical research. Lieutenants Hatcher and Wheeler discussed a memo from Doctor Astalos.

Lieutenants Mitch Wheeler and Karen Hatcher were first and foremost a part of the mission team, but their backgrounds inspired Doctor Astalos to train them to operate and maintain the time travel equipment.

They met as freshmen in calculus class at the University of North Georgia and discovered their birthdays were one day apart. It was the first of many commonalities that drew them together.

Both grew up in urban communities in large Midwest cities and completed secondary school in three years. Both excelled in math and physics. The college environment in Dahlonega Georgia was a wilderness paradise for these two city kids.

Despite his name, Wheeler was of Hispanic descent. With an olive complexion, jet-black hair and dark brown eyes, he spent most of his free time in the gym lifting weights. He was five-foot-seven on a tall day and compensated with hours of practice in the martial arts. He had a quick wit and always found the upside of any situation.

Hatcher was taller than Wheeler with a slender, athletic build. She wore her raven hair in a ponytail most of the time. Freckles she never tried to conceal augmented her nose and upper cheeks, but her bright blue eyes were her most striking feature. She was introverted and rarely smiled, but was all business when it came to her job in the military.

Hatcher was first in their PT class for hand-to-hand combat. Wheeler took second place, setting up years of competitive friendly matches between the two. Hatcher's fighting ability and direct manner earned the respect of male and female cadets alike.

While Hatcher excelled in combat, Wheeler surpassed everyone in physics and quantum mechanics. He read doctorate dissertations in his free time. His curiosity about the subjects might have been considered obsessive if he wasn't having so much fun learning about it.

Tyler was becoming impatient. *Time to get the party started. Where's that beer we ordered?* He turned to look toward the bar and saw their server hurrying to their table.

"I'm sorry, sir. We're a little backed up tonight." He set a bucket of bottled beers on the table. "Courtesy of Mr. Townsend, the owner. He's a retired Ranger."

"Thanks," Tyler said. "It was getting pretty thirsty back here."

"Yes, sir," the server said. "Sorry about that." He pointed to Kathy. "Did you decide on which wine you wanted, ma'am?"

"Yes, the house Pinot Grigio, please. Thanks."

"No problem, ma'am. I'll be right back with that." After a quick glance around to ensure everyone was happy, the server retreated to the bar.

Tyler held up his beer and announced a toast. "To the HERO Team!" They clinked their bottlenecks together and settled back to relax.

"I didn't mention it earlier," he said. "But Major McKnight told me General Drake and Master Sergeant Clary will be joining us tonight. That's probably why he's running late."

"Outstanding!" Wheeler said. Hatcher raised her beer in salute.

"I'm glad he'll be here," Kathy said. "I always learn something new when the General is around."

"Seems like everybody feels that way," Trevor said. "Have y'all been with him for a long time?"

"Not really," Hatcher said. "But he's a legend in the Rangers. But he's more than that to us. I know the Major sees him that way, too."

"It's true," Tyler said. "the Major looks forward to their meetings."

Hatcher nodded. "Yeah. Me, too. It sounds corny, but he's like a father figure to most of us. When he talks about tactics and strategy and stuff like that? I come away with new insights and perspective. You can't buy that anywhere."

"Wow," Trevor said. "Lieutenant Hatcher, I –"

"Call me Hatcher, please."

"Sure. I think I've heard you talk more today than my entire time with the team."

"I talk all the time."

Trevor shrugged. "About work, yes, but I haven't really heard much else."

Wheeler laughed. "Hatcher's just naturally blabby."

"Shut up, you ass," Hatcher said. "Unlike you, Wheeler, I don't waste my time talking about irrelevant stuff."

"See what I mean? Blabby."

Kathy and Trevor laughed as Hatcher scowled and threw a balled-up napkin at Wheeler.

Wheeler ducked and said, "And violent, too."

"Bite me," Hatcher said. She leaned back in her chair and took a long drink from her beer.

Trevor looked between the two and smiled. "Seems like you two have been friends for a long time. From school, maybe?"

A slight smile crossed Hatcher's face. "Too long. I'm thinking about killing him if he doesn't shut up." She glared at Wheeler. "You talk too much."

"Yes, since we met at UNG," Wheeler said. "We were in the same class together. We were the two dummies in the class – nobody else would talk to us. So, we just hung out together." He shrugged and took another sip of beer.

"Speak for yourself," Hatcher said. "I was one of the smart ones."

Trevor laughed. "What was it, Karen? Why did you guys connect?"

"I think most of our classmates were just trying to pass Physics. Wheeler and I liked it. We've always been physics geeks."

"True, true," Wheeler said. "She graduated with honors at the top of our class at the Academy."

"No kidding. That's impressive, Karen," Kathy added.

"It's not that impressive," Hatcher said, with only a hint of a smile. "Wheeler did it, too."

"Yes, but you did it first," Wheeler said.

"Only because my name comes before yours in an alphabetic list. We graduated in the same ceremony, dumbass."

"Oh, yeah. I forgot." Hatcher rolled her eyes as Wheeler continued. "Hatcher's unique, you know."

"How's that?" Trevor said. He smiled at Hatcher. "Not that I doubt it."

"She's second generation," Wheeler said. "The first one."

Trevor glanced from Wheeler to Hatcher and back. "What does that mean?"

"She's the first female Ranger officer with two Ranger parents." Wheeler pointed at Hatcher. "Her Dad."

"Yeah?" Trevor turned to Hatcher. "Your parents were Rangers?"

Hatcher shrugged. "Yeah, Dad's retired now. Mom's a general, about to retire."

"I'm impressed. Were there any expectations or pressures to succeed because of that?"

"No," Hatcher said.

"Yes," Wheeler said.

Hatcher looked exasperated as Wheeler continued. "What do you think? The first Ranger daughter of married Rangers, not to mention being a general's kid. C'mon!"

"It's not that bad," Hatcher said. "No more than any other military parent. I don't think about it much."

Wheeler laughed. "Yeah, right."

"So, you two hooked up in school?"

"Poor choice of words, Trevor," Wheeler said. "I'm married and Hatcher has her own love life. We work well together and we both have an unnatural love of physics."

Hatcher nodded. "That," she said, "we can agree upon."

"Okay. And after school?"

Wheeler continued. "Now Hatcher majors in time travel and rattlesnakes."

Hatcher leaned forward and glared at him. "Don't go there again, Wheeler. Please?"

Trevor sat up straight. "Now, this is the third time I've heard something about Hatcher and rattlesnakes. What's that all about?"

"You haven't heard the story?" Wheeler asked.

"Oh, that's right," Tyler said. "I think everyone else was on the team when that happened. You weren't around to hear about it."

"About what?"

Tyler started to speak, but Kathy touched his arm. "Let Wheeler tell the story. He was there."

"You want to hear it?" Wheeler asked.

"Oh, puh-lease," Hatcher said. She leaned back in her chair, sighed heavily and studied the ceiling.

"I do," Trevor said. "Is it a true story?"

"Of course," Wheeler said. "You doubt that I would speak anything other than truth?"

"Are you kidding?" Trevor said.

Wheeler laughed and clutched at his heart. "I am cut to the quick, sir." He drained the rest of his beer. "But I'll get over it if you'll pass me another beer."

A new drink in hand, Wheeler sat up straight and said, "All take heed here, as I share with thee the story of Hatcher and the Rattlesnake."

"Oh, brother!" Hatcher said, shaking her head.

"Shut up, Hatcher. I'm telling the story of your glory and bravery. Trevor, what do you know about the calibration of the Time Engine?"

"Well, nothing really. Just that you or Hatcher type in configuration data on the keyboard that somehow programs the Engine to take us to where and when we want."

"You've got it," Wheeler said. "So, we had to learn how to do that, right? Doctor Astalos stumbled upon the ability to travel, but we didn't know how to focus or control the travel. It was pure dumb trial and error. Hatcher and I spent weeks experimenting with changing one of several field parameters and recording the results to see what happens. We gathered enough data to predict where any set of parameters would take us. Follow me so far?"

"Yes, I think so."

"Okay. Here's what happened. It isn't classified now. Hatcher and I spent two months up in the Sandia Mountains in New Mexico. Clear nights and some altitude. We took the Time Engine there and practiced sending a camera on a chariot back in time to photograph the stars. Same thing, over and over. Change a configuration setting on the Engine, send the chariot back through time to take pictures of the stars' position, tag the picture with the time and settings, and send the pictures to a lab where Doctor Astalos and a team of astronomers would figure out the time, date, and position of where and when the chariot landed. After a week, the lab sent us configuration settings to try so they could see if their theories were valid."

"Okay, I get the idea," Trevor said. "So, what does that have to do with rattlesnakes?"

"I'm coming to that," Wheeler said. "One night about two in the morning, we sent the camera chariot back one hundred years. We're standing back about twenty yards and it was a little dim. I mean, you know, we had lights shining on the area, but not enough to see all that well from a distance. When we bring the chariot back this time, it looks like something has fallen on top of it."

"Uh-oh," Trevor said. "I think I see where this is going."

"Yup. I ran over to the chariot to see what's up and learned two things."

"What did you learn?"

"I learned the junk on the chariot was a really angry diamondback, and I was standing too damned close to it."

"Shit, what happened? I already know you're not dead."

"Good guess. I threw myself backward to put some distance between us. Good thing, too, because it tried to strike and missed me by an inch. But we hit the ground right next to each other, and I was sure he would get me on the second try."

"Yeah?"

"Then Hatcher scooped it up."

"She what?"

"She grabbed that sucker by the tail and started swinging it over her head."

"Oh, my God!" Hatcher exclaimed.

"Honest. She yelled for me to start up the Engine again. After I did, she slung that snake into the time bubble. It was trying to get out of the bubble when the machine fired. Cut that asshole right in half. Gave him the chance to exist in two different centuries at the same time."

"No way."

"Oh, yeah. That's how Hatcher became known far and wide as the Rattler Queen."

Hatcher sat quietly, shaking her head.

Trevor turned to her. "Is any of this true?"

Hatcher shifted in her chair. "Some of it. I don't remember swinging a snake over my head."

Trevor didn't speak for a minute. "You just picked up a rattlesnake?"

"No," she said. "I jumped on it. Grabbed it behind the head so it couldn't bite me. Once I did that, I grabbed his body near the tail so I could control him."

"What the hell did you do that for?" he asked.

"Well, if I hadn't, he would have bitten Wheeler for sure. I couldn't let that happen. Though I'm thinking now maybe I should have. But then, I would've had to carry his lazy ass down off that mountain."

"I'd have thought a rattler would be too fast for you to grab like that."

"They are, but he didn't see me coming." She pointed at Wheeler. "He was busy trying to strike Mister Personality here."

"What happened after that?"

"I know you'll have a hard time believing this," she said. "But Wheeler wanted to chat about it. We have a hundred-year-old snake, he said. Here I am, standing there trying to hold the squirming asshole and he wants to bask in the moment! I should have let it bite him."

"What about it getting cut in half? Did that happen?"

"Yeah, that happened. I threw it in the time bubble, but it didn't want to stay there. We kept poking it with shovels, trying to keep it in. It struck at me, but the Engine fired when its head and part of the body were outside the bubble. I got venom and blood splattered all over my uniform blouse. Ruined it."

"I can imagine. I think Wheeler owes you more than a few beers."

"I'd call it even if he'd just stop telling that story." She looked at Wheeler. "It gets more ridiculous every time he tells it. I'm tired of hearing it. Give it a rest, will you?"

Wheeler laughed again.

"Well," Kathy said. "I think it was a pretty brave thing to do. You go, girl."

"I'm a Ranger. Like the rest of these guys. We have each other's back, even when we're stupid." She pointed her beer bottle at Wheeler. "Which Wheeler is, more than his share of the time."

Trevor raised his beer bottle to Hatcher. "Karen, you're not just a Ranger. You're a bad-ass Lady Ranger. I, for one, am glad you're on our side. God help our nation's enemies when they get on your bad side."

"Here, here," Kathy said.

Hatcher shrugged and took another pull from her beer.

****

7:26 p.m. – June 17, 2036 – Old Town, Alexandria, VA

"Where is this place?" Drake asked.

"Sorry for the long walk, sir," McKnight said. "Seems like Old Town Alexandria is pretty busy tonight. We're almost there."

Drake made a half-turn and glanced back the way they had come. "A nice night for a walk, though."

McKnight, Drake and Clary walked the last few steps from the parking deck to the Army Mule pub.

"Sorry for making you late for the team outing," Drake said. "It's important to spend time together outside the office."

"I'm sure all will be forgiven, sir, since you and the Sergeant Major have come along. The team likes to see you, and they know they're important to you."

"Well, good. So, how's the new receptionist working out?" Drake asked.

"Very well, sir. I called Senator Owen at home. He recommended her and said he was glad she found a position here. In addition to her reception duties, she's picking up some minor office admin tasks, getting them off Doctor Wu's plate. So far, it's all good."

"Okay. During the move meeting tomorrow, please remind everyone not to put the move date on their calendars. Just in case. I don't expect us to get hacked, but let's not leave that to chance."

"Yes, sir."

They reached the front door of the bar.

"It's a regular hangout for the Rangers in town, sir," McKnight said. He opened the door for Drake and Clary and followed them inside.

The place was crowded, but it didn't take long to locate the team, seated around a table in the back. As they maneuvered through the crowd to reach them, a voice yelled out. "General Drake!"

At the sound of his name, Drake turned toward the bar. Clary and McKnight paused beside him.

The bartender waved at him, came to attention, and saluted. "It's good to see you again, sir."

Drake said, "Well, I'll be damned! Jim Townsend. God, it's been a long time. I heard you had retired."

"Yes, sir. My brother and I started this bar last year. What do you think?" Townsend spread his arms and gestured at the room around him.

"I think I'll have a drink," Drake said. He reached over the bar and shook Townsend's hand. "You remember Sergeant Major Clary, don't you?"

"Absolutely, sir. How are you, Tom?"

"Just fine, Jimmy boy," Clary said, as he shook Townsend's hand. "How's your beer?"

Townsend laughed and handed Clary a drink menu.

Drake turned to McKnight. "Come back in a few minutes, Marc. Jim's an old friend and I want to catch up." He slipped onto a bar stool as he motioned for McKnight to carry on. Clary sat next to him.

McKnight nodded at the two men. "Will do, sir." He turned on his heel and continued wading through the crowd toward the team. As he walked away from the bar, he heard Drake ask Clary to retrieve his briefcase from the car. He smiled at the thought. Drake would ask Townsend to contribute to his favorite charity and display a poster in the bar's front window.

The team was seated in a semi-circle around a couple of tables. Tyler sat on the near side of the table, next to the empty chair he saved for McKnight. Across from Tyler sat Wheeler and Hatcher. Kathy and Trevor occupied the last two seats.

The military members of the team rose as a unit and came to attention when he arrived. Kathy and Trevor raised beer mugs in his direction.

He saluted the officers and said, "As you were."

He took a chair opposite them. In any other place and time, he wouldn't take a seat with his back to the door. But he felt secure here with these three officers and two sharp civilians looking over his shoulder.

"How's it going, Winnie?" McKnight asked Tyler.

"Excellent, sir. Just waiting for you. What can I get you?"

"The usual. Thanks." McKnight turned to Wheeler as Tyler headed to the bar. "How's the baby, Mitch?"

"Great, sir. He starts kindergarten this year."

"Already? Seems like he was born just the other day."

"He's five years old now, sir."

"Wow. Time flies way too fast."

"You gentlemen are a beer or two behind us, sir," Hatcher said, as she raised her glass to McKnight.

Under Astalos' tutelage, Wheeler and Hatcher had become experts in programming and configuring the Time Engine. Both were up for promotion this year.

"Yes, we are. It's time to remedy that." Tyler handed a beer to McKnight. He lifted it in Hatcher's direction with a flourish. "Cheers, Lieutenants…and you, too, Kathy and Trevor."

McKnight took a long draft and leaned back in his chair. He turned to Tyler. "Hey, any word from Barbara Howard?"

Tyler frowned and shook his head. “Nothing. Not a word. I gotta tell you – Sarah and I are getting worried.”

“Keep me posted, will you?”

“Sure,” Tyler said. “Sarah decided to call her parents again to see if she can get in touch with them.”

McKnight nodded. “Good idea.” *This doesn’t sound good. I hope she’s okay.*

Hatcher was the first to see it coming. She sprang to her feet and strode toward General Drake. Wheeler was right behind her. As they passed McKnight, he turned in his chair and saw what had triggered them to move.

An angry drunk man stood before General Drake at the bar. McKnight recognized him as a military contractor who worked for Senator Lodge in the past. The man leaked classified information about the HERO Team and was terminated by Lodge. *What was his name? Smith? Yes, that’s it.*

McKnight and Tyler rose and followed the others. McKnight saw Hatcher signal Wheeler to go before her and spoke to him as he passed. He nodded and quickened his pace.

Smith's voice carried in the small bar. The patrons stopped talking and watched the events as they unfolded.

“You cost me my job, you asshole. Because of you, nobody will hire me for security work. I'm gonna whip your ass right here in front of God and everybody.” His voice trailed away. “Fucking Rangers,” he muttered under his breath.

Hatcher stepped to the General's side and spoke to him without taking her eyes off the belligerent Smith. “Is this gentleman bothering you, General?”

“So, what if I am?” the man said, as he turned halfway around and glared at her. “What are *you* gonna do about it?”

“No problem here, Lieutenant,” Drake said.

He looked Smith in the eye. “Sir, I humbly apologize. Here, let me buy you a drink.” He turned toward Townsend, who anticipated

Drake's conciliatory response and handed him a premium beer. As Drake offered the drink, the inebriated Smith slapped it away.

Glass shattered on the floor, and the room went deathly quiet.

Smith glared at Drake. "I don't accept anything from a Ranger," he said. "You blew your credibility with me a long time ago."

McKnight heard an awestruck voice whisper from across the room. "Oh, my God. That's General Drake!"

Drake spoke softly. "Mr. Smith, you revealed classified information related to time technology. Nobody wants a security chief who talks out of turn and loses his clearance. You cost yourself the job."

Smith was oblivious to everything else in the room. He stared intently at Drake. "After I kick your ass, I'm gonna make you–"

"Pardon me, sir," Hatcher interrupted. "But you seem to have dropped your beer. Maybe you've had enough to drink tonight. Maybe you should go home." She smiled sweetly at Smith as McKnight slipped onto the bar stool next to Drake. Smith stared at him with malice in his eyes, then turned back to Drake.

Hatcher spoke to Smith again. "Can I help you with anything, sir?"

Hatcher finally penetrated his alcoholic haze and got his attention. Smith turned to face her. "Go away, little girl, before you start to piss me off. You don't know who you're messing with."

"Neither do you," she said, a touch of ice in her voice. "You look tired. Why don't you let me help you to your car?"

"You really *are* asking for it," Smith barked. "Go home before I lose my patience and damage that pretty little face of yours."

She added a final barb to irritate him. "Better men than you have tried, sir. *Much* better men."

Smith took the bait. He pointed at Drake without looking at him and mumbled, "You're next, after I spank this bitch."

Then he advanced on Hatcher, who took one step back into a fighting stance.

Drake slipped off his stool to interfere, but McKnight stopped him with a hand on his shoulder.

"Hold on a second, sir," he said. "He's got no idea. Let's give her a minute."

"I don't think I want this to happen," Drake said.

"She'll end it faster than we could."

Smith took a swing at Hatcher, who caught his wrist, threw her hip, and pulled him past her, using his own weight to send him sprawling.

He leapt to his feet, fury in his eyes. Embarrassed now, he approached her with a smile on his face and malice in his eyes. He was no stranger to hand-to-hand combat, and he intended to do the young lieutenant significant harm. He was lean and muscular and outweighed the woman by sixty pounds.

"Mike!" Townsend called out. "You're a regular here, but so help me, you throw another punch, you'll never drink in this bar again. General Drake is my guest."

"Fuck you!" Smith said, angry beyond any reasoning. He swung twice at her and connected with Hatcher's left shoulder with the second, spinning her around. He didn't realize she was in complete control.

She continued her spin and struck him full in the cheek with a back-handed left fist followed by a right roundhouse blow and landed in a fighting stance.

Smith staggered backward but didn't go down. He touched his cheek and examined his fingers to see if she had drawn blood. Then he strode toward Hatcher and was met with a kick to the chest, which forced him to back-pedal to keep his feet.

Hatcher pressed her advantage and closed in as Smith assumed a defensive posture. He lost more ground as he fended off blow after blow with his forearms. As it became clear he was losing the fight, three men from a table across the room stood and made their way over to the melee.

McKnight and Drake moved between them and the fight. McKnight noticed Clary had returned and joined them.

The first man tried to push past Clary, who put his hands up, palms out. "It's a fair fight, friend. Let's stay out of it."

The man took a swing at Clary, who ducked the blow and struck the man in the throat. He went down on his hands and knees, coughing and gasping.

The second man grabbed Drake's jacket lapels and tried to push him away.

Before McKnight could respond, Drake kneed the man in the groin, grabbed the fingers of his right hand and bent his hand backward to the point of breaking.

The man took a feeble swing at Drake's face with his left hand.

Drake blocked it and raised the captured hand higher forcing the man onto his tiptoes. "Don't do that again," he said, his tone much like a growl. In a softer voice he said, "I presume you will be needing these fingers for work in the near future?"

The man nodded, his face contorted with pain and his breath coming in short gasps.

"Good. Let's both butt out of their business." He pushed the man away and stood for a second, palms out again.

The man nodded and massaged his sore fingers.

Behind Drake, Hatcher was wearing Smith down. Though he had more experience and size, the alcohol in his bloodstream had taken its toll. He couldn't react fast enough to fend off the flurry of blows from the whirling dervish in front of him. She was younger and faster. It was only a matter of time before his impaired reflexes failed him.

Finally, that moment came. He didn't move quickly enough to block the roundhouse kick to the side of his head. The big man went down and stayed there.

The third man approached Drake, who moved to a fighting stance.

The man shook his head and waved his hands to indicate he wasn't a threat.

"No problem here, General." To the others he said, "What the fuck is wrong with you guys? Taking on the Dragon? Are you stupid? What the hell are you thinking?" He turned back to Drake, his face a picture of humility. "I'm sorry, sir. Mike and the rest of us overdid it tonight. He gets a little mean sometimes when he's had too much."

Drake relaxed and nodded. "If he's your friend, I suggest you get him out of here."

"Yes, sir." The three men hurried past him, helped Smith to his feet, and hustled him out the door.

Townsend came around to the front of the bar and stood with McKnight and his team.

"General, I'm sorry this happened. That guy is no longer welcome in my bar. He's been a regular and, well, sometimes he drinks too much and speaks out of turn, but this is the first time he's caused trouble. Some of the stuff he says seems pretty crazy. Maybe I should report it to the police."

Drake shook his head. "Not a problem, Jim. Mr. Smith has a beef with our team and we'll never be good friends." He crossed his arms and leaned against the bar. "Tell me. What sort of stuff has he been saying?"

"Well, not a lot, but lately he's been spouting off about some big deal he has cooking. I got tired of hearing him brag so I asked him for details. He stared at me for a second and the curtain came down. I guess he realized he was talking too much and went dark. I can tell you this – I've heard him mention you and Major McKnight more than once. Until now, I thought it was just booze talking."

"Okay. Thanks, Jim. Seriously, if you hear anything else about him, please call me or Tom here ASAP. Tom, give Jim one of your cards, please."

The bartender shrugged with relief as Clary handed him a business card. "Sure, General. Let me buy a round for you and your team to compensate for the inconvenience."

"Thanks, Jim. That would be very much appreciated."

Townsend retreated behind the bar and began pouring beers.

Drake leaned toward McKnight to speak but was interrupted by the sound of the door as it crashed open behind him. They turned to see Smith standing in the doorway, his fists clenched by his sides and his face red with rage.

Hatcher and Wheeler moved to a protective position in front of Drake and Clary.

Smith's friends burst in behind him and took him by the arms. As he struggled to get free, they pulled him back through the door.

"We're not done, Drake! I'm gonna fuck you up. You and McKnight and that candy-ass Lodge." His friends won the tug of war to pull him out of the place. As the door closed behind them, he yelled over his shoulder, "Your Ranger asses are mine, motherfuckers."

McKnight sent Tyler and Wheeler to confirm Smith and his friends had left the vicinity of the bar. Hatcher moved to follow them.

"Not you, Lieutenant. We don't want to get him fired up again. Let him go nurse his wounded pride."

"Yes, sir. May I ask a question, sir?"

"Yes. Nice work, by the way."

"Thank you, sir. What's this guy Smith's problem?"

"Lieutenant, do you remember that the existence of the Time Engine was a secret for the first ten years after it was invented?"

"Yes, sir, I do," she said. "Someone leaked the information a couple of years ago."

"And what's been the result of that leak?"

"Well, I know that it's been Hell for Robert and Robby Astalos. As the inventors, they've been bombarded by the media and all sorts of folks who want to use the technology for personal gain."

"Correct," McKnight said. "And you know it was a lot easier to protect the technology when nobody knew it existed."

"Yes, sir," she said. Her eyes brightened. "Oh, was he the leaker?"

"In a word, yes. He worked security and sensitive projects for Senator Lodge at the time. He was trying to impress a female client and leaked the information. General Drake found out about it and reported it to the Senator. The Senator blackballed him in Washington and got his clearance yanked. Since then, he never got another security contract with anyone in government."

"And he blames you and General Drake?"

"That's right. It was his own fault, but his ego is too big to see it that way."

"I see," she said. "So he lost his job?"

"Well, I heard he was able to find some mercenary work, but it's a lot more dangerous and the pay isn't as good. All in all, I think you're safe in assuming he doesn't like us much."

Hatcher nodded. "Sounds like an A-number-one asshole to me, sir."

"It would seem that way, Lieutenant. But you never know a man – or a woman – until you've been where they've been. Keep that in mind."

"Yes, sir." She turned and took up position next to him and Drake. She stood there with her back to them, so she could watch the other patrons of the bar. She reminded McKnight of a lioness protecting her cubs.

McKnight turned back to Drake who was intently studying the floor. "Are you all right, sir?"

"What? Oh, yes, of course. I was just thinking. There's more here than meets the eye. I don't think we should ignore this guy. And his hatred of the Rangers feels like more than normal service rivalry."

"I agree, sir. He has something in the works and we'd better try to get out in front of it."

"Right. He made a big tactical mistake just now and we'd be stupid not to pay attention to it. Why don't you request his service record through the Joint Chiefs and let's see who he really is?"

"Yes, sir, and I'll alert the FBI and Senator Lodge's protection detail. Considering the access he had in the past through Senator Lodge, we should alert NSA as well, don't you think?"

"Yes, them, too. He's up to something and it can't be good. And I think we're in trouble if we don't find out what it is."

CHAPTER 6

1:55 p.m., June 19, 2036 – Kingstowne Center, Telegraph Road, Alexandria, VA

It was unusual for April Wu to venture to Alexandria from her home in Washington DC's Chinatown. On any other occasion, Kathy couldn't have dragged her mother out of the house to eat in a local restaurant, let alone down in Alexandria. But she insisted Kathy meet her here at this time. She wondered why.

Kathy opened her umbrella, locked her car and walked across the parking lot to the Pasara Thai restaurant. At the door, she slipped her umbrella into a bag offered there and looked around for her mother.

The place was winding down from a busy lunch hour. Bus boys were clearing the tables and the wait staff was tallying the last few bills for the remaining customers. Her mother stood and beckoned to her from a booth in the back.

Kathy hurried over and the older woman waved her into the red vinyl bench seat beside her. Her mother wasn't alone – a smallish woman near her mother's age sat across from her. Kathy recognized the face. *Mrs. Chang from the old neighborhood.* Kathy slipped into the booth, but her mother remained standing as she introduced the other woman in Chinese.

"Kathy, you remember Mrs. Chang, don't you? Her family lived in our neighborhood when you were in college."

Kathy hadn't see the woman in years. She looked much older. "Of course, I do. How are you, Mrs. Chang?"

The woman nodded and looked down at her hands, clasped before her on the table. Kathy looked back at her mother, who said, "Kathy,

Mrs. Chang has been our good friend for many years. She needs your help."

Kathy looked back and forth between the two women. "Mom, what's going on?"

"Karen is a good woman and a good mother. She believes her daughter is in trouble, and you are the only one who can help."

"I don't think I..." She paused when she noticed Mrs. Chang was on the verge of tears. Her lips trembled, and Kathy saw fear and distress in her eyes.

"I will leave you two alone to talk," her mother said with finality. She looked down at Mrs. Chang. "Tell Kathy what you told me. I will be back in forty-five minutes." To Kathy, she added, "You are my daughter and you have a big heart for others. I know you will do whatever you can to help our friend." She turned on her heel and left the restaurant.

A waitress appeared next to Kathy. "May I get you something?" she said.

"Just some green tea, if you will. Thanks."

Kathy turned back to Mrs. Chang. Her mother was right – the pain of others always pierced her heart. "Mrs. Chang, are you unwell? Can I get you anything?"

The woman's voice wavered as she spoke. "I have tea here and water. I am fine. It's my Amy."

"Your daughter, Amy?"

"Yes, do you remember when you met? You were in college, and Amy was nine years old. You agreed to babysit Amy once."

Sometimes having an eidetic memory was a curse. But not today. Kathy remembered Amy Chang. At nine years old, Amy was skinny and awkward. But Kathy had encouraged her and treated her with respect. She didn't realize until later how much the little girl idolized her.

"Yes, ma'am, I remember her. What's happened to her?"

"She's gone. I fear…I fear she is dead."

"Dead? What do you mean?"

"I saw it on TelExtraVision. She fell from a balcony. So long ago – I don't understand..." Tears rolled down her lined and careworn cheeks.

"You saw it on...Mrs. Chang, please forgive me." Kathy reached across the table to touch the woman's clenched hands. "Can you start from the beginning?"

"Yes...yes," the woman said, dabbing at her eyes with a tissue. "She always calls me every two or three days. Six weeks ago, she stopped calling. After a week, I started to worry. She didn't answer her cell phone, and she didn't call me back." Shaking her head at Kathy, she continued. "My Amy is a good girl. She'd never forget her mama."

"Mrs. Chang, does Amy have a boyfriend?"

"Yes. I talked to him. He's worried sick, too. He told me she was upset. She wouldn't tell him what, but he was sure she was..."

"What, Mrs. Chang?"

"She was afraid."

"Afraid of what?"

"He didn't know. He seems like such a good boy. I don't believe he knows anything but what he told me." The woman opened her purse and pulled out another tissue.

"Mrs. Chang, I understand why you're concerned. Have you been to the police?"

"Yes." She held Kathy's eyes with hers, and they filled with tears again. "They questioned Michael – her boyfriend. They called all her friends and all of mine. I don't know what else they could have done. They were sympathetic and helpful but...they found nothing." The tears flowed again. She paused a moment to get herself back under control.

Kathy saw quiet strength in that anguished face, but a spirit that had been bent to the breaking point. "They believe my Amy is dead, and there's no hope. They tell me to have hope, but they have none. I can see it in their eyes. And it must be true. I saw it myself. She's gone."

"Mrs. Chang, what did you mean about Amy dying? You said you saw it?"

"Yes. I didn't realize it then, but after I didn't see Amy for a few days and didn't hear from her, it came back into my mind."

"What did?"

The older woman pulled her purse into her lap, unzipped it, and gave Kathy a video cube. "Years ago, a friend sent this to me. It was a TelExtraVision series about politicians. The episode on this recording tells of a politician whose career was ruined because he had an affair with a young girl who killed herself. My friend mentioned how much the girl looked like my Amy."

"Really?"

"Yes. I forgot about it until recently. When Amy disappeared, I found it and watched it. The girl in the video is Amy."

Kathy felt the hair on the back of her neck stand up. "Does the video ever identify the girl?" she asked.

"No, it doesn't. The narrator said no one ever learned who she was. But I know. It showed a security camera film of the man and a girl in an elevator. It was Amy." She looked Kathy in the eye. "A mother knows her daughter's face. And she was wearing a dress I gave her last year. It was her. I know it."

The waiter set a cup of tea in front of Kathy and disappeared.

Kathy pulled a link cable from her purse and plugged the cube into her phone. She started the video app and watched the opening credits for the series. The lead for the story said a Chicago politician lost his career when he was found in a rented apartment from which a girl leapt to her death.

"Kathy, you can see her in the elevator scene. Fast forward to the twenty minute mark."

Kathy did so, and the elevator scene appeared.

A man and a woman were in the elevator. The man draped his arm around the woman's shoulders. She didn't act forced, but there was something odd about her manner. Kathy couldn't put her finger on it, but the scene just didn't seem right.

The video quality was better than most. She had to admit the girl resembled the child she had known.

"Do you have a recent picture of Amy?" Kathy asked.

"Yes," Mrs. Chang said. "Let me prox it to you." She touched a few buttons on her phone, and the proximity link appeared on Kathy's.

Kathy accepted it and looked at the picture, then switched back to the video and paused it. She switched the apps back and forth a few more times. She had to admit the resemblance to Amy was startling.

Kathy forgot about her cup of tea.

"Mrs. Chang, I understand why you believe this girl is Amy. Did you show this to the police?"

"Yes. They were skeptical and said they understood how I felt. They think I'm desperate and will grasp at any hope of finding her. They are right, of course. I am sick with worry. They want to help, but I fear they are doing nothing more because they don't know what to do. They made a copy of the video, but…" She shrugged and her eyes pleaded with Kathy. "You're my only hope, Kathy. I know what you do – you work with the time travelers. You can save her. Please, will you help me?"

Kathy's heart broke for the woman. More memories from the past flooded into Kathy's mind. She remembered Amy confided in her about a boy she had a crush on and another child who was mean to her. Kathy was twenty-two at the time but delighted in Amy's excitement and wonder at everything around her. She let her high school and college experiences slip away and became a child again – giggling, telling knock-knock jokes and bonding with Amy. She told Amy about her favorite pet and how much she liked school when she was nine.

As Kathy put her to bed that night, Amy hugged her and said, "You are my best friend. Let's email and be best friends forever."

Kathy promised they would keep in touch. She didn't intend to forget Amy, but she got busy with her friends and so, she thought, had Amy.

The young girl once trusted and looked up to her. Kathy felt a lump of outrage growing in her throat. If what Mrs. Chang suspected was true, her daughter was in serious trouble. And there was no way Kathy would abandon this girl if she could help it.

"I'm not sure I can do anything, Mrs. Chang. But yes, I'll see what I can do. I can't promise you anything, but I'll do everything I can to look into this. Let me think for a minute."

What could she do? Was there was a way to verify the girl was Amy? The Chicago police would have the girl's DNA. And maybe she could get a facial recognition comparison done between the video and the picture.

"Mrs. Chang, can you get something of Amy's for me? Something that might have her DNA on it?"

"I watch TelExtraVision," the woman replied. From her purse, she produced a hairbrush and held it up in front of her. "This is Amy's. Some of her hair is still on it." She clutched the hairbrush to her breast for a moment, her eyes closed. Then she handed it to Kathy. "I can find something else if you need it."

"Thanks. This should be enough."

"Thank you, Kathy. I am in your debt."

"Not at all," Kathy said. "Give me a few days to see what I can learn."

"Please, find and save my daughter."

"Mrs. Chang, I promise you I'll do everything I can."

As she left the restaurant, Kathy's brain was working overtime. She had learned to trust her instincts, and they screamed that the girl in the video was Amy and she was in mortal danger if not already dead.

By the time she got back to the HERO Team office, one thing was clear to her. Her first step was to prove the girl in the video is or is not Amy. *If it isn't Amy, it's an eerie coincidence.* The resemblance of the girl in the video to Amy was unsettling. Logic told her it made no sense.

If it is Amy, something is bad wrong here. Who would do something like this? What could they gain from it?

CHAPTER 7

3:25 p.m. – June 19, 2036 – Defense Logistics Agency Satellite Office Building, Telegraph Road, Alexandria, VA

When Kathy got back to the office, she went straight to Trevor's office. While she was a savvy mission planner, Trevor's forte was cold case investigations – that was his job at the Atlanta Police Department.

Cindy, the new receptionist, was standing by his desk, arms crossed. It occurred to Kathy the girl was using the posture to accentuate her breasts. When she saw Kathy coming, she smiled. Kathy pasted a smile on her own face. The girl was friendly enough, but she paid way too much attention to Trevor for Kathy's taste.

As she got closer, Cindy said, "Now, that's funny. Trevor, you are *so* crazy. Well, I'd better get back up front." To Kathy, she said, "Hi, Doctor Wu. How are you today?"

"Just fine, thanks. Am I interrupting something?"

"No, not at all," Cindy said. "Oh, Doctor Wu? Doctor Astalos asked me to check his calendar and schedule an appointment with his doctor, but I don't have access. Who could help me with that?"

"I can. Actually, you need access to everyone's calendar. I'll set it up later today and text you."

"Thanks," she said to Kathy. "See you later, Trevor." Turning, she walked back down the hall.

Kathy watched her for a moment, then turned to Trevor. "What was that about?"

"Huh?"

"Huh? The Blonde Bombshell."

"Her? I don't know. I guess she was bored out at her desk," he said.

Kathy bit her lip. *Shut up! This is the thinking that gets in the way of your work. That's why you don't get romantically involved with people on the job.*

"Did I do something wrong?" he asked.

"No."

"Look," he said. "I'm sorry if I upset you. It's important to me that you know where I'm coming from—"

Trevor can flirt with anyone he wants.

"You don't have to apologize to me. It's none of my business."

"I know I don't have to. But I don't want you to get the wrong impression, either."

"I'm sure I'm not. Can we focus on work for a few minutes?"

Trevor caught her eyes and held them. "You're very important to me, Kathy. Can't you see that?"

I want to. "And you're important to me, just like all the rest of my colleagues."

Trevor's face fell. He looked away and muttered something she didn't catch.

"What did you say?" she asked.

"Nothing. Just talking to myself."

"Trevor, you know I think you're a special man."

He chuckled. "I think you mean that as a compliment, but it sounds like 'buzz off, weirdo.' Okay, I get it."

"I'm trying to tell you that I like our relationship. It's very special." *How do I get this across? I don't want to mess up our working relationship.*

"Just like it is right now, you mean?"

"Yes."

He shrugged. "Okay. I'll adjust."

"What?" she said. "Oh, never mind. Look, I need your help. Do you have a few minutes?"

He smiled at her. “Sure. What's going on?”

She told him Mrs. Chang's story and showed him the picture and the video.

Trevor listened without comment. When she finished, he nodded and said, “I see. Under normal circumstances, a missing girl would be a case for DC Police. But they didn't move on it because there's no evidence of foul play, and most missing girls are missing because they want to be. Your thought is, if this is Amy Chang in this video–and it's a big 'if'–then she time-traveled somehow. That makes it our business, right?”

“Yes, that's what I was thinking.”

“Well, the timing is about right for us to investigate. It’s close to the twenty-five-year anniversary of the event.”

“Yes, I thought of that. If we go back today, that girl is still alive. We can save her life. I understand we’re not supposed to interfere with history, but if it’s Amy, then she shouldn’t be back in 2011 in the first place. Don’t we have an obligation to act if history was unnaturally changed somehow?”

“Good question.” He shook his head. “If that girl is Amy, all Hell will break loose on this one. I can hear General Drake now. 'How the Hell did a girl from Washington get murdered in Chicago nearly twenty-five years ago when she should be a toddler?' Worse, we don't know the answer to any of the questions he might ask. We're the only people authorized to have and operate this technology. We gotta figure this out.”

“Agreed. He needs to know we detected it, and we’re researching it. What's our plan?”

“Do you have the hairbrush with you?”

“Yes,” she said, handing it to him.

Trevor started the magnification app on his phone and focused on the hairbrush. “There's enough follicle and skin matter on the hairbrush to get some DNA. Let's make a copy of the picture and the video for safekeeping. I'll send the video off to my buddy Eve in

Atlanta who does excellent facial recognition work. She should be able to tell us if this is the same girl. And we should be able to compare Amy's DNA with the samples they collected from the dead girl in Chicago. You realize if we get a DNA match, they'll want to know where we got it?"

"Yes, I know," she said.

"We can't keep that from them, but I don't know what they can do with it, anyway except refer it back to us."

"Right."

"Well, let's digitize the DNA sample, make a copy of the video cube and the picture and get them emailed out to Chicago and Atlanta."

Kathy frowned. "Then we need to wait for the results to come back before we do anything?"

"I don't think so. It's a pretty strong coincidence, isn't it? The girl has been missing for a while and there's a video featuring a girl that looks like her? It wouldn't stand up in court, but I think it's enough for our team to be interested and ask questions, don't you think?

"I do," Kathy said.

"Regardless, we should get the results back in less than a week."

He smiled that smile she liked so well. *What is it about this man?* In these last few minutes, he validated her thoughts and instincts by reviewing the evidence and reaching the same conclusion she did during the ride back from lunch. *We think a lot alike.* "And then?"

"Let's start with Major McKnight. He'll want to know about any project we're working on. And he'd be pretty ticked if we knew about something like this and didn't tell him."

"You're right."

"Time is not on our side here. If that girl is Amy, her life is at stake. And think of what would happen if we find out it's Amy later and did nothing to stop it – not to mention how bad we'd feel."

Kathy stood and looked down the hall. Looking back at Trevor, she said, "Let's get the two packages out the door."

In thirty minutes, the two packages were on their way to Atlanta and Chicago and they were on their way to McKnight's office.

****

Marc McKnight was sitting with his back to the door, his feet up on the credenza, looking out the window that was the outside wall of his office. There was a picturesque stand of hardwood trees there, but he didn't see them. His eyes captured the images, but his mind was somewhere else.

In a few days, they would move their offices from this location on Telegraph Road to DLA headquarters about five miles away.

He pushed the subject to the back of his mind. *You delegated this, remember?* Tyler was planning the move and rarely made a mistake. McKnight didn't need to waste time second-guessing the plan.

A gentle knock on his door broke his concentration.

"Come," he said, as he turned back to his desk.

Trevor and Kathy entered the room and stood before his desk. "Major, is this a good time to chat for a few minutes?"

"Sure. What's up?"

Trevor looked at Kathy, who said, "We think someone may have interfered with history, or is going to."

McKnight leaned back in his chair. "Let's hear it," he said, pointing to the two side chairs across from his desk.

They sat across from him and laid out the story. Kathy spoke first, detailing her lunch with Mrs. Chang, what she knew of the daughter, and the evidence of the video cube and the picture. Trevor followed, explaining what they had done so far and why they felt it was worth pursuing.

"Okay. I understand where you're coming from, and I appreciate you bringing it to me, but until we hear from Atlanta and Chicago, I haven't heard anything that makes me think it's more than an interesting coincidence. The facial recognition would be compelling, but the DNA test will be the key piece of information. If that comes back as a match, then we have a potential mission we can take to the General or Senator Lodge for approval. Fair enough?"

"Absolutely," Trevor said. Kathy looked disappointed but nodded.

The two rose to leave his office, but McKnight held up his hand. "I don't want the DNA results to come back as a match for Miss Chang."

"I agree, sir," Trevor said.

"If it's a match, we have a much bigger problem. I want to see the results as soon as you get them back. If the girl in the picture is Amy Chang..."

Kathy finished the sentence. "Yes. If it *is* Amy in the picture... then we're not the only ones with time travel technology."

"And you're right, Major," Trevor added. "That would be a much bigger problem."

CHAPTER 8

11:23 a.m. – June 20, 2036 – Defense Logistics Agency Satellite Office Building, Telegraph Road, Alexandria, VA

Kathy and Trevor sat in her office. She typed notes on her computer pad as he sat across from her, with his feet on the corner of her desk, looking at the ceiling.

"What are you doing?" he asked.

"I'm trying to get organized. I'm documenting what we know for sure and trying to figure out what else we can do before we get the DNA and recognition results back. And you?"

Trevor grinned at her. "The same thing. Funny how different people do the same thing different ways, eh?"

"Yes." Kathy liked the twinkle in his eye as he turned his gaze back up to the ceiling. Trevor George wasn't flashy or sophisticated. It wasn't any of the stereotypical things women were attracted to. He was an intelligent man who cared about others and worked hard to do the right thing. He wasn't perfect. He was unique.

As if he felt her gaze, he looked at her with that gentle smile. "What?" he said.

"Nothing," she said. "Get your feet off my desk."

"Sorry," he said. He moved his feet, but he didn't stop smiling. "Here's something we can do."

"Yeah? What's that?"

"Why don't we run this by Doctor Astalos? He's always curious, and maybe he knows something that'll help. It's worth a try."

"That's not a bad idea." She frowned. "I don't know if he's in, but I saw him earlier."

"Let's go to the lab and see if he has time to talk."

They walked down the hall and around the corner to the lab. Trevor pressed the access disk from his hip to the security reader and allowed the zip line to snap it back to its place on his belt. The translucent doors parted to allow them to enter.

The Lab was a large open room, about eighty feet by sixty feet, and they entered through a door in the south wall. The ceiling was thirty-five feet high. To the left, a metal staircase led up to a short catwalk near the ceiling and to the roof and helipad beyond. An electronics workbench, a small sink and a conference table were underneath the staircase. To the right was the entrance to Doctor Astalos's office. Against the north wall, Kathy saw the original Engine, the new Engine and the loading dock. The familiar steel travel pad lay in front of the machines.

They walked to Astalos's office and found him sitting at his desk with his eyes closed. His arms were crossed and his fingers were lightly drumming on his arm. *He's not asleep – he's thinking.*

"Doctor Astalos?" she called, her voice a whisper.

"Yes," he said. He opened his eyes and smiled at the two before him.

"Sorry to bother you. Do you have a few minutes?"

"Not at all. I have some time. I was reviewing the call I just had with Robby."

"How is he?" she said. "Is he still in Finland?"

"Yes," Astalos said. "He's enjoying himself."

"I wasn't aware he traveled over there," Trevor said. "Is he doing research or something?"

"Yes, he is. I'm sure you remember I came back to the HERO team when we hit a dead end on our joint research for the warp drive. We decided to go in different directions to break the thinking log jam. It made sense to focus on something else for a while and let my subconscious work on problems. Robby chose to write a book about our research to this point and re-examine the work we've done. That's his approach to refocus."

"Makes sense," Trevor said. "Is everything going okay?"

"Oh, yes. He's staying in Tampere at the Sokos Hotel Tammer. We visited a few years ago and fell in love with the place. He's making progress on the book and doing some research. We were comparing notes. What's on your mind?"

Trevor looked at Kathy, then spoke. "We believe we've run across something that leads us to believe unauthorized time travel has occurred and resulted in the death of a young woman in Chicago."

"Really? Someone else is traveling? What's your evidence?"

"We have a video from an old TelExtraVision program. It shows what appears to be a woman of Kathy's acquaintance right before her death in the past. The girl is missing. She should be in her early twenties today, but in the video, she is an adult of about the same age back about twenty-five years ago. We've sent off the video and a current picture of the girl to colleagues of mine in Atlanta, and we've sent a DNA sample to the Chicago Police for comparison with the dead girl's DNA, provided they still have it."

Astalos stared at them for a moment, his face a picture of focus and concentration. "Very interesting," he said. "If she was killed twenty-five years ago, it means she will soon travel if she hasn't already."

"That's what we thought, too," Kathy said, glancing at Trevor. "It wasn't lost on us that it's been almost twenty-five years since the girl died. And Amy has been missing for about six weeks now."

Astalos looked at Kathy. "Amy? Is this a friend of yours, Kathy?"

"Yes," she said. "Well, not really. Our mothers are old friends."

The elderly man smiled. "I can see there's a bond between you. Let's see the video and picture. Then you can tell me the whole story."

"Sure," she said. She pulled the video cube from her pocket and Astalos connected it to the TelExtraVision monitor on his office wall. "If you have time to watch the whole thing, you'll know everything we do."

Astalos nodded. "Okay, good. Let's do that before we go any further. I want all the background."

As they watched the video, Astalos took a few notes and doodled in his lab book.

When it was over, Astalos said, “Amazing. Let me see the picture of the girl again.”

He searched the video for the elevator scene and froze it on the girl's face. He held the picture up at arm's length and moved forward until the face on the monitor and the face in the picture were about the same size.

“The quality of the video is not great, but the resemblance is striking. Is it just me, or does she seem to be somewhere else? I mean, it doesn't appear the man has her full attention.”

“Yes,” Kathy said. “I noticed it, too, but couldn't quite put my finger on it until you said it. Yes, she seems distant - detached from the situation.”

“That might be the case if she were upset or afraid,” Trevor said. “And, now that I see it again, the man seems a little nervous.”

“Or maybe just excited. She *is* a beautiful woman,” Astalos added. “How did you two come across this?”

Trevor spoke first. “Kathy met with the girl's mother... if she really is who we think she is.”

Astalos turned to Kathy. “Her mother? How interesting! Tell me the rest of the story, Kathy.”

They sat across from each other at his desk and Kathy told him everything she could remember, from the lunch invitation to her decision to check it out.

“I see,” Astalos said. He sat still for a moment. He turned around to his computer pad. He tapped on some keys, then turned back to them. “There may be a way to provide independent evidence that history was altered. *If* it was altered.”

“What?” Trevor said. “What do you mean?”

“Well, we've learned a lot about time travel in the last few months. After your first mission, I got interested in the impact of changes in time. Time has a rhythm and a frequency. We can measure changes to the frequency over time."

"A frequency?" Trevor said. "You mean like a musical tone?"

"Never thought about it that way, Trevor, but it's a good analogy. Normally, it shows up as a straight line. That means no changes to the timeline. Here, let me show you." He spun his chair back around to face his computer and switched it to presentation mode. A three-dimensional copy of his screen filled the air above him. He stood and selected files with hand gestures. "Okay, here we go. See this file?" He touched an icon, and it expanded to a picture before him. It showed a straight line with some tightly clustered spikes in the middle. To the right of each spike the line was slightly out of focus for a period, after which the focus sharpened again.

With an expansive wave of his hands, the spikes spread out, and Kathy saw a great deal more fuzziness between the spikes. She could now tell there were four spikes, three large and one small. "This is the time distortion map from your first mission. The three large spikes are when Major McKnight traveled, and the smaller one is when *you* traveled, Doctor Wu."

"Wow," Kathy said. "It looks like twisted wire. What's all the fuzzy stuff between and after the spikes?"

"That's the time distortion. Twisted, eh? I like that expression. Twisted time is probably a better name for it. If the line is flat, nothing happened to disturb the time frequency. That's how you tell history could have been modified. Remember how history was altered by chance on the Major's first trip and he had to go back and set it right? The spike represents time modification, and the fuzziness immediately after the event is frequency disturbance. When he went back the second time, things quieted down."

Kathy touched Astalos on the arm. "Can we look at the time when the girl dies?"

"Sure. What was the date again?" Kathy told him. Astalos reached out and, with a compressing motion of his hands, reduced the spikes to a small blip in the timeline. With a subsequent sweep of his right hand, he pushed the timeline to his left. Looking at the dates on the display as they flew by, he said, "We should be getting pretty close now." Almost on cue, a large spike appeared in front of them, with an elongated field of twisted time following it.

"Wow," Trevor said. "How did you get it to enlarge like that? Before, you had to stretch it out manually."

Astalos stared at the display. "I didn't."

"You mean the change is that big?" Kathy asked.

Astalos turned and addressed the computer. "Note to computer. Set up a cron job to search the timeline log for spikes and distortion at 0200 hours daily. Label the report as 'Twisted Time Events'. Email report to me with touch points attached to each event over one point tall. Please confirm." The computer repeated the instructions, paused, and then added the request was complete.

"Doctor Astalos?" Kathy said. "Did Amy's death cause that spike?"

"We don't know that," Astalos said, still staring at the display. "What we do know is something significant happened around that point in time and a time travel event caused it." He turned toward Kathy and smiled gently. "But if it isn't the same event, it's a very interesting coincidence."

"Well, Kathy," Trevor said, "looks like there's something going on. Not that I doubted you, but this is a strong indicator. Even without the DNA test, this should be enough to warrant an investigation. As soon as we get the results of the DNA and facial recognition, we'll take it to the Major. But I have no doubts now – there's something here that needs to be checked out."

"Ahem," Astalos cleared his throat. "There's two other items to think about. As we discussed earlier, the event date was less than twenty-five years ago, so the time travel that resulted in this murder may not have occurred yet. The ramification of this is…if it really is your friend Amy…she's probably still alive right now. There's still time to prevent it."

"That's right," Kathy agreed. "And the other item...?"

"Someone else has time travel capability, and we don't know who they are. And chances are excellent they will not appreciate us interfering with their plans."

CHAPTER 9

10:50 p.m. – June 26, 2036 – Phillips Home, Reston, VA

More than anything else in the world, Congressman Blake Phillips wanted to be President of the United States.

After two terms in the Virginia Legislature and three terms as the Congressman from District Eight, he decided to make his run in 2036. He flattered and romanced his Party's power brokers and traveled far and wide to make his name and face the most recognizable trademark in the state.

In the primaries, he waged war against the candidates of his own party. While some of his opponents still seethed at the lies and misinformation he used to beat them, they closed ranks behind him for the Party's sake. He garnered their support by making promises he had no intention of keeping.

But now he was hip-deep in the General Election campaign. Things were not going well. He tried everything he could think of and his principle opponent Wade Harrison was pulling away from him in the polls.

He couldn't beat the man on the issues because he himself had no real position. A career politician, Phillips was in it for the money and the power. More than once, his opponent cited examples where Phillips flip-flopped to be on the winning side.

He stayed in the running because he didn't make many unforced errors. He launched a comprehensive smear campaign, which backfired because the lies he told about Harrison were so outrageous the public reacted the opposite way. Harrison responded by pointing out the facts, and inviting Phillips to a debate of the issues.

Phillips agreed to the debate. A skilled orator, he was not without debating skills. He prepared well, but he had no control over the public record. Harrison used Phillips' past voting record to portray him as easily influenced by outside interests. The debate was an unmitigated disaster for Phillips.

His hopes of winning the election were all but gone.

Tonight, he sat in his home office, the only light coming from his computer pad. He glanced at the clock, aware it was after midnight. He was waiting for Rho, his mysterious chat partner.

Rho's identity was a mystery to Phillips, but he didn't really care. His information was reliable, and Phillips could always use good information.

He connected with Rho several times over the last year. Rho offered Phillips actionable information every time. The information helped him avoid problems or gain advantage over opponents in the House. Over the last few months, Phillips' reputation and prestige increased, and he began to trust the information provided by this mysterious benefactor.

Phillips didn't get elected to the House by being a trusting soul. At first, he tried to learn Rho's identity. After a while, he gave it up. Despite his suspicious nature, he wanted the advantages brought by Rho's information and couldn't bring himself give it up.

Rho hadn't communicated with him in two weeks. Tonight, Phillips prayed Rho would be online so he could talk to him. He had screwed up royally and would go down if he didn't get help.

His politician's instinct told him help from Rho would have a price attached this time. But he would pay it. He admitted to himself he would do anything–anything–to make his current problems go away.

His chat session pinged, dragging him back from his thoughts to his computer pad screen.

The session had a message from Rho. <you there? >

<Yes, I'm here. > Phillips responded. <It's been a while. >

<Yes. How are you? >

Typical of Rho to not give any reason for not contacting me. He typed on the pad, <Stressed. Worried. >

<Understandable - given the circumstances. Want some help? >

<Yes, I need some. I'm at the end of my ability. But I'm not sure what you could do for me at this point. >

<You might be surprised. What do you need help with? >

<The campaign, for one. What can I do to beat this asshole? >

<You can't. Not without help. Serious help. He humiliated you in the debate. >

Phillips typed "Fuck you" into the chat, but erased it without sending. He paused while he got his temper under control. He wanted to respond sarcastically but couldn't afford to alienate Rho.

Rho sent another message. <What are you willing to do to win? >

Phillips paused. He was about to cross a line and he knew it. Slowly and deliberately, he typed his response.

<Anything. >

Rho's response appeared after a few seconds. <Anything? Perjure yourself? Murder someone? Assuming you could get away with it, of course? >

Phillips was well aware his response would be a commitment. After a deep breath, he responded. <Yes, anything. >

Rho responded, <What about the girl? >

Oh, my God! Reflexively, Phillips typed a response. <What girl? >

<Please. Don't insult me. >

Feeling the hair stand up on the back of his neck, Phillips tried once more to deflect the subject.

<I'm not sure what you mean. > he typed.

There was a short pause. Then Rho responded. <OK. If you don't trust me... if you can't be honest with me... then I don't think we should continue our relationship. >

A part of Phillips wanted to agree, log off and not come back. For the first time, his apprehension about dealing with Rho slipped into fear.

If Rho knew about the girl, he knew enough to send Phillips to jail, maybe worse.

Panic gripped him and he saw only one clear path of action. He typed in his response as fast as he could.

<Hold on. Let's talk about this. >

<I don't think talking is necessary any longer. I wanted to help you, but I see my help is not needed. Maybe you're just fine where you are. Maybe you don't really need my help. >

Phillips felt fear and desperation creeping into his consciousness. <I do need your help. Please. I need help with the girl, too. >

<Which girl? There are two. One dead. One alive...for now. >

Shit. How did he know about that?

Rho continued. <Did you think you were the only person I don't watch all the time? I don't care about the girls. But you need the problem to go away, do you not? >

<Yes. >

<You're out of ideas. You're on track to kill the second girl, correct? >

<I thought about it. >

<Bad idea. Unless you leverage it to solve your other problem and remove any chance of getting caught. >

Huh? Phillips couldn't see a way to do that. He wracked his brain, trying to think how it could be possible. He came up with nothing that made sense. After a full minute, he responded.

<I'm listening. >

<Finally. >

It had the desired effect on Phillips. Rho was in control, Phillips was all the way in and both of them knew it.

<What must I do? > Phillips typed.

<Are you really willing to kill the second girl to solve this problem? It might come to that. I need to know if you're willing to and capable of doing it. >

Phillips sighed. He didn't have a choice. He took another long breath and typed the words. <Whatever it takes. >

<Good. More tomorrow. Make no decisions before then. You'll need the help of the contractor I referred to you.>

The chat session ended before Phillips could respond.

Rho often terminated the chat abruptly. This time, it irritated Phillips more than usual. He suspected Rho did it deliberately to keep him off balance and make him hunger for more information.

Whatever the reason, it worked. Phillips had two thoughts as he turned off the pad and headed for bed. He wondered again who Rho might be, and he knew he would do whatever Rho suggested.

CHAPTER 10

2:34 p.m. - June 30, 2036 – Defense Logistics Agency Satellite Office Building, Telegraph Road, Alexandria, VA

Kathy rubbed her temples. She was getting a headache. Too many questions and too few answers. *Assuming the girl was Amy, what was she doing in the past? How did she get there? And if she wasn't the type to commit suicide, why was she dead?*

She leaned back in her chair and looked at the ceiling. The seed of a theory was beginning to form in the back of her mind, but she couldn't quite get her thoughts around it. If the girl wasn't the type to jump off a building, then it was a murder case. Why would someone want her dead? She couldn't think of a good reason. And who? Certainly no one from the past.

What if the girl wasn't Amy? If she wasn't, what caused the time twisting Doctor Astalos found?

No. In her heart, she knew the girl was Amy. She couldn't conceive of a different scenario.

Until she had the test results, she worked on the problem she could make some headway with – finding witnesses. With a cup of hot tea, she sat at her desk with her computer pad, searching for additional information on the case.

Wade Harrison, the politician, was the most obvious witness. He was at the scene and could at least identify Amy from a picture. In the interview with police, he was disoriented, though the screen for drugs had turned out negative. He had a moderate quantity of alcohol in his bloodstream. Enough for two light drinks, but nothing to imply reduced coherence or a black out.

He was arrested and the circumstantial evidence against him was compelling. But he was from a prominent family and he had a good lawyer. After holding him without bail for two months, they set him free. Many in the law enforcement community still believed he had gotten away with murder.

He was easy to find. Despite the girl's suicide, he was elected to a city council position in Deerfield, Illinois, a Chicago suburb. His constituents praised his honesty, integrity and skill at solving complex political problems. Kathy watched two TelExtraVision interviews with him. He had a generous dose of charisma and a modest way of engaging the people around him. People who heard him speak responded to his common-sense approach to issues.

In interviews, unfriendly reporters asked him rude questions about the girl's death. He handled those interviews with humility and grace. He expressed regret for his shortcomings and thanked his wife of many years for her forgiveness and compassion. It was a deliberate and practiced response from the man, but Kathy thought she could read real regret and sadness in his eyes.

She leaned back in her chair and brought the teacup to her lips. Harrison seemed like such a model citizen except for this event. *If Amy hadn't gone off that balcony, he might have run for state senator or governor.* Her teacup shook in her hand. Thoughts and images flew through her mind at blinding speed. *What?* The thoughts in the back of her mind finally surfaced. *Could it be Amy was not the target?* Her eyelids fluttered slightly as she digested the thought.

A knock on her open door jolted her out of her reverie. Trevor stood there.

"Hi, what's up?" she said. "Oh, did you get the results back?"

"Yes. Positive ID. The DNA on the hairbrush matches the dead girl's DNA. It's Amy. Eve reported in, too. Ninety-five percent positive match on the video against Amy's picture. I briefed Major McKnight. He's off and running. To execute a mission without the required lead time and research, he'll need a Presidential executive order. When I left his office, he was on the phone, trying to find General Drake and Senator Lodge to get that started."

"Okay," Kathy said. She sat there, taking deep breaths to calm herself while her mind raced. Part of her was triumphant – she was right. Another part of her was heart-broken that a sweet, innocent kid was killed, her life thrown away like a scrap of paper. Tears welled up in her eyes.

"I'm sorry," he said, leaning against the door jamb. "But remember what Doctor Astalos said. There's still time to save her."

Trevor is always in tune with me. "We need to get started on a plan," Kathy said. "We need to interview Wade Harrison to find out all we can about what happened, and then we need to work out the timing to intercept them before the event."

"Yup," Trevor said. "And let's not forget. How did she get there in the first place? Somewhere behind the curtains, someone's pulling the strings. If she didn't jump – and we still don't know for sure…"

"I don't know why, but I just don't believe she jumped."

"But we need to keep that in mind and account for it, just in case." Trevor came into her office and sat.

"Yes, I know, but I'm having a hard time believing it."

"Okay, then we interview Wade Harrison. Who else might have information? Maybe some of the folks who witnessed her death?"

"I found two people who saw the fall. They were sitting together outside near the building. The police report says they didn't see her leave the balcony – just the end of her fall and the impact."

Trevor leaned back and looked at the ceiling. "Let's try to get an interview with them and then Harrison. We'll know more about what to do after talking to them."

CHAPTER 11

4:35 p.m., July 3, 2036 – Deerfield, IL

Kathy and Trevor walked from the parking lot into the Deerfield Police Department on Waukegan Boulevard. This would be the hardest interview on their list. They would ask a man to talk about his greatest failing. Who would want to talk about that?

It would also be their last chance to get information. The other witnesses were not helpful. Either they had blocked the gruesome event out of their memory or they didn't remember enough about what they saw.

Trevor motioned for Kathy to precede him through the revolving door on the front of the building.

How does a man live with something like this? Wade Harrison was the picture of the ideal candidate before the event. He had a beautiful wife, two kids, a growing legal defense practice and a reputation for being smart and savvy. Everything they heard contributed to the picture of a good man with a desire to serve others, a man on track to be successful politically. He had the brains, the charisma and the skills to inspire followers. He had everything to gain and was developing a state-wide following.

And yet somehow, he ended up alone in an apartment building in Chicago's River North district with a young woman. He had sexual relations with her and, while he was in the shower, she allegedly jumped to her death from the apartment balcony. And now, after all these years, he would hear some of that story might not be true.

Despite all that happened, Harrison still got elected to a position of public service years later. Thanks to a small core of loyal supporters and a supportive wife, he ran a campaign and got elected to the

Deerfield City Council. Despite repeated attempts to bring up the specter of the girl's suicide and his moral shortcomings, he developed a reputation for fair play and honest dealings.

Getting this far was a major accomplishment. But with this suicide issue hanging around his head, he would never go further.

They entered the door of his office and, after a brief discussion with his private assistant, were led into a conference room. Harrison joined them after a few moments.

“Good afternoon,” he said, with a smile. “I'm Wade Harrison.”

“Hello,” Trevor said. “I'm Trevor George. This is Doctor Kathy Wu.” He paused as the councilman shook their hands. “We're with the Historical Event Research Organization.”

“The time travel people? It's an honor to meet with the HERO team. I'm impressed by what I’ve heard about your charter and your plans. What brings you here?”

“Councilman Harrison, it's a pleasure to meet you,” Kathy said. “And I wish we were here under better circumstances.”

“Oh?” Harrison said.

The media called the dead woman 'the suicide girl' so Trevor chose the straightforward way to broach the subject.

“We want to talk to you about the suicide girl.”

Harrison's smile disappeared, his eyes fell to the floor, and his shoulders sagged. “Will I never get past this? It seems you can never escape your past. I don't think I'll ever get over it.”

“We understand, sir. May we sit down?” Kathy asked.

“Oh, yes. Sorry, I forgot my manners.”

Harrison motioned them toward a small pit group next to his conference table. He chose a chair and Kathy and Trevor sat together on the sofa. Harrison leaned back and closed his eyes. After a moment, he spoke. “It was almost twenty-five years ago, and yet I remember it like it was yesterday. I was speaking at an event at the Marriott on Michigan Avenue.”

"Councilman, we have a little different focus in mind for our meeting here. What can you tell us about the girl?"

Harrison shrugged. "They never figured out who she was. She wasn't in any of the crime databases. Her fingerprints weren't found anywhere else. It's so disturbing to think she hooked up with me for the evening and then killed herself. I still can't fathom why she would do such a thing."

"The police report says she told you her name was Amy. Is that true?" Kathy asked.

"Yes," Harrison said.

"Did she give you a last name?"

"If she did, I don't remember what it was. We were only together for a couple of hours."

Trevor shifted in his seat. "Can you start from the beginning?" he said. "We're trying to piece together what you know with new clues and anything you can tell us will help."

"New clues? What did you learn that's new? " Harrison leaned forward on the sofa. "I have been wracking my brain for twenty-five years to understand why this happened. Tell me what you've found out."

Kathy said, "Sir, I promise we will tell you anything we can. But first, we'd like to validate some of the clues we already have."

"Okay," he said, leaning back again. "I got tired of telling the story a long time ago, but I'm willing to tell it again if you'll share what you know. Or anything you might suspect that could shed light on this. Will you do that?"

Trevor and Kathy glanced at one another. Trevor nodded. "I think we can agree on that."

"Thank you," Harrison said. "What would you like to know?" His eyes moved back and forth between Trevor and Kathy.

Kathy held up her index finger. "May I first ask about your marriage? Sorry, but is there any way Amy might have expected you to be open to her advances?"

"I don't know," he said. "I'd been running hard, all over the state, trying to get my name out there. I wanted to run for office to serve Chicago or maybe even the state. My family has always been involved in the community and giving back to the city or county is in our family blood. My dad was a cop, my uncles were firemen. For us, it was all about service. Not to be the big shot, but to fight the big shot guys and clean up the town. Chicago has a reputation for dirty politics, and our parents and aunts and uncles were so tired of it they pounded ethics into us. Anyway, I was trying to see as many voters as I could. About a week before this happened, I got home a day early from a trip and found my wife Angie in bed with another man." Harrison's face showed no emotion and his gaze dropped, but not before Trevor saw the pain in his eyes.

Harrison looked back at Kathy and Trevor. "But could the girl have known about Angie? I don't see how. No."

Kathy touched his hand. "I'm so sorry," she said. "So, you felt angry and deceived?"

"Yes, and I wanted to get back at her for cheating on me." Trevor could see tears welling up. "Strangely enough, this whole thing helped us get right with each other. Angie strayed because she was lonely, and I was so focused on the goal, I wasn't giving her the attention she needed and deserved." He wiped his eyes with a handkerchief. "Sorry. It seems the older I get, the closer my emotions are to the surface."

"So," Trevor said, "you found her in a compromising situation and, a week later, decided to retaliate?"

Harrison looked up. "No," he said. "It wasn't like that at all. It just happened."

"What *did* happen, sir?" Kathy asked.

"Sometimes, it seems like it was yesterday. Here's what I remember. I had just finished speaking at the fundraiser–"

"At the Marriott on Michigan Avenue?"

"Yes. I was back in the service corridor after speaking. I didn't think the talk went well, and I was looking for my campaign manager to do a postmortem on the speech. Anyway, we were on our way out for a drink when an organizer intercepted us and wanted to discuss the next day's agenda. It was a disappointing end to a long day. I was tired, the organizer hadn't done as well as expected, and I asked my campaign manager to handle it. I decided to have that drink by myself and go home. Now that I think of it, I wasn't all that eager to get home. Angie was sorry, but I wasn't ready to forgive her yet, though I already knew I was going to." He looked up at Trevor. "Do you understand what I mean?"

"I do," Trevor said. "So, what happened next?"

"Well, I sat at a table by myself in the bar. No one recognized me there, which was a little depressing for a man running for office." He gave a wan smile to Kathy. "It didn't help my mood any. I guess I was feeling pretty damned unappreciated."

"I get the picture," Trevor said. "Then what happened?"

"I'm not sure, really." Harrison rubbed his temples, then his eyes. "I was just sitting there nursing my drink, and I realized she was standing next to my table. She was beautiful and smiling in a shy sort of way. She asked me, 'Are you Wade Harrison?' and sat down across from me when I said yes."

"So, she approached you?"

"Yes. But to be honest with you, I was a willing participant. I was down in a hole. Tired, depressed and heartsick. And suddenly there's this stunning young woman acting interested. I flirted my ass off with her. I didn't know where it was going, and I didn't care." He looked down at his hands folded in his lap. "And she killed herself." He couldn't hide the misery underneath his calm demeanor.

"How did she act toward you?" Kathy asked. "I mean, did she act like a woman on the make, or very demure, or some other way?"

"Now that you mention it, she was being forward and flirty, but seemed, well, unfamiliar with it. I mean, she was sexy and inviting, but she didn't seem experienced at it. I'd have bet real money she'd never picked up a guy before."

Kathy looked at Trevor and then back at Harrison. "Okay. So, whose idea was it to leave the bar?"

"It was hers. She told me I looked tired, stressed and desperately in need of some fun. I didn't disagree with that. She suggested maybe we should go someplace less public for a drink and maybe some partying. She didn't have to ask me twice. I paid the bill and we left the bar."

"She suggested her apartment?"

"No, we were going to a little bar and grill near Lincoln Park, up in Old Town, but she needed to go by her apartment first to pick up something. She didn't say what, and I didn't ask. To be honest, I didn't care in the slightest. I wanted to escape my life, if only for just a little while."

Trevor sensed something, an undercurrent to events he couldn't quite put his finger on. *What am I missing?* He asked, "So, the plan was to go to her apartment first?"

"Yes."

Kathy held up her hand to get Harrison's attention. "Hold up a second. You said she seemed inexperienced. How do you mean?"

"Well, it was a feeling…an impression, really. When we got to her apartment building, we walked in together, but she didn't seem comfortable to be there...with me, you know. We walked apart, like we had a professional relationship...like colleagues. Then she slipped an arm around my waist and purred like a kitten – like she couldn't get enough of me. It was like a signal to go for it. Like someone flipped a switch. Does that make sense?"

"Yes, it does," Kathy said. "Councilman, I hate to ask this, but is there any way I could get some water or something? I'm feeling dry all of a sudden."

At this, the councilman rolled his eyes and stood. "Oh, of course. I should have offered earlier. Let me ask my assistant to get something for us all. Mr. George, can I get you anything too? A soda? Tea? Coffee? Anything? What about you, Doctor Wu?"

"Yes, black coffee for me," Trevor said. "Hot tea and water for Doctor Wu, I think. Right?"

"Perfect," she said. Harrison nodded and left the room.

Kathy turned to Trevor. "Are you going to show him the photographs?"

"Yes," he said. "But not until right at the end. When we show them to him and, if he picks Amy out of the group, he'll realize we know who she is. And we won't get anything else out of him because he'll be too busy asking us questions about her. He might even get pissed and stop sharing. We need to keep it under wraps until we get all the information we can. But I think we can give him some hope of a resolution. And maybe we can prevent the event."

"I hope so."

When Harrison returned, he carried a cup of hot tea in one hand and a bottle of water in the other. His assistant followed with a coffee service and set it on the table between them. "Thank you, ma'am," Trevor said to the assistant as she poured coffee for him and the councilman. She smiled at him and left the room.

"Okay, where were we?" Harrison asked.

"You were telling us how the young lady seemed unsure of herself," Trevor said.

"Yes. Now that you put it that way, you're right. I remember thinking she looked nervous. After a few drinks, most people are less inhibited, but she seemed..."

"Measured?"

"Yes." Harrison stopped and looked at Trevor. "You think she was trying to manipulate me."

This guy's sharp. Left alone, he might figure it out.

"It's a possibility. So, you're aware there was film of the two of you in the elevator?"

"Yes. It even showed up in a documentary film, but I bet you already know about that."

"Yes," Trevor said. "Kathy and I reviewed that video. We noticed what you picked up on. What happened when you got to the room?"

Harrison paused for a long moment. Trevor guessed he was processing the possibility of manipulation and trying to fit it into what he remembered.

"Councilman?" he said. The man did not reply.

"Wade?" Kathy said in a quiet, gentle voice.

Harrison flinched. "Sorry, I was just thinking about what happened. Once we got in the room and the door was closed, she came on strong. She pressed herself against me and kissed me. It surprised me but I went with the flow. She was beautiful and I wanted the escape. Before I knew it, we were undressed and in bed. It was over so fast, I hardly remember it at all."

"How did she act afterward?" Trevor asked.

"Well, that plays to your idea of manipulation. She rolled away and turned her back. I realized she was crying. I asked her what was wrong."

"What did she say?"

"She said everything was wrong, and she kept on crying. I asked her what I could do. She told me to do whatever I wanted. She was inconsolable, so I decided to take a shower and deal with it afterward. I got up, turned on the bedside lamp, and went into the bathroom. By the time I finished the shower, I was feeling guilty. I was ashamed of myself for taking advantage of a young girl who was so obviously vulnerable and unhappy. I remember asking myself how I could be so damned stupid as to end up in her apartment when all I really wanted to do was get my wife back. I decided to get my clothes, leave and head straight home to beg my wife to forgive me. And that's when everything went to hell." Harrison had slumped on the sofa, but now he moved to the edge of his seat, rested his elbows on his knees and buried his face in his hands.

"So, you came out, and she was gone?"

"That's the strange part. I remember I opened the bathroom door. The next thing I knew, I was lying on the floor next to the bed and she was gone."

Trevor sat up on the edge of the chair. "Think hard, Councilman Harrison. Is there anything that sticks in the back of your mind? Did you have a dream?"

Harrison lifted his head and looked at Trevor. "How did you know? I dreamed I opened the door and saw the girl sitting in the middle of the bed. I thought I saw movement to my left and, as I turned, everything went white and then black. Then I was on the floor. Does that tell you something?"

"No," Trevor said. "But I can guess. Did you wake up with powder on your face?"

"What? I don't know. I didn't look in the mirror." The man stood. "What do you suspect?"

"No mention of powder in the police report, so if you didn't wipe it off, it wasn't there." Trevor looked at Wu. "Have everything you need? Any more questions?"

She shook her head.

Harrison flushed and raised his hands, palms outward. "Look, I have plenty of questions. I've shared my story. It's time for you to explain. Why are you here?"

"Councilman, you've been more than helpful. I have one more question." He extended his hand toward Kathy and she pulled three photographs out of her briefcase and handed them to him. Trevor handed them to Harrison and said, "Do you recognize any of these women?"

Harrison immediately picked out the picture of Amy Chang. "That's Amy. No question. You know who she was? Wait a second..." He turned the photograph over and read the time stamp. "This was taken last year? How is that possi.....?" He paused. "She time traveled. That's why *you're* involved. Wait! She time traveled to seduce me and then kill herself? That doesn't make sense."

Kathy took the photographs back from Harrison. “We don't believe she has traveled… yet.” Harrison stared at her in confusion for a long moment. Trevor watched as the truth dawned on him.

“She’s still alive? I mean, she hasn't traveled, so she's still alive?” Harrison became more animated. Hope shone in his eyes. “You mean, there's a chance we can keep her from killing herself?”

“Councilman Harrison, hang on a second,” Kathy said. “I can’t tell you much more now but believe me when I say we will get to the bottom of this.”

She looked at Trevor, who nodded. “We don't think Amy time-traveled of her own volition, and we don't believe she jumped off that balcony. We think she was thrown off it...” She let that information sink in, then added, “...and not by you.”

“But why?” Harrison said, his voice a hoarse whisper.

“We don't know yet, sir,” Trevor said. “But you don't remember having powder on your face when you woke up?”

“No. Is that important?”

“It might be. Twenty-five years ago, there were sedatives that could have been administered by inhalation. All would leave a powdery residue. The ones in use today deteriorate quickly, and their use is undetectable in less than twenty minutes.”

“You think someone from the future gassed me?”

Trevor shifted his position and looked the man in the eye. “I think it’s possible. I assure you we will find out what happened and who did it. The chances Amy committed suicide are dropping fast, in my opinion.”

“And Councilman?” Kathy said.

“Yes?”

“We believe you and Amy are the victims here. You didn't cause this to happen. Someone else did.”

She’s strong and assertive.

For the first time since they arrived, hope and renewed strength radiated from the man's eyes. "Thank you for that, Doctor Wu. I hope you'll soon be able to share with me what happened."

Kathy opened her mouth to respond, but Trevor held up his hand to her. "We absolutely will, sir. Now, if you'll excuse us, we'll get out of your way and let you get back to managing the city." They stood and left after promising to get back with him and share results of their investigation.

They were walking to their rental car when Kathy spoke again. "What do you think, Trevor? You've interviewed a lot of people. Is he telling the truth?"

She's sympathetic to him. So am I. "I think so. He doesn't give any of the usual liar tells, like frequent blinking or swearing on a stack of Bibles. If he's not telling us the truth, he's a very good liar. But I believe him. If he pushed Amy off that balcony, he doesn't remember doing it."

"Good. That's what I thought, too. If he did it, he deserves an Academy Award for his performance today. But I just don't believe he's lying. By the way, why did you tell him we could share what happened? I don't think the General or Major McKnight would want details to get out."

Trevor stopped and looked back at the building. "Kathy, I don't think it matters. If we fix it..." He looked at her. "*When* we fix it...history will be changed, and he won't remember any of this anyway. I think we're on pretty safe ground."

CHAPTER 12

7:35 p.m. – July 11, 2036 – Defense Logistics Agency Satellite Office Building, Telegraph Road, Alexandria, VA

Trevor George sat at his desk, reading his notes from the interview with Wade Harrison one last time. *I didn't leave anything out. It's all there.*

He filed the notes, leaned back in his chair and put his feet up on his desk. He was tired, but there was always something else to do. He tried to think of a short task to do before leaving. As hard as he tried, he couldn't think of one because what he really wanted to do was call Kathy. The problem was, he couldn't think of a good excuse. He really just wanted to hear her voice and her laugh.

He tried to push her from his mind. *She's strong and assertive.* Both good reasons not to get involved with her. *Been there, done that.* He didn't want to repeat the experience of his mother and ex-girlfriend.

But Kathy was different somehow. *What is it?* A little quiet thinking was what he needed and now was as good a time as any. He thought of her interactions with Wade Harrison and the others during their interviews. She was effective and made the interviewees comfortable. *How did she do it?* It took a few minutes before he came up with the answer. She was committed to getting information from them, but she did it with compassion and respect.

How would Mom have acted in Kathy's place? He chuckled to himself. Mom would have run over them and manipulated them to get what she wanted. That's what he didn't like about her. No matter what the subject, it was still all about her and she would work hard to get you to do what she wanted without a thought about your needs and wants. It wasn't her strength that he didn't like. It was her motives.

Not Kathy. She...

Someone was walking down the hall outside his office. He checked the time on his wall clock. Tyler and McKnight were the last of his coworkers to leave, but that was more than an hour ago. *Who could that be?*

He stood and walked to the door. He didn't see anyone, but he heard the dishwasher start in the kitchen. He walked to the kitchen and saw Cindy standing there with her back toward him. She was putting away silverware and plates. Her tailored white blouse accentuated her figure, and the fit of her blue skirt drew attention to her hips. Despite his feelings for Kathy, he was attracted to the woman standing before him.

He cleared his throat.

Cindy spun around at the sound. The look of concern on her face turned to a broad smile. "Oh, hi, Trevor. Are you leaving now?"

"I beg your pardon?" he said. The top two buttons of her blouse had somehow come undone, revealing more cleavage than usual.

"Are you leaving now? I thought I'd hang around as long as someone was here, just in case someone needed something. I think it's just you and me now."

"I'm going home pretty soon. Got big plans for the weekend?"

"No, as a matter of fact. I'm thinking I'll be pretty bored this weekend."

"You?" Trevor said. He crossed his arms and leaned against the door jamb. "I would think an attractive lady like you would be booked up all weekend."

She beamed and walked to him. "What a sweet thing to say! You've always made me feel so welcome here." She stopped before him and gently touched his crossed arms. "And how about you? Big plans? How about tonight?"

"Not to speak of."

Cindy slipped her hands up behind his neck, her breasts brushing lightly against his folded arms and chest. Her perfume was an unfamiliar scent, yet it was intoxicating. It engaged his senses like none he experienced before. As she looked up at him, her blue eyes and full mouth somehow obscured everything else from his vision. Warmth surged through his body and stirred all that was male in him. Somewhere in the back of his mind, he wondered who manufactured that scent.

"You know," she said, "we could go to the Red, White and Brew Pub down the street and have a drink or two."

Trevor felt overwhelmed and somehow out of his depth.

"It would give us a chance to get to know each other better," she said. "I'd really like that. What do you say?"

"You're beautiful," he whispered. "Another time, perhaps."

"Are you sure?" she whispered. She pressed herself more closely to him.

What would Kathy think? If I want to be with her, I can't do this. He uncrossed his arms, grasped Cindy's wrists and gently pulled them from behind his neck. "Yes, I'm sure. I can't right now. It's complicated."

Cindy smiled at him. "Another time then. You're a handsome and intriguing man. I can wait."

She stepped away and smoothed her blouse and skirt, drawing his attention to her figure. *Was that intentional?* "Until next time then."

Cindy left the kitchen. Trevor stepped into the hall behind her and watched as she walked down the hall, grabbed her purse from her desk in the reception room and unlocked the office door. She turned and waved at him, then walked out.

Trevor stood there for a moment staring at the closed door.

Damn. He shook his head and walked back to his office.

CHAPTER 13

2:50 p.m. – July 14, 2036 – Defense Logistics Agency Satellite Office Building, Telegraph Road, Alexandria, VA

The move planning meeting was scheduled for 1500 hours in the big conference room. Tyler arrived first. It was his briefing, and he had ten minutes to get set up.

The room was already prepared. Light streamed in from the transparent outside wall. Cindy brought in covered platters and hot drink urns to a table in the back of the room.

Tyler set his phone down on the desk and went to investigate the food. He lifted each of the food platter covers and discovered glazed doughnuts, chicken fingers with dip, and a fruit/veggie selection. The urns contained regular coffee, decaf coffee and hot tea. *Cindy knows her job.*

Tyler poured himself a cup of coffee and returned to his seat at the head of the table and connected his phone to the overhead projector. A few selections on the device caused the first slide of his presentation to appear on the screen at the end of the room.

Like McKnight's office, the conference room had the new wall technology upgrade. The implementation allowed the exterior wall to be transparent, translucent, or opaque with the touch of a button. Tyler picked up the room remote and switched on the overhead lights. He toggled the exterior wall to 'translucent' and the glass exterior wall turned from clear to frosted white, obscuring the outside view but letting in the afternoon light. He read his first slide on the screen and decided it was still too light in the room. To compensate, he toggled the remote to 'opaque' to block all outside light.

Kathy entered the room. "Hi, Winnie. How's it going?"

"Great," he said. "I'm just about ready."

"Anything I can do to help?"

"Nope" he said. "But you can start in on the veggies and hot tea in the back of the room."

"I timed my entrance perfectly then," she said, and headed for the back of the room.

Trevor, Wheeler and Hatcher came in together chatting about baseball results. The Nationals had been pounded again in last night's game. "Food and drink in the back," Tyler said, pointing at the refreshments.

Trevor sat next to Tyler. He always liked to be in the front of the room. Kathy handed him a cup of coffee, sat next to him and sipped her hot tea.

There was a knock at the door. Tyler clicked the projector to standby mode and said, "Come in."

Cindy stuck her head in the door. "Sorry for the interruption. Are the refreshments okay? Is there enough food and drink?"

Trevor spoke up. "It's perfect. Thanks for all your help."

"Good," she said. "Oh, may I come in for just a second before the meeting starts to fix something?"

He waved her into the room. "Sure, we're not ready to start just yet. C'mon in."

Cindy hurried to the refreshment table, moved the platters around and tinkered with the foil covers. Apparently satisfied, she returned to the door, patting Trevor on the shoulder as she passed.

"Thank you, Cindy," Trevor said.

Cindy beamed at him and closed the door.

Tyler noticed Kathy was frowning. He felt sure she wouldn't approve of anything Cindy did for Trevor.

"Is Major McKnight coming?" Hatcher asked. Before Tyler could answer, the door opened and McKnight and Astalos filed in.

"Thanks for coming, everyone," McKnight set his phone on the table and sat. "Are you ready, Mr. Tyler?"

Hatcher and Wheeler made their way back to the conference room table and sat.

"Yes, sir," Tyler responded. "Let's get started." He switched the projector from standby to active. The first slide appeared on the screen.

"This briefing covers our upcoming move from this office to the DLA HQ office just south of here. This technology has significant potential for physical and financial damage in the wrong hands, so while we haven't had any threats or incidents, it makes sense to protect it during this short trip.

"The move is scheduled for July 20th at oh-seven hundred, about one week from now. We're making the move early on a Sunday in the hope there will be less traffic. Let me transfer the details to everyone."

He tapped on his phone a few times, and each of them began opening the virtual folders on their own phones or comm pads. Tyler paused a few minutes to let them review the information.

McKnight said, "Looks pretty straightforward to me. What did you decide about security?"

"After some thought, I came around to your way of thinking, sir. I checked into the costs of executing a heavily armed convoy trip from here to DLA HQ. Bottom line is, the cost is more than I expected. So, rather than use a large armed escort that'll attract a lot of attention, I think Doctor Astalos's bodyguards with some additional firepower should be sufficient. As you pointed out, the secrecy will mitigate the risk. Earlier today I set the date, and no one outside this room knows it. I'll be making the rest of the arrangements this week. Keeping the lead time short but giving enough time to get prepared. We'll do all the packing and filing ourselves."

"Actually, that brings up a good point. Everyone?" McKnight looks around the room. "Do not put this event in your calendar. As far as the outside world is concerned, we all plan to sleep in Sunday morning. Understood?"

"Yes, sir."

"Very good," he said. "I see the convoy order. Looks good. Any questions, anyone?"

On the desk, McKnight's phone began to vibrate. He picked it up and looked at it.

"Do you need to take that, sir?" Tyler asked.

McKnight blinked, touched a button and set the phone down. "No, it's a personal call. Let's continue."

"I have a question," Astalos said. "What about the original Engine? And all my research papers?"

"Not a problem, doctor," Tyler said. "After delivering the primary Engine to DLA HQ, the truck and cars will return here to bring along the rest of the team and the original Engine. I'll be here to supervise the loading."

"I'd like to be here for the loading of the original Engine as well."

"Okay. Not a problem, sir. We'll just keep moving stuff until we get it all done."

To everyone, Tyler said, "I'll revise the schedule and send out an update this afternoon. If there are no more questions, we'll call it a wrap?"

"Thank you, Captain," Astalos said. He rose and headed for the back of the room and McKnight left the room. "I hope Lieutenant Wheeler left me a doughnut."

Tyler was still gathering his phone and papers when he saw Kathy make eye contact with Trevor and shake her head.

"What did I do?" he asked.

"Nothing," she said. "Absolutely nothing." She rose and left the room.

Tyler swallowed a chuckle.

Trevor turned to Tyler. "What was that all about?"

This time, Tyler laughed out loud. "You tell me," he said.

"She really acts weird sometimes."

"Seriously?" Tyler laughed again and pointed at the door. "Why do you think that is?"

"I don't know. She's never acted like this before."

"Maybe she never had a reason before."

Trevor looked thoughtful, as if he now had new information to digest.

Tyler stood. "Trevor, we have a couple more hours of work to do. What say I buy you a beer after work, and we'll discuss the great mystery of life?"

"Huh?" Trevor said.

"Women, Trevor. I mean women. See you in a couple of hours."

CHAPTER 14

5:30 p.m. – July 18, 2036 – Defense Logistics Agency Satellite Office Building, Telegraph Road, Alexandria, VA

In the review of Chicago Police interview notes, Trevor and Kathy learned one witness testified that Amy's body dropped 'like a limp rag.' No waving of the arms and legs, no screaming. They believed Amy was unconscious when she fell.

Trevor and Kathy were convinced Harrison and Amy were victims of a time twist by unknown persons. It was murder and Harrison was not the killer.

The one thing they knew for sure was that Amy shouldn't have been there in Chicago in the year 2011, so they conceived a plan for her rescue. They submitted their recommendations to McKnight, who went to work to get the mission approved.

Based on Kathy's planning, McKnight selected himself, Kathy, Trevor, Tyler, Wheeler and Hatcher for the mission team to rescue Amy Chang. The six of them sat around the conference table for the mission briefing.

"This morning, General Drake and Senator Lodge persuaded the President to sign an executive action order to proceed with the mission," McKnight said. "We're ready to execute, subject to any concerns or issues raised here. Doctor Wu, it's your plan. Give us the details."

Kathy handed out numbered folders and the agenda to each of them.

She set a meeting recorder in the middle of the table and switched it on. "This is Katherine Wu of the Historical Event Research Organization. This recording documents the mission briefing for mission number 20360718." She added the date, time and names of attendees for the record.

"For your reference, the mission title is 'Amy Chang Rescue.' There are three objectives for the mission."

"Objective one is to intercept Amy Chang and Wade Harrison before they reach the apartment in Chicago and warn him off. Obviously, you can't tell him who we are or where we come from, but you can imply he is in danger and you are there to protect him. Objective two is to retrieve Ms. Chang back to the present unharmed. Assuming another time traveler murdered her, objective three is to intercept and capture the unidentified subject and bring him or her back to the present. Are there questions on the objectives?"

No one spoke.

"Okay, let's walk through the mission. Let me give all the steps, and then we'll do questions. Ready?"

There are nods all around the table.

"Okay. Major McKnight and Captains Hatcher and Tyler jump into a conference room in a local Hyatt Place hotel in Chicago. They walk to the apartment building and go up to the apartment. They intercept the couple when they get there, turn Harrison away, and get the apartment key from Amy. Tyler returns to the present with Amy. McKnight and Hatcher enter the apartment with caution and take up positions. When the unsub shows up, they arrest him and bring him back to the present."

"Questions?" Kathy asked.

"Yes," Hatcher said. "We're jumping into a conference room at the Hyatt? What if there's something happening in that room?"

Kathy shook her head. "There isn't. On the target date, this conference room was under renovation. They had lighting problems and shut it down for three weeks. Since we're going in during evening hours, the place should be deserted. You two can jump in, walk up the stairs and out through the lobby – no problem."

"Okay," Hatcher said. "Chances are good we'll end up on the floor after the jump. If construction is in progress, aren't we likely to get dirty enough to stand out?"

"Good point. You'll wear disposable jumpsuits over your suits and dissolve them after landing, okay?"

Hatcher nodded.

McKnight flipped through the folder. "How far is it from the Hyatt Place to the apartment building? I don't see it here."

"There should be a map there in the folder," Kathy said. "It's only two blocks – one block west, one block south."

"Do we have any idea who the unsub is?" Wheeler asked.

"No," Kathy said. "That's why we'd prefer to bring him or her back in one piece – we want to have a long talk with this individual about where they got the technology and how they figured out how to use it."

Hatcher leaned back in her chair. "Not that I don't want to go on the mission...but is there a reason why we don't intercept the girl earlier in the day? Before she meets Harrison?"

Kathy nodded. "I like that idea, but we don't know where she'll be earlier in the day and our best chance of catching the unsub is to be there when we know he'll be there. The only time we're certain of is when Amy's in the apartment. We're taking a chance anyway, right? He might be in the hallway outside the apartment where we intend to intercept Amy and Mr. Harrison. I mean, the risk of that is low, but it's still a risk. You have to watch for anyone suspicious when you get there."

"Any more questions?" No one spoke.

"Okay," Kathy said. "Let's get moving. Lieutenant Wheeler, you'll be operating the Time Engine. In the appendices of the plan, you'll see the coordinates and time for the jump."

Wheeler turned to the back of the folder, studied the page and looked at his phone. "Then we go about...one hour from now?"

"Correct."

"Okay, any extra equipment or anything needed?"

"Yes," Kathy said. "We don't know who Lieutenant Hatcher and Major McKnight will run into in the past, but it's a safe bet it won't be someone nice. They are the two best hand-to-hand combat resources on the team and the best shots."

"The best shots?" Wheeler asked.

Kathy smiled. "You heard me, Lieutenant. Like I said, we don't know what to expect. So, besides the usual paraphernalia – sleep bulbs, c-cam, and so forth – the travelers will carry standard issue plastic Glock 9-mil automatic pistols."

"Yes, ma'am," he said.

She turned to Hatcher and McKnight. "Firing your weapon is the last thing you want to do. But, in case our unsub cares less about the impact on history than we do, I don't want to send you into what might be a gunfight without a weapon. The only reason to use that weapon is if you or someone else is about to die. Got it?"

"Yes, ma'am," they answered in unison.

McKnight shifted in his chair. "What clothes will we be wearing?"

"I've given that a lot of thought, Major. The apartment building is in an upscale area of River North in Chicago. My follow-up call with Mr. Harrison revealed he was wearing a navy-blue suit and Amy was wearing a black pantsuit with a white silk blouse. You'll be wearing similar clothing."

McKnight found the apartment floor plan in his folder and waved Hatcher over to his side. He opened and examined it while she peered over his shoulder.

"I'm betting the unsub has scouted out the place," he said. "This area here in the living area is the only place that's big enough to jump into without destroying the furniture. I'll position myself behind the entrance door so I don't alert him to our presence."

"Good," Kathy said. "If this guy gets away from you, do not chase him. The risk of history disruption goes up if you start running around. Remember, you've already prevented his mission and Amy's out of danger. Engage the beacon and come back here. Remember, we're traveling two days ahead of the anniversary date. We have about nine days to fix problems. Got it?"

The two officers nodded.

"And if you two get separated somehow, don't go looking for each other. Engage the beacon and return. Does that make sense?"

McKnight and Hatcher exchanged glances. Looking back at Kathy, they both shook their heads.

"No," he said. "Sounds too much like leaving a man on the field of battle."

"I agree," Hatcher said.

Kathy nodded. "I thought you might feel that way. Think about it this way – if you get separated and have no idea where to look for each other, doesn't it make sense to retreat and regroup? We've got time."

After a moment, McKnight nodded. "Yes, Kathy, that makes sense. I'm not crazy about it, but you're right. I can't think of an alternative."

Hatcher shrugged and nodded agreement.

"Okay, good," Kathy said. "Now, pay close attention. I have equipment upgrades for you. Here." She handed them two medallions strung on thin metal chains.

"New return beacons?" McKnight asked. "What was wrong with the old ones?"

"Nothing. These have extended capabilities. As you know, the return beacon was just a trigger for the Engine which did all the work. You travel to a new destination, squeeze the beacon, and you come back. These new beacons allow us to program in multiple time trips without coming back first.

"Here's the new beacon." She rose and walked around to their side of the table, leaned over between them and, resting her forearms on the table, pointed at the beacon in McKnight's hand. "See anything different about it?"

McKnight turned the beacon over in his hand. He pulled out his phone and activated the magnifying app and the light. “There's a slide control on it?”

“Yes,” Kathy said. “Try it, it’s turned off now.”

McKnight used his fingernail to slide the control to the left. It clicked into place. “Okay. What does that do?”

“Let's say you have three destinations programmed into the Engine. Picture them as being a list from left to right. Hold on.”

She stepped over to the conference room's white board and drew a horizontal line and then, above the line, she wrote the letters A, B and C. “Okay, if A, B and C are your destinations, then they are accessed in this order. If you move the slide control to the right, the order is A, B and C. First, you travel to A. Squeeze the beacon once, and you go to B. Squeeze it again, and you go to C. Move the slide control to the left, squeeze the beacon again, and you go back to B.”

“I see,” McKnight said. “It's now more of a destination beacon and not just a return beacon. It allows you to have a staging destination or a retreat destination. Nice. Can I skip a destination?”

“Not yet. Not without a more extensive modification of the beacon. It's on the list of enhancements.”

Hatcher spoke up. “If I'm at B and I want to abort, do I have to go through A or C first? That might not be a good thing.”

“No,” Kathy said. “All you do is squeeze the beacon twice. That overrides everything and returns you to the origin point.”

“Makes sense,” McKnight said.

“Okay,” Kathy said. “Are you comfortable with the beacon enhancements? I have a formal training package, but honestly it isn’t much more than I just told you.”

“Seems straightforward,” Wheeler said.

“We still have time before the travel event. If anyone has questions, stop by to see me and I’ll give you the formal training. That’s all for now. Lieutenant Wheeler, they’re all yours now.”

"Okay," Wheeler said. "We have thirty minutes of configuring to do, and then we'll be ready to go. Please assemble your gear, get your weapons and join me in the lab in about thirty-five."

All but Trevor and Kathy filed out of the conference room, each intent on their tasks for the next thirty minutes. Kathy sat still, staring at the folder before her.

"Are you okay?" Trevor asked.

She rose and walked over to the wall and cleared it, exposing the trees and parking lot outside the conference room. "Yes, I...actually, no. I feel like we're missing something."

"Want to go over the details again? Maybe we can find something..."

"You wouldn't mind?" she said to him, then turned back to stare out at the trees. "I'll feel a whole lot better if we could do that."

"It's no problem at all," he said.

Kathy turned around to face him.

He's always so helpful and kind. Is it possible we could work together and still…?

"We always have worked well together, haven't we?" Trevor said.

Can he read my mind? "Yes. I can't tell you how much I appreciate that."

He smiled at her. "Me, too. The opportunity to work with you was one of the reasons I took this job."

"I'm glad you're on the team, Trevor."

"Thanks. Is there a particular area of the plan that you're worried about?"

"Oh, I already know what my problem is."

"What's that?" he asked.

"With another time traveler out there, there's too much uncertainty and too much risk. Normally, we can check history and be sure we're the only variable. But this time, we have another traveler out there, and that stresses the hell out of me."

"I get it. Let me run down to my office and get the rest of my notes. I'll be right back." He rose and left the room. She watched the door close behind him.

Maybe he and I could make it work.

She turned back to the window and stared out at the courtyard and trees outside. The mission concerns flooded back into her thoughts.

She crossed her arms and shook her head. *Another time traveler...Who the hell are you?*

CHAPTER 15

8:35 p.m. – July 18, 2036 – Defense Logistics Agency Satellite Office Building, Telegraph Road, Alexandria, VA

McKnight put on the suit Kathy provided him. It looked brand new but out of style. Checking his appearance in the mirror on the back of his office door, he straightened the tie and adjusted his belt buckle to line up with the pants fly and his shirt buttons. He patted his pockets to ensure he had nothing "present-day" in them. The figure in the mirror looked alien to him. He had always felt more comfortable in fatigues than in civilian casual clothes, let alone a suit.

He checked the time on his desk clock. *I have about ten minutes before we start. I need to call Megan.*

He sat at his desk and commanded his phone to call her. After several rings, she answered.

"Hello, Marc."

"Hi. How's it going?"

"Fine."

An awkward moment of silence.

"Uh, good. Megan, I wanted to apologize for seeming so resistant to the idea of moving in together. It just caught me by surprise."

"Why would you be surprised? Where did you think our relationship was going?"

It was his turn to hesitate. He was happy with their relationship but hadn't thought about what was next.

"I guess I hadn't thought it through. We've been so heads-down busy lately—"

"Marc, that's the worst excuse I've ever heard. You're too busy to think about me and…and us. Does that mean you don't want our relationship to go any further? Or even continue?"

She thinks I want to break up. "Not at all. I—"

"You don't?"

"Hold on. I was trying to say it does not mean I don't want us to continue. I do want us to continue."

"Just continue?" she said. "Nothing more?"

"I didn't say that." *I can't say more unless I'm willing to commit. I don't know if I want that. I don't want to lose her, but I –.*

"But you did. You don't want to go any further. Geez, I feel like I'm dating a married man."

Déjà vu. This is just like what happened with Barbara.

"You know there's no one else," he said. "You have to know that."

"I believe your work is much more important to you than me. I'm not so sure I can deal with that. I mean, I love that you are passionate about what you do and sometimes it requires you to put all your attention there, but right now it always has all your attention. Do you understand what I mean?"

That's what Barbara said. He didn't want that to happen again – not with Megan.

"I'm sorry, Megan. I can do better. Don't push me away."

She paused. "Push you away? It's been a week since you called me last. What does that tell you? I would have thought you would take some time to think about us."

"But I have thought about you. Every day. I tried to call a couple of times, but I didn't want to leave a message. I wanted to talk to you."

"A message would have told me you were thinking of me. No message tells me nothing."

McKnight looked at his watch and grimaced. *I'm out of time.* "Megan, you are important to me and I want to work this out. You know I love you. I don't want us to end."

His words echoed in his mind. He knew that much was true.

"But duty is calling you right now," she said. I can hear it in your voice."

"Yes, it is. I'm sorry, Megan. This is awful timing, but I have to go. People are waiting for me and it's important. I'll call you tomorrow morning."

"Okay," she said.

"I love you, Megan."

"I know." She disconnected the call.

He put his phone in his desk, sighed heavily and stood. *If I don't call her back tomorrow, she'll dump me. I don't want that. But if we move in together, it might end up the same way.*

He couldn't think of anything else to do, so he turned off the light and left the room.

Hatcher was waiting for him outside his door. "Ready to go, Lieutenant?" he asked.

"Yes, sir." She smiled at him. McKnight noted how attractive she was. Most of the time he didn't notice. Their relationship was professional and he wouldn't allow himself to see her as anything but an intelligent and trained fighting resource.

Today, it was hard not to notice. Today, she wore a black pantsuit with a white silk blouse and pearls. The ponytail was replaced by shining black hair cascading about her shoulders. Her makeup was flawless. She looked the part of a successful woman out for a night on the town with friends.

"Okay, let's go," he said, and they walked down the hall to the lab. Hatcher applied her access disk to the security reader, and the door hissed open to admit them.

Kathy, Wheeler and Tyler stood around the new console along with Doctor Astalos, who was explaining the differences between the original and the new machine. McKnight motioned for Hatcher to precede him with a wave of his hand, and the two of them joined the others.

As they approached, McKnight heard Astalos saying, "...and as soon as this mission is over, we'll dismantle the new machine and pack it up for traveling. As you can see..." he pointed to the original Engine. "We've already started packing the old machine. The new machine will go over to DLA on Sunday morning, and the old one will go later in the day."

Turning away from Astalos, Wheeler looked Hatcher up and down and then at McKnight. Jerking a thumb at Hatcher he said, "Who's that?"

"What?" Hatcher said.

Grinning, Wheeler continued. "I mean, sir, I thought you were bringing Hatcher, not a date."

"Shut up, Wheeler," Hatcher said. "Kiss my ass."

"Oh, I'm sorry, sir," he said, grinning at Hatcher now. "I guess it *is* Hatcher."

"You're such an asshole," she said. "Shut up and let's get to work."

McKnight's spirits were lifted by Wheeler's backhanded compliment for Hatcher.

The original Engine sat on a stainless-steel table. It looked much like an old gasoline engine from a muscle car. It was made of a dull bluish metal, the top was covered with digital gauges, and a metal shaft extended about four feet from one end of the block. A cap on the end of the shaft connected to four heavy-gauge wires in a sheath that trailed down to connectors on the stainless steel plate the table rested on. The plate was about a hundred square feet in size. A huge electric cable connected the other end of the Engine to an eight-foot tall power generator.

The new Engine was the same basic shape and color as the old one but had a smaller footprint. It still had a panel of gauges, but no metal shaft sticking out of it. The wire sheath came directly out of a port at the base of the Engine and was connected to the steel plate as before.

The generator cabinet was the same height as the other but narrower. A large metal cable connected the new Engine to the cabinet.

There was a small side table between the two generators with a road case, a backpack, and some electronic gear laid out on it. McKnight recognized it as Wheeler's road kit. He recognized it from the mission at the NewT Tower in Atlanta last year.

Astalos's voice broke back into his consciousness. The scientist was talking about the new machine. "...And so there is a significant improvement. The travel sphere took about thirty seconds to spin up and trigger the time travel. Before taking off for Finland, Robby improved the travel algorithm and the power efficiency to cut that time down to ten seconds."

"So now…?" Tyler said.

"So now, there will only be ten seconds from the time you squeeze the control beacon until you make the leap."

"That's good," Tyler said.

"Yeah," Wheeler said. "Might be useful to get out of a situation. Faster is always better."

Astalos grinned at Wheeler. "I thought you'd like that."

"All right," McKnight said. "Are we about ready?" He turned to Tyler. "Captain, you've been pretty quiet. Don't you have any questions?"

Tyler looked a little sheepish. "Actually, sir, I've been here for about an hour, talking to Doctor Wu and Doctor Astalos. Most of it was a rehash for me, sir."

McKnight nodded. He couldn't hide the slight smile that appeared on his face. "I should've known better than to ask. Doctor Wu?"

"I think we are ready to go," Kathy said. "We..." She stopped, looking over McKnight's shoulder at the door. McKnight turned to see Trevor there with Ginn.

The two of them walked over to where the others were standing.

"We just received word that Miss Ginn has received her final level of clearance," Trevor said. "Probably a new world's record for approval, thanks to Kathy."

"Yes, thank you very much, Doctor Wu," Ginn said. "I'm so excited to be a real member of the team now."

"Don't mention it," Kathy said.

"Welcome aboard again," McKnight said. The rest of the team offered their congratulations.

"Okay, let's get started," Kathy said. Motioning to the others to step back from the Engine, she then turned to Wheeler, pointed at him and twirled her finger in the air.

Wheeler beckoned McKnight, Tyler and Hatcher over to the table, opened his backpack and pulled out a black pouch. "Okay, standard issue, by the checklist. Ready, sirs?"

"Ready," Hatcher said. McKnight nodded.

"Do you have your side arms?"

The three officers patted their Glocks through their jackets and nodded.

"Check," Wheeler said. He handed out items from the pouch.

"Three control beacons."

"Check."

"One sleep bulb, one packet of anti-nausea serum, and a penlight each."

"Check." McKnight stuffed the sleep bulb, packet and penlight in his pockets. The suit he wore didn't have pockets as big as the ones on his fatigues. It wasn't comfortable, but not too noticeable and he'd get used to it. Looking at Hatcher, he felt a twinge of envy. The purse that came with her outfit was perfect for carrying the gear. He noticed she was grinning at him. He gave her a little smile and turned back to Wheeler.

"Hatcher, take this," Wheeler said, and handed her a small vial of liquid.

"One dissolver for the jumpsuits," she said and slipped it into the purse. She produced a rubber band and pulled her hair back into a ponytail.

"That's it, Major. Do you need anything else?" Wheeler asked.

All three officers shook their heads.

The three of them walked to the Engine where Kathy was already standing. "Everything ready?" McKnight asked.

"Yes, sir," Kathy said, handing them three packages. "Here are the jumpsuits. Ready to go?"

"Affirmative," Hatcher said. The three of them unwrapped the packages and slipped the jumpsuits on over their suits.

Wheeler looked over Kathy's completed preparations and nodded his head. He turned to the Engine and plugged the heavy cable into the power generator, checked the lights and switched on the Engine. McKnight could feel more than hear the low-pitched hum that resulted.

Wheeler turned back to McKnight. "Sir, may I have your control beacon, please?"

McKnight took off the chain and handed it to Wheeler who removed the beacon and inserted it into the console. After a moment, the console beeped and ejected the beacon. Wheeler reattached it to the chain and handed it back to McKnight who draped it around his neck. He did the same for Hatcher and Tyler.

Wheeler held up a hand to get their attention. "Major McKnight, Lieutenant Hatcher and Captain Tyler, I've programmed your control beacons with only one jump destination – the conference room at the Hyatt Place on North Clark Street. We'll send you there initially and, when your mission is complete, you'll come directly back here. If you run into any issues, you'll travel directly back to this time and place. Understood?"

The three travelers nodded.

"Each traveler has a control beacon," Wheeler said, as Kathy joined him at the console.

"Check," she responded.

Wheeler picked up the trigger and plugged the cable into the Engine console.

"Trigger connected."

"Check."

He lifted up a small cover over the trigger and switched off the safety. "Trigger safety off."

"Check."

"All set, sirs." Wheeler said and gave them the thumbs up. "Ready when you are."

"Affirmative," McKnight said. He waved in the general direction of the others, and the three travelers stepped onto the metal plate. They knelt, leaned forward and placed both palms on the plate in front of themselves. As each got into position, they looked at Wheeler and nodded.

"Travelers acknowledge ready."

McKnight saw Wheeler turn to face Kathy at the Engine console and say, "Target time is Thursday, July 21, 2011, at 1930 point zero-zero hours."

"Check," responded Kathy, her eyes scanning the console. "We are green across the board, Lieutenant. All systems are go."

"Roger. We are go for travel," answered Wheeler. "Good luck."

"Be careful, you guys," Kathy added.

Hatcher and Tyler nodded without looking up. McKnight stared at his hands, focused on the mission ahead.

Wheeler held up the trigger. "Initiating jump in five... four... three... two... one... mark."

As Wheeler squeezed the trigger, the volume and pitch of the Engine hum spiked and continued to climb. The room's lights dimmed.

Static electricity in the air spiked and McKnight's hair stood on end. The plate glowed and the air above it surged with energy. The hum from the machine grew louder and higher in pitch – much faster than usual, he noted, just as Doctor Astalos had said. A globe of shimmering light formed and spun around them. McKnight glanced at Hatcher. Her raven ponytail flew around her face as if she were kneeling in the middle of a tornado. McKnight could feel his own short hair whipped and tugged by high winds of time travel. The globe became brighter and brighter until he could no longer see outside the sphere. The circulating wind in the globe grew stronger. He heard a loud crack and felt the familiar tug, the irresistible force that pulled him backward. Abruptly, he felt he was lifted off the ground and then falling backward through a field of stars.

CHAPTER 16

8:35 p.m. – July 21, 2011 – Hyatt Place Hotel, North Clark Street, Chicago, IL

The conference room in the basement of the Hyatt Place was quiet. Dust covered the carpeted floor. There were no tables in the room – only scaffolding and a giant tarp covering about half the floor. The paneled ceiling was under construction and acoustic tiles that normally hung from the ceiling were piled next to the south wall near the scaffolding. The air was dry and stale.

A faint breeze of unknown origin stirred the dust. A globe of bright light and spinning air appeared. The level of static electricity in the air spiked, and forms of three figures took shape within. The light went out, the globe vanished, and the three travelers fell backward onto the floor. McKnight turned the fall into a roll and came to his feet, as did Hatcher. Tyler remained on the floor, flat on his back and looking up at the ceiling.

"Are you all right?" McKnight asked.

Tyler rolled over to one side and propped himself up on an elbow. He was grinning. "Man, that never gets old." He sprang to his feet. "Do you guys see, like, stars?"

"Yes," Hatcher said, "for about five seconds. Or, at least, it feels like five seconds. Or maybe twenty-five years." She shrugged.

"Okay, you two. Get focused," McKnight ordered as he peeled off the jumpsuit. He looked at his phone. "We have about two hours before someone murders Amy. We know they're down the street at Harrison's speaking engagement right about now. It won't be long before they show up at the apartment. I want to be in position long before that happens. Lieutenant, dispose of the jumpsuits and recon the area."

"Yes, sir." She stripped off her jumpsuit and collected the two from McKnight and Tyler. She opened the door quietly, peeked around it, and stepped out into a hallway closing the door behind her.

Tyler looked at McKnight and said, "You all right?"

"What? Of course."

"Just checking." Tyler pulled his anti-nausea packet out of his pocket, tore off the end and sucked the medication out. Then he crumpled the package and stuffed it in his pocket. He closed his eyes, took a couple of deep breaths and opened them again. Looking at McKnight, he smiled and said, "Better now."

They both tensed as the door opened. Hatcher had returned.

"Nobody in sight, sir. Jumpsuits destroyed."

"Good," McKnight said, "Let's go."

McKnight strode to the door, checked the hallway, and they filed out. At the end of the hall, McKnight paused at the stairway door. "Okay, remember. We belong here. We avoid any unnecessary interaction with people we meet. Say as little as possible."

"Yes, sir."

McKnight opened the door to the stairwell and led the way up one flight of stairs, through the lobby, and out the revolving door onto Chicago's Illinois Street.

The sights and sounds of 2011 Chicago assaulted their senses. Surrounding them was the noise of pedestrians hurrying from work to home, the smell of auto exhaust from taxis darting about in the street, and the Hyatt Place bellman orchestrating transportation for hotel patrons looking for the evening's entertainment. The Chicago of 2011 didn't look much different from the Chicago of 2036. For a moment, they stood outside and drank in the environment. They looked east and west down the street to get their bearings. The bellman asked if they needed a cab. McKnight shook his head and motioned for the others to follow him across North Clark Street.

They walked in silence for a block. At the corner of LaSalle Street, they turned south. McKnight pointed at a building across the street and one block away. He stopped, and they stood in a tight group to talk.

"According to testimony, one witness was sitting right over there when Amy fell," McKnight said, pointing to the outside seating area of a bar. Looking back over his shoulder at the building, he continued, "Then ran over to where it happened. We're about fifty yards away. Let's get in position."

They walked the rest of the way to the building and passed by the door. McKnight halted them again. "I'm a little concerned we might run into a problem at the security desk. We're not residents, so we might raise a flag with security. Kathy suggested we mingle with any group of residents going into the building and socialize our way in, but I'm not sure that'll work. What do you think? Ideas?"

"Not a problem," Hatcher said. "No problem at all." She looked down the street. "Here's a group going in now. Tailgate them in. I'll go first and distract the guard." With that, she darted away to get in front of the group moving toward the lobby.

McKnight and Tyler exchanged glances, shrugged, and fell in behind the residents.

Hatcher pushed her way through the revolving door and marched to the security desk. The residents behind her continued on through the glass door, with McKnight and Tyler trailing them. Behind the security desk sat a gray-haired man. McKnight estimated his age at mid-fifties.

"Hi," Hatcher said.

"Good evening, ma'am," the guard said. "What can I do for you?"

McKnight saw her looking at a notebook on the counter. She looked up from the notebook, smiled, and waved a key at him. "My boyfriend just moved into these apartments. He asked me to meet him here tonight. Do I need to sign in with you or can I just go upstairs?"

The guard smiled. “Yes, ma'am. If you could sign your name there in the book and include the apartment number and your boyfriend's name. That’s all I need.”

“Right here in this book?” she said, punctuating her words with a toss of her hair and another big smile.

The guard smiled again and stood, moved to the book to point out where she should sign. He handed her a pen.

She thanked him and signed herself in.

McKnight glanced at Tyler, who shook his head and said what McKnight was thinking.

“Wow.” Tyler pushed the elevator call button.

“Thank you *so* much,” Hatcher said, turning to walk through the glass door. “You are *such* a sweet man,” she called back over her shoulder.

“Have a wonderful evening,” he called after her.

Hatcher arrived at the elevator as the door opened. Hatcher said, “Wasn’t he just the sweetest, most helpful man?”. They followed her into the elevator and McKnight pushed the button for the thirtieth floor. As the door closed, someone touched the crash bar to cause the elevator door to open again. A young couple stepped into the elevator, and the man pushed the button for the tenth floor.

The young woman turned to Hatcher and said, “Are you new here?”

“Why, yes, we are,” she said, slipping her arm around Tyler's. “We moved in last week. We bought a house here in Chicago, and it isn't ready yet. It should be ready in a few days. We got a short-term lease for a month, just in case.”

“What's your name?” the girl asked, a big smile on her face.

Hatcher ignored the question and said, “Do they have great parties here in the apartments? I heard it's 'party every night' here. What's the scoop on that?”

The elevator dinged to announce the tenth floor, and the man said, "Don't get her started." He took the girl by the arm and pulled her off the elevator.

She waved to Hatcher and smiled from ear to ear. "Bye!"

The door closed, Hatcher dropped Tyler's arm, and they all breathed a sigh of relief. Tyler chuckled. "Hatcher, you're coming with me on all my missions. That little maneuver at the guard's desk? Brilliant."

"Thanks," she said.

"Good job, Lieutenant," McKnight added.

The elevator dinged again, and they got off on the thirtieth floor. They walked the hallway to all endpoints to get the lay of the land and stopped near the elevator.

McKnight spoke. "Apartment 3008 is the destination." Looking up and down the hallway, he continued, "It's in the middle of the hallway. You two take up position at this end, and I'll take the other end. Listen for the elevator and try not to look like you're waiting for someone to show up. We'll converge on them before they enter the room and convince Harrison to leave, using intimidation if necessary. Then I want to talk to Amy and get the key from her." He touched Tyler on the shoulder. "Next, you engage your beacon and take her out with you, Captain."

"Yes, sir."

"Questions?" He glanced at both officers, who nodded.

"What about other residents coming on the floor? What if they go into 3008?" Hatcher asked.

"For other residents, act like you're going to the elevator until they enter their apartment. If someone else goes into 3008, we'll talk again. At minimum, we wait until they come back out. I don't relish walking into the apartment without intel."

"Yes, sir. Let's get started."

"Right," McKnight said. "Stay sharp."

CHAPTER 17

9:15 p.m. – July 21, 2011 – Apartment Building, North LaSalle Street, Chicago, IL

McKnight stood at the west end of the hall on the thirtieth floor. Since he had taken position, there had been only four instances of people arriving on the floor – one couple, two women and one man.

Self-doubt crept into McKnight's consciousness. Did he have the right night? The right year?

He told the negative voice in his head to shut up and shook his head to clear his thoughts. He focused on Tyler and Hatcher. They had it a little easier than he did. When anyone came off the elevator, they moved closer together and, for all intents and purposes, looked like a couple flirting in the hallway. The best McKnight could do was walk down the hall. A suspicious person might wonder what this tall man in a business suit was doing there.

The elevator dinged and the two officers moved close together again. McKnight again walked toward the elevator. A couple came out of the elevator and started down the hall toward him. It was Amy and Harrison.

Amy was hanging on Harrison's arm, and he was smiling at her. McKnight heard him ask her which apartment, and she pointed down the hall toward McKnight. Hatcher and Tyler broke from each other and quickly closed the gap behind the unwary couple.

Harrison glanced at McKnight and, not perceiving a threat, went back to reading apartment numbers on doors. They stopped before apartment 3008, and Amy opened her purse and reached in it.

"Amy," Hatcher said, causing the girl to whirl around.

Harrison followed her gaze down the hall. When he turned back to Amy, McKnight had stepped between them. He was so close, Harrison involuntarily stepped back. McKnight pressed his advantage by stepping nearer.

McKnight looked Harrison in the eye. “Mr. Harrison, aren't you in the wrong place?”

“What?”

“Sir, is this where you should be? You're a candidate for elected office. You wouldn't want anyone to see you here, would you?”

Tyler and Hatcher reached them, and Hatcher took Amy by the arm. “Amy, it's time to go home.”

McKnight saw confusion, then fear flash across her face. “No, no!” Amy cried. “My parents! I have to –”

“No, you don't, Amy,” Tyler broke in. “Your parents are safe. You've been lied to.”

“Are you okay?” Harrison said to Amy. He pushed forward toward her, but McKnight gently fended him off.

“She’ll be fine now that we’re here,” McKnight said. “Listen carefully to me, sir.” McKnight waited to make sure he had Harrison's full attention. Harrison tore his eyes away from Amy and looked at McKnight. Amy began to cry.

“Sir, you're in the wrong place and so is Amy. I can't explain, but people who want to embarrass you arranged this meeting. Think about it. Should you really be here?”

Between sobs, Amy spoke to Tyler. “Are they really okay? He said he would hurt them if I didn't do what he said.”

“Amy, do you remember Kathy Wu? Her mother is a friend of your mother’s. Do you remember her?”

“Kathy? Yes. You know Kathy?”

“Yes, Amy. She works with us and she asked us to come find you. Your mother came to see her. She said you were missing and she was worried about you. We figured out what happened, and we came to find you.”

"What's going on here?" Harrison said, pushing toward Amy again. "Who are you people?"

McKnight held him back and said, "We're friends, sir, and we're trying to keep you from making a serious mistake. Go home, sir. Go home to your wife. She's waiting for you."

At the mention of his wife, Harrison stopped struggling and looked McKnight in the eyes.

"Please, sir," McKnight said. "Go home to those who love you. Amy will be okay."

Harrison stepped to the side where he could see Amy better, and McKnight didn't move to block him.

"Do you know these people, Amy?" Harrison asked. "Do you trust them?"

"I don't know them," she said, her eyes darting from face to concerned face. "But I know who they are." A tear ran down her cheek as she looked back at Harrison. "They're friends of my family." Glancing at McKnight and his team again, she said. "We have nothing to fear from them."

"She's correct, sir," McKnight added. "But every minute you stay here increases your risk and her danger. Go home, and we'll get Amy back where she belongs."

Harrison looked less apprehensive, but wasn't ready to abandon Amy to these strangers, though he was very much a stranger to her himself. "Are you sure about this?" he asked her.

Amy managed a feeble smile and pulled a handkerchief from her purse. "Yes, I am. Please go. I'll be fine."

"Okay, I'll go," he said. He turned back and stood there, studying McKnight's face.

"Don't worry, sir, you'll never see or hear from us again. And we will keep Amy safe."

Harrison paused and made eye contact with McKnight again. "I think you will. I don't know why I trust you, but I feel I can." He took a step forward. "But if I ever find out you people have hurt this young lady, I will find you."

"I'll take that deal, sir. We're in agreement. Now, we're running out of time. Please go home."

Harrison turned on his heel, walked to the elevator, and pushed the call button. With a look of confusion and concern on his face, he looked back at the small group in front of apartment 3008.

Amy gave him a little wave as the elevator arrived. He stepped into it and the door closed behind him.

McKnight turned to Amy. She stopped dabbing her eyes and asked, "Are my parents really out of danger?"

He smiled at her and said, "They were never in danger. They deceived you. In a few moments, Captain Tyler here will take you back to our time where Kathy is waiting for you–"

"Our time? What?"

McKnight softened his tone. "What do you remember?"

"A few things. Some of it is fuzzy. I was drugged part of the time."

"Okay, we'll figure it out. Kathy will have some questions for you, and she'll make sure your parents know you're safe. In the meantime, I need to know a couple of things. Quickly, now. What were your instructions? What did they tell you to do?"

"He told me to get Wade to come back to this apartment with me and...uh...to...uh..."

"To seduce him?" Hatcher prompted, glancing at McKnight and back at Amy.

Amy turned to Hatcher and said, "Yes." She cast her eyes down at the floor.

McKnight caught Hatcher's eye and inclined his head toward Amy and nodded.

"Amy?" Hatcher said.

The girl continued to stare at the floor.

"Amy!" Hatcher said, with a more authoritative voice. The girl looked up at Hatcher. In a soft voice, Hatcher said, "Amy. What else?"

"Nothing. After he leaves, well, tomorrow, I'm supposed to go to the Chicago Tribune and tell them Wade spent the night with me. After that, he said I could go home."

"Who?"

"Smith, or whatever his name is."

"Smith?" McKnight asked.

"I know it's probably not his real name," Amy said. "I heard one of the others call him that."

"Others?" McKnight asked.

Hatcher looked exasperated. *She's right – let her handle this.*

Hatcher repeated the question. "There were others, Amy?"

"Yes, there were several others."

"Did they hurt you?"

"Oh, no. None of the others touched me or even spoke to me. They talked among themselves, and I heard one of them refer to him as 'Smith'."

"How long did they have you? Your mother said she hadn't heard from you in weeks."

"I don't know." She sniffed and wiped her nose. "At least two weeks. I think I was drugged because I don't remember being kidnapped, and then I was in this dark, dingy place. When I could think clearly, I started counting the days. There were at least fifteen."

"Okay, we'll talk more soon." Hatcher looked at McKnight, handing control back to him.

"Amy," McKnight said, "do you have a key to the apartment?"

"Yes, I do." She reached into her purse and handed him a key on a small ring. "Smith or whoever he is gave it to me."

"Thank you. Now, I need you to go with Captain Tyler. Winnie is his first name. He'll make sure you get back to Kathy. Just do what he says, and everything will be fine, okay?"

Tyler gave the girl his most charming smile. She smiled back and slipped her arm within his. Tyler patted her hand and looked at McKnight. “Do you need me to come right back, sir? I can if you need me to.”

“No, Captain. Relay to Doctor Wu and Mr. George what’s happened. If we're not back in ninety minutes, come back here with Wheeler. Understood?”

“Yes, sir.” Turning, he said, “Let's go, Amy. We have a long way to go.” He pulled her to the widest part of the elevator lobby, pulled his control beacon out of his shirt and squeezed it. A bright globe of spinning light formed around them. Amy gasped as Tyler pulled her closer to him. An internal wind blew fiercely mingling her raven locks with Tyler's sandy blond hair. The light grew brighter until it bulged and disappeared, taking them with it.

McKnight sighed in relief and turned to Hatcher. “What do you think?”

“Someone planned this for a while.”

“Yes, I agree. But I expect we only have one unsub coming. If they plan to kill someone, they’ll want as few witnesses as possible.”

Hatcher put her hand on McKnight's arm and caught his eye. “Smith?”

“I know what you're thinking. It’s more likely a coincidence. It’s a common alias. The guy we know is smart enough to pull this off, but I don’t see the motivation.”

“Well, why not him? Who else has any familiarity with time travel?”

“Well, he *does* know more than most people. And she mentioned another person who wasn’t there willingly. If he had help with the Engine...Well, maybe. Regardless, let’s keep our guard up.”

“Yes, sir. What's next?”

“First, we need to search the apartment to confirm he isn't already there. If he is, we need to arrest him. If not, we wait for him to show up and then arrest him.”

"What's your bet on him coming in, sir? Jumping in or coming through the door?"

"Good question. I don't have a clue. I hope he's jumping in, but if it were me, I'd jump to somewhere else and walk in." McKnight paused for a moment. "But that's just me. For now, let's get inside that apartment."

With an eye toward the elevator, they pulled out their weapons and lined up, one on each side of the door to the apartment. Hatcher stood with her weapon in both hands pointing at the ceiling. McKnight slid the key into the lock and opened the door, holding it a couple of inches ajar. Returning the key to his pocket, he pressed his back against the wall and gripped his weapon in both hands. He looked at Hatcher, nodded and pushed the door open. Hatcher darted through the door to the near side in standard room-clearing protocol and he crossed the fatal funnel behind her to go to the far side.

CHAPTER 18

9:20 p.m. – July 21, 2011 – Apartment Building, North LaSalle Street, Chicago, IL

The apartment was dark. McKnight pushed the door closed behind him. Hatcher caught it before it made contact and closed it without a sound.

McKnight checked off the floor plan in his mind's eye. One-bedroom apartment. Main room, one bedroom, one bath. Main room has a pit group, open area in the middle, kitchenette, a small pantry closet and cloak closet, sliding door to balcony, utility closet on the balcony. Bedroom has double bed, double-door closet, non-opening window to outside. Bathroom has linen closet, shower and tiny non-opening window.

There was no one there. They met in the large area in the middle of the main room.

"Okay," McKnight said. "Not here, so he's coming in later."

"Agreed," she said. "According to Harrison's interview, they had sex and then he went into the bath to shower. When he came out, he saw the girl and got gassed. I'll go set up in the bedroom for that."

"Right. I'm taking up position behind the door. That's the best place since we don't know if he's coming by Engine or through the door."

"Roger," she said. She turned and made her way to the bedroom. She closed the door and McKnight saw the light from the bedroom streaming underneath the door.

He turned off the ringer on his phone, stepped behind the apartment door, and settled in to wait.

McKnight always hated this part. He wasn't a patient person and waiting for someone else irritated him. Especially when it was a bad guy.

He checked off sounds he could hear so he'd be aware when they changed. The vehicle sounds from the street below were next. He noted the air conditioner and filtered it. Next came the television in the apartment next door and the hum of power from appliances in the apartment. He thought he heard a rodent - an indistinct scratching inside the apartment wall.

He didn't have long to wait. After ten minutes, he felt the hair on his arm stand up. *Static electricity. He's jumping in!* McKnight drew his weapon and pointed it at the middle of the room. The bright globe of light appeared there, and he could see a crouching figure within the spinning sphere. The room came alive with dancing shadows created by the light. *He's using newer technology!* The globe was progressing faster than usual.

And the globe was forming closer than he liked. The team learned through experience that contact with the globe during a time event could cause a severed limb. It hadn't happened, but he didn't want to be the test case.

He dashed to the left side where there was more room to avoid the proximity of the globe. His eyes adjusted to the brightness of the spinning air. He could see the figure inside now, crouched on one knee. There was a white patch on the man's left cheek. *A bandage?* The figure looked in his direction. *Can he see me?*

The figure scrambled to pull something from his pocket. And he had a pistol in his right hand. McKnight crouched as his mind raced. *Do I shoot him without prejudice?*

The globe would bulge out any second now, and he was still too close. He stepped back and his buttocks bumped against the sofa of the pit group. *No place to go!*

He saw the unsub drop onto his left side and roll toward him. As he completed the roll, he hurled an object at McKnight.

Off balance, McKnight deflected it with his gun hand. Before he could recover, the object exploded with a bang and a bright light. He went down.

As he regained consciousness, he heard sounds of fighting. For a moment, he couldn't move, but his senses were active. *A flash grenade! Who travels through time with a flash grenade?*

His blurry vision came back into focus. In front of him, he could make out two dark figures fighting in front of him. Hatcher had engaged the unsub. As his eyes adjusted, he recognized the man. It was Smith.

Hatcher was winning the fight. Smith was bigger, but he was older and slower. She was at the top of her game. Her youth and speed were her greatest advantages. He was tiring, and she showed no sign of letting up.

Hatcher executed a spinning kick and caught his cheek squarely on the bandage. As she regained her fighting stance, a trickle of blood ran down his face.

Smith caught her next kick and threw her back across the room. As she recovered, he pulled a control beacon from his pocket, squeezed it, and the globe formed around him. The room flooded with light.

McKnight pulled himself up to his hands and knees. Smith was getting away. He searched the area around him for his sidearm. *There it is!* Still stunned, he crawled the five feet to the gun, grabbed it and swung it toward the spinning globe.

Before he could fire, Hatcher dove into the bubble of light, crashing into the man and driving the spinning light a few feet across the room. He saw Smith trying to push her away and out of the globe. Her head bobbed out and then back inside the spinning maelstrom. McKnight had no clear shot. The spinning globe surged outward and they vanished.

McKnight rolled onto his back and stared at the ceiling, the gun still in his hand. *Damn!* He pounded the floor once with both fists. He saved Amy but failed to capture the unsub. *Smith!* Not only did he not capture him, but the battle moved elsewhere, leaving him behind. *Now what?*

He could hear people talking in the hallway. The flash grenade had attracted attention. He figured he had only minutes to clean up and get out. Struggling to his feet, he flipped the light switch next to the door. There were scorch marks on the wall and ceiling where he had deflected the grenade. *Can't do anything about that.*

The grenade itself lay smoldering on the sofa. Concerned it would catch fire, he used his pistol as a lever to sweep the hot grenade off the sofa to cool on the floor. He holstered his weapon and walked into the bedroom. He found Hatcher's jacket and holster and was stuffing them into her bag when he heard the first knock on the door.

She must have lost her pistol in the fight. She might still have it, but he was sure she would have used it instead of jumping into the globe. He returned to the main room and scanned the floor but found nothing. He dropped to his knees and looked under the furniture.

The knocking on the door became insistent. He found the gun behind the trashcan in the kitchen. A voice identifying itself as the police accompanied the next knock on the door. *Not good.*

McKnight was certain he had everything they brought with them. He used Hatcher's coat to pick up the hot grenade and pushed it in her bag. He squeezed his control beacon two times in rapid succession and was rewarded by brilliant spinning air and a windstorm inside the globe.

The knocks at the door ceased. McKnight guessed the building superintendent had arrived with keys. He hoped he would be gone before the door opened. He felt the familiar tug and went speeding home through a bright field of stars.

CHAPTER 19

9:40 p.m. – July 18, 2036 – Defense Logistics Agency Satellite Office Building, Telegraph Road, Alexandria, VA

As the bubble surged and dissipated, McKnight sprawled forward in the HERO lab. The contents of Hatcher's bag, including the still warm grenade, spilled out before him.

Tyler and Wheeler rushed to help him, but he was on his feet before they got to him.

"Report," he said, as they stepped off the Engine's steel plate.

"Amy and I got here about twenty minutes ago," Tyler said. "She's shaken up but sitting with Doctor Wu in the little conference room."

"Very good. Any sign of Lieutenant Hatcher?"

"Not yet, sir. What happened?"

"I got caught by surprise, Captain. Our unsub is Mike Smith, Senator Lodge's old security chief. He jumped in, saw me, and flash-banged me."

"He what?"

"You heard me correctly, Captain." McKnight pointed at the grenade. "I brought it back with me. We might be able to pull evidence from it. By the time I recovered my senses, Hatcher engaged him, and the two of them jumped out on Smith's beacon."

"Yes, sir. By the book, let me debrief your jump."

"Okay. Go ahead."

"Did you leave anything behind? Anything to raise questions?"

"No, I don't think so. I have my stuff and I maybe all of Hatcher's, but I'm not sure. There is residue from Smith's flash-bang, but I couldn't do anything about it."

"Yes, sir. Any point in going back to clean up?"

"No. There was a cop banging on the door as I jumped out. I'm sure people are still there snooping around. But at least we didn't have a murder."

"Right," Wheeler said. "Any idea about Hatcher's condition? Was she injured? Conscious?"

McKnight paused to replay the scene in his head. "She appeared to be unhurt when they jumped. She was winning the fight which is why Smith tried to run. But that's not what I'm worried about. If he jumped back to the present, he probably had reinforcements waiting for him, which means she's in trouble. Where's Doctor Astalos? We need to know if there's any way we can figure out where she is."

"He went home a couple of hours ago, but we don't need his help. We can recall her if she still has her control beacon on her person. Regardless, the beacon log will give us more information. Let's check it."

Wheeler dashed to his Engine console, but the Engine came on by itself before he touched it. Brilliant light from the globe flooded the room as static electricity crackled through the air.

McKnight drew his weapon when he discerned two figures in the globe. One kneeling and one on the deck.

Is this an attack? The time bubble surged and disappeared. The kneeling figure stood. It was Hatcher, and the prone figure was Smith. Whatever happened, she had prevailed.

McKnight holstered his weapon and approached the plate landing area along with Tyler and Wheeler. Hatcher had a little blood trickling from her nose and a bruise forming on the left side of her face. She pulled her long black hair off her shoulders and back into her ever-present ponytail. Trevor broke out the first aid kit.

Tyler and Wheeler pulled Smith's arms up behind his back and slipped on white plastic restraints.

"Lieutenant, are you injured?" McKnight asked.

"Not to speak of, sir," she said, looking down at the unconscious Smith. "Asshole tried to escape by jumping out."

"Understood." Pointing at Smith, he said to Tyler, "Call the MPs and get him ready for interviewing."

"With pleasure, sir," Tyler said, as Trevor thrust a smelling salts ampule under Smith's nose, and the two of them roughly pulled him to his feet.

Blood saturated the bandage on Smith's left cheek. Trevor peeled it back, cleansed the wound and replaced the bandage. "Looks like someone took a shot at him, Major. This wound looks like a bullet crease. He was lucky that day."

"But not today," McKnight said. "Captain?"

"Yes, sir?" Tyler said.

"Contact General Drake and bring him up to date. Tell him I'll call to brief him within the hour. Thanks."

"Yes, sir." They half-dragged, half-carried the still groggy Smith out of the lab.

Trevor tried to wipe the blood off Hatcher's face, but she pushed him away. "Stop it. Give me a cold pack and a bandage." He handed her both. She pressed the cold pack against the left side of her face and her expression softened. "Sorry, no offense. I'm okay." She pointed at the lab door. "I'm still mad at that asshole."

"None taken," Trevor said.

She nodded, stepped off the plate and walked with McKnight to the conference table. "Ready for my report, sir?"

They sat at the table after McKnight poured water in a solo cup for her. Trevor joined them at the table, turned on a recorder and said, "Okay, standard protocol. We need a formal record of what happened before memory fade sets in. Go ahead."

Hatcher cast her eyes at both men and began to talk. "Okay. Major, you set up in the main room of the apartment and I set up in the bedroom. First indication I got was the light. I saw it coming in under the door, so I knew he was jumping in. I decided to position by the door and wait for him to enter.

"When I heard the flash-bang, I entered the room and saw him pointing his weapon at you. I knew we wanted him alive, so I yelled to distract him and charged. I guess he was off balance from the travel, because he went down easier than I expected. I lost my gun in the process. I'm not sure what happened to his. But he recovered, and we ended up dancing a bit."

She lowered the cold bag and touched her left cheek. Grimacing slightly, she continued. "He got in a couple of lucky punches early, but it was only a matter of time."

McKnight noted that the left side of her face was beginning to swell. She grinned ghoulishly at him. "He tried to jump out because I was whipping his ass. He pushed me away and activated his beacon. I wasn't about to let him get away, so I jumped in the bubble with him. Asshole tried to kill me by pushing me halfway out."

"Lieutenant, what possessed you to do that? We covered that in travel training, right?"

"Yes, sir. I know. I just couldn't let him get away."

"I understand that, Lieutenant. You *did* realize that, since you recognized him, we could find him after we got back, right?"

"No, sir. I didn't. I mean, I didn't recognize him until after he and I jumped out. If I had, I would've shot him."

McKnight barely contained the laugh that jumped to his lips at this unrepentant honesty. He wiped his hand across his mouth under pretext of rubbing his nose.

"While he may deserve it for something he's done, I'm not ready to shoot him without cause," he said.

"Yes, sir."

"What happened next?"

"I was afraid we'd end up at his origin with a roomful of unfriendlies, but we landed in an abandoned warehouse. It was dark as hell. Low visibility. I could tell it was night, but I couldn't tell much of anything else – no idea what time or where. We fought for a couple of minutes before I got past his guard and kicked him in the head."

"Really?" Trevor said. He looked at McKnight. "Some sort of staging area, maybe? Very interesting."

"Yes, sir," she said. "There's more. There was someone else there."

"What?" McKnight said. "Who?" Trevor added.

"I didn't get a good look. But he looked familiar. It was weird."

"Okay, go back," McKnight said. "Tell us about him."

"Sure. After I put Smith down and my eyes adjusted to the dark, I took a quick look around. Since there wasn't an Engine there, I assumed a couple of things. Oh, did you notice how fast the bubble formed and triggered? That and the lack of a machine told me he was using new technology." She looked from McKnight to Trevor and back. "I thought this was brand new stuff. How did they get it? Today was the first time we used it." Her face was a picture of consternation.

The same question was forming in McKnight's subconscious mind, but her question brought it up to the surface. "I don't know," he said.

"Anyway, I was snooping around, just looking for any sort of clue or evidence. I heard a noise at the other end of the building and saw a light. I realized someone else came into the place. It was dim, but I made out a male figure. I started toward him to detain him. He thought I was Smith; he called him by name. Then he realized I wasn't, and I guess he had a beacon in his hand because the bubble formed immediately. I tried to get there before he jumped, but I was cutting it too close, so I stopped. He was wearing a gray sweatsuit. I think I recognized him, sir, but... I don't know. Sorry, sir."

"No problem, Lieutenant. Good report. Go get cleaned up."

"Yes, sir." Hatcher saluted and left the lab.

The two men watched her go. Still looking in her direction, Trevor spoke. "Not too smart, jumping in the bubble with Smith."

"Risky, but she showed initiative. I'm glad she didn't shoot him, or we wouldn't have the intel we do have."

"Right. Speaking of which, the most troubling part is they have the new technology."

"Yes," McKnight said. "And how did they get it?"

CHAPTER 20

1:20 a.m. – July 19, 2036 – Defense Logistics Agency Satellite Office Building, Telegraph Road, Alexandria, VA

McKnight and Trevor entered the small conference room. Kathy Wu was on the other side of the table with Amy Chang, a tape recorder, and a box of tissues. They closed the door behind them and sat at the table.

Kathy had her arm around the girl and nodded to her as the two men sat before them.

Amy spoke. "Major McKnight, thank you for coming to get me. Kathy told me everything, and I wanted to thank you and your team for saving my life."

"It was our pleasure, Amy," McKnight said. "But, it was actually Kathy who brought your situation to our attention. We just acted on good information. But you can pay us back by taking a few minutes to answer some questions for us."

Amy nodded. "Yes, of course. What do you want to know?"

"Let me get the tape recorder going here," Kathy said. She started the recorder and named the people in the room, the date and time, and the purpose of the interview. "Okay, go ahead, Major."

"How did you get mixed up in this? Why are you the person they brought in?"

"I asked myself that at the beginning. I think it was because of what I knew about Barbara's disappearance."

"Who's Barbara?" Trevor broke in.

"My friend Barbara – Barbara Howard. She was dating this man, and–"

"Barbara Howard?" McKnight said. "Where do you live?"

"Newport Place, near DuPont Circle. I–"

"She's your neighbor?" McKnight asked softly. The room began to spin slightly and images of the Barbara he knew played before his eyes. He stared straight ahead.

"Yes," Amy said. "She had the apartment across the hall from me at 112 Newport Place. How did you know?"

McKnight found he couldn't speak. *Barbara gone?* Barbara's sparkling eyes and brilliant smile were still before his eyes.

"Major?" Trevor said in a soft voice.

"What's the matter?" Amy said.

"Marc, are you with us?" Kathy asked.

Kathy's voice penetrated the fog that threatened to consume him. McKnight searched her face and saw compassion and worry. *Get hold of yourself.*

He took a deep breath and leaned forward. He rested his arms on the table, palms up. "Amy, please forgive me," he said. "I'm a friend of Barbara's, too. We dated for a while and it was a shock. Captain Tyler is her friend, too. We haven't heard from her and we've been getting worried. Please continue and share with us what you know."

Amy glanced at Kathy.

"Amy, it's okay," Kathy said. "Remember it was Major McKnight who led the mission to rescue you. He's worried about Barbara, just like you."

Amy nodded.

"You said Barbara disappeared?" Trevor asked.

Amy leaned forward again. "Yes, she was dating this man and then one day she was just gone. I didn't see her for several weeks, and then I ran into him at this bar, so I thought I'd ask if he'd seen her."

"Him who?" Trevor asked.

"Her boyfriend. I'd only met him once before. I saw him and Barbara together there at the same bar. On that day, he acted like a jerk. Like he didn't really want to be bothered. She introduced me, but I didn't get his name – the music was too loud."

"What bar was it, and when did you meet him again?"

"It was the Hard Rock Cafe. Downtown on E Street. When I saw him again, he was having a drink with some other girl. So, I asked him about Barbara."

"What did he say?" Trevor asked.

Amy shook her head. "He seemed irritated that I spoke to him and he didn't want to talk about her. He mumbled something about her dumping him and leaving town. I knew that wasn't true, and I called him on it. He left after that. I checked with other tenants in our apartment building, and nobody there knew anything about her moving or her boyfriend. I had almost made up my mind to go to the police, when...well, I'm not exactly sure what happened. I woke up in a little room, and I was a prisoner."

"Okay. Amy, let's back up a little and start from the beginning. Tell us about Barbara. What was her last name again?"

"Howard. Barbara Howard. She lived across the hall from me at our apartment building in Georgetown. We became friends a couple of years ago when she first moved in. We went out together a lot. You know, to bars and stuff. Until recently, that is. She got a new job somewhere last year and, after a while, she didn't want to go out anymore. I thought she was angry with me or maybe was only my friend because I was convenient. Then I found out differently."

"What do you mean?" Trevor asked. He leaned forward. "Did something happen to change your mind about it?"

"Yes. One night about two months ago, I came in from a party and saw her in the hall at our apartments. She was crying and couldn't get her door open. I could tell she was frustrated and upset. I opened her door for her. She was crying so hard she couldn't get her key in the lock. I asked if I could help her and she said no and slammed the door in my face. I decided not to let it bother me and went into my place. A few minutes later, she knocked on my door. She apologized and explained it was because she and her boyfriend had split up. I had just broken up with a guy before I met Michael, too, so I could relate, you know?"

"Yes. She confided in you."

"Yes. Anyway, I got us both a drink and we sat down to talk. I think she just needed someone to talk to. After a few minutes, she told me she found out her boyfriend was married."

"Really?" Trevor asked. It was more a statement than a question.

"Yes. I asked her if she knew how crazy it was to fool around with a married man. She said she did, but she didn't know until that night. Anyway, he told her he loved her and was going to divorce his wife and marry her." Amy shook her head.

"It's an old story," Trevor said.

"Yes, that's exactly what I told her." She dabbed at her eyes with a tissue. "But she insisted their situation was different. I knew it wasn't true, but I agreed so we wouldn't argue. Anyway, she told me she was going to confront him about when he was going to ask his wife for a divorce."

"She wanted a commitment out of him," Trevor nodded.

"I was pretty sure he would never do that. Girls hear that fairy tale all the time. That's when she disappeared." She crumpled up the tissue, tossed it aside and reached for another. Kathy patted her arm.

"She disappeared? How do you know?" Trevor asked.

"She told me she was seeing him the next night. I didn't think much about it, but then I didn't see her the next couple of days. I even thought maybe her boyfriend was sincere and they were together. But then there was a moving van out front and some men loaded her stuff and took it away. I talked to our landlord, and he said Barbara's boss called and said she was transferred to the Denver office and they were moving her."

"He did?" Trevor said.

"Yes. He said he had a note signed by Barbara that said it was okay to give access to her apartment for the move. Barbara's company paid her rent to the end of the lease in cash, along with a thousand dollar bonus to the landlord for expediting the move paperwork. They did it all in one day."

"How did you know about the bonus?"

"The landlord's wife told me."

"Did you talk to any of the movers?" Trevor asked.

"No," she said. "It happened while I was at work. But it was weird, you know? What girl moves out of state without packing her things personally? I'd never let a bunch of guys rummage through my stuff and pack it for me. That just didn't seem right to me. That's when I knew something must be wrong." She sniffed and wiped her nose.

"And what did you do?"

"Well, nothing really. I wasn't sure what to do until I ran into the boyfriend at Hard Rock. The way he acted really made me suspicious. It was maybe two days later that I went blank. I remember walking to work, but nothing after that until I woke up in this little room."

"And there you met Mr. Smith?"

"Yes."

"Okay, Amy, you're doing great," Trevor said. "What I want you to do now is tell us everything you can remember about anything he ever said to you. I also want you to please describe Mr. Smith and anything you can remember about him like physical marks, tattoos, mannerisms, accents, anything. If you think you remember anything word-for-word, please say so. Can you do that for me?"

Amy looked at Kathy, who smiled and said, "We'll use your statement to help prosecute Mr. Smith and anyone else who helped him. He kidnapped you, and he might have killed Barbara. We're going to make sure he never causes you or anyone else any trouble, ever again. After you tell your story, Major McKnight and Trevor will question him and, at minimum, he'll spend the rest of his life in prison."

"He threatened me and said he was going to hurt my mom and dad. You're telling me he planned to kill me and probably did kill Barbara. I'll do whatever it takes to make him pay."

Trevor looked at Kathy and then back at Amy. “Amy?”

“Yes.” She was looking at her hands in her lap.

“Look at me.”

Slowly, she raised her face to make eye contact with him.

“What I want you to do is tell the truth,” he said. “There is no 'whatever it takes.' He will pay for what he did. All you need to do is tell us exactly what happened to you. Don't try to guess. Don’t try to figure anything out. Just tell us everything you can remember. Okay?”

A tear rolled down her cheek. “Okay.” She sniffed again.

Trevor smiled and patted her hand. “Good girl. Look, it's going to be all right. This guy is a bad man, and it won't be hard to prove what he’s done. Just tell us everything you know and we'll take care of the rest.”

She nodded and started to tell her story as the recorder’s microphone light blinked on the table.

As McKnight listened, he fought down his personal feelings and tried to compartmentalize them. He bristled at the callousness Smith showed. He was clearly trying to protect this ‘boyfriend’, whoever he is, and Amy got in the way. And he must be a man of means. No punk would be able to afford someone like Smith to do his dirty work, not to mention the cleaning crew that removed Barbara’s things from her apartment. She was an inconvenience, and they kidnapped her. They planned to murder her to keep her from talking. He grew angrier as each minute ticked by.

He didn’t want to admit it, but his mind flew to the end of the logic. *Barbara is dead.*

He pushed the emotion down and ordered himself to focus.

Something she said caught his attention. Smith held her captive for about six weeks as far as McKnight could tell. But they kept her sedated most of the time, and she had no idea how long she had been there. Then she woke up, got healthy food and access to a shower. *Why was that significant? Could it be they didn’t know what to do with her at first?* It fit the activity pattern. First, they didn't know what to do with her. Then they came up with an executable plan.

A drugged girl would have no chance at getting Harrison up to her room. But a healthy, beautiful and charming girl with something to lose if she failed? That girl would be much more likely to succeed.

Something else she said brought him back to the present. "...Today was the first day they got it working."

"Wait a second," McKnight said. "What did you just say?"

Trevor looked at him and back at Amy. "Yes, Amy. You were saying? I asked you about the Time Engine."

"That man Smith talked to me for a few days about being with Mr. Harrison. He didn't tell me we were going to the past. He just said I had to get Mr. Harrison to come to an apartment and have sex with me or they would kill my parents. I was sure he would do it. I didn't know we were going back in time. I knew it was possible, of course – I watch the news – but I didn't realize what they had in mind until a few hours ago."

"Tell me what happened. How did you find out it was about time travel?" McKnight said.

"Well, Mr. Smith came to my room and said today was the day, and he gave me a suitcase. We walked out of my room into a larger room. That's when I realized we were in, like, a warehouse or something. There were a bunch of men there with guns. They were carrying in equipment and setting it up in the corner. There was a man telling them what to do and where to put stuff. And there was another man standing next to him with a radio telling someone what to bring in next. They did it all in one day. They carried it in, set it up, and tested it yesterday. Then Smith took me back to 2011 with a map on how to find Mr. Harrison." She looked intently at McKnight. "I've never been so scared."

"What was in the suitcase?" Trevor asked.

"New clothes," she said. "He said I needed to look successful and pretty. The clothes were nice, but all I could think about was what he was making me do. It made me sick to my stomach."

"I see. Mr. Smith wanted you to sleep with Mr. Harrison. What else were you supposed to do?"

"He told me I needed to seduce him and then go to the Chicago Tribune the next day and tell them he had raped me. Then Mr. Smith would come back and pick me up and bring me home." She paused and looked ill. "But that wasn't his plan, was it?"

"No, Amy, it wasn't. He planned to throw you off the balcony and make it look like suicide. His plan was to embarrass Mr. Harrison so he would lose his election and, at the same time, rid himself of someone who could embarrass his employer by asking too many questions."

"About Barbara, you mean?" she whispered.

"Yes."

Amy paled. She rose abruptly, ran to the trashcan, and vomited.

Kathy followed her with a wad of tissues in her hand.

McKnight and Trevor leaned toward one another to share thoughts.

Trevor put his hand on McKnight's shoulder and whispered, "Are you okay?"

"Yes, I'm fine."

"She said they brought in an Engine just like ours this morning. Does that mean they just got it or did they have it at another location?"

"I don't know," McKnight said. "Something's not right."

"Okay, let's look at it another way. Who's qualified to set up the machine? Wheeler, Hatcher, Doctor Astalos, and... I guess Doctor Wu and Captain Tyler could do some of it, but not the calibration and wiring...oh, and Robby Astalos."

"I think we can rule out Robby since he's in Finland. This feels like a dead end. Everyone else was here working on the move for Sunday morning." McKnight drummed his fingers on the table. "I think we need to talk to Doctor Astalos about this. There must be someone else who knows the technology. This just doesn't add up."

After a couple of minutes, the two women returned to the conference table.

Trevor rose to help Amy back into her seat. "Are you all right?" McKnight asked.

"Yes," Amy said, her voice little more than a hoarse whisper. "There's something else I need to tell you."

"Yes," Trevor said. "What else?"

"There were two other prisoners there."

"What? Did you know who they were?"

"No, but they knew each other. One was a little girl and the other was an older woman."

"Her mother, maybe?"

"Maybe, but she seemed more like her grandmother. The girl clung to her. And the man knew them."

"You mean Smith knew them?"

"No, the man who was helping them. My memory is still a little fuzzy, but now that I think about it, he seemed like a prisoner, too. The man with the radio? He was holding onto his arm like he might run away."

"The other two prisoners…could you hear any of what they were saying?" Trevor asked.

"Not really. The woman kept asking what they'd done to be prisoners, and the girl just kept crying. They threatened the woman to make her be quiet, then they tied us all up and covered our mouths with tape. Another man with a gun stayed with us. I got really scared for them."

Trevor smiled at her. He reached across the table and patted her hand. "We're almost done, Amy. What else can you tell us about them?"

"I can't think of anything," she said. "I'm so sorry I can't remember more. I was so frightened. Then that man Smith threatened to kill me if I told Mr. Harrison or anyone else about the other prisoners."

"Okay. One last question. Did you recognize anyone else you knew at the place where the Engine was, like maybe Barbara's boyfriend? Or maybe someone else who was in charge? Or just anything else that seemed out of place?"

"No one other than the man who helped them with the machine. He didn't seem like one of the others." Amy yawned. "Can I go home now? I want to see my parents."

Kathy nodded. "I think we can continue this discussion tomorrow. Right, gentlemen?"

McKnight and Trevor exchanged glances. "Yes, of course," McKnight spoke for them both. "We've arranged protection for you and your parents. There'll be someone with you at all times for the next few days. Mr. Smith is now in custody. We'll find out who his friends are, and we'll make sure they pay for what they have done."

"Thank you. Kathy? Could you come with me?"

"Of course." She helped Amy to her feet, and the two of them left the room. McKnight and Trevor remained at the table.

McKnight scratched his head and said, "I'm in bad need of sleep. I'm going to get some rest so I can think clearly. I have a bad feeling we're still behind the curve on this one. We caught the little fish, but not the big one. Let's set up the interview for tomorrow morning. I don't like leaving Smith any time to gather his thoughts, but we're all too tired to be effective interviewers tonight."

Trevor nodded. "I agree. Here's what I think we should do. Tomorrow, we interview Smith. I think we should involve Kathy, too. As a matter of fact, I think she should take the lead role."

"What? Why?" McKnight asked.

"Because he doesn't like you," Trevor said, with a smile. "You and Smith have history and, if you think he might have killed Barbara, there's no way you should be in the room, it's too personal for you. It's your call, but if it were mine, there's no way you'd be the interviewer. There's nothing about you that's likely to encourage him to talk to us."

"But she doesn't have much experience in interviewing."

"No, but she's smarter than both of us put together, and you've seen her talk to folks. Nobody is as good as she is at charming people. Smith will be expecting you or someone like you for exactly the reason you want to be on point. It's about adrenalin and testosterone. You'd love to lock horns with him and I think he's looking forward to butting heads with you. That's not a good recipe for getting information out of him. At minimum, it should be me talking to him instead of you. But I think Kathy is a better choice. She'll have an advantage."

"You make a good case," McKnight said, fingering his phone. "Suppose we do allow her to be on point. How does she know what to ask? And how do we get suggestions to her, like questions for her to ask him?"

"Good question. We can set up a chat session on her computer pad. He won't be able to see it, and she won't have to type anything since we'll hear and see everything from the control booth."

"Okay, that should work. So, what would be her approach?"

"This guy's history indicates he has a pretty big ego. My bet is he'll assume he's smarter than her and get careless. He'll try to intimidate her, but he'll get interested if she can banter with him successfully. He'll expect us to be listening in, but he just sees her, not us. It's an advantage. If she can get a banter going with him and not reveal much, he'll try to impress her or maybe taunt her about what she doesn't know. As a former SEAL, he knows how to resist interrogation, but he can't prevent his emotions from reacting to information. His challenge is to hide those emotions from us. Our job is to distinguish between his normal behavior and those emotions."

"You've convinced me," McKnight said. He looked down at his phone and started tapping on it. "I'm sending you the information about where Smith is. Or rather where he *will* be. When I briefed the

General, he requested we take Smith to the Pentagon. They have a detention section along with interview facilities downstairs. Remind Kathy to take her ID with her, and make sure she gets some rest before she takes this guy on. Let's see...it's after two now...let's plan it for oh-eleven hundred hours today. I don't want to wait long, but we need to get some rest so we'll be fresh when we talk to him."

"I agree. You're way past beat, I guess."

"I'm not so bad. Hatcher took the beating from Smith though I daresay she gave more than she got."

Trevor laughed. "I'll bet." His smile disappeared after a moment. "The biggest thing we need to know right now is this: there's another Time Engine out there someplace, and we need to find it."

"Yes, we do," McKnight said. "But I'm not sure that's our biggest problem. Smith is a bright guy, but he doesn't have know-how on how to operate the Engine. Someone's helping him, and that's the guy we need to find. If we don't, we're going to be in a lot of trouble. And we need to get him to tell us where Barbara is. If there's any chance that she's still alive--"

"There isn't." Trevor touched McKnight on the shoulder, then patted it. "I'm sorry, but it's a very slim chance; almost no chance. Going to all the trouble of grabbing Amy and attempting to kill her? No, I can't think of anything that gives me hope she's still alive."

McKnight clenched his jaw and slowly nodded. "If there's any chance she's alive...this is a lot to put on Kathy's shoulders."

"Yes, I know. But she's still the best choice to get through to this guy. Trust me on this."

"I am," McKnight said. "See you tomorrow."

As he walked from the office to his truck, he thought of Megan and glanced at his watch. *Way too late to call now. Better wait til tomorrow.*

He climbed into his truck, cranked it, and started the ten minute ride to his BOQ apartment. Driving south on Telegraph Road, he replayed Amy's story in his mind. *Trevor's right. It's a high probability that Barbara's dead. If Smith is responsible, I'll kill him.*

CHAPTER 21

10:30 a.m. – July 19, 2036 – Pentagon Food Court, Alexandria, VA

By the time he arrived at the Pentagon, McKnight's anger subsided to a slow burn. He decided Kathy didn't need the pressure of his anger while she interviewed Smith. It was already a new experience for her and putting more pressure on her was counterproductive. *Better let Trevor manage the interview with her.*

He passed through security and made his way through the labyrinth of hallways to the food court.

He stopped by Starbucks and got in line.

"Major McKnight?"

He turned at the voice and saw Kathy approaching.

"May I buy you a coffee?" she asked.

"No. I dragged you down here on the weekend to talk to this guy, so I'm the one who should be buying."

She smiled and said, "If you insist. Tazo Refresh for me, if you don't mind. Trevor's here already. I saw him a few minutes ago. He briefed me, and we're ready to go. Any last-minute advice or direction?"

"There are plenty of concepts I could share with you. The basics are you need him to feel like you empathize with him and establish some kind of rapport. Some folks believe you always have to be a hard-ass, but I don't think that will work in this case and, besides, that's not your style. Empathy is your strong suit."

"Anything else?"

"Hang on," he said. He placed their order, and they moved over to the pickup counter to wait for their drinks. "First, I think he'll be surprised it isn't Trevor or me talking to him. He will underestimate you, so use that to your advantage. He'll probably try to derail you by reducing you to a sex object. The implication is that you aren't worthy to interview him. Don't react to it – stay on track. He might try to taunt you with the fact you don't know what he knows. If he believes you're not picking up on what he's hinting about, he might slip up and say more than he intended. That's a good thing."

"That would be nice. I want to get a few things from him, right? We want to know where his Time Engine is, how he got it, and who else he's working with."

"And we want to know about Barbara. He had a role in her disappearance, no matter what. At minimum, he helped dispose of her body. He might even be her killer."

"Do you think she's dead?"

McKnight sighed. "I don't want to believe that, but Trevor does and he's probably right. You should proceed as if she's dead and you already know it. If he believes you already know all about it, there's a chance he may give away details."

"Okay, that's the way I'll approach it."

"One other thing," McKnight said. "I got back a copy of Smith's service record. There are some clues there about why he hates the Rangers."

"Seriously? Is it something you can share?"

"Oh, absolutely. I think we need to ask him about it. If you can get him talking about it, he might get pissed and reveal more than he plans to. It's another lever."

"Okay. What happened?"

"Hold on," McKnight said. Their order was ready. McKnight handed Wu her tea and picked up his coffee. "Let's sit down for a minute and talk about it."

The food court was becoming crowded, but they found a table slightly removed from the others and sat. McKnight pulled up the report on his phone.

"According to this," he said, "Smith and his team were captured in Afghanistan by the Taliban near Kandahar. Smith is the only one who survived. He spent three years in that prison, apparently in fear for his life every day. The formal record noted that Smith was a changed man. His attitude tanked and he would have been discharged had he not announced his intention to leave the service at his earliest opportunity."

Wu sipped her tea. "It must have been awful for him. And no bad marks on his record before then?"

McKnight scrolled back through the report. "Just a couple of clashes with the MPs for public drunkenness in Germany and Iraq."

"So we can assume that what happened in that prison profoundly affected him. Does the record say what happened?"

"Um-hmm," McKnight said. "In his debrief, he complained about how the Army Rangers left him there to rot. But there's no mention of the Rangers associated with his mission. Maybe that's what we need to ask about?"

"Okay, I can do that."

"According to Smith, his team was murdered the first day they were there. Apparently, the Taliban figured out he was the team leader and decided to extract information from him. He fully expected to be executed the next day after his interrogation."

"But–?"

"He said the Rangers knew he was there and promised to rescue him, but never did. He commented that the SEALS would never have left a man in captivity if they knew where he was."

"And you think this is why he hates the Rangers?"

"It makes sense, I think," McKnight said. "And he was right to expect the Rangers would be coming back for him. That's standard procedure. 'Never leave a man behind.' Whatever the reason, he wasn't rescued and eventually escaped after killing three Taliban – his story, anyway."

"So you think I should ask him about this and get him talking about it? Do you think dredging that up might actually get him to give away information? I would think it would have the opposite effect. You know, remind him that he hates you guys?"

"I don't know. It's a lever. If we aren't getting anything useful during the interview, maybe pissing him off will change the atmosphere and reveal something."

"Okay. I see that he's a retired Chief Petty Officer. Do I call him Mister or something else?"

"Good question. Call him 'Chief'. That should be fine."

"Okay, got it. What else?"

McKnight smiled. "That's enough, isn't it? We should get to the detention center. But, if you don't mind, I need to make a quick call. Give me just a couple of minutes."

"Sure," she said, and McKnight stood and walked a few steps away and commanded his phone to call Megan.

The phone rang six times before going to voice mail. He started to disconnect, then remembered what she said about calls. *I won't make that mistake again.* He left a message.

He rejoined Wu and they headed for the elevator to the detention center downstairs.

"One more thing," he said. "Don't provide Smith with any information he can use to re-orient himself. Nothing about where he is, what time it is, who is behind the mirror – all that stuff. He can guess. Let him. Just don't respond to it. He's smart, so he'll figure out some stuff based on questions you ask. Just don't give up any information you don't have to. Make sense?"

"Yes, it does. I'm on it."

They reached the basement detention center, signed in and headed for the interrogation room.

****

11:04 a.m. – July 19, 2036 – Pentagon Detention Area, Alexandria, VA

Trevor arrived first at the interrogation center in the Detention Area. There was a conference table in the room, accented by a platter of doughnuts, coffee carafes, cups, creamers and sweeteners. Five chairs were scattered around in mild disarray. To the right was a large observation window with a countertop and bar stools along the edge. He sat on a stool and reviewed his notes.

McKnight and Kathy entered the interrogation room.

"How's our bad little boy?" McKnight asked.

Trevor smiled and gestured at the observation window. "He's behaving up to this point. The MPs brought him in, uncuffed him, but strapped him in his chair. He can move his arms and legs, but he isn't going anywhere."

Kathy stepped over to the booth window and looked in. She met Smith briefly in Atlanta when the team investigated the murder of Senator Lodge's father. Back then, he was a security consultant for the senator.

She frowned. "He looks pretty beat up. Did the MPs do that to him when they brought him in?"

McKnight joined her at the window. "No, I believe you can thank Lieutenant Hatcher for that. He put up a fight and she had to subdue him. It took a few minutes."

"Wow," she said. "Remind me not to piss her off."

"Yes, I know," McKnight said. "I've sparred with her a few times in PT, but never when she was pissed off. She's fast and strong. I'd have no qualms sending her after just about anybody."

"No kidding. I'm impressed." Turning to Trevor, she said, "Are we ready to get started?"

"Yes. Let's set up a chat session between your comp pad and mine so I can pass you questions from the Major and myself. Don't let Smith see it. I'm sure he'll be able to read upside down if you give him the opportunity. And don't forget to disable the message alert ping."

"Okay."

Trevor set up the chat, aware she was studying him closely. When the task was done, he handed her a large folder stuffed with paper.

"What's this?" she asked.

"It's his file."

"Why didn't I see it before?"

"Because it doesn't exist. Whenever you talk to a subject, you always take his file in with you. If you don't have one, you create it. Sometimes it's a pile of old papers or maybe junk documents from a file cabinet. It gives the impression you know them and already know what happened. Since they aren't sure what you know, they tend to stay pretty close to the truth so you don't think they are lying to you. It gives you a slight edge on them."

"Won't this guy know better?"

"He should, but it'll still have a subconscious effect. Let's stack the deck as much as we can, right?"

"By all means, I'll take any help I can get." She laughed, but it seemed a little forced. Trevor saw the worry in her expression and posture.

"Kathy?" he said.

"Yes, Trevor?"

"You'll be fine. We're right here. He can't touch you, and we'll be in there in five seconds if he gets unruly."

"I know," she said.

Trevor stepped closer to her. "You can do this. You're our best chance to get good information from this guy."

"I know," she said. She squared her shoulders and looked up at him.

He took both her hands in his. "You got this," He said. "You rock, as usual."

She gave him that smile he loved to see. In her eyes, he saw determination, vulnerability and courage under pressure.

"Okay," she said, pulling away. "Here I go."

She put her comp pad on the big folder, then picked up both and cradled them under her arm. She grabbed her paper cup of tea and walked to the door.

McKnight opened it for her, then sat on a stool at the counter at the observation window.

Trevor sat next to him with his comp pad before him. "I hope we're doing the right thing, having her interview him," he said.

McKnight turned to him. "Having second thoughts?"

"No, not really. I still think she's our best chance to get him to talk to us." He shifted his weight on the stool. "I just hate asking her to do it without the experience."

"She's one tough cookie, I'll tell you that. And she remembers everything. And I mean everything."

"How long have you known her, Marc?"

"A couple of years. She impressed me with her organization and planning skills while we ramped up the project, but you really get to know someone when they get tested on a mission. In Atlanta, her planning was perfect, even though we rushed into the mission without enough lead time to do proper research. When we got new info, she adapted and overcame. Tyler couldn't have done it any better. She never lost sight of the objective. But you were there. You know."

"Yes, I do. I'm not forgetting that."

He saw Kathy enter the room and approach the table where Smith sat. She stopped before the table and set the folder and comp pad on it. Under his breath, Trevor said, "You got this."

McKnight smiled and turned back to the window.

Trevor noted with satisfaction that they achieved surprise. Smith could not keep it from showing on his face, but recovered quickly and replaced the look of surprise with one of amusement.

"Hello, Chief," she said. "I'm sorry to meet you again under such unsavory circumstances." She slipped into her seat with an elegance designed to cover her nervousness.

"What are you?" he asked with a leer on his face. "The T and A warm-up? When does the main event start?"

"T and A?" she asked, then smiled sweetly. "I'm sure you must have me confused with someone else. I'm here to ask you a few questions."

"I'm not confused at all. You're Doctor Wu. I remember you from the Lodge case. You're a fine-looking woman. Play your cards right, and you might get to see more of me. You can call me Mike."

"Great!" she said. "And you can call me Doctor Wu. Let's have a chat, shall we?"

"I'm sorry, little lady, but my after-hours appointment book is pretty full. If you asked me nicely, I might tell one of the girls to go home early, and you can take her place."

Trevor felt his jaw tighten. He would have happily shot Smith to death at this point without a second thought.

Kathy laughed out loud. "Me? With you?" She shook her head and smiled. "Thanks. I needed a good laugh. Oh, one of your bimbo friends came by here earlier, looking for you. I told her to come back in fifty years. You should be able to take visitors by then."

Trevor looked at McKnight, who was grinning. "I think she'll be okay," McKnight said.

Trevor looked back into the interview room.

Smith was smiling. "Where *is* here, by the way?" Smith asked and examined his fingernails.

"Oh, it's the weekend vacation condo. I wanted to make sure you were safe. We wouldn't want anything to happen to you, now would we?"

"Of course not," he said, a smile on his face. "Who is we?"

"I was using the 'royal we.' But in fact, we identified several bimbos who care passionately about your safety. I'm not sure why, but we'll try to take care of you for their sake. But then there's Lieutenant Hatcher. She begged me to let her come talk to you."

"Who?"

"Oh, *you* know! The lady you met in the bar last week and who also brought you back from 2011."

Smith's face darkened for an instant, then returned to his broad smile.

Trevor grinned. *She's holding her own. Atta girl.*

"Speaking of which, where is that asshole, McKnight?" Smith asked. "Still nursing his wounds from the beating I gave him last night?" He continued to look around the room and smile. "I'll bet he's right behind the window there." He waved at the mirror on the wall. "Hi, Marky. How you doing, buddy? Are your ears still ringing?"

He's pleased with himself.

Trevor glanced at McKnight, who said, "I wish it *was* me in there. He wouldn't dare provoke me like this if I was close enough to do something about it. Can we let him escape so I can catch him and break every bone in his face?" Before Trevor could respond, he waved his hand in dismissal and said, "Yeah, yeah. I can dream, can't I?"

They turned their attention back to the interview.

"I was really hoping to get to talk to McKnight, sweetheart," Smith said. He continued to smile at the window, blowing kisses and waving derisively at it.

"Maybe I can arrange for him to come by later, Chief. When do you have free time?"

Smith laughed out loud. "That's all I got, baby. Lots and lots of free time. Tell him to bring backup. He'll need it."

"I'll relay that to him. Now, what do you know about the murder of Barbara Howard?"

Smith turned his attention from the window to Kathy. "Who?"

"We have most of the story already. I'd like to know your side of the story before we turn you over to the DC cops for investigation and indictment."

Smith chuckled. "I have no idea what you're talking about. I didn't kill… Barbara? Was that her name? In fact, I haven't killed anyone lately."

Kathy caught his eyes and held them. “Be careful what you say. When what you say doesn’t match what we know to be true, it makes you look like a liar. That makes it harder to believe you when you tell the truth.”

“Ha! I don’t give a shit. I didn’t kill what’s-her-face. You’re grasping at straws, Doctor. Come back when you have some real information. I think this interview is about over.”

Smith went back to making faces at the window and waving.

“Very well,” she said. “I’ll pass your response on to the powers that be.”

Smith threw a response over his shoulder. “Please. Tell them to knock themselves out looking for a connection. There isn’t one.”

Trevor typed on the chat. <Move on. He’s not biting on this. Ask about the technology. >

Kathy nodded involuntarily. “Well, I can arrange an interview for you with Major McKnight. I’m sure he’d love to talk to you.”

“I’d be happy to talk to him. But, honey, you’re still a good substitute. I’ll talk to you any time.”

“Well, thank you,” Kathy said. “So, tell me, where did you get the time travel technology?”

Smith whipped his head around to look at her. He smiled at her and then turned his gaze back to the window. But he couldn't take back the expression that flashed across his face. He continued to smile and wave at the window. “Why, Doctor Wu, whatever do you mean?”

Trevor didn't miss the expression. *He was surprised at the question. Why wasn’t he expecting that question.*

“Oh,” she said. “I’m sure it didn’t drop out of thin air. Where did you get it?”

Good. Keep him on that subject.

“Well, my goodness,” Smith said. “Believe it or not, I found it in my closet.”

“Your closet?”

"Yep. There I was, looking for a clean shirt and, lo and behold, there it was!"

Trevor noted Smith's eyes were darting around, looking at nothing and everything. He guessed the man was assessing, running through options.

"Well, *that* must have been a happy surprise," Kathy said.

"It was. My fondest hope was I would find a crisp, laundered blue shirt. But there it was – a Time Engine. Right there in my own little closet."

"It must have been heavy. How did you get it downstairs? Did you have friends over?"

"How'd you guess?"

"It was a stretch. Frankly, I *am* surprised to learn you have friends."

"Ah, you've pierced me to the heart." Smith fidgeted a little. "Well, my neighbor owed me a favor. I loaned him my leaf blower two weeks ago, you see." He gave Kathy a knowing smile and continued with a lilt to his voice. "I felt justified in asking him to return the favor. He went the extra mile to help me out."

"I'm sure," Kathy said.

Shit! We aren't getting anywhere with this. Trevor racked his brain for another approach.

"I apologize for doubting you, Chief," she said. "You're a man of significant resources, and I underestimated you."

Smith gave her an amused look, but not quite as disdainful as before.

Kathy glanced down at her comp pad. "I was looking at your service record. You had a lot of success in the military–Chief Petty Officer in the Navy SEALS, a stint in Special Forces, time in Iraq and Afghanistan." Looking up at him, she continued, "Your degree at Annapolis was in electrical engineering. Did you get to use it much in the military?"

"Not that much. I mostly got shot at. You ever been shot at, Doctor Wu?"

"Not yet."

Smith laughed. "There's no feeling like it. After someone shoots at you, there's not much else that can scare you. Economic pressure, threat of being sued...threat of jail, for example. Anything else pales in comparison."

"I hope it never happens to me. So, after the military, you joined a contracting firm to provide security?"

"No, I joined a contracting firm for a lot of money." He grinned at her. "Make no mistake. Being in the Navy is a noble thing. But the pay isn't worth it, and the politicians have no problem throwing blood and treasure at a political problem that has nothing to do with national security. It's all about the money. I wised up, that's all."

"I see. Makes sense, I must say. So, the pay was good?"

"Oh, yes. You wouldn't believe it."

"Try me," she said. "How good?"

"About three times what the military pays, plus tons of benefits. The client usually provides everything. Cars, entertainment, vacation trips. Whatever you want, as long as you produce the desired results on your missions."

Kathy let out a low whistle. "Wow. I had no idea. Sounds like you made a smart decision there. And, it sounds like you didn't have many expenses. What did you do? Invest the extra money?"

Smith smiled.

Did he just puff up a little? Maybe she found a lever.

"I've been getting some great investing tips from a…benefactor, a friend who gives good investing advice. He sends me a lot of tips. I have a big damned portfolio," he said, locking eyes with her. "Nothing you can touch or affect."

Kathy looked pained as if he had insulted her. "I can't imagine a threat as trivial as that would concern a man like you, especially one who's been shot at."

"Correct," he said.

She shook her head. "But I'm getting off track here. Being an electrical engineer, I guess it was easy for you to get the Time Engine technology to work. I mean, I've seen it used. Seems easy...you know, to run it. You turn it on, and it works."

"Ha. You might think so. There aren't five people in the world...well, you know. You have your Doctor Astalos. Or rather, your *Doctors* Astalos. It's not as easy as you might think."

In the control booth, McKnight and Trevor looked at each other.

McKnight pulled out his phone, but it rang before he could make a call. Trevor watched him shake his head and decline the call. He looked distracted.

"Was that something important?" Trevor asked.

"What? No, Megan was returning my call. It'll have to wait."

"Okay. I think you were going to call to check on Robby and Robert Astalos?"

"Yes, I was." He speed-dialed a number, then spoke into the device.

"Mr. Tyler...Has Robby Astalos checked in with us from Finland during the last two days...Can you check? I'll wait." Looking at Trevor, he said, "I should have thought of this. We should have made a list of the people who could help Smith do this. This guy isn't big enough to pull this off alone. Even with a double-E degree, I doubt he could do it without help. We should pull our assets back home to make sure they're protected. I think we need to do that at minimum."

"Yeah, I'm with you. Let me get back to monitoring this interview. You do what you need to do."

"Right."

Turning his attention back to the phone, McKnight said, "Yes, I'm still here... Okay... he hasn't checked in? All right, Mr. Tyler. I need you to go find him. Get Wheeler to keep trying to contact him, but you go to Finland and bring him back now. I'll call the General and see what help we can get from the Finns...Understood...What?...Okay, how far along is that planning?...Okay. It sounds like Wheeler can pick up the planning for the move tomorrow and execute it. Give it to him and get your ass to Finland…Yes, right now…Good luck."

McKnight disconnected the call and turned his attention back to the interview. Kathy and Smith were chatting about American military policy.

He looked at Trevor, who turned and smiled at him. "Amazing, isn't she? She's engaged him in debate. She's stayed away from the topics, but she's getting on his side of the table. It may take a while, but she'll get under his skin, and he'll talk to her without even realizing he's doing it."

"How soon?"

"Weeks, maybe." At the look of dismay on McKnight's face, he added, "Look, this guy is like steel… Navy SEAL. Special Forces. Other than being a total asshole, he isn't that different from you."

"Thanks a lot," McKnight said. "We're nothing alike."

"I'm serious," Trevor said. "If we were trying to get information out of you that you didn't want to share, how hard would it be? As a SEAL, Smith's had training similar to yours and more. And when we *do* get to the truth, he's most likely going to jail for a long time, so he isn't in much of a hurry to start that. As long as we're in this phase, he has a chance to work a deal. Believe me, it's going to take a while."

"Okay, I get it. What can we do in the meantime? I guess we can keep chasing the physical evidence, what little there is. What else?"

"What about the supposed betrayal of the Rangers? Let's ask about that."

"That's a good idea. Might as well get it all out on the table," McKnight said.

Tyler typed into the chat. <Ask about the Afghan prison and the Ranger promise. >

After another three minutes of small talk, Kathy glanced down at her comp pad and shifted in her chair.

"Changing the subject," she said. "May I ask you about something I'm personally curious about?"

"Does it matter if I mind?" Smith grinned at her. "Go ahead, I don't have anything else to do."

"Well, it's kind of personal. I'm thinking of writing a book about people who have been imprisoned in the Middle East. I read that you were captured and locked up in Afghanistan for three years."

Smith's face darkened and his eyes narrowed. "Not something I like to talk about," he said.

"I'm sure it's not," Kathy said. "But do you mind? When I write the book, I'll list you as one of my sources and include contact information. At some point, you might want to go on the lecture circuit and—"

"Me? I don't see that happening."

While his words didn't support it, Trevor thought he was pleased by the thought.

Smith leaned back in his chair and shrugged. "I'll make an exception in your case. Ask away, Doctor."

"Thank you, Chief. As background, may I ask how you were captured?"

"Yes. I don't suppose it's classified any more. I was on a mission with four other SEALS. We got intel that a Taliban leader would be meeting a woman near Kandahar without a protection detail, so we went in to see if we could kidnap him. Our intel was faulty, or it was a trap. I'm not sure which. But we got surrounded by a superior force and surrendered after losing one of our guys in the fighting."

"Oh, my God," she said. "So you and those three surviving SEALS were all in prison for three years?"

"No. We were marched to the prison and they executed the other three to motivate me."

"They killed them? What does that mean – to motivate you?"

"It means they guessed I was the team leader, which was correct. When I refused to give up anything, they shot my team dead in front of me. They held a gun to my head last and the leader stopped them from killing me. He gave me twenty-four hours to give up information or die. It was theater, of course. They tossed me into a small cell to think about it or to prepare to die."

"How horrible! Were you scared?"

Smith laughed. "Are you kidding? I was petrified. But I knew it didn't matter if I told them anything or not. In the morning, they were going to blow my head off, no matter what. So I decided to be a good soldier and take it like a SEAL."

Kathy smiled at him. "I don't know if I could have done that. I would probably have told them everything I know. If there was any chance of survival, I'd probably have spilled my guts."

"It's an effective motivator, but once you tell them what you know, they have no use for you. No reason to keep you alive except maybe as a hostage, but that usually brings a Special Forces operation and they don't want that."

"But you survived. What happened?"

"That night, I didn't sleep a wink. No food, no water. Every sound in that dark hole might have been them coming to get me. I didn't know which moment would be my last."

Trevor smiled. *I wonder how many times he's told this story to impress some lady?*

"What happened?" Kathy asked.

"I had a visitor. I heard scratching on the door of my cell and went to the door. I figured it was my jailors so I said 'fuck off' in English. I heard a voice answer in English. 'Army or Navy?' I thought they were trying to trick me, so I said, 'Fuck off, raghead.'"

"Oh, my God," Kathy said.

"Then I heard what I didn't expect. He said he was a Ranger. I remember him like it was yesterday. Sergeant Randall." Smith's expression hardened, then relaxed. "I told him a Ranger Grunt was too stupid to find his way into a Taliban camp."

Trevor wrote down the name.

"Bastard," Smith said. "He said they knew I was here now and they would break me out. I told him it had to be now because I was a dead man tomorrow. He said he copied and would be back before dawn. He swore he would come back for me. The Rangers never leave a man behind, he said. Even a Squid, he said and laughed. I told him to get fucked and we both laughed."

"Amazing," Kathy said. "Then what happened?"

"He asked me my name. Then he left and never came back. The bastards left me there to rot. Not even a hint of a rescue attempt."

"Obviously, you're still here. What happened in the morning?"

"I fully expected to die, but they didn't do it. After asking questions that I didn't answer, one of them pulled out a pistol and waved it at me. The leader started yelling at him in a dialect I didn't recognize. Anyway, they put me back in my cell and gave me some water. For some reason, they decided not to kill me. Maybe they knew they had been penetrated. Who knows? But the damned Rangers never came back. They left me there."

"I'm so sorry to hear that. But you eventually escaped…"

"Yes. I watched their security patterns for holes for three years. After a couple of months, they stopped trying to get information from me and left me alone. I considered myself lucky that they remembered to feed me every couple of days. Anyway, one day they left my cell unlocked. I couldn't believe it. Turns out it was a trap…one of the guards wanted to kill me for sport. I was in a weakened condition, but he underestimated my ability to fight. And he didn't think to get any of his raghead buddies to back him up. To his significant regret."

"You killed him?"

"What do *you* think? Anyway, I managed to sneak out and stole a vehicle that barely qualified as a car and drove out before they knew I was loose."

"That's quite a story. Why didn't your command come looking for you?"

"They did. The guys who took us did a good job of hiding what happened. To Command, we disappeared into thin air. Usually, there is some evidence or the Taliban brags and word leaks out, but not so in this case."

"I see. Chief, that's a great story. They ought to make a movie out of it. Tell me…I see you left the service not too long after that. Was it because you were in prison for so long? I mean, that has to take a toll on anyone…even you."

"It's no secret that I'd had enough of fighting over there. I couldn't see how it was helping my country's security. I changed my mind about a lot of things. Sitting in a dirty rat hole for three years does give you some serious thinking time. So when my tour was up, I bailed. Don't feel sorry for me. It's been pretty lucrative up to now."

"Sounds like it. Thanks for sharing that with me." She looked at her comp pad for the time. "Let's take a few minutes break. Want some coffee?"

"Sure," he said. "What time *is* it?"

"Time for a break," she said. "I'll be back in a few minutes. Relax." She picked up her comp pad and left the room.

Trevor watched Smith closely through the one-way glass. The man slumped back in his chair, glanced at the glass and sat up straight. *Good. He's not getting much back from Kathy.*

Kathy came into the control room. She looked tired.

"You okay?" McKnight asked.

She shrugged. "I can see why he doesn't like the Rangers. Sounds like they left him there. There must be more to the story. But what he has done…" She glanced back through the glass into the interview room. "Or what he planned to do…gives me the creeps. Do you think we're making any progress?"

"Yes," Trevor said. "You're frustrating him, though he's trying hard not to show it. Despite himself, he's opening up to you. We'll get to him eventually."

"And we have another piece to the story about why he hates the Rangers," McKnight said. "If we can find out more about that Ranger Randall, we might get a lever we can use to get more from him. I'll get some research done to find out about that guy, if he really exists."

Trevor nodded. "I think that's a good idea."

"What else can we do?" Kathy asked.

"We keep asking and listening. As long as he's talking, there's a chance he'll give us a clue. We need to pay attention to everything he says." He turned and pointed at the computer console in the corner. "We're recording everything he says and does. Eventually, he'll slip. He'll get careless, or he'll get too smart for his own good. He might not even realize it, but he'll give us something we can use."

"Okay," she said. She poured some coffee and tea and went back into the interview room and sat. Smith leaned forward on the table, his fingers interlaced before him.

McKnight and Trevor went back to the window and sat.

"Okay. So, we listen," McKnight said. "I wish we could get something sooner. Somewhere out there, people are trying to change history to their advantage, and Smith is our only clue." McKnight looked Trevor in the eye. "That's a helluva note, isn't it? This asshole is only the muscle, but he's all we have."

CHAPTER 22

5:32 p.m. – July 19, 2036 – Pentagon Detention Area, Alexandria, VA

The interview continued for six hours. Kathy looked fatigued. Trevor reflected on the results. Smith didn't even acknowledge he time-traveled, even though he was caught in the act. When Kathy asked about the other man Hatcher saw, he smiled and apologized for not knowing what she was talking about. And he still denied knowing anything about Barbara.

They hadn't learned much, but they made progress because Smith was warming up to Kathy. Or at least his demeanor had moved away from the derisive comments he made at the beginning of the interview.

The most interesting thing happened when she asked him about the cut on his cheek. He seemed surprised at the question and replied, 'Some asshole shot me.' It wasn't what he said, though. It was how he said it. *Was he surprised by the question?* Before he answered her, he looked from her to the window and back again. *He's aware that he knows something we don't.*

At the end of the day, Smith told war stories. At first, Trevor thought he was bragging to impress Kathy. *Maybe he is. She's beautiful and sympathetic. Why wouldn't he want to impress her?*

But something else came through to Trevor. There was a consistent pattern of professionalism in Smith's speech, the way he glossed over details that were likely still classified, but recalled other mission events in detail. And his love for the men under his command was there, too. It occurred to Trevor that Smith was proud of being a SEAL and he wasn't completely without honor, regardless of the persona he seemed determined to portray. In spite of his bluster and posturing, there was still a US military officer in there somewhere.

Kathy was the picture of patience. She listened and responded to every word Smith said.

Trevor typed on their chat. <Time to call it a day. >

Kathy was listening hard to Smith but glanced down from time to time. This time, the message was only thirty seconds old before she caught it.

As he brought the latest tale to a close, Kathy stretched and yawned. She was tired, and she made a show of it so he wouldn't think she was getting bored.

Rising, she said to Smith, "Well, that's enough for now. Please don't go anywhere. I'd like to talk to you again. But it's getting late and I have a date." She smiled at him and started for the door.

Trevor could see the tenseness in her posture. *Smith won't miss that.*

Smith called after her. "Where are you going on your date this fine Sunday evening?"

She looked back at him and bit her lip, but said nothing. Smith smiled at her.

Before she left the room, Smith had one last thing to say.

"Hey, how's General Drake? Tell him I said hello, would you?"

She looked back at him and opened her mouth to speak but stopped.

Smith was not looking at Kathy. He was staring at the observation window.

"I will," Kathy said.

Smith didn't respond. He put his hands together on the table and stared at them.

Kathy closed the door and hurried to the observation booth.

****

Kathy joined Trevor and McKnight at the observation window and watched in silence as the MPs escorted Smith from the room. Trevor retrieved the interview tapes and pushed them into an envelope.

Kathy said, "Do you want to do a postmortem on the interview?"

Both men looked at her. McKnight was the first to speak. "You did well. You got him talking. It may be a while, but we'll get something out of him."

"We already did, right?" she said.

"I think so. But tell me what you observed."

She glanced back and forth between them. "Well, maybe I'm mistaken, but...okay, here's what I think. Number one, I think he expected me to know who shot him and was a little unnerved when I didn't. But then he changed the subject again. That's weird."

"Yes, I thought so, too," Trevor said. "What else?"

"We learned about why he hates the Rangers. We need to find out about this Sergeant Randall. Who is he and why didn't the Rangers try to rescue Smith or let the SEALS know where he was?"

"Right," McKnight said. "I'll send out an inquiry tonight to see what happened."

"Good idea," Trevor said. "What else, Kathy?"

"I think he's telling the truth about Barbara. I don't think he killed her. But he's very careful with his words. He didn't say he knew anything and he didn't say he didn't. But he was adamant that he didn't kill her. And I believe him."

"Yes," Trevor said. "I picked up on that, too. He might not have killed her, but I think he knows what happened to her. We still need to drag that out of him."

"Give me a few minutes with him," McKnight said. He held up his hands, palms out. "I know. Not good investigative technique. But I believe he knows who killed her, and that's the son of a bitch I want to talk to."

"Yes, I know, Major. I know she was a friend and we'll get the truth, I promise you. What else, Kathy?"

"It's less clear. He was talking about how hard it was to get the Time Engine working. He said something about us having the 'Doctors Astalos,' like there's a competition going on between us and him. Remember?"

"Yes. The Major noticed it, too," Trevor said. "He's sent Captain Tyler to bring Robby Astalos back from Finland. We'll keep Robert right here with us. And what's the third thing?"

"Right there at the end. Did you notice? He was trying to get me to tell him what day it was."

Trevor smiled. "Yes, that's right."

"We need to figure out why that was important to him."

"And we will," McKnight said. "But not tonight. You're exhausted and you need sleep. I do, too. We have that move to DLA HQ tomorrow. Anything else?"

Trevor and Kathy looked at each other. "No," they said.

"Well, then. If you two will excuse me, I need to report to General Drake and hit the rack." He rose from the stool by the observation window, set his coffee cup on the table and left the room.

Kathy stepped over to Trevor. She touched his chest gently, then withdrew her hands. Trevor responded by pulling her into his arms. She looked up at him and smiled. "How'd I do? Do I still have a job as chief interviewer?"

Trevor kissed her forehead. "Of course. You held your own with him. Everything he said to you...you responded or countered. With a little training, you'd be magnificent at interviewing."

"Good."

"Did you enjoy yourself? Seems like you did."

She looked thoughtful. "Yes, I guess I did. Smith is a complex person. There are things in Smith to respect and things that repel me. I can see now why he hates the Rangers, but we only have one side of that story." She paused. "Yes, I did enjoy myself. Tell me, is it normal to feel sympathetic and angry with a subject at the same time?"

"Yes, it is. In the beginning, before you get jaded. If you talk to guilty people all the time, you tend to lose the sympathy part and just be angry. Try not to let the angry part push away the sympathy. In this case, he feels your compassion, no matter what he says. It comes through."

She slipped out of his arms and said, "That sounds like good advice. Thanks."

"Good."

They stood there for a moment, looking at each other.

"Well, then...may I buy you a drink?" he said.

"If you want to. If you don't have other plans."

"I wouldn't ask you if I didn't want to."

"That's nice to know."

"Kathy, I know I don't always act like it, but…"

"Yes?"

"You're the reason I …I mean, I took this job because…Well, I really like the job, too, but…you know what I mean."

Kathy smiled. "I think I do, but it's nice to hear you express it with such clarity."

"Huh?"

She smiled and slipped her arm inside his. "Let's go."

He nodded, then stopped. "Say, don't forget the audio from the interview to take with you? You still want it, right?"

"Yes, I do. I'll review it tomorrow morning."

"Perfect." He picked up the tape envelope and handed it to her. "And tomorrow night after the move, we'll take another whack at getting Mister Smith to rat out his buddies."

CHAPTER 23

4:32 a.m. – July 20, 2036 – Kathy's Georgetown apartment, Washington, DC

Kathy opened her eyes and looked at her bedside clock. The time was 4:32 a.m. She was through sleeping for the night – her mind was active and already thinking about the day's tasks.

But there was more to think about. She remembered the night before. *Or was it a vivid dream?* She held her breath and listened. The sound of deep breathing continued. As gently as possible, she rolled over to see Trevor's sleeping form. She smiled in spite of herself. Inhaling deeply, his scent reminded her of last night. *It's real.*

She tried to piece together the events that led to this. She couldn't blame it on the alcohol, because they only had a couple of drinks apiece. It was partly physical, because he was physically attractive.

She liked the way he treated her at work. He asked for her thoughts, treated them as important, and measured them against his. It was respect. He valued her contribution.

And he treated her the same way when they talked about personal things. He listened and asked questions. There was no doubt that he wanted to understand her.

And he opened up to her as never before. She was glad he too was uneasy about the pitfalls of their relationship. She told him she was worried about the impact on their work life. He said he wasn't afraid of that, but was concerned about being run over by a strong-willed partner.

Who, me?

She invited him home with her because they connected in body, mind and spirit.

So they slept together. Though she feared things would now be awkward between them, she couldn't help but smile at the memory. For a first time together, it was good. Trevor was kind, gentle, and focused on her wants.

But what would she find when they were both awake and conscious of what happened between them?

This might be awkward.

But this wasn't what awakened her this early. Something was stuck in her mind about the interview with Smith. She couldn't put her finger on it, but there was something she missed, and she needed to find it. She wouldn't be able to rest until she found it or convinced herself it wasn't important.

She slipped gently out of bed and into the bathroom. After showering, she slipped on a pair of jeans and a tee shirt. She pulled her blue-black hair into a ponytail.

I need caffeine. She made a single cup of tea, then glided into her office and pulled up the video files.

A sense of determination set in. *It was near the end of the interview. There's something there and I'll find it.*

She slipped in her ear buds, double-clicked the first file on the list and leaned back in her chair to watch.

****

<u>6:01 a.m. – July 20, 2036 – temporary HERO offices, Alexandria, VA</u>

Wheeler stepped out of his car, locked it and walked to the back door of their Telegraph Road complex. If all went well, this would be their last day at this location. After today's move, they would report to the DLA HQ building tomorrow. This building was old and laid out like a maze, but he would miss its character, compared to the new and polished halls of DLA HQ.

Captain Tyler delegated the move project to him and he was determined to do the best job possible. He checked the time. Tyler was already on his way across the Atlantic to Finland. *Man, I'd have loved that duty.*

He used his access disk to enter the building, climbed the steps to the HERO offices on the second floor and stopped by the kitchen for coffee. He usually made the first pot of the day, but he found McKnight already there, sipping from a white mug.

"Good morning, Lieutenant," McKnight said.

"Morning, sir. You beat me to it this morning."

"Yes, I did. I've been here about twenty minutes. I thought I'd get here early and take a few minutes to get organized before the day starts."

"Yes, sir. That's why I come in when I do."

"Any word from Mr. Tyler? What time did he finally get off?"

Wheeler checked his phone. "They took off a few hours ago. It's an eleven-hour flight from here to Helsinki. Tampere is about the same distance. They should get there some time around 5:00 p.m. local time – faster if they have a good tail wind."

McKnight took another sip of coffee and said, "Okay. I'll feel better when he's on the way back here. What's happening with the move?"

"We should be about ready to go. I talked to the load team an hour ago. They completed crating all components and were ready to load them on the truck. I'm headed to the lab now to see how close we are to starting out."

"I'll go with you." McKnight gestured toward the door with his coffee cup and rose.

Entering the lab, they found Hatcher and the load team sitting around the conference table. Cindy was serving them coffee and egg and cheese sandwiches. The two Time Engines sat in front of them. The new Engine was crated up and waiting to be loaded on the truck. The old Engine was disconnected and partially disassembled. Through the open door to Doctor Astalos's office, they could see General Drake sitting in one of the side chairs.

"Mitch, get the status," McKnight said. "I'll go see what's up with the General."

"Yes, sir."

As McKnight headed for the office, Wheeler walked to the conference table and sat next to Hatcher. "Good morning, Lieutenant. What's the status here for the load?"

Hatcher waved and swallowed the last piece of her sandwich. "Hi. Everything's ready to go. The security team is outside, staged and ready to go. We're waiting for the truck to be in position." She shifted and looked over his shoulder. "Ah, there we go."

Wheeler turned to see Sergeant Franklin waving from the loading dock.

"Okay, let's go," Hatcher said to the load team.

They stood as one and hustled over to the new Engine and moved the crates onto a mini-forklift. Hatcher supervised the load.

Wheeler nodded his head at the scene. A voice from behind said, "They sure are efficient, aren't they?" He turned to see Cindy standing there with coffee in hand, nodding her head in approval.

"Yes, they are," he said. "Thanks for picking up the sandwiches, by the way. I knew I wouldn't have time to do it."

"On the contrary. Thanks for thinking of me. I want to be a good team member and you know I could use the overtime."

"Yep," Wheeler said. "Well, I guess I'd better go see what's happening in Doctor Astalos's office."

"Good idea. I'll get this mess cleaned up. Have a great day."

Wheeler waved over his shoulder as he walked to the office. As he reached the doorway, he came to attention and saluted.

Drake returned the salute and said, "As you were, Lieutenant. Come in. I'm throwing a wrinkle into your move plans."

"No problem, sir." *Uh-oh.*

Drake laughed. "Just kidding, Lieutenant. Or at least, it's not a big wrinkle. It's just that Sergeant Major Clary and I are coming along with your team today. We're riding with the doctor."

"Yes, sir. It would be an honor to have you with us, sir."

"Good. I don't think you need to change any security details. It looks fine. The Major approved it?"

"Yes, sir."

"Okay, then. When do we get started?"

"Should be in the next half hour, sir. If you'll excuse me, I'll go check with the load team and see if we're ready."

"Very good. Thank you, Lieutenant."

****

<u>6:58 a.m. – July 20, 2036 – temporary HERO offices, Alexandria, VA</u>

Wheeler checked the convoy arrangement again. He was being anal, but he wanted to check everything off once more to confirm he missed nothing. He walked down the line from the back of the convoy of armored black Suburbans to the front.

Last car – car number five – Sergeants Vincent and Andrews – bodyguards. Vincent behind the wheel.

Car number four – Doctor Astalos's car. Sergeant Edwards behind the wheel. And now the General and Sergeant Major Clary.

Wheeler looked toward the building door and saw Hatcher there. Her task was to let Astalos and the others know it was time and escort them to their Suburban. He signaled her that all was ready. She turned on her heel and went back inside.

Car number three – the Marine escort – Sergeant Clinton behind the wheel and four Marines to protect Astalos and the Time Engine.

Car number two – the Time Engine car – a flatbed truck carrying the dismantled Engine in a set of large wooden crates. Sergeant Franklin behind the wheel.

And car number one – the lead car – Sergeant Lauer behind the wheel and accompanied by Sergeant Quarrels and me.

He stopped and looked back down the convoy. Hatcher opened the door on the fourth car and General Drake, Sergeant Major Clary and Doctor Astalos slipped inside. She closed the door and waved to Wheeler.

He glanced forward and waved to the two motorcycle officers who would lead the convoy to their destination. Satisfied, he slid into the back seat of car number one. Sergeant Lauer lifted his radio and made his third radio check in the last thirty minutes. All cars and motorcycle units could "read" each other. All Lima Charlie – loud and clear.

Wheeler's phone beeped. It was McKnight. He accepted the call with his thumb and said, "Yes, sir?"

"Lieutenant, someone just time-traveled into Smith's jail cell and tried to kill him. I need you to investigate. These guys can handle the move without you. If there are any logistics problems, I'm sure Sergeant Clary or the General can straighten them out."

"Yes, sir." *What the hell?* He got out of the car as he disconnected the call. He waved the driver on and watched as a soldier in white gloves stopped traffic in both directions on Telegraph Road to allow the convoy to enter the road as a unit. Their route led down Telegraph Road to Beulah Street, then southeast to cut through the Fort Belvoir Golf Course and on to the DLA HQ complex.

He watched until the convoy was out of sight. He sighed and trotted back to the loading dock door.

As he entered the lab, McKnight was on the phone. He put his hand over the microphone and said, "Get down to the Pentagon and find out what happened. Move him so it doesn't happen again. I want a full report. If we lose this guy, we have nothing. I'll be there in two hours to talk to him."

"Yes, sir," Wheeler said. He turned on his heel and dashed out to the parking lot. *Geez! What else could go wrong?*

****

7:02 a.m. – July 20, 2036 – Kathy's Georgetown apartment, Washington, DC

Kathy watched the high definition video of the Smith interview. A beam of light filtered into her office through the window drapes.

She looked for subtle cues from Smith, like posture and vocal inflection.

Two cameras captured the video record of the interview. One camera was stationary to capture his body language and movements. The other was computer-controlled to maintain a tight focus on his face to capture every twitch and facial inflection, voluntary or involuntary.

She noticed Smith didn't blink often. At first, it was just an impression. She tried not to blink while she waited for him to. She rarely succeeded, but it was a successful experiment because it established a baseline on his responses. Any variation from that baseline would show Smith might be stressed or agitated.

At this point in the video, however, Smith appeared confident.

"I'd be happy to talk to him," Smith said. "But, honey, you're still a good substitute. I'll talk to you any time." He winked at her. She missed that during the interview. But then he looked back at the window and smiled. He blew kisses and waved at McKnight, whom he rightly assumed was behind the observation window. As far as she could tell, the man felt totally in control.

Then she heard herself speaking over the soundtrack. "Well, thank you. So, tell me, where did you get the time travel technology?"

This time, she saw something unusual. Something out of place.

In the video, he glanced at her for a second then turned back to the window and continued waving. "Why, Doctor Wu, whatever do you mean?"

What the hell? What she said got his attention and he looked back to the window to hide it.

She stopped the recording and rewound it a few seconds. She wanted a closer look at his reaction. *I asked him where he got the technology, he glanced at me and then tried to cover it. Why?*

She replayed his response. *Is that surprise on his face?* She replayed the scene at half speed and found what she was looking for. Smith recovered, but the high-speed camera captured his glance at her, the narrowing of his eyes, an 'out of rhythm' blink and the rapid switch to a smile. She stopped the video. *No doubt about it. The question surprised him. He wasn't expecting it.*

She stopped short, her mind racing. *Why didn't he expect that question? It was the most natural question in the world. It was the obvious question. Yet, he didn't expect it. Why not?*

She considered other things that were out of place. *Who shot him, who set up the machine for him, and what day was it?* Smith was surprised she didn't know the first two and actively attempted to find out the last.

Her mind raced through the possibilities. She pushed herself back from the desk and forced herself to breathe. Her left hand went to her mouth in shock.

"They got it from us," she whispered. In a hoarse voice, she corrected herself aloud. "They *get* it from us."

Where's my phone?

"Trevor!" She dashed into the kitchen and found her phone on the counter next to her keys. She speed-dialed McKnight.

George came into the kitchen from the living room shirtless, half-walking and half-hopping as he pulled his slacks up over his briefs. "What? Are you okay?"

She glanced at him and said, "No, I'm not." She turned her attention back to her phone.

"Major?... Thank God, I caught you. Is the move to DLA HQ in progress?... No, I believe they're going to be attacked. Remember Smith was surprised we didn't know who gave them the technology and who shot him?... He didn't know what day it was. He was surprised we didn't know answers to questions... Remember we went to intercept him in the past, but we started out two days before the event anniversary? We captured him on a timeline two days before the technology was stolen. On our timeline, he hasn't stolen the Engine yet. On his timeline, it's the day after." She paused to let that sink in. "Yes, he thought it was later...Forget all that. We need to warn Doctor Astalos... What?... The General is with him? Not good… Okay, I'm on my way there now."

She disconnected the call.

Trevor stood before her, a grim expression on his face. She read the truth in his eyes and tears filled hers.

"We're too late, aren't we?"

He extended his arms toward her, and she moved into his embrace. She buried her face in his bare chest and feared the worst.

CHAPTER 24

6:30 a.m. – July 20, 2036 – Intersection of Beulah Street and Telegraph Road, just south of Alexandria, VA

Mike Smith stood on top of a building and looked over the intersection below. He chose this location because it was the best of several poor choices. This operation was risky, but he had enough men and he was confident of success.

The building stood in the southwest corner of the intersection. The convoy would come from the north on Telegraph Road, turn east on Beulah Street and continue on a half mile to Fort Belvoir.

A corn field lay behind the building where he stood. There were woods on the southeast corner.

Across Beulah Street in the northwest corner, a ditch ran north along Telegraph Road. The roadside of the ditch had a gentle slope, but the other side was steeper and higher.

Diagonally across from his position, in the northeast corner, was a small fallow field with woods to the east. The assault would come from these woods, across the field to the road. Four hours before, his team planted Minimore explosive devices in the ditch to cut off retreat. The result was a compact kill zone.

Smith expected a call at any moment from Rho, his mysterious benefactor. He never met or talked to Rho in person. They only communicated through texting or a synthetic voice transmission. While Smith trusted no one, his association with Rho was the closest thing he had to a trusting relationship.

Over the last eight months, the financial tips from Rho had tripled the size of his portfolio. The introduction to Representative Phillips and the subsequent wet work pay nearly doubled his holdings. Smith nearly laughed when Phillips told him to treat any order from Rho as if it were coming from him. It was okay with Smith if Phillips didn't understand who was working for who.

In this case, Rho showed much more knowledge of tactics and strategy than Phillips. And unlike Phillips, he wasn't a wimp.

Somehow, Rho got information about the HERO team and passed it to him. Smith didn't understand where or how, but he trusted the intel.

He set up security in all four directions to stop traffic when the time came. His spotter's trailing car was back down the route toward Alexandria. When the convoy rode by, the spotter would call Smith and follow it to the intersection. When the attack started, the spotter would block any escape back down Telegraph Road.

Smith did another survey of the area with binoculars, though he didn't need them – the engagement area was small. The sniper Jones sat on the roof next to him, his back against the low wall, his knees drawn up and his rifle cradled in the crook of his arm. Smith's rocket launcher lay close at hand on his other side.

When the time came, Jones would take out the driver of the lead car as Smith fired a rocket to disable it. The spotter would destroy the last car with a rocket, thus immobilizing the convoy and setting up the kill zone. His men would attack the convoy from the east and kill everyone except Doctor Astalos.

The team was ready.

One by one, he checked communications with each group. Each responded the same. 'I read you Lima Charlie' – loud and clear.

His phone buzzed. The caller ID read 'Unknown.'

"Yes?" he said into the receiver.

"Are you in position and ready?" The clipped timbre and buzz of Rho's artificial speech.

"Affirmative. We are go. Do you have details for me?"

"There are five vehicles, four armored Suburbans and one truck. The Time Engine is on the truck. First vehicle has two occupants.

Second vehicle is the truck with the Time Engine. Other than the driver, it should not be targeted. Third vehicle is security detail of five men. Fourth vehicle is a driver with Doctor Astalos and General Drake with aide. Fifth and final vehicle has two occupants. Take Doctor Astalos alive. Repeat. Astalos must be taken alive. All others are targets. Do you copy?"

"Roger," Smith said, and then repeated the information back to Rho. *Drake delivered into my hands.* He smiled at the thought. "I count thirteen to kill, one to snatch, fourteen total, correct?"

"Affirmative. Priority one: The mission is a total failure if Astalos is injured or killed or the machine is damaged. Do you copy?"

"Roger. I copy. Astalos must be taken alive and unharmed, the machine must not be damaged. Are they on the move?"

"Affirmative. They're pulling out of the Telegraph Road office now. Do you copy?"

"I copy. We're on it."

"Don't fuck up," the synthetic voice said.

"We won't," Smith said. "Anything else?" he asked.

Silence. Rho had already disconnected.

He relayed the information to his team. He did a final ready check with the security teams.

Smith smiled. *Drake will not survive the day.* With luck, he might get to do it himself.

****

7:08 a.m. – July 20, 2036 – Temporary HERO offices, Alexandria, VA

McKnight disconnected from Kathy and speed-dialed Drake. Disaster was right in front of him. It might already be too late.

Hatcher chatted with Cindy on the other side of the lab. He whistled to get her attention and motioned her over to him. He put his finger over the phone microphone and said, "Weapons."

Hatcher turned and sprinted to the weapons locker.

The phone buzzed the open ring signal in McKnight's ear. He cursed and whispered into the device, "Pick up, dammit!"

The call went to voicemail. The sound of Drake's familiar VMS greeting filled him with dread. He ended the call and called Quantico's Hostage Rescue.

Hatcher returned with side arms and a machine pistol for each of them. They rushed through the loading dock door and jumped in McKnight's truck. He jammed it into gear and the truck fishtailed out of the parking lot as he accelerated south on Telegraph Road.

Hatcher checked the weapons as they drove, and McKnight tried again to call Drake. Still no answer.

"I see smoke," Hatcher said, pointing ahead.

McKnight nodded. Cursing himself for not recognizing the risk sooner, he slammed his foot on the accelerator. His horn blared as they blew through a red traffic light.

****

7:08 a.m. – July 20, 2036 – Telegraph Road, just south of Alexandria, VA

Smith's earpiece clicked. "Coach, batter is up." The convoy was approaching his position. The spotter followed it as a squad rushed to stage a street maintenance roadblock.

"Roger, Scout." He squinted as he looked down Telegraph Road toward Alexandria. No sign of them yet. A tight smile crossed his face. *Come to Papa.* If he hustled, he could be in position in time to kill Drake himself. *No, don't alter the plan. Discipline. Let the team do their job.*

His phone buzzed. The caller ID showed Scout's number.

"Go," Smith said.

"Approaching home plate." The line went dead.

He smiled and whispered into his comm unit. "Umpire, are you ready?"

"Yes, sir." Smith nodded at Jones, who rocked forward off his haunches and turned around to bring his rifle to bear on the intersection.

"Stand by, Umpire. Less than one minute." Umpire stood at the traffic signal control box across the intersection. His job was to stop the convoy with a red traffic signal.

"Roger," Umpire responded.

Smith looked up Telegraph Road. The first car of the convoy came into view. *Just like Rho promised.*

"Do it now, Umpire," he said, and watched the traffic signal turn red for traffic on Telegraph Road.

"Ready, all bases," he whispered into his phone as he shouldered the rocket launcher. The first car of the convoy slowed to a stop at the traffic signal. He glanced at the sniper next to him. Jones knelt with his rifle trained on the face of the driver.

****

Drake and Astalos were enjoying the ride to the new offices.

Clary was reviewing his notes.

Astalos commented on what a beautiful morning it was.

Drake relaxed and looked at the scenery. He was tired and reflected on how long it had been since he had taken time off. *Maybe it's time to take a little vacation and... What?* His attention jerked back into sharp focus. The convoy was slowing, and he could see a construction worker standing at the traffic signal control box closing the cover. *What's wrong with that?*

Ahead and to the right, he saw figures on top of a building. He leaned forward to look past Astalos to the woods on the left and saw movement. "Shit," he said under his breath. *Ambush!* He punched the button on the intercom and said, "We're under att–"

A rocket hit the first car and exploded, shredding the body of the driver, already dead from the sniper's bullet.

"Oh, my God," Astalos said.

Drake opened the documents panel in the seat back before him and removed the two .45 automatics Hatcher placed there. He handed one to Clary, who was already assessing the open field to the left of the convoy. Drake pulled a small caliber automatic from the back of his waistband and handed it to Astalos, who took it with trembling hands.

Drake heard the automatic gunfire coming from the left. "Robert, listen. If these guys know what they're doing, we're dead. The only question is whether we'll take some of them with us. If anyone you don't know gets near you, kill 'em."

"Okay." The old man examined the weapon, found the safety, and pushed it to the off position. He cocked the weapon and held it with both hands.

"Our only chance is to get out to the right. It looks clear, but... No matter what happens, stick with me and Tom."'

As Drake opened the door, blood splattered against the Plexiglas between the vehicle compartments. Their driver was dead.

****

Smith took a long breath and whispered into his comm. "All bases. Home run. Home run." He exhaled and pulled the trigger on his rocket launcher. The sniper rifle beside him discharged with a cough. His rocket struck the lead car in the grill and it shivered with the force of the explosion. His team charged out of the woods to the east, laying down withering fire at the convoy. Two seconds after the first explosion, the trailing car bucked from a rear impact. The spotter did his job. There would be no escape now.

He dropped the rocket launcher, ran to the ladder on the back of the building and slid down it. His desire for revenge overcame his discipline. If Drake was there, Smith wanted him to know who killed him. He rounded the structure at a dead run. His team focused on the middle car – the one carrying the Marine security detail.

A staccato rattle of machine pistol fire erupted from the convoy - the Marines were returning fire.

****

The mercenary moved with his teammates and sprinted across the open field toward the middle vehicle. His squad's job was to take out the bodyguards there. He leveled his machine gun and sprayed a burst at the car as the team spread to stay out of each other's line of fire. The vehicle's windows shattered. A spray of blood from the driver's window confirmed at least one casualty.

Seconds before he died, the barrel of a machine pistol appeared in the rear window and began firing. He took three rounds from it – one through his throat, one into his vest and one through his wrist, severing the band of his wrist phone. As the impact of bullets spun him around, the phone slipped from his wrist and landed several feet from his body. His team ran past him and concentrated their fire on the rear window until the defensive fire ceased.

****

As he crossed Beulah Street, Smith saw the defense breaking down. *It won't be long now.* One of the Marines ran by Astalos's Suburban and retreated across the ditch – a fatal mistake. Smith glanced back toward the rear of the convoy, looking for his engineer. He drew his sidearm when he saw Astalos, Drake and Clary crawl out of the car on the west side.

Astalos started into the ditch, and Smith felt a thrill of fear. If the engineer blew the Minimores now, Astalos would be killed.

But Clary caught Astalos by the arm and restrained him.

Smith smiled without humor. Clary guessed the Minimores would be there and saved Astalos. He reminded himself to thank Clary before he killed him. The engineer blew the Minimore by the car and the Marine's body, shredded by the explosion, slammed against the far embankment of the ditch.

The rate of gunfire was slower than before. It meant the drivers and security team were all dead or dying.

Smith spoke into his comm. "Clear the dugout" – the team's signal to check each casualty and execute a kill shot to any who still lived.

Drake took Astalos by the arm and dragged him toward the exploded Minimore – now the safest way through the ditch and the only remaining escape route.

Clary followed them, still facing their rear – gun trained on the horizon.

The escape route was only an illusion. A team waited there to cut off escape.

Smith ran past his team and over the top of the embankment. He intended to be the one who ended Drake's life. The team scrambled to follow him.

Astalos couldn't move fast, but he moved well enough for a man of his age. They were climbing up the embankment when Smith crested the top and pointed his weapon at them.

Drake was half pulling, half dragging Astalos up the embankment when he came into Smith's view. Clary was behind them facing the rear with his pistol raised in a two-handed grip.

When Drake saw Smith, he raised his weapon, but Smith had the advantage of surprise and the high ground.

He fired twice, both bullets striking Drake in the chest. The force of the impact knocked him off his feet and back down to the bottom of the ditch.

Clary spun around trying to bring his weapon to bear on this new threat, but he was too slow.

Smith fired twice again, the rounds striking Clary in the chest and neck.

Astalos whirled to see Drake's body land at the bottom of the ditch, the breast of his uniform discolored by the growing burgundy stain. He slid down the embankment to where his friend lay and knelt beside his body.

Smith holstered his weapon. He and his team followed Astalos down into the ditch. He surveyed the crippled convoy. He heard isolated pistol fire – the kill shots. Astalos was now the lone survivor of the attack.

Smith spoke into his comm. "Back to the clubhouse." He stood over Astalos and said, "Doctor Astalos, if you'll come with me–"

Astalos whirled, moving faster than Smith expected.

One of the team yelled, "Gun!" Smith ducked and threw up his left arm in self-defense.

The pistol in the old man's hand discharged in Smith's face and a searing pain erupted in his left cheek. His left eye stung as if it was on fire. His senses reeled from the shock of a weapon fired so close to his face.

When Smith regained his senses, there were two men in front of him holding Astalos's arms by his side. The old man's chest heaved with the exertion and fury distorted his face.

Smith's left cheek stung like it was on fire, and his left eye was full of tears and pain. One of the team held a gauze pad against his cheek. He was lucky – the bullet only creased his cheek. He might need stitches, but there was no structural damage. His eye stung, but at least he could still see.

"Thank you, Doctor," he said, taking the gauze pad from the team member. He glanced at it. There was a little blood, but not much. "I'll remember this when you're no longer useful."

"Might as well kill me now," Astalos said. "It'll be a cold day in hell before I help you with anything."

“We'll see,” Smith said, waving at his team. “Let's get moving. The MPs will be here any second.” The team scattered in various directions, each to his assigned duty.

One trooper jumped onto the running board of the truck that carried the Engine, unscathed except for bullet holes in the door and a dead man behind the wheel. The truck engine was still running. He opened the door and yanked the man’s body out of the cab, letting it fall unhindered to the pavement. He moved the vehicle back and forth until he could maneuver it out of the convoy and escape to the south on Telegraph Road.

At the top of the ditch, Smith turned and looked at the bodies of Drake and Clary. *Mission on track with a bonus.*

He could hear sirens in the distance. He nodded with satisfaction and trotted to his escape vehicle. The entire event had taken less than five minutes. The latest model of the Time Engine was no longer under the control of the HERO Team.

****

7:21 a.m. – July 20, 2036 – Telegraph Road, Alexandria, VA

McKnight's truck roared down Telegraph Road. They were getting close to the source of the smoke. After a bend in the road, they saw the carnage from the attack. At first glance, it appeared all vehicles were destroyed. His heart leapt when he saw some of them were still intact. He accelerated the vehicle as long as he could before slamming on brakes and skidding to a stop a few feet from the fifth car. Emergency vehicles from Fort Belvoir arrived near the front of the convoy, sirens still blaring. He heard more sirens in the distance.

McKnight and Hatcher emerged from the car with weapons drawn and began clearing the scene, wary of anything that moved. McKnight motioned for Hatcher to clear the right side as he cleared the left. The fifth car was destroyed from behind by a rocket – he had seen enough damaged vehicles in war zones to recognize the telltale signs. In a separate compartment of his brain, he counted the human costs. Sergeants Vincent and Andrews, two of Doctor Astalos's bodyguards. Dead. The two charred bodies in the front seat were family men who treated their protection duties as a blood oath. McKnight's mouth drew into a tight line across his face.

They rounded the wreck of the fifth vehicle, and Hatcher called out to him. As he passed between the fourth and fifth cars, he saw Hatcher kneeling with her head down next to Drake. His worst fear was fact. The General was lying at the bottom of the ditch, his jacket and shirt covered with blood. Clary lay on the near side of the ditch in a large pool of blood. He glanced down at the rest of the convoy and ran to her side and said, "Clear the rest of the convoy, Lieutenant. And don't get shot by the MPs."

She looked up at him with tears in her eyes, then ran back up the slope of the ditch to the convoy, her automatic weapon ready.

McKnight stood over his mentor. There were two wounds in his chest, just right of center. Well placed. Very professional. If Drake was still alive, it would not be for long.

His legs grew weak. He dropped to his knees, closed his eyes and forced himself to take deep breaths. He could smell the sweet warm morning air and freshly mown grass mingled with two other smells he knew too well – blood and burned flesh.

McKnight opened his eyes and felt Drake's neck for a pulse. *He's gone. First Barbara, now the General.* Tears rolled down his cheeks. He wiped them away and cursed. *Focus, dammit! Assess. Analyze.*

He looked back up the slope and saw evidence the body had slid down to this point. *He was trying to escape with...?*

For the first time since he found Drake, McKnight remembered Doctor Astalos. He swung around, scanning the ground for other bodies and clues. The attackers had policed the area before retreating. There would have been a gun in the car – Tyler would have insisted. But there was nothing in sight now.

They took him. He glanced toward the front of the convoy and confirmed what he already knew. The truck carrying the Engine was missing. *Kathy was half right – they were after the Engine, but they needed Doctor Astalos, too.*

Activity surged around him as he stripped off his blouse and placed it over Drake's face and upper torso. The emergency response effort was in progress, and the MPs were busy cordoning off the scene and collecting evidence. He walked forward along the length of the damaged convoy to survey the damage.

They knew we were coming this way.

Hatcher walked back toward him, her sidearm holstered and the machine pistol slung over her shoulder.

"Report," he said to her.

"Textbook convoy assault, sir. Thirteen dead. Doctor Astalos is missing, unless he's back over in the field there," she pointed to the other side of the ditch, "which I doubt. My bet is they took him. All the dead have a coup de grace head shot except for the General and the Sergeant Major."

McKnight felt his fury rising. *Smith said he didn't kill Barbara. He forgot to mention he killed thirteen others.*

"The Engine is gone," Hatcher said. "Looks like they pulled it out and around the lead car and back onto the road. We notified Virginia Highway Patrol with a description. My bet is they won't find it. Most likely they've already switched it to another truck."

Hatcher hadn't bothered to wipe the tears off her face. "How did they know we were moving today, sir?"

"I don't know, Lieutenant." He turned to look at the devastation around him. "This wasn't spur of the moment. They knew we were coming."

"How?"

"I don't know. But we'll figure it out."

"There's somebody on the inside," she said.

"Yes. Someone from our team."

She shook her head. "Not one of us, except maybe…?"

"Who?"

"Cindy, sir. She's the only person on the team we don't know well."

"That's not enough, Lieutenant. Has she done anything to raise your suspicions? I don't see how she could have orchestrated this. She didn't know the date until last night when Wheeler called her to bring in breakfast."

"I don't know, sir. I'm still thinking about it."

"Let me know what you come up with. Word got out somehow, so we can't rule out anyone, including the two of us."

"Who was behind it, sir? Was it that asshole, Smith?" she asked.

"Most likely. Or at least he executed the attack. Yes, I'm sure that's the case."

"We're sure? I thought we had him in custody?" She spat out the words. She trembled with anger, struggling to keep control. Her eyes were hard and cold.

"Yes. We still have him." McKnight stared at the bodies at his feet.

"The bastard killed the General and Sergeant Major Clary."

"Yes."

"Smith's a dead man. I wish I had killed him when I had the chance."

"You had him after the fact, Lieutenant. This happened before we caught him in the past. We need to focus on what's next."

"Yes, sir."

Hatcher looked down at Drake's body. Her body shook with rage.

McKnight sighed heavily. This was almost too much to bear.

Hatcher glanced at him and saw the pain in his face. Her expression softened, and she blinked as more tears came. "I'm sorry for your loss, sir."

McKnight sighed again and raised his eyes to meet Hatcher's. She looked devastated. Drake was a mentor and father figure for McKnight, but Hatcher and the rest of the team idolized him.

"It's your loss, too, Lieutenant. Are you with me?" he asked.

Fire came back to her eyes. "Yes, *sir*. One hundred percent. I want that asshole. What about Doctor Astalos?"

"Taken. I think I know how Smith got that wound on his cheek. Either Drake or the good Doctor got a shot off at him."

"Good for them." She searched his face. "Do you think the Doctor is still alive?"

"Yes, I do. At least for now. He'll stay that way as long as they can use him. When they decide they can run the Engine without him? Not long. Let's make sure we catch up with them before then. The bigger question is why did he help them? How did they get him to cooperate?"

"Threat to life and limb, maybe?"

"Maybe, but I don't see it. At least not quickly. He's a tough old guy despite his personality. I guess we'll find out."

"Understood. What are your orders, sir?"

"First, get on the phone and warn Captain Tyler. If they have Robert Astalos, they might want to grab Robby, too, or maybe put him out of commission." He waved to include the scene. "This was a professional job. I'd expect Smith to anticipate and eliminate any chance we have of recovering the machine. That means Robby is a risk. Tell Captain Tyler they may come at him with deadly force."

"Yes, sir."

"Then get back to the lab. We've still got the old Engine. If we can get it reassembled and back up and running, we have time to go back and stop this before it happens. That will be up to you and Lieutenant Wheeler. Are you up to it?"

"Yes, sir. Wheeler puts all configurations and adjustments in his notes and copies me. We can do it together, no problem."

"How long?" McKnight asked. He was regaining his cognitive reasoning after the shock. It was devastating to see the General dead. *But if I can go back in time and prevent it...*

"Four or five hours. We'll need to unpack it first, then reassemble and test. Who's going back to warn them besides me?"

"Not you, Lieutenant. I need you and Wheeler to be on point for running the Engine. I know the Doctor scavenged parts from the old machine. It might not be functioning up to par and you guys may need to make emergency changes in a short time frame. We can't risk a problem."

Her gaze fell to the ground.

"Lieutenant?"

Her attention jerked back to him. She glared at him with tears and anger in her eyes but didn't speak.

"I know how you feel, Lieutenant," he said. "I have to put the best qualified resources in the right places. You and Wheeler are the right choices to run the Engine."

She nodded and wiped her eyes.

He nodded back. She was a soldier and she obeyed orders.

She pulled herself to attention. "Yes, sir. Who will travel, sir?"

"Mr. George and me. I want to go back to about six thirty this morning."

"Yes, sir. I'm on it."

"Very well. Get back to the lab and get started. Take my truck. I'll hitch a ride back with the MPs. Let me know if there are any issues. I'll wrap up here."

"Yes, sir."

Hatcher saluted and turned to walk away.

After she took a few steps, McKnight spoke. "And, Lieutenant?"

She stopped and turned back to him.

"Yes, sir?"

"No matter what, whoever is responsible for this will answer for it."

"Hooah, sir." She nodded and walked away.

CHAPTER 25

12:30 p.m. – July 20, 2036 – Defense Logistics Agency Satellite Office Building, Telegraph Road, Alexandria, VA

McKnight sat in his office with his feet on the credenza looking at trees outside his transparent wall. A sandwich and a soda sat untouched on his desk behind him. He wondered what else he could do to make things happen faster.

Wheeler was on his way to the Pentagon when he received the call from Hatcher to return to the lab. Up to this point, he and Hatcher had unpacked the old Engine, taken inventory and began the re-assembly. She estimated it would be sixteen hundred hours today before they could test it and another hour before they could make the trip back. McKnight turned and looked at the clock on his desk. It was ten minutes since the last time he looked.

Although Hatcher talked to him already, McKnight felt the need to contact Tyler in flight over the Atlantic and discuss the attack with him. *He'll blame himself for this. I'd probably feel the same way if it was my plan.*

It was a hard call to make.

"Winnie, this is Marc."

"Yes, sir."

"I wanted to call you. Did Hatcher get in touch with you?"

"Yes, sir, she did. It's like a bad dream. Is he really gone?"

"Yes, he is. But we're working on preventing it. Wheeler and Hatcher are working on the old Engine to get it operational. You know it wasn't your fault, right?"

"Begging your pardon, sir…my plan, my fault."

McKnight feared this would be the case. *He's hurting. Beating himself up. And he's going formal on me.*

"I can see why you might feel that way, Captain. May I remind you that your original plan called for more troops and firepower, but I pushed you to do it with fewer people and maintain secrecy?"

"Yes, sir, but it was my decision to make."

"And mine to approve. Besides, you didn't know the General would go along. Had you known that in advance, you would have insisted on more protection. So would I."

"Yes, sir."

"You'll remember I had Wheeler relieve you so you could go get Robby. So it was no longer your responsibility, anyway. Yes, your plan, but the circumstances put Wheeler and me on point for it. For now, I need you to forget about it. I need you to be focused when you get to Tampere. There's a good chance they'll make a move on Robby since he's the only expert on the Engine we have left."

"Understood, sir. I'm on it."

"Good. Questions, Winnie?"

"Yes, sir. How did they know when we were coming? I can't believe anyone on our team leaked the date and time."

"It's hard for me, too, Winnie. But we'll deal with that after we figure out how to reverse it."

"That's great, sir. I wish I was there to help kick their collective asses."

"Hurry back and you might get your wish. But let's secure Robby first."

"Will do, sir. I have no other questions. I'll check in later."

"Good. Thank you, Captain."

"Yes, sir."

McKnight broke the connection. Tyler idolized Drake and was both furious and distraught. But he would get the job done.

He turned back to his comp pad and the Pentagon security report on the display. He'd talk to them later, but the report showed him what he needed for now. It included a video clip from a security camera so he could see the attack on Smith for himself.

Smith was reclining on his bunk as the clip started. The first sign came from him. He raised his arms and stared at them. *Static electricity! He knows someone's coming.* McKnight watched as Smith jumped from the bunk, dashed to a corner of the cell and crouched, his hands covering his head.

A time bubble formed in the middle of the cell, engulfing part of the bunk. A standing figure appeared inside the bubble. Part of the bunk disintegrated, and the rest of it collapsed.

The traveler turned toward Smith. He had an automatic pistol in his hand. When the bubble bulged and vanished, the man fell backward as Smith charged him.

The traveler didn't crouch to prevent falling. *He's a rookie. No training.*

The fight was brief and conclusive. Smith disarmed the assailant and manipulated him into a sleeper hold. In six seconds, the man was unconscious and Smith let his body slip to the floor. He pulled out the man's boot knife and paced around him, brandishing the knife and breathing heavily.

McKnight knew what was coming.

Smith held the knife up to the camera for a long moment before plunging it into the man's chest. He extracted it, held it up to the camera again, and then pushed it out through the food window of his cell. The knife clinked as it hit the floor outside the cell. He nodded and walked to his corner.

After ten seconds, a time bubble appeared again around the body and Smith jumped up onto the toilet. It surged and disappeared taking the body with it.

The video clip ended.

It occurred to McKnight that Smith could have jumped inside the returning time bubble to escape. *No. Bad plan. Whoever sent the guy wouldn't be glad to see him.*

The security report said they salvaged a blood sample from the knife and sent it to be analyzed. It concluded by advising that Smith be moved to an undisclosed location to prevent another attempt on his life.

It was a hard phone call with Senator Lodge. He wasn't the first to alert the Senator to Drake's murder, but he was the first to give details. Lodge chewed him out for letting Drake get killed. The Senator's words still stung like fire.

Could he have planned in more protection? Yes, but Drake would have criticized him for undue caution. With the secrecy, it should have been enough.

Lodge's ass-chewing was not the first of the day. General Flynn had called within an hour of the event to demand an accounting. McKnight tried to explain what happened. When he realized Flynn didn't want to hear it, he stopped talking and let the man vent. Flynn was Drake's friend and was feeling the same pain he was feeling.

As expected, Flynn ordered a full report to be on his desk tonight.

The only thing that eased McKnight's pain was the knowledge he would go back to the past and prevent the raid. He had no doubt Smith was the architect of the attack. The assault method was taught in the US military academies and schools. Smith's background and proximity was too compelling to be coincidence.

In contrast to Flynn, Lodge was not Drake's friend. In fact, they butted heads frequently. While Drake ran the HERO program, Lodge was the chairman of the Senate Oversight Committee for the program. This arrangement occasionally put them at odds with each other.

The contention between Lodge and Drake escalated when Lodge used his influence to force the team to investigate the unsolved murder of his father. Smith worked for Lodge at the time but was fired when Drake's team determined he was leaking information about time travel technology to the public.

Drake handled that situation with grace and dignity. He chose not to embarrass Lodge when it would have been easy to do and Lodge had not forgotten this courtesy. He and Drake still crashed into each other regularly, but there was mutual respect and trust.

While Lodge was not always happy with Drake, McKnight came away from the call knowing Lodge was angry that someone had attacked and killed his program leader. Lodge promised to provide any aid possible to determine who was responsible and bring them to justice. McKnight took him at his word and resolved to call on the Senator if necessary.

Drake hand-picked him for this job, and the team respected and revered him. Now Drake was dead, and it was up to McKnight to set it right.

He tried to sort through the emotions and facts to decide the best course of action for now. He was unsuccessful.

McKnight picked up his phone and called Trevor George. He needed someone to bounce thoughts off and Trevor was the ideal person for that.

Trevor came to his office and they settled in to brainstorm.

"Let's start with what we know," Trevor said. "They have the new machine and Doctor Astalos. Presumably, they convinced or forced him to help them operate it to send Smith back in time with Amy sometime in the next week, correct?"

"Yes. We also know they have a sizeable force of men at their disposal and hostages in a warehouse somewhere close by – it can't be too far away, right? They need to assemble and test it before they can use it."

"Yup. We're pretty sure Doctor Astalos is helping them but showing Amy a picture of him would wrap that part up. I don't think there's any doubt, though." Trevor shook his head. "They'll have it up and running in no time with his help. I wonder what could be so powerful a lever to get him to help?"

"Let's call Tyler. He's on the ground in Finland now. He can ask Robby about that." McKnight picked up his phone and called. Tyler's number rang open until voicemail picked up the call. He left a short message for Tyler to ask Robby about leverage.

"What else can we do?" Trevor asked.

"We could interview Smith again. Since someone tried to kill him, he might be more open to persuasion."

"I'd say so. Somebody wants him dead. Worth a try. Before we do that, are we sure we can tie him to the attack?"

"What do you mean?" McKnight asked. "Our Time Engine was stolen and we caught him after he time-traveled to the past…Oh, I think I see."

"Tell me."

"We captured him in the past. Things learned during time travel aren't admissible in court because the event can't be corroborated – it's his word against ours."

"That's a good point," Trevor said. "but there's a more compelling argument the defense attorney could make. What does Joe Blow Juror know about time travel?"

McKnight shifted in his chair. "Not much, I'm sure."

"I think the defense attorney can generate sufficient doubt by pointing out we had Smith in a jail cell during the attack. I can hear it now. He points at the defendant and says, 'Ladies and Gentlemen of the Jury, how could my client be leading a military raid on that Sunday when he was in fact in the custody of the US Military? Do you think maybe they let him go home for the day?' Something like that – we'd spend weeks trying to explain it to the jury."

"Oh, no," McKnight said. "Are you saying we have nothing?"

"No, I'm not. It's hard to keep everything under wraps with an operation this big. There's bound to be evidence somewhere. He will understand that. If we can tie it to him, he's on the hook for ambushing and killing thirteen men. We'll find it, but it may take more time than we have. If he gives up the Time Engine and his employer now, and the victims aren't dead, the charges against him might be greatly reduced."

"All that makes sense, Trevor, as long as he doesn't fear his employer more than us. That's a factor, too. But I agree – there are several compelling reasons for him to talk to us."

"Yes, I –" Trevor froze in place.

"What?" McKnight asked.

Trevor rose and paced back and forth across the room. "Wait a second. There should be a bunch of loose ends that lead to evidence against Smith. Some of his cronies from the bar fight might be willing to talk. What about income statements? Where was his money coming from? Phone records? His calendar over the last few weeks? There should be a ton of evidentiary data we can collect." He stopped and turned toward McKnight. "How sharp is this guy Smith? Would he be stupid enough to leave a trail of evidence?"

"No," McKnight said. "He might have become less disciplined and has a big ego, but he *was* a Navy SEAL, for God's sake. He's not stupid. What are you thinking?"

Trevor started pacing again and McKnight considered his question. Smith wasn't brilliant, but he was smart enough to plan the mission and take the evidentiary trail into account. Leaving so many clues behind was sloppy planning. *Unless...*

"Trevor?" he said.

Trevor stopped and stood facing the office wall. He held up his hand toward McKnight. "Just a second. I'm close to…something."

McKnight could feel it himself. Something was off in their reasoning. No way Smith could avoid the evidence they would have. *Unless...*

Trevor pivoted and slid back into his chair. He leaned forward and said, "There's no way Smith can get away with this, despite the evidence unless…unless it doesn't matter."

McKnight blinked in surprise. "What?"

"Yes," Trevor said. "What if evidence isn't a factor? What if it doesn't matter?"

"I don't get it. If we have the evidence, we can bring him to trial and put him away."

"Normally, yes. What if we can't? What if he's untouchable?"

McKnight shifted his weight in his chair. *Untouchable? How could he accomplish that? There can't be that many options.*

One way would be to disappear. This scenario was unlikely. If the U.S. government wants to find you, they will. No question about it.

The other scenario would be protection by someone who could call off law enforcement.

McKnight leaned forward toward Trevor. "I get it. Who could call off law enforcement?"

"Now we're getting somewhere," Trevor said. "Political clout. What if Smith was working for someone with a political agenda? Why did Smith need the Time Engine? He wanted to kill Amy and ruin Harrison's career. Kathy and I talked to Harrison. He seemed pretty guileless to us."

McKnight shook his head. "But he's only a minor politician. What possible reason…" The look of wonder on Trevor's face stopped him. That look turned into excitement.

"Marc, have you listened to or looked at the news at all since we rescued Amy?"

"No, I haven't." *What history got changed because we rescued Amy? Harrison would be affected.*

"Neither have I."

McKnight sat up straight, turned around to face the large TelExtraVision monitor and called up the automated search engine. "A-S-E?" Trevor moved around the desk to look over his shoulder.

An image of a young woman appeared on the monitor. "Yes, Major? What can I find for you?"

"Search for 'Wade Harrison' and 'Government.' Associate and correlate."

"Please wait," said the automated search engine as the image turned dark. Then it reappeared. "Major McKnight, there are 28.456 hits. Do you wish to refine your search? I have suggestions."

"Okay. Show suggestions, A-S-E."

A list appeared on the monitor. The first two leapt out at McKnight. They were 'Governor Wade Harrison' and 'Governor Harrison Front Runner in Presidential Run'.

"A-S-E, please select 'Governor Wade Harrison' as refinement." An article and a picture of Wade Harrison appeared. The man in the picture looked different, but it was the same Wade Harrison Trevor and Kathy interviewed a few days ago.

"He looks good," Trevor said. "More carefree and less haggard than he did when we interviewed him. Amazing what the removal of twenty-five years of guilt and bad memories can do to your appearance, isn't it?"

A quick scan of the article revealed Harrison was a two-term Governor of the state of Illinois. He was generally credited with changing the state's political climate and cleaning up the corruption that plagued the state for decades. His support of traditional values and his relentless pursuit and elimination of corruption in government was praised throughout the country.

"A-S-E? Go back and refine search again with 'Front Runner in Presidential Run.'" Another article appeared. This one featured a picture of Harrison, Senator Lodge and President Wanda Taylor. The President was patting Harrison on the back. McKnight and Trevor read the text.

"Damn," Trevor said. "The President's all but tapped him as her replacement. This is what Smith was trying to prevent."

"Stand by, A-S-E." He turned around and looked through the wall.

Trevor returned to his seat. "Now we know why. But who?"

Turning back to the report on the monitor, McKnight said, "A-S-E, scroll down."

The article rolled up on the monitor revealing more text. “Again,” he said. The article moved again, revealing the last two paragraphs and the byline. There, in the last paragraph, was a list of the potential candidates for President.

McKnight smiled. “Here's a rich set of suspects. We need to see if there’s a financial connection between any of them and Smith.”

“Or Smith needs to give the man up. He has incentive now.” Trevor’s face brightened. “Hey, what about Hatcher’s report? She saw a guy in the warehouse where she captured Smith. If one of them is the man she saw, we’d have him.”

“No, wait. That happened during time travel. Not admissible.”

“Fine. But knowing who he is would help us know where to look, right?”

“Yes. Okay, could you get Smith’s phone and bank records so we can see who he’s been communicating with?”

“No problem,” Trevor said. “I’m on it.” He left the office.

McKnight leaned back in his chair. *This is my next priority after preventing the attack. Who do I call?*

Normally, it would have been Drake. *Okay. Senator Lodge then. He'll brief the President, and we'll get all the help we need.*

CHAPTER 26

6:03 p.m. GMT+2, July 20, 2036 – Tampere-Pirkkala Airport, Tampere, Finland

Tyler landed at the Tampere airport at six in the evening. As he got off the chartered jet, two soldiers approached him. If he read the Finnish army uniforms and insignia correctly, they were a major and a sergeant.

Tyler saluted the Major and shook his offered hand.

"Hello," the officer said. "You are Captain Tyler?"

"Yes, sir, I am. And you are?"

"I am Major Janne Jylha. I am assigned to serve as your guide and interpreter." He gestured at the sergeant. "This is Staff Sergeant Ellonen, our escort." Ellonen executed a crisp salute. "I am told we are to help you find an American doctor named Astalos and return the two of you to the airport safely. Is that correct?"

"Yes, sir. Thank you, Major. Is the hotel far from here?"

"No. The towns Tampere and Pirkkala share this airport. The hotel is sixteen kilometers from here. I have a car waiting for us."

"Good. Could we drive there now? We have reason to believe someone might try to kidnap or kill Doctor Astalos. I need to find him as soon as possible."

"Very good. If you please, let us go to the car." He gestured toward a door in the terminal. As they walked, he continued. "Yes, we were told he might be in danger. We have a man following him, but we have no information about contacting him. We did not know if we should make him aware of our surveillance."

"Yes, sir. It would've been fine but no problem either way."

They reached the car and got in the back seat.

The sergeant jumped in the driver's seat and fired up the engine. He skillfully maneuvered the car through the airport traffic and onto a freeway toward downtown Tampere.

"May I ask you a question, Captain?" Jylha said.

"Of course," Tyler responded.

"It is a surprise for Doctor Astalos that you are coming? I wondered why you did not call him and have him come to us for protection."

"Well, we tried to call him, but he is famous for turning off his phone."

"He is... famous?"

"Sorry. By that, I mean the people that work with him all know he has a habit of turning his phone off and forgetting it. We called the desk of the hotel and asked them to give him a message to stay in the hotel until we get there. They have not found him as far as we know. Doctor Astalos may know we're coming now, but he didn't when we left Virginia and no one has communicated to us that he responded. To be honest, I'm not surprised. He likes people and may be walking around in your beautiful country, talking and experiencing your culture."

"I see. Thank you. But our man is with him always."

"Major, are you in contact with your man who is following Doctor Astalos?"

"Yes, of course. Just before you arrived, he advised us Doctor Astalos is in the Koskipuisto Park right next to the hotel."

"Really? Good. May I ask if you could get your man to meet us at the hotel and lead us to him, sir?"

"Of course. Sergeant?"

"Kyllä herra!" Ellonen said, and then he whispered into his phone. After a moment, he said, "It is done, sir. He will meet us there."

They rode in silence during the first few minutes. Tyler gazed at the countryside they passed as it went from rural to suburban to urban as they approached downtown Tampere.

In an effort to relax, Tyler studied the young officer. "Your English is very good, Major," he said.

"Thank you, Captain. Most of us speak at least some English. Much of our TelExtraVision programming comes for the United States. I am also fluent in Russian and Swedish."

"That's fantastic," Tyler said. "Tell me something. It seems unusually light here. Back home, it's dark by this time of day."

"Yes, we are 500 kilometers from the Arctic Circle. The summer solstice was just last month. Our days are long at this time of year."

"Oh, right," Tyler paused before changing the subject. "Tell me, sir. You were a friend of my General Drake, Major?"

"No, sir, I never met him. My commanding officer worked with him in Germany ten years ago. He called me this morning and asked me to please assist his friend's colleague. I offer my condolences, sir. I am sorry for your loss."

Emotion welled up in the back of Tyler's throat, and he paused so his voice wouldn't crack. "He will be missed. Doctor Astalos is our friend, and we hope he'll be able to help us find the men who killed the General."

"We'll do anything in our power to help, sir. Our orders are to protect you and Doctor Astalos at all costs."

"I see." Tyler saw determination in Jylha's face. "Well, I appreciate your help, Major. Thank you."

"It is my pleasure. Ah, here is the hotel. Sergeant, please park the car."

Tampere is a small industrial town in central Finland. It is situated on a small isthmus of land between two large lakes, the Näsiselkä and the Villilansalmi. A small river, the Tammerkoski, connects the two lakes. The lower lake is fifteen meters lower in elevation, so the river flows over several waterfalls as it flows through town.

The Sokos Hotel Tammer was in downtown Tampere at the corner of Satakunnankatu and Rongankatu. About forty meters to the west, the Tammerkoski River flowed through town. As the car slowed in front of the hotel, he saw Koskipuisto Park. The park was a green area about 75 meters by 150 meters east of the river and south of the hotel.

Sergeant Ellonen dropped them off at the hotel and drove away to park the car.

A man descended the hotel steps as they arrived. Jylha introduced him as Harri Kulmala, a police detective with a military background.

Kulmala shook Tyler's hand and pointed south from the hotel steps. "Your Doctor Astalos is relaxing in the park. I spoke to the hotel clerk when I heard you were coming today. He tells me the doctor likes to sit in the park and work on his computer pad. He is there now. Shall we go see him?"

"Yes," Tyler said.

The three men walked to the park. After a few moments, Sergeant Ellonen joined them, a rifle slung over his shoulder.

The sun was high in the western sky. The park was peaceful and quiet. Only a few people were in their field of vision – couples enjoying the day together, an elderly couple out for a stroll and young mothers with their toddlers on a playground. The smell of grass and trees filled Tyler's senses.

He scanned the park and spotted Astalos fifty yards away sitting on a park bench that faced the river.

Astalos was looking down at the comp pad in his lap. As they got closer, alarm bells went off in Tyler's brain. Three men stood in a small group near Astalos. One of them was pointing in his direction.

For one heartbeat, everything remained calm.

Tyler glanced at Jylha and said, "Major…" but Jylha and the others had already noticed the danger. They leapt into action.

Kulmalla drew a weapon from his waistband and sprinted toward the men.

Sergeant Ellonen dashed five yards to the right and took aim with his rifle.

Tyler called out to Astalos. The three men drew weapons and turned toward Tyler.

One man fired at Kulmalla, who returned fire at a dead run. His shot missed the man.

Astalos spun at the sound and crawled under the bench.

Jylha quietly said, “Sergeant?”

Ellonen's rifle cracked instantly, and the bullet’s impact blew the second gunman off his feet. Ellonen worked the bolt to load another round.

The other two gunmen reacted. One of them turned and ran. Kulmalla gave chase.

The last gunman aimed his pistol at Astalos.

Ellonen shot the second man as he fired his weapon at Astalos. The bullet smashed into the bench. It blew one of the bench slats in half and showered Astalos with splinters. Astalos covered his head with his hands and pulled his knees to his chest.

Jylha and Tyler ran to the park bench to check on Astalos.

Ellonen ran to the two gunmen on the ground. He swung his rifle back and forth between the two as he approached and kicked their weapons away from their bodies. Convinced they were no longer a threat, he searched them for identification.

Tyler found Astalos motionless on the ground and feared the worst. “Robby?” he said. At the sound of his voice, Astalos rolled from under the bench.

“Oh, my God, Winnie,” he said. “What the hell was that? Were they trying to kill me?”

Tyler helped him to his feet. “I think so. That's why I’m here. We were afraid they might try something.”

At the sight of Jylha, Astalos hesitated. “He's with me,” Tyler said.

“Are you injured, Doctor Astalos?” Jylha asked.

“No, I'm okay. But my nerves are shot.”

“You are shot?”

Tyler laughed. “No, sir. He means he’s frightened. I don't blame him.”

Jylha grinned. “Good, Doctor. I am glad you are not hurt.”

Tyler pointed at Sergeant Ellonen. “What about those two?”

Ellonen made eye contact with Jylha and shook his head.

“I am sorry, Captain. They are both dead. Sergeant Ellonen is my best marksman, but he did not have enough time to aim to injure.”

“No problem, sir,” Tyler said. ‘I’m grateful he saved my friend's life. We are in his debt and, if we have time, I'd like to buy him a drink.”

“Thank you, Captain. It is unnecessary, but we can drink together in honor of a new professional bond between us.”

“Yes, sir. I look forward to it.”

Jylha cocked his head as if listening. Tyler picked up on the sound of sirens pulsing in the distance.

Jylha smiled at Tyler and Astalos. “Ah, but not this visit, my friends. You must go. You have no guilt for what happened here, but the police will delay you, and I know you must get Doctor Astalos back to Washington. Sergeant Ellonen will drive you back to the airport. I will take care of details here.”

“But I have nothing packed,” Astalos said. “I need my clothes and my notes.”

“We can't wait, Robby.”

“What’s this all about? Why did they try to kill me?”

Tyler took a deep breath to steady himself. “It’s not just you. There’s been an attack in Virginia. They kidnapped Robert and killed General Drake. We need your help back at the lab.”

“What? But why?”

“I'll brief you, but right now we need to get the hell out of here.”

“I will ensure your notes and clothes are sent to you, Doctor,” Jylha said. “Go! Hurry or you may be delayed for days.”

“He's right,” Tyler said. “You’ve got your comp pad. Won't that be enough for the next couple of days?”

Astalos's initial hesitation vanished. “Okay, let's go.” He picked up his comp pad.

Tyler, Astalos, and Sergeant Ellonen jogged up the hill to the car.

The police arrived and blocked them before they could pull out of the parking lot. Ellonen flashed his identification, and they were allowed to leave.

On the way back to the airport, Tyler told Astalos about the ambush and how Smith had murdered the security detail, the General and the Sergeant Major.

Astalos's face grew red, and fury glinted in his eyes.

When they arrived at the airport, Tyler gave his contact information to Sergeant Ellonen and thanked him again for his help.

The Sergeant, stoic as before, nodded to Robby and saluted Tyler. He trotted to his car and left.

Tyler checked his phone as they boarded the plane. There was a missed call from McKnight. *He called me during the attack.* He sat in the back of the plane, called his commander and gave a quick briefing on the attack. When he finished his report, McKnight ordered him to ask Robby about Robert's motivation.

When the plane achieved cruising altitude, Tyler moved from his seat to a seat next to Robby. Robby sat with his eyes closed. His fingers drummed on the tray table next to his comp pad.

Tyler smiled. Robert did the same thing when he was thinking. He fastened his seat belt and nudged Robby, who opened his eyes and said, "I just can't believe it."

"What?"

"General Drake is dead. We're going back to prevent it… right?"

"That's the plan," Tyler said. "Lieutenants Hatcher and Wheeler are reassembling the old Engine, and they are targeting a jump for around 5:00 p.m. tonight, DC time."

"Do you think they'll be successful?"

"I hope so. At least we have the option to try." Tyler shifted in his seat. "Robby, I've got a somewhat delicate question for you."

"Delicate? What do you mean?"

"Well, these guys grabbed Robert and the Engine, and they got it up and running damned quick. That was unexpected. Major McKnight and I talked about it and we thought Robert would have stalled them."

"And you're wondering how they got the Engine up and running so fast. Under normal circumstances, there's no way he'd help them – there must be leverage in play. Is that what you're wondering?"

"Yes. We don't understand what that leverage could be."

"I can think of only one thing. I need to call Virginia. Is there a way to do that?"

"Of course." Tyler handed Robby his phone.

"Give me a few minutes," Robby said as he rose and walked to the back of the plane.

Robby called a number and waited as it rang. Then he frowned, pulled out his own phone to look up a number, and made another call. This time, someone answered and he spoke. After ten minutes, Robby ended the call and returned to his seat. He looked pale as he handed the phone back. He sighed and said, "Yes, they had plenty of leverage."

"Tell me."

"They have our daughter."

"Your what?"

A tear tumbled down Robby's face, and he wiped it away with his sleeve. "Our daughter. She and her guardian are missing."

Stunned, Tyler said, "You have a daughter? I didn't know that. When the hell did that happen?"

"A long time ago. About eleven years. Or thirty-six years. Or sixty-one years, depending on how you measure our life. Whatever. Anyway, I called their neighbor. He said Nancy called him two days ago to say Robert wanted to spend a few days with them. They had to hurry and pack because he sent a car for them. A limo picked them up, and they haven't been back."

"Nancy is your daughter?"

"No, she's Laura's guardian."

"Laura's your daughter."

"Yes, correct."

"Could they be at Robert's?"

"Nope. He would've told me they were coming. They're my family, too, you know. My bet is Smith kidnapped them for leverage against Robert."

"Shit."

"Yep. So, did Robert help them voluntarily? Absolutely. If it would keep Laura and Nancy from harm, he'd do it in a heartbeat. No hesitation. So would I."

"Okay, I need to alert Major McKnight. Sorry, but he needs to know what he's dealing with."

"No, I insist you do that. Otherwise, his actions could get them killed."

"That's right," Tyler said. He fingered his phone for a few seconds. "Okay, I have to ask. I thought the three of you were laying low since you were all in the same time space. Having a family isn't exactly laying low."

"Well, it's a long story."

"We have ten hours before touch down in DC. Plenty of time."

Robby looked Tyler in the eye. "Winnie?"

"Yes?"

"They'll kill them all, anyway, won't they?"

Tyler sighed. "Yes, they will."

Robby nodded and stared out the window.

"Robby? Listen. Robert knows that, too. There is hope. They won't hurt them while they need Robert's help. He'll use that to delay. With luck, we'll get this timeline reversed and find them before anything happens."

Robby smiled weakly. "I hope so."

"Look, if there's any way, the Major will find it. And we'll be there soon to help. Why don't we do this? While I call the Major, why don't you get us both some coffee and sandwiches from the galley?

After I give my report, we'll settle down, and you can tell me about your daughter."

"Okay," Robby said. He walked to the galley in the rear of the plane.

Tyler called McKnight and gave his report.

Robby returned with the coffee and sandwiches, and they settled in to talk.

"Robby, I advised the Major about Nancy and Laura. He said to tell you thanks and he will do everything he can to get everyone back safe."

Robby nodded. He stared at the ceiling of the aircraft for a moment, then turned to Tyler.

"I'm sure you heard the story about how Robert discovered time travel, right? How he was experimenting with warp drive Engines and jumped back twenty-five years?"

"I believe I've heard it all."

"Okay. Let me give context because details are important. Genetically, Robert, Rob and I are the same person. We're from different times in our collective life. Rob was from twenty-five years ahead of me, and Robert is fifty years ahead. We were born on November 16th in 1979. I was twenty years old when the other two came into my life in March of the year 2000. Robert traveled back from 2025 and met himself, the man we call Rob. Over the next twenty-five years, they leveraged what Robert already knew and worked together to create a functional machine. Then they jumped back to join me so the three of us could work together on the warp engine. With me to this point?"

Tyler nodded.

"Except, the last time they traveled, other people heard the commotion, saw the three of us together and guessed what happened. The government classified the science of time travel, and we became government wards. They kept the three of us isolated but, to their credit, we weren't prisoners. And they gave us a reasonable amount of freedom after we convinced them we could keep a low profile. It didn't hurt our case to threaten to stop research if they didn't agree.

"Anyway, they swore the witnesses to secrecy under threat of government prosecution, and our work was kept under wraps for the next eleven years, until last year. You know the rest of that story. Together, the three of us brought the technology to where it is today with the help of some other people Washington gave us access to."

Tyler shifted in his seat. "But what about your daughter?"

"I'm coming to that," Robby said. "In 2000 when Rob and Robert showed up, I was twenty years old. Rob was forty-five, and Robert was seventy. In Robert's first passage through the year 2024, he met Adele Fox. She was forty years old then. Robert had never met anyone like her. She was beautiful, intelligent and a free spirit. She captured his heart. Mine and Rob's, too. He was five years older than her when they met. They fell in love and conceived a child named Laura. But Robert didn't know Adele was pregnant. Before she could tell him about it, he disappeared into the past. But she never knew he was gone because Rob… then I… replaced him in the timeline. More on that in a minute. Adele knew about his work, but she knew nothing about what happened. Laura was born in September of 2025, six months after Robert traveled the first time."

"That must have been uncomfortable for y'all," Tyler said. "How did you deal with it?"

"Robert was smart about it. You have to understand. He loved Adele with all his heart. He would've been thrilled to be Laura's father and participate in everything that goes along with fatherhood. All of us would have. Being thrown back in time was a great professional experience for him, but it devastated his personal life. After the shock of being jerked back twenty-five years into the past wore off, he realized he could never go back to his old life. What could he do? Go find Adele and explain what happened? She was fifteen years old in 2000."

"I see what you mean. I'm sorry," Tyler said.

“Winnie, you see, right? Robert waited. For twenty-five years. And as the time to meet her approached, he had second thoughts about seeing her. She was forty years old, but he was now seventy. He decided Rob should meet her, not himself. It was hard, but it was the only thing to do. He remembered the date when he and Adele met. Before 2024, he coached Rob on how he had lived his life. This was a joint effort to ensure the past wasn’t changed. That part wasn't very hard. He stayed out of the way and let Rob do what he himself did. And when the time came, he stayed in the background while Rob met Adele for the first time. Rob asked him about her then, but he refused to advise on it, struggling to stay neutral. Robert didn't want to influence his younger self. He wanted Rob to act as he himself had acted twenty-five years earlier. No matter what happened, Robert told Rob he was right on track. After they traveled back to get me, they did the same thing for me.”

“Wow, this is amazing,” Tyler said. He waved a hand at Robby and rose from his seat. “Keep going. I'll brew some more coffee.”

“You're not getting bored with this sob story?” Robby asked, as he followed Tyler to the aircraft's tiny galley.

“Not by any stretch of the imagination. Please continue.” Tyler dumped the used coffee container in the garbage and held up his hand. “Wait a second. I'm curious. How did Robert convince Rob to leave her to go back in time to add you to the group?”

“Good question. It was Rob’s idea.”

“Really?”

“Yes, after some reflection. When it came down to the decision, he balked. But his dedication to the two Engines overcame his concern when he realized she wouldn’t be alone. In fact, she wouldn't even know he had gone. Except it would be me who met her and became Laura's father this third time around. Depending on how you look at it, you could say Laura has three fathers. Not really, but we all feel like her father for obvious reasons.”

Tyler stood motionless for a few moments. “I don't know what to say... Do Adele and Laura know there are three of you?”

“Yes. When the rest of the world found out we discovered time travel, we broke the news to Adele. She was a little freaked out at first, but she understood it and got used to the idea.”

Tyler sensed something was wrong. It took a moment to realize what it was. *Past tense. He's using past tense.*

The two men stood in silence while the coffee brewed. “What else?” Tyler asked. “What else happened?”

Robby raised his head to look at Tyler, and a tear ran down his cheek. “She's... gone. She passed away.”

“Adele? How?”

Robby struggled to get the words out. “Adele...” The tears flowed now. “Snowy day... driving home from work... car wreck.”

Tyler put his arms around his friend. “I can't tell you how sorry I am.”

Robby tried to speak, but no words came. He nodded and stared at the floor.

Tyler released him and poured him a cup of coffee. “Do you want to stop talking about it?”

Robby wiped his eyes, blew over the coffee to cool it and took a sip. “No, I want you to understand. Laura knew about us from an early age. I'm not sure she understands, but she sees me as her Dad and Rob and Robert as like two grandfathers. She's been told we're all the same man, but I don't think she understands it.”

“I'm sure she doesn't. I'm not even sure I understand it, it's so counter-intuitive. But I guess we don't have to. It is what it is.”

Robby nodded and took another sip of coffee.

Tyler sighed. “I see now Robert had no choice. And now it's even more complicated. Finding Robert isn't enough. We have to find him and Laura and... what's the guardian's name?”

“Nancy.”

“Nancy. Who is she?”

"Adele's sister. She never married and doted on Laura. She begged us to let her be Laura's guardian. We were reluctant at first. But then she reminded us what would happen to her when the world found out. You can imagine what the tabloids would do with it, right? – 'Young girl has three fathers' and all that. We understood she'd have a normal life with Nancy. We both visit her about once a week and sometimes have them visit for the weekend."

"I see," Tyler said. "We need to find all three of them before we can rescue any of them. Too dangerous otherwise."

"Yes, I agree."

"Okay. Why don't you get some sleep? I need it too, but I want to think some first."

Robby nodded and walked to a seat in the rear of the plane. He turned off the overhead light and closed his eyes.

Tyler watched his friend for a few minutes. Then he poured his coffee into the sink and made his way to the front of the aircraft. He sat in a seat behind the pilot and tried to relax, but sleep eluded him. He tried to imagine how Robby felt right now. His child in the hands of... someone? Smith was in custody. Were Laura and her guardian tied up somewhere waiting for Smith to come back? Had they caused their death by capturing Smith? How long has it been? At least three days. *No. He hasn't left yet.* He hoped Smith had accomplices who didn't panic and bolt when Smith didn't come back.

We've got to find them, and soon. Their lives depend on it. The mission planner in him took over his thoughts. Details of the situation kept flashing through his mind. Some slowed down long enough for him to examine, but most sped past without allowing him to give them more than a brief consideration.

How would they find them? Smith was their best hope, but they needed another option. There had been an attempt on Smith's life. What if they succeeded on the next try? He called McKnight again to share his concerns and to ask for someone to watch Smith twenty-four seven.

Frustrated by his inability to focus along with lack of answers, he cursed Smith and his partners. *They will not get away with this.* He perceived he was losing effectiveness and his need for rest. He tried to thrust all details out of his mind for a few minutes.

Somewhere, at 36,000 feet over the Atlantic Ocean, he fell asleep.

CHAPTER 27

04:42 p.m. – July 20, 2036 – Defense Logistics Agency Satellite Office Building, Telegraph Road, Alexandria, VA

"That's it," Wheeler said. "The low-power test was successful. Do you agree, Hatcher?"

"Affirmative," Hatcher said. "Let's run it up to full power with nothing on the platform to see what the numbers look like."

"Good idea."

Wheeler twisted the power dial up to time jump levels. The old Engine had to be back into working condition for the rescue mission. Drake was like their grandfather and Clary a crusty, beloved uncle. *Their deaths are only temporary if we can get this thing working.*

The Engine surged with power, an audible hum rising in pitch. The sound dragged him back to the present.

Wheeler engaged the bubble generator so it would test separately from the power. He scanned the dials on the Engine. All green. It was ready to go.

"Okay. Let's shut it down and go see the Major," he said.

"Right… wait a second. Wheeler, look at this," she said, pointing at the bubble stability gauge.

Wheeler stared at the green and white dial on the Engine. The needle that should hold steady was pulsating, surging higher with each pulse. He looked up at the bubble. The shape of the usually perfect sphere distorted and developed a wobble as it spun.

"Oh, not good," Hatcher said. "Power is spiking, but transfer to the Time Bubble isn't consistent." She glanced at the cables coming out of the power cabinet. They were melting. A thin wisp of acrid smoke rose from the back of the Engine. “Shut it down! Shut it down… Now!”

Wheeler smelled melted circuit board. He heard the clicking sound of rapidly heating metal. “Shit,” he said, as he slammed his fist down on the emergency stop button. The bubble dissipated. The hum dropped in pitch and lapsed into silence.

Hatcher scanned the Engine’s dials while Wheeler grabbed an electrical fire extinguisher and opened the back panel. Acrid smoke poured from the panel and the pungent odor irritated his nose. He crouched down and sprayed CO^2 into the Engine.

“What the hell did we do wrong?” Hatcher asked.

“Not a damn thing,” Wheeler said, still peering into the electrical compartment. “Looks like someone exposed the wiring and wrapped copper wire around it to cause a short. It looks pretty fried in here.”

“How long?”

He shrugged. “Too long. Robby or Robert hand-wired many of these circuit boards. We'll need their help to fix it. Let's disconnect the power and update the Major.”

He unplugged the still smoldering power cables from the junction box to the power cabinet. Hatcher helped pull them loose and positioned them away from the box. When they completed the task, he said, “Yes, you're right.”

She turned to him. “Sabotage?”

“Yup. I can’t imagine how it could be anything else. Makes sense, too. Steal the new Engine and destroy the old one to take away our ability to fix what they did. Let's go.”

Out of long-established habit, they fell in step with each other as they strode down the hall.

****

McKnight sat at his desk. He was searching the net for photos of Harrison's political rivals. He had nearly completed his task when the expected knock came on his door.

"Come in," he said.

Hatcher and Wheeler filed into the room.

"Are we ready?" he said.

"No, sir. We've been sabotaged," Hatcher said.

"Seriously?" he said, looking back and forth between the two.

They nodded.

McKnight fought to keep his anger and disappointment from showing on his face. "Close the door and sit down."

Hatcher closed the door and joined Wheeler in the two side chairs in the office.

Wheeler told McKnight about the copper wire and the massive burnout.

McKnight spoke. "Okay. Who had access?"

"Only the people on the team," Wheeler said.

"And Cindy." Hatcher added. "She's my bet."

"What? Why?" Wheeler asked.

Hatcher leaned forward in her chair. "She's smarter than she acts. And she's been throwing herself at Mr. George. She's up to something."

"Why do you say that? Maybe she's just attracted to him," McKnight said.

"Because she acts too sincere and nice to everybody. She seems intelligent and sensitive around everyone else. But then she goes all goo-goo eyes around Mr. George and doesn't notice Doctor Wu has a thing for him?" She leaned back in her chair. "Puh-lease."

"I picked up on that, too," Wheeler said, "but I chalked it up to hots for Trevor. Couldn't that be her motivation?"

"Maybe, but I don't think so. Call it women's intuition or whatever. Her behavior seems inconsistent. Smart and collected one minute, all syrupy sweet the next. Up to something... or bat shit crazy. Take your pick."

"Okay," McKnight said. "Just for the sake of argument, let's say she's the traitor. How did she know the date and time of the move?"

"I've been thinking about that, sir," Hatcher said. "She came into the planning briefing before you arrived and fooled around with the refreshments. I watched her. She just moved the platters around. I don't remember her being so exacting before. Maybe she planted a bug in the conference room and overheard the date and time? It's possible."

"You think she planted a bug in a briefing while surrounded by the participants?" McKnight said. "That's pretty thin. Do you have any evidence?"

"No, sir. But I don't trust her. We should at least consider it a possibility."

"Oh, I agree, but let's not sentence her to death without more evidence. What do you suggest?"

"I'm ambivalent, sir. I don't want her here, but I don't want to let her out of my sight either."

"Okay, you get your wish. Have her take the rest of the day off but put her under surveillance. She wasn't scheduled to work today, anyway. Call in and get help from Senator Lodge's office. Hand it off to the FBI and get back down here. But keep an open mind if the evidence points elsewhere. We don't know yet."

"Yes, sir."

"But before you go..." He tapped on his comp pad and projected pictures up on the wall. "See anyone who looks familiar, Lieutenant?"

Hatcher scanned the pictures. "Yes, sir. Top row, center picture."

McKnight double-clicked the photo to enlarge it. "From the warehouse when you captured Smith?"

"Yes, sir. I'm positive. That's the guy I saw. No question. Who is he?"

"That is...." He looked up the name in his list. "The Honorable Blake Phillips, Congressman from the great state of Virginia."

Hatcher and Wheeler looked at each other. "Can we go get him, sir?" Wheeler asked.

"Not yet. It occurs to me the old Engine being fried might be a blessing."

"Sir?" Hatcher said.

"Think about it," McKnight said. If we travel back and stop the attack, things go back to where they were before. But now, their operation is blown and Smith and his people have no reason to keep Amy alive. In fact, they have every reason to get rid of her and Doctor Astalos's daughter. We have to find them first before we can move."

McKnight paused for a long moment, then slapped both thighs with his hands. "Lieutenant Hatcher, go ahead with my previous instructions. Lieutenant Wheeler, get with Trevor and find all communications between Smith and Phillips. Or any communications between Smith and Cindy or Phillips and Cindy. Also see if we can find any communication between Phillips or Smith with that guy Smith killed in his cell. Maybe we can get a clue about where they're keeping their prisoners."

"Yes, sir," the two said. They saluted and left the room.

McKnight stared at the picture of Blake Phillips. The man was young and wholesome looking. He had that winning smile that charms and influences others. *Barbara's murderer? What kind of man kills a woman and sentences an innocent girl to death to cover it up?*

He used the remote to switch off the display and change the wall to the 'transparent' setting. A view of trees replaced the beige wall.

He tried to piece together what he knew.

This is about politics. Phillips must be at the bottom of this. He's ambitious and wants to beat his competition. Needs a solution, but in the meantime, screws up on the personal side. He kills Barbara and uses Smith to cover it up. When Amy shows up and threatens his plans, he has her kidnapped.

Then he comes up with the perfect way to solve two problems. He uses Amy to seduce his opponent in the past and fakes her suicide to discredit him. Now she can't expose the connection to his murdered girlfriend and his rival is no longer a threat. Brilliant.

He pulled on his lower lip. What crime could he get Phillips on? The reality of the whole thing gnawed at him. None of the evidence discovered during time travel was admissible in court. With Amy's help, McKnight could get him for killing Barbara. *Probably.*

If he left things as they are, he could get Phillips and Smith for the murder of Drake and the rest of the convoy. He'd get life in prison or a lethal injection. But then Drake, Clary, and the rest would still be dead.

If he stopped the convoy massacre, they might never find Amy or Robby's daughter.

The course of action was still as clear and simple as it was a few moments ago when he gave his team their orders. *Clear and simple, but difficult.*

There were two ways for them to stop the massacre. Find the new Engine or fix the old one. Robby would be here soon to help with the later, and Wheeler was on the other.

I'm not using all my firepower. He called Trevor. When he answered, McKnight asked him and Kathy to assist Wheeler.

Trevor agreed and said they would set up a war room in the big conference room.

McKnight disconnected the phone. *What else can I do?*

He checked his email and found the reply to his inquiry about Sergeant Randall. He opened it.

Sergeant Christopher Randall was on assignment in the area of the Afghan prison. He was listed as BNR. *Presumed dead but body not recovered.* McKnight cross-referenced it with the date of the alleged meeting with Smith. *Same day.* Looking at Randall's service record, he learned Randall was a deep cover operative who was adept at passing himself off as an Afghan and infiltrating Taliban bases. In his last communication with Command, he advised he planned to infiltrate the prison and collect armament and strength data. *He went in, but he never came out.*

McKnight leaned back in his chair and put his hands behind his head. *No mention of prisoners or troop capture.* McKnight scanned the rest of the record. Randall was cited posthumously for his bravery and his recon work.

McKnight dropped his hands to his side and sat up in his chair. *Randall didn't go in to help Smith. He didn't even know Smith was there. He found him while he was inside and made contact, but didn't make it out to report it.*

He forwarded the report to Trevor and Kathy, picked up his truck keys and left his office. *Maybe if Smith knows the truth about Randall…it's a lever. Maybe I can get him to talk to me.*

CHAPTER 28

07:23 p.m. – July 20, 2036 – Fort Belvoir Stockade, Alexandria, VA

McKnight sat in the waiting room at the Fort Belvoir Stockade where the security team transferred Smith as a protection measure. It was a logical move and would do for the short term, but McKnight doubted he'd be safe here for long.

He hoped the assassination attempt changed Smith's perspective. He was now a liability and expendable to his employer. Therefore, he might be open to new options.

It always took time to move prisoners from one facility to another. When McKnight arrived at the stockade, they didn't have Smith in their records yet. Halfway through his discussions with the desk sergeant, the computer updated the records and Smith appeared in their database.

"Oh, here he is," the desk sergeant said. "Hang on a second, sir. They checked him in."

"Thanks," McKnight said. He leaned against the counter and watched as the sergeant tapped commands into the ancient computer terminal and read the output.

"Sir, it looks like it will be another thirty minutes before his processing is complete. Would you like to come back? There's a Starbucks over near the hospital. It's more comfortable than here."

"If it'll only be thirty minutes, I'll hang around, Sergeant." McKnight looked around the room. "Is there any coffee around here?"

"Depends on what you call coffee, sir." The sergeant grinned. "There's a machine down the hall. Not the best, but it's hot and caffeinated to hell and back."

"Thanks, Sergeant. I'll wait. Expedite anything you can for me, will you?"

"Yes, sir. I'll let you know when he's available for interview."

"Thanks again."

McKnight walked down the hall. The coffee machine was older than most of his team. And the sergeant was right; the hot liquid barely qualified as coffee, but he sipped it and pondered his approach for the interview.

He began to second-guess his decision to talk to Smith without Trevor and his interviewing skills. After a few minutes of dressing himself down, he closed his eyes and took a few deep breaths. He relaxed and allowed the ire and frustration to drain from his mind and body.

What do I need to accomplish? He focused on that question. *I need a connection to Phillips and whomever else is involved, and I need to find the Time Engine so I can prevent the attack on the convoy. That would erase everything except Barbara and the kidnappings.*

The sergeant behind the counter interrupted his thoughts. "Major?" He looked back down at his computer screen as he motioned for McKnight to approach the counter. McKnight rose and stepped forward, carrying his comp pad in his left hand.

The sergeant looked up from his display. "We have him in interrogation room four for you now, sir. Will you require any assistance?"

"No. Where do I go?"

"Right down the hall, sir. I'll buzz you in." He pointed at McKnight's sidearm. "Can I check that for you, sir?"

McKnight looked down at his waist and chuckled. He unbuckled the belt and handed it to the man. "Yes, that would be a good idea, Sergeant. I forgot I had it on." He pointed down the hall. "Right down this way?"

"Yes, sir. When you get to the access door, wait for me to buzz you in. He's in room four."

"Thank you. Will the interview be recorded?"

"Yes, sir, that's SOP. The recorder has been on since Smith entered the room."

"Perfect. Thank you." McKnight walked down the hall and entered the interrogation area. He found another coffee machine and bought a cup. *An act of kindness never hurts.* He bought one for Smith, too. He went to interrogation room four and waited for the buzz. Balancing two cups in his left hand and his comp pad under his arm, he opened the door and stepped inside.

The metal table and two chairs in the center of the room were the same nondescript gray as the room itself. Smith was wearing prison orange and sitting at the table, his manacled hands clasped together before him on the table.

"Well," Smith said. "I wondered when we'd have our little talk." The smile on his face was not warm or welcoming.

McKnight smiled. "That's a good color on you." He set the two cups on the table next to the pad and pushed one over to Smith. He sat down, opened his comp pad and checked messages. Smith cupped his hands around the coffee cup.

Nothing from Trevor and Wheeler yet.

He looked up at Smith and held his eyes. "You killed General Drake and thirteen other good men."

Smith blinked once and said, "I can't imagine what you mean. I'm good, but not that good. Besides, I've been in custody the whole time."

"Where is Doctor Astalos?"

"What? The scientist? How would I know? I've been incommunicado for more than two days. I'd like to talk to a lawyer."

"And you might get one someday. I can put you at the scene."

"Scene? Sorry, I'm drawing a complete blank here. What scene?"

Smith studied his fingernails as if bored. McKnight checked it off. *Okay, that was the rehearsed speech. Let's try something else.*

"I heard you had a visitor."

Smith jerked his eyes back to McKnight.

Ah, he's still pissed. “Where's the loyalty? Didn't take 'em long to write you off, did it?”

Smith's eyes glinted. “Motherfuckers. Sent a goddamn amateur in to do me.”

“What happened?”

“It was a clusterfuck. As soon as the static electricity started, I knew somebody was coming in. Ha! I thought they were trying to bust me out. I remember thinking the idiots hadn't thought it through – in that confined space, the time bubble could cut me in half. I jumped up on the toilet in the corner so it missed me by two feet. When he materialized, I realized it wasn’t a rescue attempt. He had his weapon in his hand and he pointed it at me. I thought I was dead meat, but the asshole didn't shoot right away. Dumb fuck didn't realize he could shoot before the bubble dissipated.”

“How'd you know?”

Smith's voice turned sarcastic. “Because I *learn*. I threw a flash bomb at you, remember? It was a gamble, but it paid off. Until that bitch lieutenant showed up.”

McKnight chose not to remind Smith how that ‘bitch lieutenant’ had kicked his ass. “What happened next?”

“Nobody told that fucking moron about falling backward when you arrive at a new time and place. When I realized he was there to do me, I rushed him. He got off a shot but missed me by a mile. I got to him before he recovered.”

He paused and drew his manacled hands across his throat. “Killed him with his own knife. He was JV. Amateur! That’s probably why they sent him. No big loss if he failed.”

“And then?”

“They recalled the bastard. He wasn't there five seconds. As soon as the static started again, I jumped back up on the toilet. They must have figured the bubble would get me. If not, he could shoot me and jump out again. Five seconds was enough time if he had known what he was doing."

"Why didn't you stay in the bubble and jump out?"

The corners of Smith's mouth curled up. "I could have, but I didn't like my chances. I figured I had a pretty good chance of being dead if I jumped out and a better chance of survival if I stayed here."

McKnight nodded. "Yeah, that was probably a good decision."

The two men sat across from each other, looking like matching bookends with their posture and focus. Two seasoned warriors with everything in common except the quality of their choices. They leaned forward, hands clasped before them and stared at each other.

McKnight broke the silence. "I can put you at the scene of the ambush."

Smith leaned back in his chair. "Again, I'm drawing a blank here." He picked at a piece of lint on his orange trousers.

"They'll try again, you know," McKnight said.

"Probably."

"They *will* try again. I could move you if I had any incentive. Have you considered the consequences?"

"Yes, Major. But I'm not convinced you can protect me."

"You might be right," McKnight said. "But I'm your only chance."

"Debatable. But you're probably right. Still, I don't see what you can do for me that I can't do by myself."

"If you cooperate, I might be able to keep you away from a lethal injection."

"I guess that's a fair point. What's on your mind?" Smith leaned forward and put his hands back on the table, listening.

McKnight leaned back in his chair and took a slow deep breath. He had to convince Smith he was sincere. And he was. It was the best path.

"Here's the bottom line. First, you're aware that, no matter what I learn or do during time travel, JAG can't use it in a court of law. Nothing you did or said can be used against you because it can't be corroborated. You understand that, right? If nothing else, I'm confident JAG can nail you for the ambush on the convoy. Felony murder. Thirteen counts. If they do, you'll probably get the death penalty. At minimum, you'll never see the light of day or breathe free air again." McKnight paused for effect.

Smith stared at McKnight as if he were looking for a sign of deception. After a long moment, he bobbed his head in acknowledgement. "What are you offering?"

"Tell me the story of Barbara Howard's murder," McKnight said. "Who killed her? What was your part? Tell me where the Engine and the hostages are. I'll go back in time and stop the convoy from moving. Everything goes back to a much simpler situation. That leaves just the kidnapping charges and, if they're still alive, nobody is dead by your hand. And I'm sure your other self will figure out what happened and disappear to an island in the South Pacific with hula girls and lots of sun."

Smith nodded. "What else?"

"I can't guarantee anything except Blake Phillips will take the fall for the murder of Barbara Howard. You'll have time tacked on for being an accessory, for trying to hide her murder. Who else was working with Phillips?"

Smith's eyes narrowed.

Shit. I gave away knowing who his employer is. Is that good or bad? Did I just blow it?

Smith twisted in his seat, but his face was an unemotional mask.

Maybe it's good...maybe it'll convince him there's no way out. Or maybe we're wrong about who he works for.

Smith drew himself up in his chair. "Sounds inviting, but I don't trust you. You or any other Ranger. Full of promises, but no follow through. You're wasting your time. Go find somebody who's stupid enough to believe you."

Afghanistan again.

"It must be terrible to labor all these years under a misconception that stems from a lack of information."

Smith looked him in the eye. "What? Like what? Like Rangers are actually angels in disguise – ready to leap into action to help the helpless? Save it for the recruiting posters."

"Like why Ranger Sergeant Randall left you in prison in Afghanistan."

"Blow it out your ass. They chose to leave me rather than risk their own. No great mystery there."

"I don't know why they would leave you, but they never had a chance to make that decision."

"Bullshit."

"I don't think so. I've seen the record. Nobody knows for sure, and I'm reading between the lines of the report, but it seems clear to me what happened. Randall's mission was independent recon. He was out in the field, gathering info. His Command didn't even know where *he* was, much less where *you* were. They didn't *know* about you, Mike. It wasn't a rescue mission. He was scoping out the prison. The only explanation is this: he infiltrated the place to recon and found you by accident. Apparently they caught him before he could report or get out of the prison. He never made it back. He's listed as BNR on the day you said you were contacted by him."

"That's all bullshit," Smith said, shaking his head. "They planned to kill me and they didn't. They must have captured him and learned that I was worthy of being rescued, so they kept me alive, at least for a while."

"That's one idea. I had that thought myself. Here's another. After discovering you in the prison, he tried to escape to report, but was caught. He knew he was a dead man, but maybe he could give you a fighting chance by telling them you were an important asset and a rescue would be attempted. I don't know, but it sounds more plausible to me. Regardless, the record shows that his Command didn't know where he was and there's no mention of American prisoners in the report."

"That's just speculation."

"No more than what you assumed. It's probably more likely, in fact."

"I don't buy it."

"I didn't expect you to, but I hoped you'd consider the possibility. We have a lot in common, Mike, even if we are on different sides of this table."

"If you're not my enemy, why am I wearing handcuffs and you get to walk out of here?"

McKnight shrugged. "The quality of your life choices, I guess. You killed American soldiers on American soil. Unforgivable. Unless you take steps to walk it back. I've already told you how to do it."

Smith leaned forward in his chair again, his manacled hands clasped before him on the table.

McKnight didn't see the emotion he hoped for in Smith's face, but he recognized the emotion the man struggled to suppress. It was fear.

Smith spoke with an unsteady voice. "What happens to *me* if I help you?"

"I told you... your earlier self will figure it out and haul ass. Disappear. Take off. What do you mean?"

"No," Smith said. He blinked twice and paused.

When he spoke again, his voice was thick and unsteady. "*This* me." He pointed at his chest with the thumbs of his manacled hands.

McKnight understood the man's fear now. If the convoy isn't attacked, Smith could not travel back to 2011 and therefore would not be captured. This timeline would no longer exist.

Doctor Astalos spoke of this in a training session. The inventor of time travel posed a rhetorical question to challenge the team and remind them of the seriousness of time travel. *What happens to timelines that are abandoned or made impossible by history changes?*

Do they continue in another dimension of time and space? Or do they cease to exist?.

McKnight looked Smith in the eyes and said, “I don't know what happens. The same goes for me. It’s not knowable.”

Smith sat back and his hands dropped into his lap. He looked down at them and didn't look back up again.

McKnight paused. *He looks hopeless.* “Will you help me?”

Still looking at his hands, Smith said, “I don't want to take the chance. I like being alive, even if not for long.” He didn't speak again.

McKnight sighed. He had nothing else to say, no other card to play. After a long moment, he closed his comp pad, slipped it under his arm and left the room.

****

<u>08:36 p.m. – July 20, 2036 – Fort Belvoir, Alexandria, VA</u>

McKnight picked up his sidearm from the front desk and left the stockade. He walked to his truck, put his comp pad inside and closed the door. He leaned against the truck and looked up at the sky.

Until now, he was still in shock from the loss of Drake and Clary, functioning on adrenalin and training. Now that he was alone and quiet, the full impact of it slammed into him. His mentor. His friend. The man he loved and respected more than anyone else was gone. In his mind, he saw Drake and Clary lying at the bottom of the ditch back on Telegraph Road.

He slid down the side of the truck to the ground and buried his face in his hands. Tears rolled down his cheeks. He allowed the grief and loss to roll over him. He saw flashes of Drake’s face, now serious, then laughing, now deftly handling politicians and soldiers, and sharing philosophical and military wisdom. He smiled at these visions of Drake, then they were replaced by the scene from Telegraph Road. *What do I do now?*

He was unaware of how much time passed, but eventually reason returned. *As long as time travel is possible, there's a chance to reverse this.*

He stood and wiped his eyes. He needed a few minutes of escape. A mind reset.

Here in this suburb of Washington DC, he didn't expect to see any stars due to the abundance of light from the city. His thoughts leapt across the country to his home in the mountains of eastern Oregon. He pictured himself back home, looking up at the Milky Way and a million stars. He allowed himself to get lost in that memory. The serenity and beauty of that Oregon sky was a source of calm. It helped a little.

He rubbed his eyes with the heels of his hands and remembered that Drake and Clary weren't the only casualties.

He thought of Barbara. A stream of memories came unbidden to his consciousness. He recalled how much fun they had together when they were dating. She was bright and funny and so pretty. He closed his eyes and, for a moment, he could see eyes that sparkled when she laughed and feel the warmth of her when they slow-danced together.

Barbara is dead. She was a good person, completely innocent and didn't deserve this.

He opened his eyes and tried to piece together how this horrible situation had come about, tracing what he knew from when he last saw her to today. The relationship lost when they stopped seeing each other, dealing with loneliness, being charmed by a married man, dating him, and being murdered for being in the wrong place at the wrong time.

If I had treated her right. If I had let her know how I felt about her, she'd still be alive.

The realization plunged him into a dark place. *It's my fault. If I had been more present, she would never have met that guy and she'd still be here.*

He closed his eyes again and wallowed in the guilt and pain. *We were good together and I blew it because I didn't act. I was waiting for a clear signal from – where? The universe? God? Who knows? And now there's no way to make it right.*

Nonetheless, if he had been less selfish and more understanding, she might not have come to this end. She was a good person that he cared about and he would find the person who did this. Her death wasn't his fault – it was the fault of whomever was operating Smith. If that person is a US Congressman, then so be it.

McKnight reined in his emotions and told himself the truth. He liked, admired, and respected Barbara. And he missed her. But now that he really examined his feelings, he admitted the extra spark to push him over the edge into love for her just wasn't there. He cared immensely for her, but not enough to commit.

And another realization struck him.

I love Megan and I'm treating her the same way I treated Barbara. And I'm blowing it, just like I did with Barbara.

He drew his phone out of his pocket and commanded it to call Megan. She picked up after four rings.

"Hello, Marc."

"Hi. I wanted to talk to you earlier, but couldn't. I—"

"Work, right?"

"Yes. It's been a bad day."

"Well, I'm sorry you're having a bad day."

"Megan, it's not just bad," he said. *How do I talk about this without crying?* "We lost two of our team today."

"You mean they quit the team?"

McKnight struggled to control his voice. "No, they were killed."

"What? Oh, Marc, I'm so sorry. What happened?"

"They were moving some technology equipment to our new offices in Fort Belvoir. On the way, they were ambushed by people who wanted our technology."

"How awful! I'm so sorry. So they were members of your team?"

“No. It was General Drake and Master Sergeant Clary, his aide.”

“Oh, no! I know you were close and General Drake was your friend.”

“More than that,” he said, and struggled to continue. “I…We’re devastated by this.”

“I know you are. Marc, I can’t tell you how sorry I am. I wish I was there with you. What can I do to help? Is there anything I can do?”

Tell her how you feel. Make her understand.

“Megan, just hang in there with me a little longer. Wait for me. I have to do what I can to fix it or catch the people who did it. After that, I want to—”

The announcement of an incoming call rang in his ear. He checked and saw that Trevor was trying to call him.

“Marc, are you there?” she asked.

“Megan, I have to go. They’re calling me with information. Just, please, don’t write me off. I’ll call back as soon as I can.”

“Go do what you have to do,” she said. “I love you.”

She disconnected before he could say anything else.

His phone rang and he answered it.

“Major?” Trevor said. “Any luck with Smith?”

“I'm more certain he's involved than before. I tried everything I could, but he didn't give me anything.”

“Yep, that's what I figured. Well, I have good news. We may have a break here. Stand by a second.”

McKnight heard muffled voices in the background. He made out Trevor 's voice and occasionally Hatcher's and Wheeler's. He grew impatient. He started the truck, backed out, and headed toward the Telegraph Road office. Then, he heard Trevor say he agreed with them and came back on the line.

“Major? Sorry about that. I needed to make sure I understood what we had before relaying it.”

“No problem. What do you have for me?”

"Your call to Senator Lodge worked wonders. He engaged the FBI, the NSA and some telecom providers. We started with Smith's cell phone records for the last three months. One untraceable line called him a few times. Fifty other people called or were called by him. One was Blake Phillips. We got to work correlating those numbers and who they had called. The NSA and the telecom providers together pieced together who called who and where they called from."

"Good," McKnight said. "What have we learned?"

"We may be on to something. We found distinctive patterns. Phillips got several untraceable calls."

"Untraceable? For the telecom guys? That's troubling."

"Yes, sir, it is."

"What patterns did they find?"

"Well, for example, sometimes Phillips got an untraceable call and called Smith. There were also times when Smith got untraceable calls and called people on the list. Got me wondering who's in charge. Maybe Phillips isn't the brains behind this. Maybe it's someone else."

McKnight turned his truck back onto Telegraph Road and drove by the scene of the ambush. There was no sign anything had happened there except for some strips of yellow crime scene tape.

"Who?" he said.

"No idea. Funny thing is we got the NSA guys to look at the untraceables. They were cooperative at first, but then they went dark on me. I kept asking about it, and they kept giving me the roundabout. I couldn't figure out if they were stonewalling me because of who the call came from or because they didn't *know* who it came from. The first possibility pisses me off. The second scares the hell out of me."

"I'm not so happy about it either. Did we get any location data?"

"That's the good news, Major. At the scene of the convoy ambush, they found a broken wrist phone. Looks like it came from the one casualty suffered by the attackers."

"We had a body from the firefight?"

"No, sir. Looks like the phone was broken, and it had blood on it. The owner was probably killed. We expected them to carry out their casualties, but they must've missed the phone. Anyway, we had the blood analyzed and traced it back through military records. The blood belonged to a guy Smith and Phillips had called."

"Where was it found?"

"In the open field at the ambush site."

"Good. If nothing else, we can tie Smith to the ambush."

"More than that, Major. We got the telecom vendors to triangulate locations for almost all the calls. We got calls from all their homes, from the woods and fields around the ambush site, from Phillips' office and from a warehouse owned by Phillips down in old town Alexandria."

"A warehouse? That sounds promising."

"Better than that. Remember that guy who jumped into Smith's cell and tried to kill him?"

"Oh, did you find him?"

"Nope, and I suspect we won't. But there was blood left behind in Smith's cell, and it was traced, too. The dead, would-be assassin was one of the men Smith was talking to. They sent one of his own guys in to kill him."

"Nice people. What else do we have?"

"Several of those guys made calls from that warehouse, some as recently as twenty minutes ago."

"Mr. George, you're saying it's reasonable to expect that…"

"That it's where the hostages are? Yes, Major... Oh, hang on a second."

Trevor came back on the line after two minutes.

"Marc, where are you?"

"I'm on Telegraph Road less than ten minutes from the office."

"Okay, get here fast. General Flynn and Senator Lodge just walked in, asked for a status and scrambled Hostage Rescue from Quantico based on Wheeler's report. They're on their way here now. You need to be here when they show up if you want to be involved."

"On my way," McKnight said and disconnected the phone. He gripped the steering wheel and pushed the truck's accelerator to the floor.

CHAPTER 29

08:50 p.m. – July 20, 2036 – Defense Logistics Agency Satellite Office Building, Telegraph Road, Alexandria, VA

McKnight's truck skidded to a stop in the parking lot. He leapt from the cab and was at a dead run after two steps. He bounded up the stairs at the loading dock, typed in the access code on the door and stepped inside. He dashed down the main hall and found the team in the big conference room. Wheeler, Kathy and Trevor sat around the table while Hatcher drew a diagram on the whiteboard.

"Report," he said.

Hatcher took the lead. "Senator Lodge and General Flynn just left. They asked for a status every hour until we resolve the situation. Hostage Rescue is still on the way here." She glanced at her watch. "They should be here in ten minutes. They won't be ready to go yet though. We don't know enough about the place yet, but the perps don't know we're coming. We have time."

"Where are they?" McKnight asked.

"We traced them to a warehouse between Wales Alley and Prince Street in Old Town Alexandria," Wheeler said. "We're still assessing the impact, danger to locals, strategic positions, and such. Whatever we determine, Hostage Rescue will go first and we'll come in right behind them."

"Okay. Priority is the hostages. But we want to make sure they don't wreck the Engine. If they do, we have no chance of reversing what they have done. The priority is hostages first, Engine second and take prisoners third. If anyone makes a move to scuttle the Engine, orders are to shoot to kill. Anyone disagree?"

No one moved.

"Good," McKnight said, looking around the room. "Now for Plan B. Robby Astalos should be back here in the U.S. with Captain Tyler in an hour. I hope he got some sleep because we're putting him to work on the old Engine as soon as he gets here."

"I hope he can salvage it, sir," Wheeler said. "It looks pretty fried."

"Understood. After we rescue the hostages, we'll see what we can do. With luck, we'll have Robert Astalos back safe."

"Anything else?" Trevor asked. "What can Kathy and I do?"

"Good question. I'm taking Wheeler and Hatcher with me to the warehouse. Why don't you call Captain Tyler and Robby Astalos on the plane and find out what you can do in advance? Just setting out the tools would help. I know Doctor Wu will have ideas."

"Yes," Kathy said. "We can do that. And I'll start calculations for the new Engine to send you back to stop the convoy. I'll send them to Lieutenant Wheeler when complete. Do you plan to bring the machine back here? The machine is set up and operational. If you want to bring it back here, we must disassemble it, pack it up, bring it back and unpack it, reassemble and test. There's risk of damage or delay in each step. We should consider jumping from there."

"Okay, good point. I'll let Doctor Astalos make that decision if he's... Well, we'll deal with that when we have to. Pack your gear and go to the warehouse. Anything else?"

Someone knocked on the door. The front desk security guard stuck her head into the room. "Hostage Rescue is here. Shall I bring them in?"

"Yes… thanks," McKnight said.

She pushed the door open, and a Marine Major in black fatigues entered the room. McKnight rose and walked around the table to greet him. They saluted each other, and McKnight stuck out his hand. "Major, I'm Marc McKnight. This is my team."

"Good to meet you, Major," said the man, taking his hand. "I'm Roger Kirby. General Flynn tells me you have people in a hostage situation in a warehouse in Old Town?"

"Yes. We need to get there as soon as possible. But it's more complex than the rescue alone. We have other considerations."

"No problem. My recon team is on site now. Your Lieutenant Hatcher sent us the address."

Hatcher stepped forward and saluted. "I'm Hatcher, sir." Kirby returned her salute. "Good to meet you, Lieutenant."

McKnight said, "Forgive my manners." Pointing to the rest of the team, he said, "This is Lieutenant Wheeler, Doctor Wu and Trevor George."

"Good to meet you," Kirby said, nodding toward the others. "Who's in the warehouse?" he asked. "And what are the other considerations?"

"We believe Doctor Robert Astalos, his daughter and her guardian are being held–"

"Astalos? The time travel scientist?"

"Yes. And two others."

"Okay, so this is a National Security issue?"

"It's more personal to us, but yes, it is."

"Ah, that's why General Flynn was so excited. Hang on." He held down the mic button on his commlink and turned to the side. "S. B.?... Please be advised one hostage is VIP. He's classified as a national security asset... Yes, that's affirmative, and I'll pass details ASAP... Out." He released the commlink button and turned back to McKnight. "Any idea how many bad guys?"

"No, sir. These are the same guys who hit our convoy this morning and killed thirteen good men. I estimate about forty mercenaries. But I'll bet most of them are paid and gone by now. There are too many people involved to hide all the clues. They're smart enough to know that. We believe their leader is Mike Smith. He's a former Navy Seal, and he's tough."

Kirby nodded. "Jack... Sergeant Clinton… was a good friend of mine. Our kids play on the same baseball team. We'll get these guys. What's the other event?"

"We plan to go back in time and stop the convoy so the attack doesn't happen. But we need to secure the hostages first. Otherwise, they'll have no use for them and get rid of the evidence. But we can't go back yet because they have the only working machine. So we need to take it back from them in one piece."

"I don't understand," he said. "But, I don't have to. What do we need to do?"

"We need to get in, take the bad guys out and rescue the hostages without damaging the Engine. With luck, it's ready to go. If not, Wheeler and Hatcher can make it operational, once the warehouse is secure. Then we can go back to stop the convoy."

"Okay, we can help with that. Get you in and on your way, and we'll watch the fort."

"It's near the exact anniversary of the time event, I wonder if we might..." McKnight paused, his mind racing. "Kirby? There's something else. There might be another person there and we need to take him alive. The good news is he won't be armed."

"Who's that?"

"Congressman Blake Phillips."

"A Congressman?"

"Yep, and we can circulate pictures of him to your men. Long story, but Lieutenant Hatcher got a glimpse of him earlier. There's strong evidence he's behind this whole thing and we believe he also murdered a woman named Barbara Howard. We know he time travels, probably at the same time as Smith. If we could catch him with the mercenaries, there's no way he can talk his way out."

"Okay," Kirby said. "What else?"

"Now that I think about it, you may not see Smith. If their time travel mission is in progress, he won't be there and he won't be back. But if they haven't traveled yet, he'll be there and will pose a threat. He's the smartest of the bunch. If he gets wind of you guys, he'll bolt. I'm sure he'll have an escape plan."

Kirby stared at him. “Maybe yes, maybe no? Man, I hate surprises. Okay, we need to take one of these guys so we’ll have up-to-date Intel. We need to know what we're dealing with. Let me get on the horn and see what we can do. My team set up a command post two blocks from the place. Let’s go there now so we’ll be ready to move when the time comes.”

McKnight looked around the room. “You heard him, people. Let’s move.”

Hatcher stood and dashed for the door. Over her shoulder, she said, “Wheeler, I’m getting weapons for us.”

“Good deal,” he called after her. “I’ll go pack Engine gear, notes and tools.” He ran from the room. Kathy and Trevor followed them out, leaving Kirby and McKnight alone in the conference room.

McKnight offered his hand to Kirby again. “Thanks again for your help, Major.”

Kirby shook his offered hand. “No problem, Major.”

McKnight pulled on his lower lip. “Major, we're at a place most people never get to. We have a disaster and a chance to fix it. In fact, if we get there before they travel, we can prevent it happening at all. But everything depends on us saving those people and securing the Engine.”

Kirby looked thoughtful. “What if we do get there before they travel? If we’re sure of that, couldn't we destroy the machine and stop everything that way?”

“No. We could stop them from carrying out the rest of their plans but not from attacking the convoy. We still need to do that.”

“Ah, right. Man, this time travel shit is too much for me.”

McKnight patted Kirby on the shoulder. “You're not used to thinking about time-related alternatives, Kirby. Believe me, it *is* an acquired skill. With any luck we'll fix it, and you won't even remember it.”

“I look forward to that. Jack Clinton was a good friend.”

"Yes, and General Drake meant a lot to us. He didn't deserve to die in a damned ambush. Let's put it back like it was. And I won't forget what Smith did here."

CHAPTER 30

09:21 p.m. – July 20, 2036 – The Christmas Attic, Old Town Alexandria, VA

"How did you guys find this place?" McKnight asked. The smell of wreaths, spices and Christmas permeated every corner of the little shop.

Lieutenant Burnette grinned. "My wife shops here. They aren't open this time of year, but I got the owner to open for us so we'd have a place close to the warehouse."

McKnight liked Kirby's second-in-command from the moment he met him. His choice of this place was perfect. They were less than fifty yards from the warehouse. The storeroom in the back of the store was small, but they gathered there as Burnette gave the recon briefing.

McKnight listened as Burnette described the layout of the warehouse. The building was constructed of brick and a plank floor in the mid 1700s. It was set back from the street on the property with a narrow alley as the only access to the building. The main room was one hundred feet long and one hundred feet wide with windows along the sides and both ends. A small room housed the office and a bathroom at the east side of the warehouse. A storeroom spanned the width of the building on the west side.

"There's one sentry," Burnette said. "I doubt Smith set up the security for the building. Or else they bugged out before he thought they would. But all the sentry can do is walk around the place since he can't cover it all from one place. And he has another problem. He's in Old Town Alexandria, so he can't openly carry a weapon. That's a big problem for him and an advantage for us.

"So, we got close and reconnoitered the place between the sentry's laps around the building. As far as we can tell, there're only five bad guys – the sentry and four guys inside. Three of them are in the main room, looking relaxed but alert. Like they're waiting for something. The last guy is in the storeroom. The main room is empty except for one area. Near the office, there is a big power cabinet, some other equipment and some packing boxes." He looked at McKnight. "Your time machine, I presume. That part of the warehouse has heavy lamps focused on the machinery. The rest of the warehouse is dim. No other lights except in the storeroom."

"Did you see the hostages?" McKnight asked.

"That's the good news. They're being held in the storeroom. One guy guarding them. He's armed with an Uzi and a sidearm. There are windows in the storeroom big enough to serve as entry points. We'll take that guy out and go in. First priority accomplished – hostages rescued. From there, we assault the main room. If they're smart, they'll surrender. If they fight, they're dead. But it'll be a little tricky for us because the only cover is the boxes around the equipment. We can't fix that, but we can mitigate it. Some of the building's side windows are next to the power cabinet so we'll have crossfire to makes those positions untenable. That helps, but when we open fire from there, they could shoot back and hit the equipment." He glanced at McKnight. "I'd like to get you some prisoners, sir, but if we want to protect the equipment, we may have to take them out."

"Understood, Lieutenant," McKnight said. "Do what you can."

"Yes, sir." Burnette turned to Kirby. "Anything else, sir? We're ready to go when you give the word."

Kirby nodded and looked at McKnight. "Anything else, Major?"

McKnight looked thoughtful and glanced at Wheeler and Hatcher.

Wheeler nodded, but Hatcher spoke to Burnette.

"Lieutenant? Did you say the three around the Engine looked like they are waiting for something?" She looked at her watch. "Twenty-two hundred... That's probably about right. It's about the same time as when we ran into them the other night. Maybe they won't come back to the same time, but they might."

"What are you saying, Lieutenant?" Kirby asked.

"Sir, they might be waiting for Smith and the Congressman to return. I saw the Congressman after the fight with Smith and he time-jumped away. These guys don't know what happened, right? Anyway, we shouldn't be surprised if the Engine comes on during the assault. We captured Smith. So if it lights up, it'll be the Congressman returning."

She's thinking outside the box. Good.

"Good point," McKnight said. "It's worth watching out for. Forewarned is forearmed. Burnette, can you tell your men the time traveler is probably unarmed? Try not to kill him. I'd much rather prosecute him for kidnapping and murder than report his death in the assault."

Burnette nodded. "We'll do our best. But if he makes any threatening moves we'll take him out, no matter who he is."

"Understood."

Kirby pointed a finger at Burnette. "One other thing. We'll do SOP and go on signal, but if the guy guarding the hostages leaves the room, go in and secure the hostages. Once you're in that room with a superior force, they won't consider retaking the hostages. They'll be thinking about their own skins. Got it?"

"Yes, sir."

"Kirby," McKnight said. "What can we do to help?"

"Just sit tight until I send the 'all clear' signal. Let us do our jobs, and we'll get your people and your equipment back." He paused for a second and then smiled. "But thanks, anyway. I know you and your people have a lot at stake here and would love to help."

The assault team left the room.

McKnight and his team donned comm units so they could hear the attack in progress. *This won't take long.*

Kathy and Trevor arrived with the gear they needed to configure the Engine.

McKnight decided Kathy Wu assessed correctly. *Better to try the time leap from here than to disassemble the Engine, transport it, reassemble it and then leap. Especially if Doctor Astalos is hurt or otherwise unable to help.* He shook his head to clear it. *First things first. Let's worry about keeping the hostages safe.*

Five minutes later the teams were in position. Burnette had taken out the sentry without killing him, and there were team members at each window.

McKnight heard Kirby's team members report their ready status. *Won't be long now.*

CHAPTER 31

10:45 p.m. – July 21, 2011 – River North district, Chicago, IL

Blake Phillips was walking as fast as he could down North LaSalle Street. His destination was the warehouse Smith designated as their rendezvous point. The more ground he covered, the angrier he became. Smith promised to solve his problems and, so far, he hadn't come through.

He accompanied Smith back in time to this date and stood on a street, watching the windows of a high-rise apartment building. But nothing happened. Smith told him to watch the windows for the big flash of light of time travel, the girl falling from the balcony and another flash of light. He saw not two, but three flashes. More importantly, no girl. Something went wrong.

He reached the warehouse and slipped down the alley to the loading dock door. After checking again to ensure no one was around, he slipped through the door they pried open earlier. Once inside, he paused to let his eyes adjust to the dim light that filtered through the windows from the street outside.

He heard a sound from the other end of the warehouse. *Smith should be here. I saw the light flash. It must be him.*

"Smith?" he called, as he made his way in the dark toward the rendezvous point at the far end of the warehouse. Now he could make out a shadowy figure walking toward him. *Why didn't Smith say something?* Phillips peered into the dimness, trying to make out Smith's form.

There was motion around the figure's head. *Long hair? It's not Smith!*

He grabbed the return beacon around his neck and pressed it once. As the static electricity spiked up, the time bubble formed. He saw the figure break into a run toward him.

“Shit,” he said, under his breath. The intensity of the light surged, and he realized with relief he would be gone before his potential assailant got close enough to stop him.

The running figure skidded to a halt outside the bubble. Phillips squinted through the bright light. It was a woman in a dark pantsuit. Then the light went out, and he fell backward through a field of stars.

****

<u>10:45 p.m. – July 20, 2036 – Phillips’ warehouse, Old Town Alexandria, VA</u>

The time bubble formed in the warehouse area. As Phillips materialized inside it and became aware of his surroundings, he could see Smith's men standing around the Time Engine. He wondered why there were so few.

The globe of light bulged to twice its previous size and went out. He fell backward, sprawling on the platform. He laid there on the wooden floor for a few seconds, grateful for having escaped.

Smith's second in command, Jones, was among the three men waiting for him.

Phillips rose from the platform. “Where is everybody?” he asked.

“Smith paid them all but twenty-five percent of their pay,” Jones said. “He expected them to hang around for the rest, but I guess most of them decided it was too risky. Good way to save money. Maybe that was part of the plan. Where is he? I thought he'd be coming back with you.”

“He isn't coming. The mission went south. Last time I saw him he was lying on the floor of a warehouse. Maybe dead.”

“Fuck,” Jones said. “We need to get out of here ASAP.”

A door closed and a voice called from the storeroom. "Jones, what the hell's going on?"

"Get back to your post, asshole!" Jones yelled. "I'll keep you posted."

The man across the warehouse showed Jones his middle finger and opened the door to the storeroom. He called out as he tried to pull his weapon off his shoulder. Silhouetted against the light from the room, they could see his body jerking in response to bullets from a silenced automatic weapon. He fell back into the main room and didn't move again.

Jones and the others took cover behind the crates around the machine.

Phillips dropped to the floor and crawled behind one.

A commanding voice came from the storeroom. "United States Marines. Lay down your weapons."

Jones and the others responded by opening fire.

Phillips sprawled on the floor. *No! I can't be caught here. I gotta get out of here!*

A memory flashed through Phillips's mind. When he was eight years old, he overheard his father talking about an escape tunnel added by smugglers in the eighteenth century. His youthful sense of adventure demanded it be found. He found a hidden door in the bathroom and explored the escape tunnel and the sewer beneath. He still remembered the anger in his father's voice and the scolding he received for that dangerous adventure.

Desperate to escape, Phillips leapt up and sprinted for the small bathroom and the escape tunnel. He tore open the bathroom door and went inside. He locked the door and dropped to his knees. Yanking open the cabinet beneath the sink, he breathed a sigh of relief when he saw the tunnel access door. Thank God no one had closed it off in all those years.

He squirmed through the door and pulled himself into the tunnel, almost losing his grip and falling into the filthy sewer below. With any luck, he would get away.

The sound of gunfire stopped. He didn't have much time.

Unlike when he was a child, the water in the tunnel was low – a dank, smelly trickle down the middle of the pipe. The tunnel was smaller than he remembered. He stooped to walk without scraping his head. His mind raced as he moved through the pipe. *If there were people at the warehouse attacking us, then our plans are exposed. If I show up anywhere, I'll be arrested.* He exhaled sharply. *Or eliminated.* The more he thought about it, the more he understood his only option. *Disappear.*

When he reached the end of the pipe, his hopes evaporated. He had forgotten the ancient metal grate that secured the opening to the river.

In frustration, he cursed and kicked the grate with his foot. To his surprise, he felt it give a little. He kicked it again, lost his balance and fell in the foul water. His sweat suit was soaked and covered with filth. He looked up at the gate again and saw it was looser than before. His energy renewed, he jumped up and kicked it again and again.

Finally, the grate swung loose on two rusted hinges. The old metal groaned and creaked as he pushed it open. He clambered his way up the embankment to the wharf.

Bruised and filthy with slime and excrement from his escape, he walked the five blocks to his car. His anger at Smith and his cohorts turned to fear. If captured and exposed, he'd be facing multiple counts of capital murder, not to mention kidnapping charges. If alive, Smith would want to shut him up. He was afraid to think what measures Rho might take to cover his involvement.

Run! He focused on his options for getting out of the country. He had resources he could call on, people who owed him. People who could get him identification and anything else he needed.

He was a survivor. By this time tomorrow, he would be in South America.

****

11:00 p.m. – July 20, 2036 – Phillips' warehouse, Old Town Alexandria, VA

"The warehouse and the hostages are secure, sir," Burnette said, as he met Kirby, McKnight and the rest of the HERO team at the warehouse front door.

Wheeler, Hatcher and Kathy headed for the machine, eager to check it out.

Trevor hung back with McKnight to hear Burnette give status to Kirby.

"Doctor Astalos and two other hostages – a woman and a girl child – are safe. They're over there," Burnette said, pointing. "We encountered five unsubs. Three were dead, one captured and one unaccounted for. We're trying to identify them now."

"One unaccounted for?" Kirby asked.

"Yes, sir. We didn't have the plans for the warehouse before the mission, but I doubt it would have mattered. There was an escape tunnel we didn't know about beforehand. We believe the unsub who got away was Congressman Phillips. He matched the description and arrived through the machine."

"Smith won't be here," McKnight said. "He was time traveling, and we captured him already." Looking at Kirby, he said, "Sorry, Kirby. Your mission."

"Okay," Kirby said, getting back to business with Burnette. "Walk me through it."

"Yes, sir. We had all the storeroom windows and doors covered. We were ready to attack when we had a stroke of luck. The guy watching the hostages left his post to go back into the main room. Sergeant Walton reported that the time machine came on and a man jumped in, so that must have been the reason. Anyway, I gave the 'go' signal, broke the window and crawled through. The guard returned, and Sergeant Callahan took him out. We secured the three hostages–"

"Three?" McKnight interjected. "Which three? We expected four."

"Doctor Astalos, a little girl named Laura and her nanny, a Miss Nancy Fox. The young lady, Miss Chang, was not there. Was that not what you expected?"

McKnight paused and looked up at the rafters above them. "We're too late. We have to do it again."

"What?" Kirby said, looking irritated.

"Nothing yet," McKnight said, holding up his hands. "We need more information. Pardon me, Lieutenant. You secured the hostages?"

"Yes, sir. We secured the hostages and the storeroom." The man turned back to Kirby. "By the time we finished, the mercenaries took cover behind some boxes. We identified ourselves to them, and they responded with fire. We held ours since their cover was right in front of the equipment. Sergeant Walton was in the flanking position and opened fire. He killed one of them and drove the other two out into the open. We opened fire, as did Sergeant Hodge on the other flank. Both men went down. One of them is still alive somehow. There's an ambulance on the way."

"Good," Kirby said. "What about the one that got away?"

"Yes, sir. As I mentioned, the guy bolted for the room on the far wall when the shooting started. We didn't shoot him because we thought it was the Congressman and, therefore, not a threat. We thought we'd have him trapped."

"And?"

"Callahan and two others surrounded the room and called for him to come out. He didn't, so they broke in and found a little door under the sink. The door led to a ladder down into the sewers. Callahan crawled down and tried to find him, but he was gone. He found fresh footprints in the mud outside the culvert, but nothing else."

McKnight turned to Trevor. “Can we get someone looking for the Congressman? He’s no fool. He’s likely on his way out of the country now.”

“Sure can,” Trevor said. He turned aside to make the call.

“Thank you, Lieutenant,” Kirby said. “Well done. Post sentries, just in case we get more company and have the rest of the team stand down over there.” He waved his arm at the far side of the warehouse, away from the equipment. “Depending on Major McKnight, we may have more work to do.”

“Yes, sir,” Burnette said. He executed a perfect about face and strode away barking orders to his team.

McKnight nodded. “Let's find Doctor Astalos and see what he has to say.”

McKnight and Kirby walked across the expanse of the warehouse, headed for the storeroom. Trevor followed them talking quietly into his phone.

As they entered the room they found Astalos, Laura and Nancy sitting on a sofa. Astalos sat between the two, his arms around them both and their heads resting on his chest.

The Marine charged with guarding them saluted as McKnight and Kirby entered. “At ease, Sergeant,” Kirby said. “Assemble in the main area with the team.”

“Yes, sir.” The Marine saluted again and left the room after a nod at Astalos.

Astalos disentangled himself from the others, stood and stepped toward McKnight. There were tears in his eyes. “Marc, I'm so sorry for all the trouble I've caused.”

“What do you mean, sir?”

“They killed General Drake and Sergeant Major Clary to get me and the Engine.”

“None of that is your fault, Doctor.”

“It's my Engine, isn't it? They killed Mike and all those other men because of me. They came up with this plot, and none of it would have happened if I hadn't built it.”

Astalos wrung his hands and stared at the floor. “I shouldn't have helped them, but...I should have let them kill us rather than permit this. I was so afraid for…” He choked up, and his tears glistened on his cheeks.

His hand trembled as he gestured back at Laura. “My child...I fear I have lived way too long.”

“Robert?” McKnight said, and waited for Astalos to meet his gaze. “All of you are safe now. But we’re only half done. Now we need to go back and prevent the convoy’s ambush. You can help undo all that happened.”

Astalos took a deep breath. It seemed as if he was starved for oxygen, and the breath rejuvenated him.

“What can I do to help?” he asked.

“Hatcher and Wheeler are already checking out the Engine, and Doctor Wu has all the configurations worked out. I'm sure they'd love to have your help.”

“I can do that. Marc, you understand you need to rescue them again, right?” He pointed at his daughter and Nancy.

“Yes, I do. Even if I stop the attack, they still kidnapped them beforehand, and they will still have them here. And Amy Chang, too. I have to go back early enough to stop the attack, and also get a rescue mission over here. The good news is, we know where the Smith and his team will be at a certain time so we could rescue the hostages while they’re elsewhere. With General Drake's help, we can catch the bad guys in position for the ambush, too.”

“There is another risk,” Astalos said.

“What's that, sir?”

“If you jump from here, and stop the Engine from being stolen, then it won't be here anymore. It'll be back at the lab. We've never tried a jump where the Engine has been moved before departure and returned. When you use the return beacon, it's supposed to reach out and look for the Engine's signature and home in on it. But we've never tested it. It should work, but I can't guarantee it. Oh, wait!"

The old man held up his hand. "The Engine should be down, right? It'll be packed up, ready for the move to DLA HQ."

"Yes, but not the one here in this time." McKnight gestured at the Engine. "It's here and operational. Won't that work?"

"Yes, of course. Yes, I think we have a plan."

"Good. Can you assist Wheeler and Hatcher in getting the machine ready?"

"It should be ready now, provided no one put a bullet in it. I'll go check it and do the configuration. It should take about fifteen minutes."

"Good. Thanks for your help. By the way, Robby should be here soon. Tyler went to Finland to get him. It's a good thing, too. There was an attempt on his life."

"Is he all right?"

"Yes, he's fine, but he was worried about you and Laura." McKnight paused and put his hand on Astalos's shoulder. "He told us about Adele. I'm terribly sorry."

"Thank you, Marc. I appreciate it."

"Well," McKnight said. "We've all become somewhat of a family here. You guys are all I have." His voice caught. He felt his emotions rising to the surface.

"I feel the same way, Marc."

"Well, anyway…" He patted Astalos's shoulder. "Let's get this done and set things right."

"Yes, let's fix it. Thanks." The old man strode out of the room.

McKnight saw renewed vigor and energy in the old man's step as he walked away. *Purpose does that for you.*

McKnight glanced at Laura and Nancy. The older woman had pulled her niece into her embrace and was gently cooing and rocking the little girl.

He turned and left the room. He found his way to the office and sent status to Senator Lodge and General Flynn. Then he sat down to record the case activities through his phone, knowing it would all disappear if his mission succeeded. *But if it didn't...*

Don't think about that. He relaxed and let training take over. *Document and save.* When he completed the task, he transmitted the report to the HERO server at the lab. Now, he was ready to act.

He realized he forgot to ask Doctor Astalos an important question. He found him where he expected, huddled over the Engine with Wheeler and Hatcher.

As he approached, Astalos looked up from his comp pad and smiled. "Good news, Major. One bullet hole, but it went straight through the power cabinet without impacting the equipment. The Engine is ready to go."

"That's great news, Doctor. I have a question for your daughter or Nancy."

"Three," Astalos said, as he typed on his comp pad.

"What?"

"You were going to ask them how many men were left to guard them during the raid on the convoy."

"Yes."

"Three."

"How did you know I was going to ask that?"

"You needed to know it, right?"

McKnight rubbed his nose and then stood with his hands on his hips. "Of course."

"It made sense you'd need to know so I asked." The old man smiled. "I wouldn't have let you leave here without telling you. But, they didn't know where they were in the building. All they knew was that they heard our Mr. Smith tell three men to stay there and watch them."

McKnight smiled. "Thanks, Doc." He looked around. "Can you, Trevor and Kathy handle this end? I want to take Hatcher and Wheeler with me to work out the details."

Astalos spread his arms and turned from side to side, as if to embrace the Engine and everything around it, and he grinned. "Hey, what am I? A rookie? I only invented the damned thing." He waved McKnight away. 'Get out of here. I got this."

Hatcher and Wheeler exchanged grins.

McKnight chuckled and waved for the two lieutenants to follow him to the warehouse office.

CHAPTER 32

12:33 a.m. – July 21, 2036 – Phillips' Warehouse, Old Town Alexandria, VA

McKnight, Hatcher and Wheeler sat in the tiny warehouse office. There was a knock on the door.

"In," McKnight said. The door opened, and Tyler stuck his head in.

"May I join you?" he said.

"Yes, Captain," McKnight said. "Welcome back. How's Robby?"

Tyler came inside and sat on the desk. "He's fine. He made a beeline for Laura when he got here. Then he and Robert started talking. Comparing notes, I'm sure." He gave a wave of acknowledgement to Hatcher and Wheeler.

"Good. You get any sleep?"

"Yes, about five hours on the way back."

"Want to go with us to stop the convoy?"

"Yes, sir, I do."

"Okay. Tell Doctor Wu to configure the Engine for the four of us. When you get back, we'll review the plan."

"Will do." Tyler left the room.

"Here's how I see it," McKnight said. "I got to the office at about oh-five-thirty yesterday morning. Before the convoy left the lab. Doctor Astalos and General Drake were already here. So were Hatcher and the load team. The convoy left at about oh seven hundred. If it were any other situation, I think we would need at least two hours or maybe more to get organized to capture Smith's team *and* free the hostages. Get there early, call in the Marines and hit this warehouse."

"But this isn't a normal situation, right?" Tyler asked.

"Right. They got word from our saboteur, whoever it is—"

"Cindy," Hatcher said. "I'd bet my bars on it."

"Maybe. Where is she, by the way?"

"I talked to the guy tailing her about twenty minutes ago, sir," she said. "She's at home, playing with her phone. It appears she's reading and texting. We're trying to get a trace fix or data capture on her phone, but no success so far. I've never heard of a phone signal that can't be found. Weird."

"How did she react when you told her to take the rest of the day off?"

Hatcher shrugged. "She thanked me for giving her some of her Sunday back. She said she only came in because Wheeler asked her to bring in breakfast for the team at the last minute. Then she left."

"Did Wheeler corroborate that?"

"Yes, sir. He told me he realized last night he didn't have time to do it and called her."

"Sounds legit. Anything so far? Do we have any evidence she has done anything wrong or has been less than truthful with us?"

"No, sir. She looks squeaky clean. But she feels… off. There's more to her than we're seeing."

"Okay," McKnight said. "We'll come back to that. They knew which vehicles to attack and which ones held the General and Doctor Astalos. We get everyone in the office into the same room together and stay there until after the attack. Then we go to the warehouse to rescue the hostages. We might take along some help from the team."

"What are you saying, sir?" Hatcher asked. "Do we travel back to the moment that the convoy starts?"

"No. Twenty minutes before. We need to get there in time to stop the convoy, keep everyone safe and then get over here while all the bad guys are still in position for the ambush."

"Sounds good," Tyler said. "But if Smith got word about the convoy and this time they don't, what do they do? If I were them and I didn't get word, I'd assume things went south and bolt. I'd head back to the warehouse and reassess. That would at least put us up against a superior force and maybe get the hostages killed."

McKnight considered this. "I think you're on track, Captain. If we go back twenty minutes before they leave, is there any way to mitigate that risk?"

"I don't see how. They get word or they don't. I guess the real question is when do they get that word? Do they get it before the convoy departs or does the traitor call after the convoy leaves?

"Okay, let's switch it around." He turned toward the others. "Hatcher? Wheeler? If you were the bad guys, how would you do it? When would you want to get the word?"

Hatcher looked at Wheeler, then turned back to McKnight. "I wouldn't want to hear at the last minute. If I did, and my team is out of position, I would only have five minutes or less to adjust the plan. Not good."

"Yes," Wheeler said. "I think I'd want an earlier call to give the lineup and then be ready for a last-minute call if anything had changed. That way, you can plan for the attack but be ready to make adjustments if you get the follow-up call."

McKnight turned back to Tyler. "There you have it. What do you think?"

"I see it," Tyler said. "We go back at the fifteen-minute mark, pull the team including Cindy together to prevent any more communication, sic the marines on the attack team and get our butts over to the warehouse? No, there's a better plan."

"Tell me."

"I'm surprised we didn't think of it before. Where were you at this time yesterday?"

"At my apartment. Asleep. I see where you're going."

"Me, too," Hatcher said. "You go back by yourself and tell yourself what happened. Lay out all the details. Your other self will call General Drake who makes a few calls, gets the Marines involved to hit both places, or maybe catches them all at the warehouse and prevents a pitched battle down on Telegraph Road."

"Close, Lieutenant," Tyler said. "An assault on the warehouse would give us a good chance to catch all the bad guys, but there's more danger for the hostages. I'd be inclined to wait for the bad guys to leave, and catch them on the way to the scene, and then hit the warehouse when they only have a small guard detail. We can still prevent the pitched battle by capturing them on the way. A sort of reverse ambush."

"I like it," McKnight said. "Do we have coordinates to send me to my place?"

"Yes, sir," Wheeler said. "Doctor Wu mandated we collect the home coordinates for everyone on the team right after she got here."

Tyler laughed. "Well, don't forget to tell yourself to reassemble the Engine and turn it on."

"I won't. Hopefully, we'll have this behind us by tomorrow. Let's get moving. Lieutenant Wheeler, please tell Doctor Wu to reconfigure the Engine to send one person. Me. Back twenty-four hours to my place."

"Yes, sir," Wheeler said. He saluted and left the office.

"Lieutenant Hatcher, I should be back in about an hour. Meet me back at the lab. Please make sure that Doctor Astalos, Robby and the girls make it home okay."

"Yes, sir."

McKnight leaned back and put his hands behind his head. "Lieutenant?"

"Yes, sir?"

"What have we left out?"

Hatcher looked thoughtful, then smiled. "The saboteur, sir. What about the saboteur? We still haven't addressed that aspect."

"Right. That's what I need you to do. We need to address that first. There's no telling what mischief that asshole might get into if we don't take steps. We know about when the old machine was damaged, right?"

"Well, yes, sir. It was rigged to short circuit as soon as we applied power to it."

"Right. And when was the last time it worked?"

"Day before yesterday when we tested it before packing up the new one."

"Okay, so you know what you have to do?"

Hatcher leapt to her feet. She was almost gleeful. "Yes, *sir!* I'll travel back to the day before yesterday, hide out in the lab and watch the Engine."

"And?"

"After it gets sabotaged, I'll leap back to here at the exact time I left and give my report."

"Good. And no interference, right? As big as the temptation will be to take out the saboteur, you need to leave him…or her…for later."

"Yes, sir."

"Perfect, Lieutenant. Then I'll report your finding and everything to my other self. On your way."

"Yes, sir." She saluted, executed a perfect about-face and left the office.

Tyler chuckled. "You were right," he said.

"What?"

Tyler smiled. "When you picked those two."

"Yup. I've patted myself on the back on a weekly basis since then."

"That's what I like about you, Marc. You're so humble."

McKnight smiled and said, "Ain't it the truth?"

Tyler laughed. "What can I do, sir?" he asked.

McKnight switched back to mission mode. "Glad you asked, Captain. We're flying blind here. We didn't take the time to see what shape history is in right now. There's been so much going back and forth, who knows what problems we've caused with our travel, let alone Smith and his. He's in custody now. But as soon as we prevent the convoy attack, that timeline disappears. He'll still be free and dangerous in this timeline. Who knows how he'll react when his plans go to shit?"

"Yes, sir."

"Can you get with Doctor Wu and try to figure out what we can expect from him? It would be nice if we can anticipate where he'll be next and stop him before he has time to think and make new plans."

"Yes, sir. On my way." Tyler rose, saluted, and left the office.

McKnight turned back to the desk and started his list. He wrote down all the things he needed to tell his earlier self about the attack and what to do to prevent it. He knew himself well. Once he made the list of items to cover and looked at it, he wouldn't need it.

When he completed the list, he leaned back in the chair and closed his eyes. He ran through the list once more in his mind. *Got it. Now I need ten minutes of sleep.* He set the timer in his phone and set it on the table beside him. He closed his eyes and relaxed. Now that he had a plan, sleep came fast.

CHAPTER 33

1:48 a.m. – July 21, 2036 – Phillips' Warehouse, Old Town Alexandria, VA

When he awoke, McKnight went to find Hatcher. She was stuffing provisions for two days into a small satchel. *She's been awake and active for over eighteen hours. And now she's going on a surveillance mission. Not an optimal situation.*

"How's it going, Lieutenant?" he asked.

"I'm good, sir. Ready to go."

"Tired?"

"No, sir. I'm one hundred percent." She buckled the satchel and slung it over her shoulder.

"Hold on. You need another piece of equipment." He stepped over to the miscellaneous gear cabinet and pulled out a small box.

"Ah, good idea," she said, as he handed it to her. She opened the box and pulled out a surveillance motion detector. She checked the batteries, then slipped it into her satchel.

"Try to get a little sleep as soon as you can. The detector will help, so use it and be smart. Get rest and stay sharp."

"Yes, sir."

"One more thing, Hatcher. Remember, you are there to observe, not prevent. You'll want to take out the saboteur and reverse the event. Don't give in to that want. Stick to the mission. We have a plan now and any intervention on your part might screw it up."

"Yes, sir, I copy. I got it when you said that a while ago."

McKnight shrugged. "Better you hear it twice than not at all."

"Yes, sir. I'll do you proud, sir."

"I know you will. I'll see you back here in about ten minutes, my time." He waved at the Engine. "On your way."

She saluted and stepped onto the platform. She turned back toward McKnight. The travel beacon resting on her uniform breast reflected light like a silver pendant. She waved and nodded to Kathy, who stood at the console with the Engine trigger in her hand.

"Okay, we are green across the board," Kathy said. "Target destination is July Seventeen, 2036, at oh two hundred hours. Power requirement is high but still in the green range. Traveler, please acknowledge."

Hatcher knelt, stretched her hands out before her and nodded.

"We go in five... four... three... two... one... zero." She pressed the trigger, and the hum of the Engine ramped up, filling the big room with static electricity. The bubble of light formed around her, and her raven hair whipped and swirled violently around her face.

The bubble grew so bright he could barely look at it, but McKnight saw the determined look on Hatcher's face and… a smile. He wished he could go with her. *Don't be stupid. You can't do it all yourself. Use your resources. That's leadership.*

The bubble of light surged outward and dissipated. The room seemed dark now. She would be back any moment now.

****

<u>2:00 a.m. – July 18, 2036 – HERO lab - Defense Logistics Agency Satellite Office Building, Telegraph Road, Alexandria, VA</u>

Hatcher fell backward through the star field. The fall was brief and void of cognizant thought. Nothing but the awareness of falling and stars speeding past. The spinning globe of light formed, bulged, and disappeared, leaving her on the steel platform in the HERO lab. She stood and did a slow, 360-degree turn to check the environment.

The only light in the room came from a few security lights recessed in the ceiling thirty feet above her. It seemed alien for this busy place to be dark and quiet. In the stillness, she heard the antique analog clock ticking softly on the wall of Doctor Astalos's office.

She selected a hiding place before she traveled. She turned on her penlight and shined it up at the roof hatch, then traced the steel staircase down for there. From the hatch, the stairs dropped eight feet to a catwalk attached to the wall. The catwalk led to the room's southwest corner, turned left for ten feet, then yielded to a steel staircase of thirty steps that reached to the floor.

She shined the light back up to the catwalk. There, in the southwest corner, was a cubic recessed area about four feet deep and four feet square. Just as she remembered it. She guessed the space was intended to be a storage area, but was never built out.

She switched off her light and went to the sink to get paper towels. After wetting half of them, she tiptoed up the stairs to her intended hideout. As she expected, it was full of dust, so she used the paper towels to wipe it down. Satisfied, she crawled into the area and pulled out her water bottle. She took a sip and stowed it. While this little hiding place was the perfect platform for surveilling the lab below, she expected it to be an uncomfortable place to spend the next few hours. Or days.

With a sigh, she broke out the motion detector McKnight gave her. She crawled out of her hiding place onto the catwalk and clipped the sensor to the edge. After she pointed it toward the old Engine in the room below, she plugged the speaker wire into the unit. *Now for a test.*

She slipped the earpiece into position, balled up the used paper towels and tossed them toward the old Engine. The paper ball passed in front of the sensor to the floor below. A soft beeping sound came from the earpiece.

Hatcher smiled. *He knew I needed rest.* She removed the earpiece and tiptoed down the stairs. She retrieved the ball of wet paper and tossed it in the trash. After one final look around, she climbed the stairs to her temporary home.

Slipping the earpiece back in place, she curled up in the confined space and fell asleep.

****

6:35 a.m. – July 20, 2036 – HERO lab - Defense Logistics Agency Satellite Office Building, Telegraph Road, Alexandria, VA

Two days passed, and nothing happened. Down below her, she saw the team, including herself, getting ready for the convoy. Her emotions tugged at her. She wanted to run down the stairs and warn them of the impending disaster. It was hard for her to sit and not act.

She shifted position, trying to get a better view of the room below without drawing attention to herself. Struggling to remain calm, she took a deep breath and let it out slowly.

She watched Wheeler knock on the door of Astalos's office, stick his head in, then walk away, leaving the door ajar.

Doctor Astalos, Sergeant Clary and General Drake came out of the office.

General Drake!

Her mind flashed back to four days ago–seeing their bodies lying in a ditch surrounded by grass and dirt stained with their life's blood. The urge to run down the stairs returned. She pushed it to the back of her mind with effort.

Hatcher reminded herself to stay focused. Nothing for two days. It had to be soon. When they came back from the convoy, there would be too much traffic in the lab. No opportunity to sabotage the Engine.

Everyone moved to the doors and went outside except for McKnight, who sat at the table.

Abruptly, he pulled his phone out of his back pocket and spoke into it. She couldn't hear what he said, but he stood and paced while on the call. He disconnected and placed a call.

Wheeler came back into the room. *Ah, yes. The call was about Smith being attacked.* After a short conversation, Wheeler dashed out of the lab into the office area. She remembered nearly bumping into him in the hallway.

She waited. McKnight's phone rang again. *This must be the call from Kathy.* She saw herself step into the room.

McKnight pointed at her other self and said, "Weapons!" She turned and sprinted through the glass doors. Moments later, she returned with machine pistols and side arms. They strapped on the weapons and ran out the door.

Hatcher leaned back in her little box and wept silent tears for the men who would die in mere minutes.

The surveillance monitor that beeped constantly for the last hour was now silent. Time was short. She was feeling stiff and cramped. She had barely moved for two days except for stealing down to the bathroom late at night.

Doubt crept in. What if no one showed up? Had their logic been faulty? Could the Engine have been tampered with already? Her imagination began to run wild. If it was already set up, that meant it had been sabotaged before her watch, which meant Wheeler was the culprit. She shook her head, refusing to consider that.

Did we somehow cause this ourselves? She grew angry. *Stop it!* She pushed the negative thoughts away and breathed slowly and deeply to calm herself.

The motion detector beeped once, and Hatcher froze. *Here we go.*

With a slow, deliberate motion, she leaned forward and peeped out from her space. Cindy Ginn stood by the lab door with a paper cup in one hand and a screwdriver and metal strip in the other. She was motionless for a moment, sipping from the cup. Then she crumpled the cup, tossed it in the trash can and strode to the old Engine.

She pulled out her phone and made a call. It lasted only five seconds. Hatcher couldn't hear what she said, but she broke the connection almost immediately and turned her attention to the Engine.

The entire event took three minutes. Cindy expertly removed the access panel to the wiring compartment. She pulled a cloth from her pocket and wiped the strip down, positioned it inside the compartment and replaced the panel. Finally, she wiped down all spots she had touched on the panel and left the room.

Hatcher's temper boiled over. She wanted to run down the hall after Ginn, beat her senseless and tie her up for McKnight to find when he returned. Reason and discipline slowly overcame her rage.

We'll get her. There's still time. She gathered her gear and walked down the stairs to stand in the middle of the room.

She glanced at the glass doors again and then at the loading dock door, knowing she and the others would be returning soon. And the General would be dead. She tried to fight it off, but a tear ran down her cheek.

"Dammit," she whispered, and wiped her sleeve across her eyes.

She walked to the trash can, removed the crumpled cup and pushed it into her pocket. She looked back at the lab doors.

"I'm coming for you, bitch," she said softly, and squeezed the control beacon once.

CHAPTER 34

1:50 a.m. – July 21, 2036 – Phillips' warehouse, Old Town Alexandria, VA

McKnight could already feel the tickle of increased static electricity in the air. Hatcher was returning. The globe of light formed, and he saw a figure inside it.

After a moment, the figure solidified and he saw raven hair swirling around the face inside the sparkling, spinning globe of air. As the globe bulged and went out, Hatcher stood.

McKnight and Kathy rushed onto the platform. Kathy tried to take Hatcher's arm to steady her. Hatcher shrugged her off. "I'm fine. Don't fuss." Kathy nodded, smiled at the younger woman and left the platform.

"Are you all right?" McKnight asked.

"Yes, sir."

"Get any sleep?"

"Some, sir." She remembered herself and came to attention with a salute. "Yes, *sir*."

McKnight returned the salute and said, "As you were. Report, Lieutenant."

"Yes, sir. The server was sabotaged after you and I left to chase the convoy. It was Cindy, sir."

"Cindy?" he asked. In his mind, he breathed a sigh in relief. *Of course. Who else could it be?* She was the only stranger in their midst. He was relieved the traitor wasn't one of his own team.

"Yes, sir. She's never been a secretary. My opinion, sir, but she got into the Engine and out in less than three minutes. She knew what she was doing."

"You think she's an engineer?"

"Yes, sir, I do. Or well trained in sabotage."

"Okay. Thank you, Lieutenant. I'll relay all that to... me."

Despite her fatigue and anger, she smiled.

"You need rest," he said. "And so do Robby and Robert Astalos. I'll ask Wheeler to take them home to rest. I'm sure they'll want to move the Engine to DLA HQ ASAP."

"Yes, sir."

He waved her and the others over to the pile of crates next to the Engine. He laid his comp pad on top and opened a file.

"Okay," he said. "I want to go over the things I need to relay to myself in the past. First, there will be an attack on the convoy to steal the Engine, led by Smith and planned by Congressman Phillips. Second, I need to pass on the location of the warehouse and the number of people guarding the hostages. We have a good idea of the size of the attack team based on the evidence. Third, we know Smith's team regrouped at the warehouse after the assault and then dissipated, but we don't know what they'll do if the event doesn't happen. And fourth, I need to pass on the word that Cindy is the traitor."

"What?" Trevor said. "Cindy? Are you sure?"

"No question," McKnight said.

"I find that hard to believe."

"It's a fact, sir," Hatcher added. "I witnessed it myself."

"There's no doubt?"

"No question," McKnight said.

Wheeler spoke up. "I can't think of anything else, sir. You have it covered. But I do have a question. What do you plan to do? Are you going to stay in the past for a while and help? Or are you coming right back to the present?"

"I'm not sure yet. I don't want to get in the way or change something, but I don't want to come back if there's information that's critical but hasn't been shared. I'll play it by ear."

"In the meantime, make no moves and don't reveal to our friend, Cindy, that we're on to her unless it becomes clear she's about to run. Understood?" Heads nodded around the room.

"Okay, Doctor Wu. Is the Engine ready for my jump back to my apartment about twenty-four hours ago?"

"Yes, sir. We're ready when you are."

"Very well." He rose from the table and walked to the platform.

Wheeler handed McKnight the control beacon, and he hung it around his neck.

McKnight knelt on the platform as Wheeler and Kathy took their normal positions at the Engine controller and ran through the checklist.

McKnight struggled to relax. The thought of facing himself was unsettling. *I can do this. I'm up to this. Piece of cake. No problem.*

He realized Kathy was speaking to him. He broke away from his thoughts and focused on her. *What did she say?*

"Major, are you ready to go?" Concern tinged her voice.

He nodded. "Yes. I'm ready."

Wheeler pushed the trigger. The Engine hummed to life and the travel process began. He could make out his team through the spinning globe of light, standing there, trusting him to get the job done and hoping for success.

Then came the stars of time travel.

He fell backward when he landed and rolled over to a kneeling position. He looked up to see, inches from his face, the business end of a Glock 21SF pistol.

CHAPTER 35

12:15 a.m. – July 20, 2036 – Major McKnight's apartment, Alexandria, VA

McKnight awoke with a start. It took a moment to get his bearings, to realize he was in his own apartment. He sat up on the side of the bed. The clock on his dresser displayed the time in pale green letters. It was oh-two-fifteen hours.

He had that same dream again. It was the only thing he dreamed about. He was back in that dark hallway again—the one with several doors and low hanging lamps every fifteen feet. As usual, he was out of breath and stressed. He knew somehow that escape lay beyond the door at the end of the hall, and he had to get through it. He took a deep breath and told himself to move, but fear paralyzed him. Willing himself to overcome it, he sprinted down the hallway. He was farther down the hall than ever before. *I'll make it this time.*

Something snagged his arm and threw him off balance. He staggered and went down as he felt strong hands grip his biceps and forearms. His arms were pinned against his side and his hands pulled behind his back as he was pulled to his feet.

He looked down the hall for the man who always appeared. It seemed to take longer this time, but a dark figure emerged from the shadows. He could make out none of the man's features as he advanced through alternating areas of deep shadow and harsh light bulbs. He wore a fedora pulled low over his eyes so a little light would fall on the tip of his nose, but nothing else. And, he carried the same ancient Webley pistol he carried in every version of the dream.

The man stopped five feet from McKnight. For a few moments, he stood there.

Abruptly, he strode the last two steps to McKnight and snatched the control beacon from around his neck. "You won't be needing this, Major," he said, as he shoved the beacon and chain into his pocket. "Take him, lads."

With that, strong hands dragged McKnight in the opposite direction and into darkness.

The dream always ended that way. He was sure it meant something, but he told no one about it. As usual, he could not go back to sleep for a while. He stood and stretched. Checking the time again, he entered his closet and slipped on a pair of jeans, some moccasins and a tee shirt. *Might as well read something.*

He poured himself a glass of ice water and sat on the sofa. He pulled up his email on his phone.

In a few hours, they would move the Engine to their permanent offices in the DLA complex. Tyler and Wheeler had done a good job setting it up. Wheeler and Hatcher were gaining the skills they needed to advance. They would both make Captain this year. Tyler had been promoted earlier this year.

He felt the hair on his arm stand up. *Static electricity. Somebody's jumping in.*

Had Smith made another trip to this time to take him out before traveling to kill Amy? He ran into the bedroom for his weapon. Had the would-be assassin made a mistake, jumping in later rather than earlier? He couldn't imagine Smith would make that kind of error.

He drew his weapon from the bedside table, checked the magazine, and drew back the slide to chamber a round. When he came out of the bedroom, a spinning globe of light formed. The figure inside was kneeling. The globe surged outward and disappeared. He leapt forward to confront and subdue the time traveler.

****

12:31 a.m. – July 20, 2036 – Major McKnight's apartment, Alexandria, VA

Present McKnight looked down the barrel of his weapon at the man who time-jumped into his living room. His own face looked up at him.

"When are you coming from?" he asked, lowering his weapon.

"Tomorrow," Future McKnight said. "Mind if I get up?"

Present McKnight offered his hand and helped the other man up. "Why are you here?"

"To warn you," Future McKnight said. "The mystery of all this, the Amy Chang thing, comes together later today. And it isn't pretty."

"Tell me."

"We were wondering where Smith got his Engine." He checked the time on his phone. "Kathy figures it out a little while from now, but too late. They ambush the convoy on the way to DLA HQ today. Very professional. They get the Engine and Doctor Astalos."

"How bad?"

"Thirteen dead."

Present McKnight frowned, and his face was a picture of sorrow. "Wheeler? He was going along."

"No. I pulled him at the last minute to chase an attempt on Smith's life. He's okay."

"Other than Astalos and Wheeler, there were eleven people planned for the convoy. You pulled Wheeler, but still thirteen are dead. Who else got killed?"

Future McKnight paused. His voice cracked as he spoke. "The General and Sergeant Major Clary. They decided to ride along with Astalos at the last minute."

Present McKnight swore and looked up at the ceiling with tears in his eyes. He didn't attempt to hide them.

He motioned Future McKnight to the sofa and sat next to him. "Okay, give me everything. How do I prevent this?"

Future McKnight filled him in on the details.

"Okay. I need to call the General. We need to get troops involved. I'd like to catch these guys in the act."

"Me, too. But there's more. They get word."

"Yeah? I was pretty sure there was a traitor in our group. Who is it?"

"Cindy."

"The receptionist? She didn't seem the type."

Future McKnight frowned. "All of us missed it except for Kathy and Hatcher. They were suspicious of her from the start. I thought it might be jealousy, but it's confirmed. Later today, we find out she short-circuits the electronics in the old Engine. Hatcher took a trip back and observed her in the act. As a matter of fact, Hatcher's here now, hiding in the lab and observing. But the sabotage hasn't happened yet. When it does, though, it's a quick and professional job. No fingerprints or anything."

"Should we pick her up now?"

"Your call. But we're pretty sure she gave the convoy lineup to Smith. No way she could know in advance so she must have observed it and called him just before the assault. If he doesn't get that call…"

"Then he knows the jig is up. I need to wait to pick her up until she gives the word. Then we'll be sure Smith and his team will be in place."

Future McKnight considered this. "Maybe not. Another option might be to intercept Smith and his team in their vehicles on the way to the scene… if we have time. You'd be more likely to have them contained and prevent a battle in a residential area. But, they may already be in position. I would be. We do, however, want to catch Cindy sending word if we can. Up to this point, we don't have anything on her that isn't circumstantial."

"Okay, I'll see what I can do. What about Amy Chang? Do we know where she's being held?"

"Yes. In the home base. And there's more."

“What?” McKnight slid to the edge of the sofa and half-turned toward the mirror image of himself.

Future McKnight paused. “Smith had expert help to time-travel. He stole the new Engine, and it was Robert Astalos who provided that help.”

Present McKnight looked up sharply. “Why? Why would Astalos turn traitor?”

“He didn't. Smith had additional hostages. Believe it or not, Astalos has a daughter. Smith kidnapped her.”

“A what?”

“You heard me,” Future McKnight said. “There's also a guardian, a lady of his acquaintance who is raising his daughter. Amy and those two are being held at the base during the assault. If possible, we want the bad guys to believe everything's okay and head out to do the assault so you can hit the base and rescue them.”

“A daughter? His? Or Robby's? Or Rob's for that matter?”

“Yes. Doesn’t matter. Family.”

Present McKnight pulled on his lower lip. “Too many variables. We hit the team and Cindy at the same time and as soon as possible. If we wait and try to get cute, we might let things go to the point we can't prevent the attack or loss of hostages. What do you think?”

“You're probably right.”

“Okay. Where do we start?”

Future McKnight rubbed his temples and then his eyes with the heels of his hands.

“You look beat,” Present McKnight said. “When did you sleep last?”

“You just woke up, right? You’re not going back to sleep, are you?”

Present McKnight shook his head.

“Right. It’s okay. I’ll catch up when we’re done. We need to find out where Cindy and the assault team are right now. Cindy should be easy; Hatcher put someone on her. The assault team is either at the warehouse, in route to the attack site or already in place. We need to get both under surveillance and then look for opportunity. If we can catch the team in route, that's the best option. The warehouse is next best, even though it's more dangerous for the hostages. At the attack site is the worst scenario. They'll be in position, and we'll never catch them all. Not to mention the possibility of a pitched battle in a DC suburb."

"Yeah, you have a point there."

Future McKnight handed McKnight a data pin for his phone. "All addresses and details, along with a timeline, are on the pin. Check it to make sure you can read the data."

Present McKnight inserted the data pin into his phone and tapped in his access code. He studied it for a moment. "Looks like it's all here."

Future McKnight stood. "I'm going back. Make me proud," he said with a smile.

"You bet. Thanks for the heads-up." Present McKnight watched as the other pressed the control beacon once. After a few moments, the bubble expanded, and he saw himself disappear with a flash.

For a moment, he stood there in his living room. It seemed darker than ever before, but it was his eyes recovering from the brightness of the time bubble. *What do I do first?*

He asked the Telextravision to call the General.

CHAPTER 36

4:10 a.m. – July 20, 2036 – Phillips' warehouse, Old Town Alexandria, VA

The Chairman of the Joint Chiefs of Staff scrambled Quantico's Hostage Rescue. In less than an hour, Kirby's team surrounded the warehouse.

Microphones and surveillance cameras penetrated three locations along the edge of the warehouse. Kirby and Burnette observed and developed the best opportunity for capture of the mercenaries.

In the alley behind the warehouse, an old school bus waited to carry the mercenaries to the ambush site. Once they loaded onto the bus, they were vulnerable to capture. Kirby led the Falcon team to the warehouse roof to provide elevated positions and had two other vehicles ready to pin the bus in the alley. The result would be an efficient kill box. Burnette assembled the Rescue team outside the storeroom where the hostages were held.

Kirby's men pulled back from the alley to avoid contact before the mercenaries boarded the bus.

Their surveillance paid off as Kirby watched the mercenaries jog out and climb into the bus. When the driver boarded, he whispered into his comm unit. "Target is moving. Go Falcon, go Rescue."

From opposite directions, two troop carriers turned into the alley. The bus was boxed in, trapped behind the warehouse. Three spotlights came on and illuminated the bus and the surrounding area.

Kirby turned on his loudspeaker and spoke: "Attention the bus. This is the United States Marines. You are surrounded by superior firepower on high ground. Surrender or pay the consequences. Leave your weapons and gear on the bus and come out with your hands on top of your head."

Kirby could hear voices inside the bus.

Kirby spoke again, pleading with the men in the bus. "Don't be foolish. There's no reason to die today. You are completely boxed in. There's no way out. Surrender or die."

More voices from inside the bus.

"Attention the bus," Kirby called. "Do you surrender? There's nowhere to go."

A voice called from the bus door. "We surrender. We're coming out. Don't shoot."

"Put your hands on top of your head," Kirby said. "Make no sudden moves. Come off the bus and line up outside it."

Twenty men climbed out of the bus and lined up against it. Kirby rappelled off the roof and dispatched a squad to frisk and cuff them.

Kirby spoke to the first man. "Who's in charge here?"

The man shrugged. "I don't know what you mean. We were just going for a bus tour of Alexandria when you guys showed up."

Kirby smiled. "I hope it was worth it." Kirby turned to the squad leader. "Lieutenant, clear the bus."

****

When Kirby gave the "Go, Rescue" order, Burnette peeked through the window at the hostages. There were three guards watching the hostages. From his vantage point, he could see an elderly man, two women and a little girl. His squad waited by the windows. Three sharpshooters trained their guns on the guards.

When the guards heard Kirby's loudspeaker, they panicked and moved to grab the hostages for protection. Burnette spoke quietly into his comm unit. "Shoot."

Three silenced weapons fired as one and the guards went down. The women and the child screamed and the old man ducked.

Two Marines broke a window and climbed into the room with the hostages while the squad provided cover. The hostages looked at them with fear until they identified themselves. One of the Marines checked the guards, pushing their weapons away from their bodies. He need not have bothered. The other Marine went to the storeroom door and cautiously looked out into the main room. Then he waved at Burnette. All clear.

Burnette nodded and waved the rest of the team through the window and into the storeroom. "Secure the warehouse." He walked around the building to find Kirby.

Kirby was standing by the bus. He saluted and said, "Hostages are secure, sir. No losses on our side. Three enemy casualties, all dead."

Kirby nodded. "Thank you, Lieutenant. No losses on either side here."

"Any clue what all this is about, sir?"

"Just what I told you in the briefing. I'll tell you what, though… These guys weren't your average terrorists."

"What do you mean, sir?"

"Come look at this." They walked to the rear of the bus, where four Marines were unloading and cataloging gear. "What's the tally, Gunny?"

A sergeant with a clipboard looked up at Kirby. "So far we have twenty Minimores, four rocket launchers, good quality comm gear, and a shitload of ammunition. These guys came to party, sir."

"Any maps or anything that might suggest a target?"

"Yes, sir. We found three copies of an assault plan. Looks like they planned to hit a convoy."

"Thanks, Gunny." Kirby led Burnette away from the bus.

Burnette said, "Looks like a successful mission, sir."

"Yes, well done," Kirby said.

****

5:10 a.m. – July 20, 2036 – Beulah Street and Telegraph Road, south of Alexandria, VA

McKnight knelt by a gardenia bush for fifteen minutes to let his night vision develop. He hoped he was being watched.

The assault team was in custody, so now it was up to McKnight to capture Smith and Cindy.

From the surveillance reports, McKnight knew Cindy was on her way to the office. They could pick her up any time so he focused his full attention on capturing Smith. He didn't expect it to be easy. If possible, he wanted the man to survive so he could testify against Phillips. Smith wasn't a fool. He didn't want to die. With luck, he could avoid a fight and capture him alive.

The attack plan was to scale the building from two sides and force Smith to split his attention. McKnight would approach the building, allow himself to be seen and Hatcher would approach in secrecy. Once they had him covered from two sides, Smith would recognize it as a no-win situation and surrender. However, Smith had shown himself to be creative and therefore unpredictable.

It was still dark as McKnight crept up on the building at the corner of Telegraph Road and Beulah Street, but dawn was approaching and couldn't be more than a few minutes away. As he expected, there was a ladder leaning against the west side of the building. McKnight climbed it. He was near the top when a shadow of a man with a shock of white hair appeared on the roof above the ladder. In the low light, he could make out the weapon in Smith's hand. He froze.

"Well, don't stop now, Major," the figure said. "Come on up and let's chat." McKnight heard the distinctive sound of the pistol's slide as it was cocked. "Slowly."

He climbed the rest of the way up to the roof and faced his adversary. He stood still, trying to gauge the man's mood without antagonizing him.

"Using two fingers, pull out your weapon and put it down," Smith commanded. "Then step back."

McKnight did as instructed.

"A little further back, please," the man said, and McKnight complied.

Without taking his eyes or his gun off McKnight, Smith knelt and picked up the weapon. He slipped it into his pocket. He smiled and said, "Well, since you're here and my team isn't responding, I'm presuming they aren't coming."

"Probably a good assumption. Some are dead and the rest will be late. By fifty years or so."

Smith shrugged and stood. "Well, that's how it goes. You just can't get good help these days. That's what I get for trusting that asshole Phillips."

"For the record, we found him, too, but he escaped. For now."

"Shouldn't take you long to find him. I'm curious. How'd you know?"

"This is our second pass through this time. We caught you after the assault and took the Time Engine back."

Smith shook his head. "So, we were successful in taking the machine during the first pass?"

"Yes. And you caused casualties and damage."

"Well, break a few eggs… right? Tell me, what tripped us up?"

"A grieving mother," McKnight said. "I didn't think Phillips was smart enough to pull this off. Did he have help?"

Smith shrugged. "Phillips? He's lucky he can find his way home at night. He's an ambitious dick but doesn't have the guts to execute his plans."

"Who, then?" McKnight asked, edging closer to Smith.

Smith quickly extended his hand with the gun pointed at the center of McKnight's chest. "I believe I asked you to step back."

McKnight raised his hands higher, nodded, and stepped back. Smith didn't lower his weapon.

"And where's Barbara Howard?" McKnight asked.

"Who?" Smith asked.

"The missing girl. Amy's friend. Where is she?"

"Oh, that one." He shook his head.

"Do you know where she is?"

"Boy, you sure have a lot of questions for a guy with a weapon pointed at him," Smith said.

"I'm naturally curious."

Smith smirked. "Why should I tell you anything? You can't give me what I might want."

Okay, Hatcher. Now would be a good time to show up. He didn't dare look away from Smith for fear of revealing their plan.

Smith glanced from side to side, then behind him, still training his weapon on McKnight. "I know you didn't come here without backup. Where are they?" He continued to scan the edges of the building, McKnight, and the darkness beyond.

"I'm not sure exactly," he said. "I brought Lieutenant Hatcher with me. You remember Lieutenant Hatcher, don't you?" Smith's face told McKnight he remembered her very well.

"Where is she? I'm not exactly sure." McKnight turned slightly to his left and pointed back over his shoulder. "She said something about getting up in those trees there with her sniper's rifle."

Smith's eyes followed his gesture.

Then McKnight pointed back to the east. "Or maybe it was over there."

Smith glanced at the faint pink beginnings of the sunrise in the east.

McKnight shrugged. "She might have changed her mind. You've seen what happens to a body that's been hit by a .30 caliber sniper round, right? It blows apart before you even hear the report."

Smith looked again in both directions and lowered his weapon, but kept it pointed in McKnight's general direction.

C'mon, Hatcher.

"Well," Smith said. "You have my attention." He glanced behind again and met McKnight's eyes. "Again, I don't think you have anything that I want."

"Maybe I do. After your interview with Dr. Wu the other day, we were able to piece together the rest of the story of you and Sergeant Randall."

"Who gives a shit?"

"I agree. Maybe nobody. But I thought you might like to know what exactly happened and how he came to be in the prison that day."

"What, you talked to him? How *is* the bastard? Dead, I hope."

"Yes," McKnight said. "Or at least BNR – 'presumed dead and body not recovered'. He went missing the day you met him. You were probably the last American to see him alive."

Smith scratched his chin with his free hand. "I'm listening."

"I'm piecing together stuff, okay? I read your briefing report on your captivity and I reread your interview with Dr. Wu. I also read Randall's service record and his CO's report that goes with the BNR. So I don't know what happened for sure, but the evidence points toward my conclusion. Are you with me?"

"So far."

"Good. Randall specialized in deep cover recon. Under most scrutiny, he could pass for a native in Afghanistan. Some people are really good at that stuff. According to his service record, he was one of those people. His missions could last for weeks and, most of the time, his own CO had no idea where he was.

"Here's what I know for sure. Your unit disappeared without a trace. Until you escaped and told the story, no one knew what happened to them. Randall's last check-in was the day you were captured. He reported that he found a stronghold of some kind and he planned to gain entry and scout out the place. He didn't report the location, or at least it wasn't in the report. He didn't mention a prison or anything about captives."

"Meaning?"

"He didn't know you were there, Chief—"

"Don't call me Chief. I'm not a SEAL anymore."

"Once a SEAL, always a SEAL, Chief. You earned the rank. No one can take it from you unless you give it away."

"I got past that long ago, Major. You were saying…?"

"Just this, Chief. Nobody but Randall knew you were there, but he only knew it because he found you while doing recon. Since he never reported on the place, it stands to reason that they caught him before he could get out."

"Why didn't they just throw him in a cell like me? You think they killed him outright?"

"No idea. But you know these people as well as I do, Chief. Probably better. You get caught by them, you're dead meat unless they think you're worth something, either as bait or for ransom. Since they planned to kill you and didn't, he must have changed their minds somehow."

"You think he convinced them otherwise?"

"I don't know for sure, Chief. But I gotta believe he expected to be killed as a spy. But maybe he thought he could give you a fighting chance if he managed somehow to convince them you were valuable enough to keep alive for at least a while. If that's the case, it worked."

"That's a pretty fine story, Major. You're very creative."

"It's the truth. But I guess maybe I wouldn't buy it either if I were in your shoes."

Where are you, Hatcher? He didn't dare look anywhere except at Smith's eyes.

Smith glanced at the trees beyond McKnight. "I'm starting to wonder, Major, if your support is really out there. Seems to me she would have shot me by now if she was." He smiled. "Maybe she fell asleep up in her tree."

"Don't make me kill you, Chief," Hatcher said. "Sorry I'm late, Major. It was harder to climb the building than I expected."

Smith looked back over his shoulder and turned slightly toward her.

"Careful now, Chief," she said. She stood five yards behind and to the side of Smith, her service weapon trained on him.

At her voice, Smith raised his weapon to point at McKnight's head.

"Unh-uh, Chief," she said. "I'd rather not kill you, but I will and I'll sleep like a baby tonight. Please surrender your weapon to the Major and get on your knees, hands behind your head."

Smith looked from McKnight to Hatcher and back again. He shrugged and released his grip on the weapon, allowing it to dangle from his trigger finger. McKnight stepped forward and took it from him. Smith knelt and put his hands behind his head.

Hatcher pulled his hands behind him and secured them with a nylon tie. She stood behind Smith when she finished.

"Lieutenant, call the MPs up here," McKnight said and took a knee before Smith.

"No place to run or hide, Chief. You're in this up to your ass. If you help me, I'll see what I can do to mitigate the charges. You have kidnapping charges against you and maybe conspiracy, but Amy and Astalos and the others are safe and I don't think you killed anyone. Or did you?"

Smith smiled at him and said, "I didn't, but I'm not sure I can prove it."

"So who were you working for?"

"I don't have much that will help you, but I guess it doesn't matter. I got my instructions from someone named Rho."

"How'd you meet him?"

"He contacted me online, gave me some lucrative tips in the stock market, then offered me a job."

"What does he look like?"

"No idea. Never met him face to face."

"And you just went to work for him?" McKnight shook his head. "You're mighty trusting of someone you don't know."

Smith nodded. "Well, he knew some things about me that I didn't want some people to know. Let's just say he had leverage and leave it at that." He looked down at the roof surface before him.

"Okay. What was the job?"

"To be on call for a politician when he needed help."

"Phillips?"

Smith nodded.

"What kind of help?"

Smith looked up at him. "Well, you know those guys, right? There's always something they want to go away or that they don't want the public to know about. I just took care of those things for Phillips."

"You cleaned up his messes."

"You might say that," Smith said. "There were four or five little scrapes I got him out of."

"Like what?"

"Like a hooker who wanted money or she'd reveal their relationship. I just paid her and told her to get lost or else."

"What else?"

"An ex-business partner. He was threatening to sue Phillips for some issue from years ago. He thought he'd have more leverage since Phillips was running for President."

"What did you do?"

"One of my team broke his leg. We paid his medical expenses in exchange for his promise to lay low."

McKnight thought he knew the answer to his next question. "Was Barbara Howard one of the messes? Did you kill her to help him out?"

Smith shook his head. "No, I didn't kill her. Phillips did. He called me in a panic the night it happened. It was probably an accident."

"What happened?"

"When I arrived, he was pretty upset. She was on the floor, dead. I got a cleaner to come in to do the scene and a couple of my guys to help."

McKnight felt himself growing angrier by the second. Barbara's eyes and smile flashed through his mind. "What did he do with her body?"

"Nothing," Smith said. "He doesn't know where she is."

"Who disposed of her body?"

"I did," Smith said. "Or rather, my guys did."

McKnight fought to keep his temper down. In a rough voice, he asked, "Where is she?"

Smith nodded toward McKnight. "Right behind you. In the field. It isn't an active farm anymore, so very little chance of the body being found or disturbed."

"Where exactly?"

"I don't know. I wasn't with them when they buried her. Provided they're not dead, I can point you to the men that buried her. Sorry, but I don't know any more about that."

McKnight frowned. "So you subcontracted to Phillips?"

"Not at all. Rho told me to let Phillips think he was calling the shots, but I ran everything by Rho if I had time."

"Tell me about Rho. What did he sound like?"

"Just a synthetic voice on the phone."

"Male or female?"

Smith paused. "Hmm. Never thought about that. Either, I guess. I always assumed he was a guy."

"What about Cindy? What does she know?"

"Who?"

Now it was McKnight's turn to hesitate. "Cindy Ginn. You don't know her?"

"Never heard of her."

McKnight stared at Smith. He couldn't tell if he was lying or not, but Smith would try to implicate the biggest rat in the pack in hopes of reducing his exposure.

"I'm not feeling very reassured," he said finally. "What else can you tell me about Rho?"

Smith rocked slightly on his knees. "One thing that always bugged me about Rho—"

"Yes?"

"Now that I think about it, he knew I hated the Rangers. More than once, he called his mission a chance to get revenge on the Rangers. And he knew stuff that I didn't see how he could know them. I mean, like his stock picks. He told me exactly what to invest in and when. But the money was so good, I didn't question his methods."

"Maybe you should have," McKnight said.

"Yeah, maybe so." Smith shook his head and his shoulders shrank down.

Rho counted on Smith's anger at the Rangers. He manipulated him.

McKnight considered this new information. Finally, he said, "You're saying the attack on the convoy was Rho's idea."

"Yes. Look, Major, I wish I could help more, but that's all I know. Sorry."

Smith stared at the roof surface as McKnight rose and faced the east. The sun would peek over the horizon any moment.

The two men who were mirror images of each other were gone. In their place was a man who had fallen to ruin and another who personified what he had lost.

"Lieutenant, let's get him up."

Hatcher and McKnight each took an arm and helped Smith to his feet.

McKnight checked the man's pockets, and removed his wallet and his phone. The MPs arrived and took Smith down from the roof and off to a van. McKnight and Hatcher followed them down the ladder.

"I'm sorry about your friend," Hatcher said.

"Thank you. He told me where she is. Small consolation, but at least she hasn't disappeared without a trace."

"I'm glad for that, at least. And you got the name Rho."

"Yes. And Rho is apparently the brains behind the operation, not Phillips."

"And he didn't know Cindy," Hatcher said. "Sounds like separation of efforts. Rho kept the members of his team separate so they can't give each other up."

"That's what it sounds like. And Smith said Rho was a synthetic voice."

"So Rho and Cindy…"

"…might be the same person." McKnight pulled on his lower lip. "Let's go get her and find out."

"Yes, sir."

"Where's our vehicle, Lieutenant?

Hatcher pointed. "It's over there, sir. And, sir?"

"Yes, Lieutenant?"

"I want you to know I thought about what you said. Back in the bar, I thought Smith was a low life asshole that needed to be put down. But I was wrong. If I were in his shoes, I might have made some of the same crummy choices. I'd like to think I wouldn't, but who knows what choices you might make when the pressure's on. I'm glad I didn't have to kill him."

"That's true, Lieutenant. But remember, in the previous timeline, he killed Amy and the General. He did go bad. He isn't an innocent victim of fate or whatever. But your attitude about it is right. To judge well, we have to understand that there is always more than one possible reason for behavior and we have to use discernment."

"Being an officer is harder than I thought, sir."

McKnight smiled. "Yes, it is, but you're on the right track. So, let's go get Cindy."

CHAPTER 37

6:58 a.m. – July 20, 2036 – Defense Logistics Agency Satellite Office Building, Telegraph Road, Alexandria, VA

Cindy entered the big conference room, closed the door behind her and walked to the wall control. She dialed it to transparent, and the pale beige color turned clear. She saw the convoy lined up outside. After a moment's inspection, she nodded, drew her phone from her left pocket and speed-dialed a number. She held it up to her ear and began to pace.

The number rang open. She pulled it away from her ear and looked at it. "Sixty seconds! Where the hell are you, Smith?" She switched the device's mode to text and typed in a short message. <Where are you, Smith? > She stared at the phone for a few seconds. There was no response.

The convoy pulled out of the parking lot and turned south on Telegraph Road.

She swore and sat in one of the conference chairs. She closed her eyes and breathed deeply, gripping the phone with both hands. With effort, she leaned back in the chair and let her hands fall into her lap, leaving the phone on the table.

The phone pinged. Her eyes flew open, and she grabbed it. She read the return text from Smith's phone.

<Hi, Cindy. Smith isn't here. >

She blinked twice. She leapt to her feet, ran to the door and tore it open. McKnight, Hatcher and Wheeler stood in the doorway.

"Oh," she said, taking an involuntary step backward. "You startled me."

She ran her hands down the sides of her dress, accentuating her hips and tiny waist. She checked the time on her watch. “I lost track of time. I was just going to make some more coffee.”

“Really?” McKnight said, as he entered the room. Hatcher and Wheeler followed him in. Cindy stepped farther back as the two lieutenants flanked her.

If she noticed the two moving to position, she didn't show it. “Why, yes. That's my job. Unless you have something else you need me to do?” She smiled and assumed an expression that was the picture of innocence and attention.

“Actually, I do,” McKnight said. “I want you to talk to me… about this.” He held up the phone that had been Smith's.

“What's that?” she asked.

“This phone belonged to Mike Smith. But you know that, don’t you?”

She frowned. “I don’t know who you’re talking about?”

“Because you just called him and then texted him. May I see your phone, please?”

She looked a little puzzled, then handed it to him.

McKnight noticed she took that instance to glance around the room. *Looking for an escape route? A weapon?*

“Talk to me,” he said. “Why?”

A pained expression crossed her face, and she began to cry. She stepped backward and collapsed into a chair. Tears rolled down her cheeks.

“He has my daughter... Smith... he threatened to kill us both if I didn't help him.” She looked up at McKnight, then her eyes darted around the room, searching for a sympathetic face. “You've got to believe me,” she pleaded. “There was nothing I could do.”

Trevor and Kathy entered the room.

Cindy said, “Trevor! Please! I had no choice.”

“How did Smith first contact you, Cindy?” McKnight asked.

She looked back at him, and her expression radiated misery. Her lips trembled and the tears continued. When she spoke, it was with a trembling voice.

"Right after I started working in your office. Somehow, he must have found out I worked for you. He came to my house one evening, forced his way in, and, well, you can guess the rest."

McKnight nodded. Kathy produced a handkerchief and handed it to Cindy. She took it with her left hand and dabbed her eyes with it. McKnight turned and looked at Kathy.

Kathy shook her head and said, "All I can say is, she's the best damned liar I ever saw."

Defiance showed in Cindy's eyes when she looked at Kathy. "You're just jealous because Trevor likes me," she said, and buried her face in her hands.

"I read through your records," Kathy said. "Or rather, Cindy's records. I have a talent. An eidetic memory. But it took me a while to figure out what bugged me about you. Today I figured it out. Cindy Ginn's profile says she's right-handed, but you're not. I just spoke with Senator Owen and he said the strangest thing. He told me Cindy is so right handed, she rarely uses her left hand for anything. And yet, you took that handkerchief in your left hand, used it to wipe your eyes and you're still holding it. How strange."

Cindy glanced at the handkerchief and continued to cry.

"So I showed him your picture," Kathy said. "He said you sure looked like Cindy and asked if you were related to her. I explained that you were Cindy, but he disagreed. He said the resemblance was close, but he was sure you're not her."

Cindy shook her head and the tears continued.

"But the last straw was this," Kathy said. "Hatcher saw you sabotage the Engine and collected a coffee cup with your DNA. There's no question about it. You're not Cindy Ginn."

Kathy paused. Cindy's sobbing stopped and she was staring at the floor.

"Who are you, really?" Kathy asked.

Cindy raised her head. The tears and hurt expression were gone, replaced with an icy stare.

She stood and glared at Kathy, who backed away. Trevor pulled her behind him.

Hatcher and Wheeler edged closer to Cindy on each side.

McKnight said, "You might as well tell us the truth. It's over."

Cindy smiled and squeezed her right forearm with her left hand. "You assume too much, Major. It's *not* over. I'll be back, and I'll stop Harrison." She pulled herself up straight and defiance radiated from her.

"Stop Harrison? What do you mean?"

"I'll tell you later. Maybe."

An aura appeared around Cindy's body. It was the same intensity and color of a time bubble, but it enveloped and clung to her body at a distance of two inches.

She winked at McKnight. "Gotta go. I have plenty of Whens to go to. See you soon, Marc."

Wheeler took a step toward her, but she swung at him and he dodged the blow. McKnight saw a flash of metal. It was a neck knife, a two-inch blade designed to kill at close range. It missed his throat but sliced his chin.

Hatcher rushed her from behind, reaching around to grab both arms by the wrists. When their bodies collided, the aura expanded to envelope both women.

McKnight lunged forward.

"No!" Kathy screamed, and the two women vanished.

McKnight landed on his hands and knees in the space their bodies occupied an instant before.

"Dammit," he cried in frustration, jumping to his feet.

Cindy had escaped. And wherever she went in time and space, Hatcher was there without a beacon.

"We need to go back two hours and fix this so Cindy doesn't get away," McKnight said.

Wheeler cried out. Trevor had pushed him into a chair and was applying pressure to the deep, bleeding cut on his chin. Kathy ran for the first aid kit.

Wheeler tried to speak, but Trevor's hands hindered him. He shoved him away and said, "The Engine! They'll try to take it out so we can't try again."

McKnight called Kirby.

When he got him on the phone, he said, "Alert your detail protecting the Engine at the warehouse. Tell them an attack is imminent."

****

7:10 a.m. – July 20, 2036 – Phillips' warehouse, Alexandria, VA

The squad of Marines assigned to protect the Time Engine focused their attention on the entry points of the building.

The blinding white silhouette of a time traveler appeared next to the Engine and resolved into a lone figure.

The light alerted the Marines and two of them sprinted to the Engine.

An aura appeared around the traveler and he vanished. He was in the warehouse less than three seconds.

The Marines advanced with weapons ready. One of them looked under the Time Engine and gasped. "Grenade!" he shouted.

The explosion that killed him turned the Time Engine to scrap metal.

CHAPTER 38

01:32 p.m. – July 22, 2036 – Reagan National Airport, Washington, DC

The man with the green windbreaker and Washington Nationals baseball cap waited patiently in line to check in for his flight. The Delta kiosk recognized the payment token on his phone and completed the transaction. It printed out his baggage token and transferred the boarding pass to his phone. He attached the token to his bag, breathed a sigh of relief and carried his bag to the bag drop. *Just a few more hours and I'll be out of reach. They can search everywhere for Congressman Phillips, but they'll never find me.*

He had just handed the bag to the attendant when he felt a pinch from behind in the small of his back. Irritated, he turned but the attractive blonde woman behind him smiled. Her perfume was intoxicating. All he could see were her blue eyes and full mouth. Warmth spread throughout his body. But there was something else there, too.

"I'm so sorry," she said. "I wasn't looking where I was going. I didn't mean to crowd you."

"Not at all," he said, with a smile. "Best thing that's happened to me all day."

The woman blushed. "How sweet!" she said. "Thank you. Well, I guess I'd better go catch my plane. Have a nice day."

He watched as she walked away. He felt strangely abandoned by the absence of her scent. He shook his head to clear it and turned back to the bag attendant.

"I've got it, Mister..." He looked at the ID tag on the bag. "er...Johnson. One checked bag and one carry-on. Enjoy your flight."

"Thank you."

"Sir, did you know that lady?"

He looked after her, but she was gone. "Sorry, no, I don't."

"No problem, sir. She forgot to leave her bag. Maybe she decided not to check it. It happens. Have a nice day, sir."

Phillips picked up his carry-on bag and walked to the security line. Five minutes later, he was sitting at Gate 16 waiting to board his flight. He took a magazine from his bag and began to read. He didn't notice the two security men until they were standing in front of him.

"Mr. Johnson?"

He looked up at them. "I beg your pardon?"

"Sir, are you Mr. Paul Johnson from Reston, Virginia?"

"I am. Is there a problem, officer?"

"Not at all, sir. Just a little issue with your luggage. Could you please come with us for a minute? We need to open your bag, and you need to be present when we do. Federal regulations, you know."

"My plane starts boarding in fifteen minutes. I won't miss my plane, will I?"

"No, sir. Your plane won't leave without your bag, and we'll make sure you're back here before it gets on the plane. Could you follow me, please?"

Not good. "Certainly," Phillips said. He stood and fell in step behind the man as he turned and walked away.

The other man paused for a moment and followed him as they walked. At a secure door, the first man entered a code and opened the door. He waved Phillips through, then walked past him to an office on the right. He opened the door and directed Phillips to a chair.

"Have a seat, sir," the officer said, gesturing to a metal chair next to a table.

The other officer closed the door and leaned against the wall.

"Where's my luggage?" Phillips asked, in a shaky voice.

"Sir, you know I don't have your luggage."

Phillips leaned forward on the table and clasped his hands together. "I guess you're not really Airport Security."

"No, sir, I'm not. I'm Special Agent Kennedy with the FBI and this is Special Agent Timmons."

"I see." He took off the ball cap and wiped his brow. "So, why am I here?"

The man stared at him for a few seconds and then spoke. "I think you know exactly why you're here, Congressman Phillips." He paused and smiled.

Phillips shifted his weight in the chair and shook his head. "I think there's been some mistake here. I'm Paul Johnson. Mr. Phillips is my congressman, but I've never met the man."

"Did anyone ever tell you that you look just like him?"

"Why, no. Really?"

"He's your congressman, but you've never noticed the resemblance?" Kennedy rolled his eyes. "Spare me." He stood and leaned forward over the desk.

"I have a warrant for your arrest, Congressman. For the murder of Barbara Howard and the kidnapping of Amy Chang and two others."

Kennedy said, "Please stand up, Congressman Phillips, and put your hands behind your back." He walked around the desk and stood next to him.

Phillips looked up at the man. "Surely there's some mistake."

"Stand up now, sir. Please."

Phillips slowly got to his feet. He passed his hand over his eyes and shook his head. *Why do I feel so groggy?* He put his hands behind him, and the agent slipped a pair of handcuffs around his wrists.

Agent Timmons took Phillips' arm and pulled him toward the door.

Phillips moved slowly. His brain was flooded with a mental fog. He shook his head as they walked through the door. *It's hard to breathe!* Halfway down the hall, Phillips staggered to the left and ran into the wall, his face and left shoulder pressed up against it.

“Congressman, are you all right?” Kennedy asked.

Phillips finally understood what was happening to him. He shook his head weakly. His last conscious thought was of intoxicating perfume. He vomited on the wall.

Timmons caught him as he slid down the wall to the floor. Kennedy rushed to help gently lay Phillips on the floor.

The agent pressed his fingers against his neck. After a few seconds, he cursed. “Call an ambulance. Not that it’ll do any good. He's dead.”

CHAPTER 39

07:42 a.m. – July 22, 2036 – The White House, Washington, DC

McKnight sat next to Mike Drake on a small bench outside the Oval office. He was reviewing his notes. Last night, he received a call from Drake informing him he would brief the President before breakfast. He spent the night pulling together the facts and creating a brief to give the President an accurate picture of the events.

An aide approached them and said, "The President will see you now."

McKnight and Drake rose together and followed her into the Oval office. It was only the second time McKnight had met the President of the United States.

Wanda Taylor sat at her desk, reading. She wore an immaculate dark gray suit with a blue blouse. As they entered, she rose and met Drake in the middle of the room.

"Hey, Mike," Taylor said, shaking his hand. "It's good to see you. How are you doing after all this excitement?"

"I'm fine, ma'am. May I present Major Marc McKnight? He's the operational lead of the HERO Team. Thanks to Marc and his team, I'm here to tell the tale, so to speak."

Taylor extended her hand to McKnight and said, "I believe we have already met, the Major and I. Didn't we meet last year after your project in Atlanta?"

"I'm flattered that you remember me, Madame President. I know you see a lot of people every year."

"I do," Taylor said. "But I always remember the interesting stories and yours certainly was that. And I understand you have a new adventure to share with me?"

"Yes, ma'am, I do."

"Let's get to it then." She motioned them to the sitting area, where two couches faced each other over a coffee table. As they sat, the President said, "Coffee, gentlemen? I'm worthless without it in the morning."

"Yes, ma'am, I'm sure we both do," Drake said.

The President poured coffee for them from a silver service. "Cream? Sugar?"

"Black for me, ma'am," Drake said.

"Cream and sucralose for me, ma'am. If you've got it," McKnight said.

Taylor smiled and produced two small silver vessels and handed them to McKnight.

"Mike, do you want to start?" Taylor asked.

"No, ma'am," Drake said. "Marc has all the details and I don't want to waste your time. Shall we proceed?"

"By all means," Taylor said.

Drake looked to McKnight and nodded.

McKnight pulled his laptop out and opened it to his presentation. He set it on the coffee table so that both Drake and Taylor could see it. The first page had an executive summary of the event. McKnight read it and stumbled over the second sentence. His second time through the sentence wasn't much better. *I'm blowing this.*

The President glanced between McKnight and Drake.

"Sorry, ma'am," McKnight said. "I didn't have time to rehearse before coming in—"

Taylor leaned forward. "Marc, it's okay. How much sleep have you had in the last three days?"

"Not enough, ma'am, but I'm functional."

Taylor searched his face and smiled. "Okay," she said. "Put your presentation aside and tell me the story like you told General Drake here. You can refer to the presentation if you need to. I'm a quick study."

"Yes, ma'am." McKnight took a deep breath and began the story. "One of my team members was contacted about a missing girl and followed up on the circumstances…"

It took fifteen minutes for McKnight to tell the story and, in spite of his initial nervousness, he was satisfied with his performance. Once he relaxed, training kicked in and his report flowed in a coherent and logical stream. Looking back on it, he forgot some minor details, but the important parts were all there.

The main point of the briefing was that Congressman Phillips plotted to discredit Governor Harrison and win the election. Even without the illegal use of time travel charges, there was enough evidence to prove Phillips killed a woman and conspired to kidnap three people to cover it up.

The President rose from the couch and said, "Thank you for the briefing, gentlemen. Mike, as always, you have overseen successful protection of the integrity of our government. It's much appreciated." She turned to McKnight. "Marc, thank you for the report. Good job. Now, go get some sleep."

"Yes, ma'am."

As they turned to leave, Taylor picked up her phone. Before they left, they overheard her ask her aide to get the Speaker of the House and the Senate Majority Leader on the phone.

****

04:42 p.m. – July 22, 2036 – United States Capitol Building, Washington, DC

McKnight walked with Senator Lodge through the tunnel from the Senate offices to the Capitol building. Behind them walked a small group of DC police and military officers. Ahead of them walked the most powerful woman in the world with a Secret Service escort.

A few minutes before, McKnight learned the FBI arrested Phillips and he died under mysterious circumstances.

"Senator?" McKnight said.

"Yes, Major?"

McKnight pointed at the President. "What's she going to do?"

The Senator looked surprised. "Lay out what happened for everyone and his brother in Washington. What did you think she's going to do?"

"No, I mean, are they going to whitewash this? You know, push it out of the public view so it isn't an embarrassment to the party?"

The Senator chuckled. "That would be normal procedure, wouldn't it?"

McKnight nodded.

"It's what I would do." The Senator paused for a long moment as they walked. "You don't know Wanda Taylor very well, do you?"

"No, sir."

"She's a political animal like the rest of us. But in certain areas, she's the biggest damned goody-two-shoes you ever met."

"Yes, sir."

The Senator produced a handkerchief, blew his nose into it and pushed it back in his pocket. "Damned cold. Always gives me the sniffles. Yes, she'll drill a political opponent right between the eyes and never think twice about it. But this? Killing a young girl and kidnapping a child? No, she would never put up with that."

"Yes, sir."

The Senator placed a big hand on McKnight's shoulder. "In this case, my friend, she gets the best of both worlds. She rids the country of a crooked politician and gets a chance to fix something she doesn't like. And, as a fringe benefit, she advances the career of the man she thinks should be her successor." Lodge chuckled. "This is one of those rare occasions where the President's conscience and political aspirations are in perfect harmony. Yes, sir. Wanda Taylor is a happy woman today."

McKnight was aghast. "You mean she got rid of Phillips?"

"Figure of speech. No, I don't believe she did. The President has the FBI turning the city upside down looking for the person who killed Phillips. They used a poison no one can identify. Not that she isn't happy about it, but she doesn't want some asshole running around town killing off politicians either."

"I see. What's she going to fix?"

"You'll see. There's this project she's been working on for a while. I don't necessarily agree with it, but it's something we politicians can fight about when we don't want to address something else."

McKnight paused before he spoke. "I'm not sure I want to be part of this."

"Oh, it'll be okay. It is the right thing to do. Everybody knows it. They just don't want to do it."

They reached the end of the tunnel and stopped.

President Taylor and Kirk Nixon, the Speaker of the House, stopped to speak with the DC Chief of Police. The man nodded, spoke to them and waved for them to continue.

They walked across the House lobby to the main hall and stepped inside.

The Sergeant at Arms announced the entry of the President, and Taylor made her way to the podium, shaking hands, laughing and talking to supporters and opponents alike.

McKnight climbed the stairs to the gallery to hear the proceedings.

After five minutes of socializing, Speaker Nixon approached the lectern and introduced Taylor, who joined him there. After a brief round of applause, the President addressed the joint session of Congress.

"Mr. Speaker, members of the Senate, members of the House, honored guests and citizens of our beloved country, I come before you today to talk about a sad and shameful day in our history and to launch an effort to change how we do business here in Washington. We have become what our forefathers wished to avoid. Their intention was that men and women would enter government service to do that and nothing else. Serve. Government service is supposed to be a position of trust. A pledge to invest their time here to make things better and then retire in honor and pride for their good works.

"Instead, men and women have come here to enrich themselves. They usually come here with good intentions, but are seduced by power and financial opportunities presented to them. Soon, they're deciding for their own advantage, not for the good of the people. It becomes about the power and the money for them. A Congressman accepts a contribution for a few hundred thousand dollars from a lobbyist and votes that man's way to make his employers millions of dollars richer. That's a good investment for a company but not for America. We together, you and I, are going to stop this now."

McKnight scanned the audience. You could have heard a mouse squeak in the room. Wanda Taylor had their complete attention.

"About three hours ago, one of your colleagues was arrested and charged with felony murder and kidnapping."

The room erupted with voices and sounds of men and women twisting in their seats in attempts to figure out who was missing from the hall.

Speaker Nixon pounded his gavel to restore order. McKnight thought he heard someone say the name Phillips.

The President waited. When the noise died down, she resumed her message.

"This man was from my own political party and was a colleague of mine. But we will not sugarcoat this, and he won't receive any cover because of his position. If anything, we should be stricter with the men and women charged with implementing the will of the people. They should set the example for the rest of us, not treat their position as a money-making proposition.

"What leads a person to do such a thing? Maybe it was lust. Or maybe it was fear. But I believe, beneath whatever other motives he had, there lies a cancer that affects us all. A cancer of greed and the lust for power. None of us is untouched, and many of us have acted on these longings. It's clear that, for many of us, our government branches have regressed to where we civil servants are in the business of enriching ourselves to the detriment of those we're elected to serve.

"Let me hasten to add that I'm not pointing my finger at this Congress alone. I'm also pointing it at the Executive Branch and the Judicial Branch. And at the bloated bureaucracy that supports us all. None of us are blameless. I'm asking you to join me in changing the way we work. I'm spending the next few minutes to outline a plan to make things better. It won't be perfect, but I believe it's a step in the right direction. I'm open to suggestions from both sides of the House and Senate as long as the spirit of the proposed legislation is preserved. I don't propose to have all the answers, but I believe together we can do what is needed. So, let us begin.

"The legislation I'm proposing will be available for review at the end of next week. Speaker Nixon has agreed to sponsor it. I'm not going into great detail today – I'll just speak to the main points.

"First, I'm proposing a Constitutional amendment that limits all members of the House and Senate to twelve years of elected service. The objective is to eliminate government service as a career choice and turn it back into a service an individual performs and then goes back to private life. This will also apply to Supreme Court Justices and all senior levels of the government bureaucracy."

McKnight heard faint murmurs from the ranks of the legislators.

"Second, all members of our Executive, Judicial and Legislative arms of the government will check their fortunes at the door. They'll have appropriate budgets to manage residences and staff, but their personal finances will be placed in a blind trust. This trust will be tied to a public stock index that tracks the health of the country's economy while they are in public office. When they leave office, the trust will become theirs."

McKnight whistled. *Ooh, I'll bet that hurts.*

Sounds of disagreement coming from the floor were rising in volume.

"What?" Taylor said. "I hear your dissent. But consider this. If you're doing the people's work—improving the state of the national economy and keeping the people safe—then your fortunes will be safe. During your tenure in office, they'll track with the country's fortune and the wellbeing of the people you represent. I welcome your input to make this a good deal for everyone but understand this…the purpose of this is to separate your finances from your work as the people's servants. No one should profit from performing service for our country.

"My fellow Americans...my colleagues…" Taylor paused and looked over the floor and then up at the gallery. "My friends. I know this is a big change. It will change everything about how we operate our government. But look around you. Don't we need a change? Congress's approval rating has been under fifteen percent for about fifty years now. The people don't trust us and for good reason. We've become what our Founding Fathers feared. And it's time we fixed it. Again, I welcome your input. Thank you."

Taylor left the lectern without further words.

The room erupted with voices, a roar of dissent mixed with approval.

News reporters sprinted from the hall to set up their cameras for the inevitable interviews with Congressional leaders. Each was eager to report their reactions to the President's proposal.

Taylor shook hands with Speaker Nixon and strode toward the door. Her Secret Service escort struggled to stay ahead of her through the press of legislators and reporters who wanted to speak to her.

McKnight sat still in his chair as the gallery emptied. Everyone around him talked about the speech, the topic moving from Taylor's presence before cameras to her speech and to argue the impact of her words.

It would change much. The number of government jobs could diminish sharply if the President succeeded. He wondered if it was a good thing or a bad thing.

McKnight rose from his seat and made his way to the stairs. His hand glided along the polished mahogany bannister as he walked down the stairs to the lobby.

To his surprise, Senator Lodge was waiting for him at the bottom of the steps. "Well, Major? What did you think of her plan?"

"It's ambitious, sir. Do you think she can pull it off?"

The Senator smiled. "I don't know. Part of me says no way. It'll take much more than this to change the direction of government."

"Yes, sir."

"But I do have to admit... well, there's a small voice in the back of my mind that leapt with joy at her courage and conviction. It takes a special person to resist opportunities to feather their own nest. One day, I think we'll look back on this and say Wanda Taylor was one hell of a great President. You know, most of us come here to do the right thing. The push to compromise your principles is constant and irresistible. I wish her luck, but it'll be a bloody fight to get it done. We'll see."

Before McKnight could respond, a group of cable journalists crowded around the Senator, asking for his comments.

The Senator held up his hands and reminded them he hadn't seen the proposal either. He told them he would comment as soon as he reviewed it.

McKnight backed away from the crowd and paused long enough for Lodge to catch his eye and nod.

He nodded back, turned on his heel and walked away.

CHAPTER 40

10:04 a.m. – July 23, 2036 – Defense Logistics Agency Satellite Office Building, Telegraph Road, Alexandria, VA

Robert Astalos, Robby Astalos and Marc McKnight sat with General Drake in his office. Clary sat in a side chair taking notes.

Trevor George stood in the doorway. After a day of reviewing details and researching events, they were still trying to understand what had happened.

"First, let's go over what we know for certain," Drake said. "Robert, can you give a report on the Time Engines?"

"Yes," Robert Astalos replied. "As of now, both Time Engines are incapacitated. One is a total loss. The other can be repaired, but not in less than a month. We still have all our data and the diagnostic computer, but that's all."

"Not soon enough to go back and make another try at capturing Cindy, or whomever she is?" McKnight asked.

"No, Major, I'm afraid not. We'll have to find another way to rescue Lieutenant Hatcher. I'm sorry."

"Thank you, Robert," Drake said. "We'll talk more about that in a few minutes. What happened to Smith?"

"He's in custody, sir," McKnight said. "We captured his team at Phillip's warehouse, and he wasn't with them. Lieutenant Hatcher and I found him at the assault site. We were able to take him into custody without a fight. He'll testify against Phillips when the time comes."

"I didn't expect him to be with the team, either," Drake said. "He was the leader. He would have been on site before them anyway. Plus, working with mercenary troops is somewhat risky. Some of them were borderline professional, so it made sense for him to stay away except during the attack. He'd want to minimize his contact with them."

“We have too many variables,” Trevor said. “There’s more going on here than we know. I keep thinking we’re trying to solve a puzzle with half of the pieces. Cindy's disappearance with Hatcher has me baffled. I mean, there was no globe of light. How did she travel?”

“I’ve been thinking about this, Trevor,” Robert Astalos said. “You all said she had an aura similar to the light globe. But it worked faster, according to what you all witnessed.”

Trevor nodded. “And she never touched a beacon, as far as I could see.”

“And the ripple in time created by their disappearance is different,” Robert said. “I checked.”

“What’s the bottom line here? What does all that mean?” McKnight asked.

Robert scratched his head. “I have a theory that might explain it. As you all know, I’ve been tracking time blips when something happens in time ever since we started this team. I looked back over the history we have collected for changes. The ripples I see here are inconsistent with what we’ve seen before.”

Drake had been leaning back, relaxed, but this statement brought him up to the edge of his chair. “Meaning?”

“Meaning that what the team witnessed appears to be technology more advanced than what we have. I think the ripple we see now is the result of Hatcher no longer being in our history. I don’t think she’s dead. I think they jumped to the future.”

“The future?” Trevor replied. “Are you saying Cindy came here from the future?”

“That's what the evidence suggests.”

“What the hell was she doing here?” Trevor asked.

“I'm not sure,” Robert said. “But it appears she came here to change the present – her past. There's other evidence.”

“What?” McKnight asked.

“Congressman Phillips. They took him into custody, and he died shortly after. It looked like a heart attack, but he projectile-vomited beforehand, and they found an unidentified substance in what he threw up on the corridor wall. They're still working on the autopsy, but we think he was injected with something extremely toxic. The doctor said it was the damnedest thing he'd ever seen. And they couldn't identify it – it's not in their database."

"Okay," Drake said. "So, the evidence supports your theory of future time travel?"

"Yes. Unidentified poison, new time travel technology, no time ripple in the past…"

Drake paused. "I think I understand something here. Robert, I'm thinking you might be on to something. Cindy, or whomever she is, joined us so they could steal the time travel capability and help Phillips influence history. But we know she had time travel capability of her own. Why didn't she just give her technology to Phillips and Smith? Maybe she didn't want to share or interfere directly, but she *did* want Phillips to be successful. She wanted him to be President of the United States. That's directly influencing American history. What scares me is, she wanted to put a crook like Phillips in the highest office of the land instead of a good guy like Harrison."

"I didn't think of it that way, sir. If it's true, we're in trouble," McKnight said.

"Yes, I think so," Drake added. "And I can't see any reason why she won't be back. And soon. She failed this time. Next time, we might not be so lucky. "

McKnight shifted in his chair. "Sir, I'm pissed off by all this, no question. But we need to find Hatcher and get her back. Shouldn't that be my first priority?"

"Not necessarily, but our only clues are associated with her. Or more specifically, associated with Cindy. The most important thing is the security of history and our country. It's hard enough to keep a political system functioning without interference from outside forces. Up to now, we've only worried about the Russians, the Chinese and a few others. Now we have to look out for people in the future who have the benefit of hindsight guiding them to our vulnerable spots."

"But we don't ever leave a man behind," McKnight said.

"That's right," Drake said. "Like I said, our only clues lie in the direction of her rescue and Cindy's apprehension. For now, our personal and national priorities lie in the same direction. It's where we need to start."

"I might be able to help with that," Robby said. "Robert, I think you know what I'm talking about. Each person who travels through time has a frequency signature, right?"

"Yes, that's true," Robert said. "Are you saying there might be a way to track it?"

"There may be. Every time someone travels, there is a frequency signature residue, or FSR. It's composed of the personal signature and the destination signature." Robby waved his hands at them. "After Cindy and Hatcher disappeared, I checked the time slice and captured the FSR for their travel.

"Remember we talked about this once before? We were theorizing that we could use an FSR to track down the destination of a travel we didn't initiate. We've collected dozens of FSRs for the team. And we have their personal signatures and their destinations. In this case, we don't have Cindy's signature or the destination, but maybe we can review the existing FSRs and use them to analyze the FSR from the jump Cindy and Hatcher made? There might be something there we can use to determine where and *when* they went. Then we can go after them, provided they haven't solved the problem of the twenty-five-year restriction."

A voice came from behind Trevor. "I'd like to volunteer to follow them, sir."

Mitch Wheeler peered over Trevor's shoulder into the office. A bandage covered his chin. "Sorry for the interruption, sir. And I didn't mean to eavesdrop, but Hatcher's my teammate and the best soldier I know. I want to be on the team that brings her back."

McKnight met Drake's eyes and saw the compassion and determination there.

What would I have done if he had been killed and I couldn't fix it? Drake would not allow Hatcher to be left behind.

McKnight stood and turned toward the young lieutenant at the door. “Mitch, I think this is a job for both of us.”

Drake nodded. “Agreed. This cannot stand as is.”

“Yes, sir!” Wheeler said. “When do we leave, sir?”

McKnight looked at Robby and Robert Astalos. “As soon as we have an Engine and a destination, Lieutenant.”

The two scientists nodded.

“Tonight, we get some sleep,” McKnight said. “Everyone needs rest. Tomorrow, we start the Engine repairs and figure out where and when. Then we go looking for Lieutenant Hatcher.”

“There’s one more thing of concern,” Drake said. “The charter of this team has been to do research, not fight battles across time.”

“Respectfully, sir –” McKnight began, but Drake held up his hand.

“Let me finish, Major, and I think you’ll agree. My next stop is Senator Lodge and, with his help, then to see the President. Our political system is under attack from unknown persons in the future and we don’t have any idea who they are or what they’re planning. They’ve already shown that they aren’t above using murder as a tool.

“Under our current operating procedures, we can only play defense. That’s what we did, and we were lucky to survive it with the damage we have. We might not be so lucky next time. Playing defense doesn’t win this game. I’m going to request the President’s support to modify our charter so we can lawfully operate and fight this proactively. Does anyone disagree?”

“No, sir,” several voices said.

“Here’s another thing to chew on. I believe they were successful in attacking us because they have history to draw information from. We can’t rule out that they can uncover our strategy if they have access to our records in the future. So we need to find another way to share information between us, other than traditional methods. Our plans need to be invisible to history. That will take some thought."

"General Drake, I'd like to take that on," Robby Astalos said. "If I can have Captain Tyler and Doctor Wu to assist me, we'll figure something out."

"Good. I'll leave that with you if it's okay with Major McKnight. Right now, I'm headed to see Senator Lodge. Tom, you're with me. Marc, you, too, I want to ask you about something. Get some rest, everyone. Tomorrow we have a new mission, beginning with the rescue of Lieutenant Hatcher."

The team scattered to their individual offices.

Drake, Clary and McKnight left the building and stopped in the parking lot to chat.

"Marc, I need your opinion on something. Remember the security guard from the NewT Communications case in Atlanta?"

"I do and I see where you're going."

"Could that woman have been Cindy, or whomever she is?"

McKnight scratched his chin. "I've been thinking about that. I'm not sure. Maybe. Her facial structure was different, but I guess a clever makeup job could give that illusion. It *could* have been her."

"Okay," Drake said. "Keep going through that first encounter in your mind. The way the guard walked. Her eye contact. Her voice. Anything you can remember. Does any of it fit Cindy or maybe remind you of her? I can't shake the feeling that we don't have the full picture here."

"That's it. That's what was bugging me. I thought Cindy was trying to influence Trevor to deflect suspicion, but if she was the guard, then how could that appearance be about Trevor? She must have had a different purpose."

"Exactly."

McKnight shook his head. "If it was her…still a big if…there's something bigger going on. And how did she know so much about us?

She knew about my mission in Atlanta and she arranged to be our receptionist here. If it was her, there's more to come."

"Good. Now you're thinking about the same things I am. We need to stay vigilant and prepared. I don't think we've seen the last of her and I don't think our reunion will be fun."

"No, sir," McKnight said. "I don't, either."

"Well, I'll leave you to it. See me early next week with a plan for our next steps."

"Yes, sir." McKnight saluted Drake and stepped back as they got in their car and drove away.

McKnight walked back to the building and stood by the loading dock. The summer sun was already heating up the day.

He looked up. There wasn't a cloud in the sky. He smiled at the woods surrounding the DLA facility. It felt a little like Oregon.

For the next few moments, he needed to push his thoughts of Hatcher, Cindy and all the rest into the back of his mind. He sat on the loading dock steps and took several deep breaths and held them in, forcing himself to relax.

He drew out his phone. "Call Megan," he commanded, and held the phone to his ear. He kicked at a clump of dirt and grass on the pavement.

"Hi," he said. "I'm sorry for all the delays this week, for not calling, and especially for the way I made you feel…You're exactly right and I want to make it up to you. If you'll still have me, I want to set a target date for moving you up here…Yes, I'm serious…I don't know…I guess sometimes I'm my own worst enemy when it comes to expressing myself. But I'm trying to get better at it…Yes, I realize there are no guarantees, but I love you and I'm willing to risk it if I can be with you…What do you say?"

****

Trevor stopped by Kathy's office. The door was open and she was staring at her comp pad.

"Hi," he said.

She turned toward him and offered a tentative smile. "Hi."

"Got a few minutes?"

"Sure." She waved him into her office.

"Not here," he said. "Let's go outside. It's a beautiful day."

"Okay." She stood and together they walked down the hall and out the building's front door. They walked to the garden area. In truth, it wasn't much of a garden – just an iron bench underneath an enormous live oak tree to the right of the parking lot. The bench overlooked Telegraph Road and the woods across the street.

Kathy sat on the bench and Trevor, after glancing around, joined her. After a moment of awkward silence, he turned toward her.

"With all that's happened, we haven't had a chance to talk about the other night."

"Yes, I know."

"We shouldn't feel so awkward," he said. "We're the same people we were a couple of days ago, but everything seems different. I'm not sure what to say to you."

"Do you regret what happened between us?"

"Oh, God, no," he said. "But I worry that maybe you do."

She looked him in the eye and frowned. "Not really. Part of me worries because I see all the risks associated with this kind of relationship and part of me thinks it was a bad idea, but most of me is glad it happened."

He smiled. "I guess I should see that as a positive."

"Yes, you should."

He nodded. "So you know where I stand…" He turned toward her. "I'm not sorry it happened. In fact, I'm glad it did. When I look at you, I see a witty, intelligent, sensitive woman that is so unreadable—" He held up a hand before she could interrupt. "That's not exactly right. What I mean is that I can't wait to hear what you say next. I can't wait to learn the next thing about you. I'm so intrigued and…and terrified at the same time."

"Terrified? Of me?"

"Yes."

"But why?" she asked.

He turned his body to face the street and rested his elbows on his knees.

"This isn't easy for me, but let me try to explain. I was engaged once. To a nice girl that was pretty and popular and…well, pretty much my mother's dream for me. She and my mom were both assertive and bright. Between the two of them, they had my life all planned out. I loved them both, but I couldn't see myself living the life they planned." He glanced at Kathy. "It got to where I had to fight them for everything I wanted for myself. That's no way to live. Who wants to struggle with the person you love for control of your life every day? So I broke off the engagement. My fiancée found someone else and my mother barely speaks to me. But I don't regret it."

"And you're worried I'd be the same? That's not who I am."

"I know. You're the smartest person I know and courageous. And you can be assertive. But you also have compassion they didn't have. They wanted things a certain way for themselves, not for anyone else. There was a little coldness there, like a predator. I'm exaggerating a little, but you know what I mean. But I don't see that in you."

"Thank you. It's a mistake to start a relationship if you expect to change the other person. In the end, no one can really change someone else. They only change in response to you and only if they want to. I don't want to change you. If I can't accept and care about you as you are, then we have no business being together."

"Right, that's how I feel. I hope I never wake up one day to find you are like them. That's my worst fear. But from what I see in you now, there's nowhere I'd rather be than right here with you."

She smiled. "I'm glad to hear that. I hope you don't feel obligated now, or committed—"

"But I did make a commitment," he said. "When we were together the other night. The act of making love with someone you care about creates a bond that should be respected. There's no one else I feel this way about."

"But what if things change? That's what I worry about. Will we still be able to handle working together if you find someone else? Or I find someone else? I don't know if I could stay here if this new situation gets bad and we can't work together anymore." She blinked a couple of times. "It's really good to work with you, Trevor. I can't tell you how much I appreciate that."

"Me, too. All the more reason to work out any problems," he said. "But for now, let's just be here, with each other, one day at a time."

"Will you tell me if you change your mind about…us?"

"Only if you promise to do the same."

"I do promise."

"Good. You know, if we were back in Atlanta, they'd say we have an 'understanding' together. That's what we call it anyway."

She laughed. "That's a good word for it. There's just this one thing. Do you think we could go for a drink again sometime soon?"

Trevor rubbed his chin and said, "Hmmm. I'll have to check my schedule. I—"

Kathy socked him hard on the arm.

"Ow!" he said, rubbing the impact point. "Well, okay, I think I can move some things around."

"You think you're so funny." She laughed again. "I may have to reconsider my decision here."

"I was just kidding." He reached out and took her hand. "I can't wait to see what happens next."

CHAPTER 41

Time: unknown – Location: unknown

A splitting headache was Hatcher's first sensation as she became aware again. She moaned and tried to move but felt constrained. She wasn't awake enough to understand why. She tried to focus. It took a few minutes.

She was lying on her left side on a metal floor, her face pressed against the cool rough surface. She was stripped down to her panties and tee shirt. Her hands were bound behind her back with plastic strips. Her legs and feet were wrapped together with duct tape.

There was little light in the room, but she perceived it was large. Packing crates were all around her. She wondered if she was in a warehouse.

How did I get here? She tried to concentrate. *I grabbed Cindy and then the star field.* Nothing after that. *Where am I now? And when am I?* There was no way to know without some frame of reference.

And where's that vibration coming from? She could feel it through her left cheek. The floor was vibrating at a low frequency. She struggled into a sitting position and found a wall behind her. She leaned against it and got a stronger sense of the vibration. *Am I on a ship?*

Time passed. She wasn't sure how much.

She took stock of her options. They took her weapons, her fatigues and her boots. When they came back, she would ask for the fatigues and boots. *If* they came back.

She didn't give a damn about the clothes, but she wanted the boots. She designed them herself. Each heel contained a small blade and some lock picks, all of which would be useful now.

She shivered. It was cool and damp in the room—she estimated it to be in the low sixties Fahrenheit. It was musty, too. She must be in a ship's cargo hold.

She heard a sound at the other end of the room. A small amount of light filtered into the room. *A door opened, maybe?*

High above her, lights came on. She craned her neck to look at them. The ceiling was thirty feet above her. She saw the walls better, and their dull dark color and surface texture were consistent with her cargo hold theory.

Somebody's coming. She could hear out footsteps coming toward her.

Two figures came into view.

The first was Cindy Ginn, dressed in dark slacks and a white blouse. She wore a security badge on a lanyard around her neck, but Hatcher couldn't make out what was written on it.

The man with her was middle-aged with a "high and tight" haircut. He was dressed in slacks, a white shirt and a loosened tie. He wore a shoulder holster and no security badge. He looked more like a cop more than anything else.

They stopped ten feet from her and stood there for a few seconds.

"Thanks for dropping by," Hatcher said in a hoarse voice. "What can I do for you?"

Cindy chuckled. "Welcome back. You had a nice long sleep." The man leered at her.

"How long?"

"Long enough. I have a proposition for you, Karen."

"Blow it out your ass." Hatcher spat out the words. "Where the hell am I?"

When Cindy spoke, the hard, cold look was back. "Somewhere safe for now. The proposition is simple. Join us or die."

"Well, now that you've explained it to me. Sure, I'll join...cut me loose and let's talk about it."

Cindy laughed without humor and moved closer. She knelt beside Hatcher and leaned over her until her face was inches from Hatcher's.

Hatcher could read her security badge now. The name on it was Rachel Patterson. *At least we have a real name now.* She blinked. *If I ever get loose to tell anyone.*

The badge was almost identical to her own. *What the hell?* The organization on the badge was Federal Time Services. The badge's issue date was 11/10/2079.

"Your reputation precedes you, Lieutenant," Patterson said. "No, I think we'll leave you as is for now. We'll work on your attitude and motivation and then talk. I'm sparing your life because I think you'll be useful to us. Step out of line once and you're dead. Got it?"

Hatcher nodded. "Cindy, can I have my fatigues and boots back? It's cold and damp down here."

"Down here?" Cindy/Patterson asked. After a wry smile, she continued. "We'll see. Maybe later. You'll be under my colleague's care here for the next few weeks, so I guess he'll accommodate you when he's ready."

"What's the date and where are we?"

"You don't need to know," the man said.

Cindy/Patterson turned to the man. "How long will it take?"

"About six weeks, sir. By then, she'll be ready to listen."

"Okay. You're aware of what's at stake?"

"I am."

"Good," she said, as she turned and left.

The man stood still until Hatcher heard the door close at the far end of the room. He removed his shoulder holster and his tie and laid them on a crate. He dragged a chair over to where Hatcher lay. Almost lovingly, he lifted her and positioned her in the chair. There were two sets of straps on the chair, which he used to bind her arms and feet to it.

He walked slowly around the chair as he rolled up his sleeves. When he was directly behind her, she felt his collar touch the back of her neck. The whiskers on his chin brushed gently against her ear.

"Comfy?" he whispered.

Then he came around in front of her and leaned over slowly until his nose was two inches from hers. She could smell tobacco and coffee on his breath. He smiled at her, then reached behind her head and took a handful of her raven hair in his fist.

"I'm Freddie," he said. "Let's get acquainted."

He stepped back and struck her hard on the left cheek with his fist.

EPILOGUE

Navy Chief Mike Smith remains in isolated custody at the Hampton Roads brig. He is moved to a different cell every day and no record is kept of which cell he occupies.

After two days of searching the field behind Smith's convoy attack site, Barbara Howard's body was found and exhumed. It was respectfully prepared by Fort Belvoir's CID team and the post coroner. She was buried in the Ivy Hill Cemetery near her family home. At the request of General Drake, an Army Ranger squad in dress uniforms escorted the casket and her family to the cemetery. In addition to family, the funeral was attended by Amy Chang and her parents, President Taylor, Governor Harrison, Senator Lodge, General Drake, Major Marc McKnight and the rest of the HERO Team. The news media was excluded. President Taylor spoke a few personal words at the funeral.

The whereabouts and status of Lieutenant Karen Hatcher is unknown. She is currently listed as MIA/BNR (Missing in Action/Body Not Recovered).

A Note From The Author

Thanks for reading THE TIME TWISTERS. I hope you enjoyed reading it as much as I enjoyed writing it.

Who was your favorite character? Drop me a line at: kim@www.AuthorKimMegahee.com.

If you're so inclined, I'd love it if you would post a review of THE TIME TWISTERS – Loved it, hated it. Whatever — I'd just like to hear your feedback. Reviews can be tough to come by these days, and you, the reader, have the power to make or break a book. If you have the time, please post an honest review of this book. Here's a link to my author page, along with all my books on Amazon here: https://www.amazon.com/~/e/B086N5Y73J

This is how authors find out if they did a good job. The only real evidence is the honest review left by a person who invested in the book on faith and took the time to give feedback.

Regardless, thanks again for reading THE TIME TWISTERS. It is much appreciated.

Cheers and Regards,
Kim

The Marc McKnight Time Travel Adventures

Book 1 – TIME LIMITS

Book 2 – THE TIME TWISTERS

Book 3 – TIME REVOLUTION

Book 4 – TIME PLAGUE

You can find these books on Kim's website at:
https://www.authorkimmegahee.com/book-store

ABOUT THE AUTHOR

Kim Megahee is a writer, musician, and retired computer consultant. He has a degree from the University of Georgia in Mathematics Education. His background includes playing in rock bands, teaching high school, and much experience in computer programming, security and consulting.

In addition to writing, he enjoys hanging out with his wife, reading, boating on Lake Lanier, playing live music, and socializing with friends. Kim lives in Gainesville, Georgia with his soulmate wife Martha and Leo, the stubborn red-headed toy poodle.

www.AuthorKimMegahee.com
Facebook: author.kmega
Twitter: @authorkmega

Made in the USA
Columbia, SC
27 March 2022